THE GEM CONNECTION

(A C. J. Cavanaugh Mystery)

Also by Michael R. Lane

THE GEM CONNECTION

(A C. J. Cavanaugh Mystery)

Michael R. Lane

BARE BONES PRESS
P.O. Box 9653, Seattle, WA 98109

Published by Bare Bones Press, Seattle, Washington

The characters and events in this book are fictitious. Any similarity to real persons, living or dead, is coincidental and not intended by the author.

Design: Bare Bones Press
Production: Bare Bones Press
Cover Art: Todd Engel

Bare Bones Press
P.O. Box 9653
Seattle, WA 98109

www.michaelrlane.com
www.barebonespress.com

Second Edition: September 2023

This work is dedicated to those who act upon their dreams.

CHAPTER ONE

A sapphire Jaguar XJS convertible cruised onto the circular driveway of a Mediterranean-styled, Southwest Hills mansion with all the stealth and agility of its namesake, its headlights beaconed through light rain and descending fog. Water beads reflected like liquid diamonds upon its shimmering shell. Maneuvering around the concrete fountain, it whispered past a blind statue of Apollo, banking smoothly toward six connected garages east of the mansion. Clinton Windell pressed his fat thumb on the wide red button of his electric garage door opener. The Jag coasted into a well-lit space, wide enough for two of its kind. The garage door automatically closed. Minus the whispering engine, the garage was as quiet as a tomb.

Windell grabbed his alligator briefcase, calfskin gem bag, and Baitz doll out of the trunk. To his left was the Bentley Sedan. To his right were the 1965 Alvis TE21 saloon, 1952 Lambert Simplicia, and 1924 Dagmar petite sedan. The missing Ford Explorer meant Genevieve was not home. He would tell his wife his great news as soon as she returned.

Windell walked down the corridor that connected the garage to his mansion. Motion sensors turned lights on and off as he entered and exited their detection fields. The walk gave him a chance to reflect on his good fortune. It had been a glorious day. Amsterdam was his *coup de main*. When he told the Bellingham Jewelers board he would personally handle the next major purchase, his enemies had been delighted. Those who called for his head had falsely wished him well with energetic handshakes and cynical smiles. His friends counseled against such a plan in light of mounting dissatisfaction amongst board members who wanted him ousted.

Clinton showed them he was still on top of his game. Delivering twenty-million dollars of first-rate gemstones, once cut, polished and set into precious metals would be worth twenty times as much.

The mutinous board members who blamed Clinton Windell for dwindling sales of the largest fine jewelry chain in the northwest would be shamed into silence. Even Andrea Bettencourt, who wanted his CEO spot bad enough to kill for it, would not have sufficient votes to unseat him. Delaying his overthrow would buy him enough time to complete his plan. After which, Andrea Bettencourt could have his seat with his blessings.

Clinton was dismayed upon entering the kitchen, and then irritated that his butler, Edward, was not there to greet him. Through the kitchen, dining room and living room he walked with a confidence many correctly perceived as arrogance. A tailored Armani suit gave his thick, tall body elegance he could achieve in no other way. When it became apparent his butler was missing, Clinton resolved he would fire Edward for leaving his daughter alone.

Second door to his left at the top of the carpeted stairs was his daughter's bedroom. The master bedroom he shared with his wife was next door.

Clinton set his gem bag alongside his briefcase outside the master bedroom door. He heard familiar voices coming from his daughter's room. He crept up to his daughter's bedroom door holding the Baitz doll behind his back. When he looked in on Pamela, she was asleep in her Pocahontas pajamas curled up with Soochow, a doll Clinton had brought back for her from Canton. The Wizard of Oz was on the TV screen watching Pamela. Dorothy had accidentally doused the wicked witch of the west with water.

"Aaaeee! You cursed brat!" the wicked witch screamed. "Look what you've done! I'm melting! Melting! Oh what a world. Who would've thought a good little girl like you could destroy my beautiful wickedness?" Clinton watched the witch melt like hot candle wax until all that remained was her black dress, black cape and pointed black hat heaped amongst hissing steam.

Clinton placed the Baitz doll on Pamela's dresser. He stopped the DVD and turned off the entertainment system. Gently, Clinton lifted Pamela from her bed. His six-year old daughter was as light as a bag of cotton in his hands. In the cradle of his arms, Pamela stirred briefly.

Clinton threw back her Cinderella bedspread and tucked her in. "Sweet dreams, precious," he whispered, kissing her forehead. He positioned the Baitz doll on the dresser so Pamela would see it when she awoke, turned off her lamps, and softly closed the door behind him.

When Windell switched on the master bedroom ceiling light, he noticed his wall safe was open. Two steps later, he felt a dull pain near the base of his skull. Dazed, Windell fell to his knees. The second blow propelled him into darkness.

A man wearing a Woodstock II T-shirt, blue jeans, tie-dyed ski mask, black leather jacket, gloves and dusty Doc Martens closed the door. Another dressed in crisp military green, polished combat boots, black ski mask, and black leather gloves put away his blackjack and checked Windell's pulse. The assailants stared at each other. Their identical clear blue eyes met. They smiled identical smiles. Woodstock checked the gem bag. Military knelt by the unconscious body. A nod from Woodstock made them smile again. Military turned Windell over. Each man grabbed Windell under an arm and sat him upright on his bed. Clinton looked as if he had fallen asleep reading or viewing television.

From customized blue leather cutaway holsters hidden beneath their jackets, the two men detached silver forty-four Smith & Wessons fitted with silencers. Military squeezed off a shot. The forty-four spit a bullet that ripped through Windell's left temple, obliterating the right side of his face. Woodstock followed with one through the heart.

They holstered their weapons assessing their gruesome work. Side by side with calm fascination, they regarded the speckles and rivulets of lambent blood, splattered flesh and splintered bones juxtaposed against that, which remained whole of Clinton Windell. Woodstock whispered into Military's ear, "While life often imitates art, death is an original masterpiece." Military grinned and nodded. Each man grabbed an arm and crossed it over the now crimson torso of the deceased. With a thumb's up, they agreed, their masterpiece was complete.

Woodstock closed the wall safe. Military picked up the gem bag. Woodstock switched off the light and closed the door behind them.

***

Six rain soaked weeks I'd been following Antonio Farhletti everywhere except the bathroom and had nothing to show for it. The former 1990

Miss Oregon, Roxanna Farhletti, suspected her husband was having an affair. So did I, several in fact, but I had no proof.

I'd tailed the President of Diva Computer Software to the elegant Tea Room at the posh Heathman Hotel. The downstairs held about sixty people and was three-quarters full, Farhletti sat at a round white marble table in front of the glowing fireplace that had an original Claude Gallee' hanging above it. He was having a dry martini—stirred, not shaken—with Judith Hardy, vice-president of the Software Development Division. I remembered her from a brief meeting they had earlier that day. Farhletti had just fired her boss, Andrew Tollman and the president of International Marketing, Deborah Slade. Hardy was next in line for Tollman's position and this meeting was set up to discuss her promotion. I sat in the mezzanine with a clear view of the whole scene.

Hardy had changed out of her double-breasted business suit into a tomato red, cashmere mini-dress, polished red pumps, small ruby earrings, and a tasteful ruby necklace. A tiny silver ankle bracelet rounded out her ensemble. The dress complimented her sleek figure. She had undone her French braid so her thick red hair fell onto her slender shoulders like a fine mink collar. Away from the office, she seemed a different person. Her smile was less restrained, more generous. Her freckled skin appeared to glow and her oval face came alive with expression. If I didn't know better, I would have assumed her no more than a bright-eyed college student rather than a hard-nosed, dynamic V.P. of one of the largest software companies on the West Coast.

Antonio Farhletti was another story. He wore a tailored gray herringbone suit, smoky gray silk tie, white tailored shirt with engraved silver cufflinks, waxed black leather shoes, platinum Rolex, and his plain 24 ct. gold wedding band. His slicked back, short, raven hair made him resemble a hustler rather than the debonair sophisticate he really was.

Though Farhletti sat with his back to me, I could see his reflection in the glass screen in front of the fireplace. Clean-shaven, angular face, beak-like nose, narrow brown eyes and narrow mouth was a face that I had become all too familiar. He was a regimented man of meticulous habits. Every morning he awoke at five. By five-thirty, he began his five-mile run. Monday morning he met with his domestic executive staff via teleconferencing, on Monday, Wednesday and Friday afternoon his personal trainer took Farhletti through a workout designed to tone and strengthen. Tennis on Tuesday and golf on Thursday doubled as business meetings with high-end clients. In between, he had private meetings with executive officers and spoke with his international executive team via videoconferencing. Monday through Friday, he took his wife to dinner at Brasserie Montmartre. On two of those nights, he met with Karen Carbo, president of Manufacturing, and Deniece Thomas, president of Research & Development at their homes.

When I discussed his late night pow-wows with Mrs. Farhletti, she said she was well aware of her husband's private meetings. She mentioned it was common for Antonio to meet with his officers at their homes. Even so, she admitted, she had barged in on both Carbo and Thomas during one of their private sessions only to find them fully clothed and hashing out some company business. Like me, she still believed something was amiss. Like Mrs. Farhletti, I was unable to get the goods on her husband to prove it. The only things that seemed out of character for Farhletti this week were the firing of two Division heads and this public meeting with Hardy.

Back at the Heathman Hotel, The Dave Marshall Trio was playing a mediocre rendition of "In A Sentimental Mood." Having settled into the soothing ambiance of vibrant conversations, music and soft lights, it was difficult for me not to relax. I had to keep reminding myself I was there for one reason, to nail an adulterer.

I don't usually take domestic cases. They are too convoluted for my investigative taste. Insurance companies, financial institutions, corporations, they pay well and on time when you do a job to their satisfaction. Private clients are far more finicky and less profitable. My only reason for taking this particular case was that six of the Pacific Northwest's finest PI's had come up empty on this guy. That intrigued me, that and the grand a day plus expenses.

Hardy sat across from Farhletti. Smoke from the cigarette she held in her left hand, curled about her face. When I was ten, I had a deaf uncle who taught me to read lips. The key is to forget sound and watch the mouth form the words. In the beginning, I could only pick off a few words. Gradually sporadic words flowed into concrete sentences. Then one day, it became as easy as dreaming. I've not only mastered the skill but the ability to prevent people from realizing what I'm doing. It's a secret I keep from even my closest friends. Hardy's cherry red lipstick made it easy.

Most of the conversation centered on finalizing a software package called U-T, expanding into foreign markets, increasing domestic sales and sizing down. Hardy asked Farhletti about Benton Lawson. She said he was still causing problems at the Beaverton Research Complex. Farhletti's response brought a sinister smile to Hardy's face, the type I'd seen plastered on Colombian drug members who had permission to kill someone who'd been a pain in the ass. Right then I knew Hardy was not only good at what she did but that she enjoyed it.

We were in the middle of our respective drinks when a man joined them. A well-groomed corporate type, wearing an expensive suit, moved as if he were in an ingratiating spotlight. Farhletti seemed indifferent to his presence. Hardy greeted him as though she expected him. The stranger took the seat to the right of Farhletti. That put him in position for me to read his lips. The man made small talk. Hardy appeared interested. Farhletti was gracious but seemed bored. Farhletti excused himself. The man waited until Farhletti was out of sight before he spoke again. He told Hardy all had gone as planned and they could proceed with the next step.

"No hitches," was his response to an apparent question from Hardy, whose mouth was obscured by her coffee cup. The man removed a sealed, padded manila envelope from his inside jacket pocket and handed it to Hardy under the table. On the man's manicured left pinkie was an enormous emerald ring. Hardy quickly slipped the envelope into her purse.

"Everything you need is in that package," the man said.

I watched the man with the enormous emerald ring leave, not knowing what to make out of what I had just witnessed. Farhletti returned. He asked Hardy what their visitor had wanted. She smiled seductively and said, "Her body." Farhletti said he could understand his interest in such an admirable asset, and then moved to sit at the right of Hardy.

Hardy and Farhletti toasted with a glass of expensive champagne, kissing after taking a sip. Hardy looked around. I tapped my hand on the table while looking at the band, which were playing a tolerable rendition of Billy Strayhorn's "Passion Flower." When I checked my watch, I could see out of the corner of my eye that Hardy was still staring in my direction. I looked around, appearing annoyed, as if searching for someone who was late. It seemed to work. By the time I took a sip of my Club Soda and lime, Hardy's interest in me had ceased.

Farhletti caressed Hardy's cheek. Hardy kissed his palm. Farhletti placed his hand on her knee and whispered something into her ear that made her green eyes light with anticipation. When Hardy put a slender arm around Farhletti's shoulders, I thought they were going to do the nasty right there. I waited a few minutes before I left. My instincts told me I would need my telephoto lens. I already knew what they would be doing, and where.

CHAPTER TWO

Back at the office, I sat staring at my computer monitor. The Farhletti report was giving me fits. It had been foolish of Farhletti and Hardy to fuck in Hardy's living room with the curtains open. I suppose the beautiful night and their drunkenness got the better of them. They might as well have invited me in. My problem was maintaining a professional tone of a salacious encounter while not scrimping on incriminating details, not my forte.

The Impressions were coming from the radio. They took me away with their lilting promises of a train to Jordan. I closed my eyes for a moment and got on-board.

***

I started in this business five years ago when I left the federal government, ending a ten-year career as a narcotics agent for the DEA. Before the Agency, I was a military man, two years as an M.P., the last three as an Army Intelligence officer. The first thing I did after my premature retirement from the DEA was to realize a dream. I'd always wanted to take a cross-country train trip. I boarded a train in my hometown, Pittsburgh, and wound up in Portland, Oregon. I liked it, stayed, and set up shop.

I'd done a little insurance investigation on the side while I was with the DEA. It was easy money then and it's easy money now. A lot easier than dealing with thugs, murderers, drug cartels, corruption, con men and junkies.

***

I leaned back in my chair pondering how to proceed with the Farhletti report when the front door opened.

"Renita?" I yelled.

"Yep!" Renita answered. Renita Harris is my junior partner. I was looking for clerical help when she answered my ad. Renita has a Masters Degree in Computer Science. She made it clear she was interested in the P.I. biz and agreed to take on a clerical position temporarily if I'd teach her the ropes. A couple of years later she was a full-fledged private dick.

I heard the familiar clicking of her Peugeot racing bike as she wheeled it across the carpet of the outer office. When you enter the Cavanaugh Investigation Agency, Renita's office is directly ahead, mine is to the immediate right. To the far left is a room that doubles as our shower area and exercise room.

A low grunt meant Renita was lifting her bike onto its wall mount. The coarse separation of Velcro followed, first to take off her bike helmet, then her gloves. All of this was background noise along with the soulful music coming from my radio as I replayed that steamy sex scene between Farhletti and Hardy in my head.

"You're late," I said as Renita appeared in my doorway.

"Miss me?" Renita asked, leaning against the doorframe toweling herself off.

Her latté skin shined. Her baby brown eyes were beaming with youthful energy. She was wearing spandex bicycle shorts and a matching spandex halter.

"Just because we have a light caseload doesn't mean you can stroll in anytime you please," I said.

"Sorry, I overslept, hiked the Cascades this weekend. Did you hear anybody in the hall this morning?"

"Not a peep."

"I found this on the floor outside of our office." Renita walked in and laid a sealed manila envelope on my desk. She watched for my reaction. I didn't have one to give her. Written on the front in black marker was "Cedric Joseph Cavanaugh." My business cards read C. J. Cavanaugh. I'm listed the same under Investigators in the yellow pages and on the internet. Whoever went through the trouble of finding out my full name obviously wanted to make a memorable impression. I opened it. Renita stood beside me reading the letter over my shoulder.

A reliable source referred you to us, Mr. Cavanaugh. A person who vouched that you are trustworthy, discreet, and efficient. These qualities are critical for what is necessary to rectify an injustice. A man has been murdered. It is our expectation that in solving his homicide you will resolve our problem as well. Believe me when we say this is a matter of the utmost urgency for a great many people. We have taken the liberty to deposit the first installment of your fee into your agency's account. You will find it quite generous. The remaining $200,000.00 will be paid to you upon completion of this case.

You have two months to solve this crime. If within that time you fail to do so, our relationship will be terminated and the $200,000.00 will remain ours. The retainer, of course, is yours for services rendered. Do not trouble yourself attempting to trace the bank deposit. We will not tell you why it is impossible but take our word for it.

The homicide victim's name is Clinton Windell. Accompanying this letter is a DVD. It contains everything you will need to know about Mr. Windell. Should you have any questions place them on our website: www.boswell.com and they will be promptly answered. Aside from Ms. Harris, no one is to know of our arrangement. Not even Detective Pendleton. Should any of our guidelines be violated this relationship will be immediately terminated.

Time is short. You had better get to work. A word of caution: step lightly Mr. Cavanaugh. Land mines are everywhere. We will be watching.

"This is some kind of joke," Renita said. Normally I would have agreed with her but this party was too well informed. They knew about my relationship with Destini Pendleton, which meant they knew a great deal about me. My days as a DEA agent and Army Intelligence officer taught me many things. One of them was that you could find out anything about anybody if you know who to ask or where to look. These people were clued in to both. That made me curious and nervous.

"I don't think so," I said in answer to Renita's comment.

"This guy's a nut case."

"How did they know about Destini?"

"That U.N.C.F. benefit last month," Renita said. "The one you took Destini to instead of me. Your pictures were in *The Skanner's* society page. This crackpot could have seen it."

"Clinton Windell was murdered last night," I said.

"Who doesn't know that by now? It's not every day a multimillionaire gets robbed and murdered in his own home."

"It sounds like an execution from what I've read."

"Rich man, powerful enemies. He probably pissed off the wrong people on a business deal."

"Business people don't go around whacking each other because of bad deals Renita; if they did, most of 'em would be dead by now—and why go through all of this trouble?"

"Nut cases do this sort of thing," Renita said. "It's how they get their jollies. This dude's probably spotted Elvis singing a little ditty on Broadway."

"There's more than one person involved from the way this letter reads."

"So it's a nut pack. They could be involved in Windell's murder for all we know."

"One thing we can find out for sure."

"See if a deposit's been made to our account?"

"You got it."

Renita left. I eyed the DVD for clues. It had no labeling, distinctive markings, or packaging. I loaded it by the edges in case our mystery person had left any prints. The first thing to appear on the monitor was a picture of Clinton Windell with his resume. I paged through to get an idea of what I was dealing with. Judging by the amount of information I saw, I decided it would be easier to comprehend on paper. It was still printing when Renita returned.

"Well?" I asked.

"Fifty-thousand dollars was deposited by Boswell Industries into our account this morning."

"Confident aren't they."

Renita nodded.

"Ever heard of Boswell Industries?"

Renita shook her head.

"Probably a dummy corporation," I said.

Renita glanced at the laser printer.

"Printing copies for each of us," I said.

"This could be an all-nighter," Renita said with a smile, "Dinner at my place?"

"I'm having dinner with Destini tonight."

"When am I going to get my shot?" Renita tried sounding disappointed. She wasn't very convincing.

"You know the story."

"One of these days you're going to see things my way. When you do, I'll never give you up."

"Destini is all the woman I need."

It was about six months ago Renita caught her fiancé in bed with another woman. She immediately ended the engagement after breaking three of her ex-fiancé's ribs and pummeling his face. I did what I could to ease her pain. She mistook my paternal support as romantic interest. She has been on my case like skin on a peach ever since.

Renita leaned over me. I cut my eyes in her direction. Her cleavage was in my face. Close to four years, Renita and I've been working together. In all of that time, we haven't so much as kissed. I'm in love with Destini but I'm not dead. Sometimes when I see Renita's athletic body dressed in tight clothes, I have to practically run away to prevent that from changing.

"The future is ours my sweet," Renita whispered.

"Whatever," I said sarcastically. "Can we get back to work? We've got two months to collect on two hundred grand and I'm not about to blow it."

Renita pulled a chair next to me. I directed her to move it back to the opposite side of the desk.

"Let's pool our facts," I said.

"Not much to go on."

"An anonymous letter, a murder-robbery victim, and fifty-grand deposited into our bank account."

"That about sums it up," Renita said. I raised an eyebrow. "No pun intended."

"See what you can dig up on Boswell Industries. Also, check our client list to see if there's any connection with Windell or Boswell

Industries. Maybe we can get a lead on this reliable source they mentioned in the letter. I'll get started brushing up on Clinton Windell."

"Mind if I shower and change first?"

"Please do," I said. Renita narrowed her eyes.

"I make you sweat," Renita said. She was right but I'd never admit it.

"When you're done you can finish writing the Farhletti report since I was up late nailing him and still managed to make it into the office on time."

"Having trouble describing some of the spicy details?" Renita asked. I twisted my mouth to one side pretending to be preoccupied by what was on my computer monitor. "Let me guess," Renita said, standing, "a little hot and steamy sexual romp?"

"Yeah," I said trying not to look as embarrassed as I felt. Renita smiled and shook her head. "Give me what you have and I'll take it from there."

I handed Renita my notes and a flash drive containing the photographs I had taken.

"Don't forget to close the report so I can get into it," Renita told me.

"Will do."

"Which do you want done first?"

"Do the Farhletti report first, that'll free us up to concentrate on Windell."

Renita was leaving when I made the mistake of saying, "I owe you one." Renita turned and gave me a flirtatious look and said, "Once is all I ask."

Two copies of the DVD information had finished printing. One hundred twenty-three pages each. I grabbed my sports jacket. I needed a place where I could concentrate without interruption. That meant home. I heard the shower. I placed the second copy of the printout on Renita's desk with a note where I would be, taking care to lock the front door behind me when I left.

CHAPTER THREE

Home is that place you wish to be more than anywhere in the world, says my mother. My English cottage in a peaceful northeast Portland neighborhood is for me that revered domicile of which she speaks. Hardwood floors, spacious rooms and an abundance of windows make for a very inviting stay. The living room, kitchen, den, and study are decorated with Kpelle art and artifacts. My bedroom and the two bathrooms are done in Iroquois motifs. The two guest bedrooms are of a Scottish flavor. I chose those particular themes because they represent the proud sum of my heritage. I want to be reminded of it every moment I spend in my sanctuary.

In the spring, my red brick house is a remarkable sight. At the front a sloping green lawn parallels a brick walk winding up toward my pediment doorway. Beneath the study and living room windows, Coxswain roses bloom. The backyard is a sizeable grass rectangle hemmed by Canadian hemlock. At the west end of the yard white Japanese wisteria set inside the hemlock and create a shady area for summer reading and afternoon naps. Red orchids, leopard's bane, white narcissuses, and pink astilbes grow in a square patch of rich soil beneath my kitchen window. Tending the roses and my personal garden are the only yard work I do. My gardening service handles the rest.

Booker and Andrew greeted me as soon as I opened the front door. Destini had given me the twin Scottish terriers as birthday gifts. She claimed my tropical fish were not enough to keep me from being lonely when she wasn't around. A couple of months later Renita presented me with four lively Zebra finches to celebrate our four-year partnership, and—as she put it—to add a light tropical ambiance to my otherwise overly cultivated place. As much as I love my pets, if I didn't have maid service to liberate me to care for them, they'd probably be dead from neglect by now.

On the coffee table was a signed note from Becky informing me she had done the additional cleaning I had requested and that I would be billed accordingly. I didn't care about the extra cost. What I wanted was for everything to be perfect for my dinner with Destini.

I fed my tropical fish and my singing finches: Toussaint, Coretta, Claude, and Truth. Andrew and Booker have the run of the house. In the north corner of the basement are two pieces of flexible pipe each clamped to the bottom of two plastic hoppers mounted to my basement wall. Each hopper is filled with dry dog food. Alongside each hopper are attached garden hoses connected to water spigots I installed on my water lines. The hoppers are rigged to release single servings of dog food into Andrew and Booker's dishes every four hours. When I turn on the taps, the hoses fill with fresh water. I've attached a pinchcock on the end of each hose. Every day before I leave I open the pinchcocks enough to half fill the water bowls then tighten them so a small drip keeps the bowls full. In the south corner of the basement is a self-made wooden sandbox filled with kitty litter. The litter is there in case the twins don't want to venture through the pet door to the backyard to do their business. I close the basement door and personally attend to all of Booker and Andrew's needs when I'm home. They know where to go for food, water, and relief when I'm not. According to my watch, and their empty dog dishes, it was time to take Andrew and Booker for our morning run.

After a breakfast of peanut butter on raisin toast, orange juice, grapefruit, and coffee, I dusted the letter, the envelope it came in, and the jewel case for prints. Except for Renita's and mine, they were clean. I turned my attention to the report.

Clinton Windell came from a blue-collar background. He graduated high school then joined the Navy. During his time overseas, Windell developed a fascination for gems. After an honorable discharge from the Navy, he enrolled at James Madison University where he earned a bachelor degree in Geology, and one in Business Administration. While working on his master's in Mineralogy at the American College of Switzerland, he met Geoffrey Bellingham, president and owner of Bellingham Jewelers. According to my phantom source, Windell became the son the widower Bellingham never had. Bellingham bankrolled Windell's education with the agreement Windell would work for him when he completed his thesis. Under Bellingham's tutelage Windell learned everything there was to know about the jewelry business. By the time Bellingham retired, Clinton Windell did what he was groomed to do. He stepped into a burgeoning jewelry business and expanded it into the most prestigious jewelry store chain on the west coast.

That was Clinton Windell's professional life in a nutshell but the report didn't stop there. Windell had fathered three illegitimate children by three different women and there was an assault charge in West Virginia that was suspiciously dropped. Whoever compiled this jacket on Windell did not assemble it from bits and pieces of various sources. There were specific details of persons, places, and events that convinced me they had tracked and backtracked this man for quite some time. A guess would be since his association with Bellingham. My knuckles tingled. When that happens, I know I'm into some heavy shit. If these people were capable of trailing a man like Clinton Windell for that many years what the hell did they need me for?

CHAPTER FOUR

I don't recall if it was the second or third Saturday in September when Destini and I first met. What I do remember are the details of that particular day. Saturday Market was brimming with a buoyant crowd casually browsing arts and crafts booths, enjoying the multicultural music and cuisine. I glanced over from a Dream Catcher I was contemplating buying when I saw her. It made me wonder if the good spirit dreams had blessed me while I was awake.

A tall woman with mocha skin, clear hazel eyes, lush lips, a modest round nose and fine black braids flowing down to the small of her sinewy back stared back at me. The air was crystal clear and nippy, yet I felt feverish all over. My stomach became jittery and my palms started to sweat. Up until then I believed love at first sight was a silly myth. Clearly, I was mistaken. It was either love or an anxiety attack.

I turned away and tried to gain control of myself. She approached to ask what I was looking at. I managed to say the most beautiful woman in the world. She liked that. It made her smile. Her dimpled smile made my anxiety worse.

Maybe Destini noticed my condition and felt sorry for me.

Maybe she noticed the sincerity in my timorous voice.

Maybe she liked me from the start.

I don't know and I don't care. All I know is she took over from there. Destini hung in there until I could give more than single syllable answers to her questions and respond sensibly to her open-ended comments. Before I realized what was happening, we had spent the entire afternoon together.

That night we met for dinner at Genoa, one of the finest restaurants in Portland. Destini entered wearing a bolero jacket and tube skirt that turned heads and once again left me speechless. I remember her confident walk, her upbeat mood, her sultry voice and feminine gestures, her entrancing perfume, her radiant skin, her infectious laugh, her inviting lipstick, her engaging eyes and mesmerizing smile. I didn't get lucky that night in the conventional context that phrase is often used in reference to romance. What I got was roped and tied. She's pretty much been running the show ever since.

***

Destini and I hadn't seen each other in a month. She had been busy finalizing half of her caseload and I had been doing a lot of surveillance work on the Farhletti case. Our three-year anniversary had passed without celebration, and although Destini wasn't upset about it, I wanted to make it up to her nonetheless.

She was late. She could have called. It was unlike Destini to be inconsiderate and my mood swung between anger and concern with each tardy minute. I'd made a special Tanzania dinner that would have to be refrigerated if she didn't show soon. I decided not to tell her about my involvement in the Windell case. It was a difficult decision. For the moment, I saw no other recourse.

At the beginning of our relationship, Destini told me she was an executive sales rep for a cosmetics firm. Six weeks later, I discovered she was a homicide detective for the Portland Police Bureau. Destini confessed she had misgivings about telling me the truth because she knew she was in love with me and she figured I'd bolt. She was right. I hate death. During my South American stint as a DEA deep cover operative, I saw enough dead bodies to last me through hell and back. Her job's still our biggest sore spot. It was quits between us for a while but I found I was miserable without her. Destini vowed never to keep secrets from me again. Implicit in that agreement was that I would do the same. I was betraying her trust and I knew it. In the end, I could only hope to find some way to make amends.

When Destini arrived, Booker and Andrew were ecstatic. I took care of Destini's coat and purse while they basked in her attention. She played with the terriers until I ordered them away to have her to myself.

Destini apologized for being late. She didn't have to, the high heels, rubied halter dress, my gift pearl necklace and Cerruti 1881 she was wearing was all the apology I needed.

I seated Destini at my solid oak dining table covered with a handmade lace tablecloth, and table settings of Waterford Crystal, fine bone china, sterling silver and lace Scottish napkins. Then I lit the dinner candles, turned on the soulful mood music, dimmed the lights, and served the mtori with coconut cream and chilled banana wine. I was wearing my Dakar skullcap, leather sandals and silk kibr with next to nothing underneath. After my shower, I had splashed on some Boucheron. Destini's favorite.

Destini was impressed. She told me so. I asked Destini to elaborate on what impressed her. She said she wasn't clear of my meaning. I told her to expound on what about me had impressed her at that moment as opposed to any other day she'd seen me. Destini smiled. I could tell she thought the whole idea was silly. So did I, but what the hell. She was slow to respond. I prodded Destini by telling her to imagine she was seeing me for the very first time. "How would you describe me to your friends?" I asked.

"There would be no need; all of my friends have met you."

"Let's say there was one or two that hadn't." I stood erect with my hands behind my back looking as if I were staring out into the distance at some intriguing spectacle. Destini took me in for a moment before she spoke.

"I would describe you as a hard bodied, square shouldered, six-four caramel treat with a handsome clean-cut baby face."

"That's all," I said feigning disappointment. I wasn't going to let Destini off that easy.

"That would be for starters," Destini said taking the bait. "Then I would tell them about your dimpled smile, full kissable lips, strong square jaw line, dreamy brown eyes, large manicured hands and large pedicure feet, and you know what large feet mean." Destini stopped.

"And," I said.

"And then I'd tell them about your cute little round ears and that darling Roman nose of yours."

"It may be longer than your average snout but my nose is not Roman."

"I adore it just the same."

"And my ears are not cute."

"They are to me," Destini said.

"What about my hair?"

"You don't have any hair, C. J. You have it cut so close you're almost bald—*but*, on those few occasions when you've let it grow a little I've noticed it is jet black with a few whispers of premature gray."

"You didn't mention my head."

"It's square honey, normal size square. What else needs to be said?"

"And my scar?"

"Yes of course. And I would adoringly tell my friends about the ruggedly handsome scar under your powerful square chin."

"You can't leave out the story behind the scar." I lifted my chin higher. Destini rolled her eyes.

"He has this adorable scar on his chin that is a memento from the twenty-seven stitches he received after a bar fight he was in while a young man in the Service."

"Why was I in that bar fight?"

"Defending a lady's honor," Destini said.

"And how many men did I fight in Biloxi, Mississippi where that bar fight took place?"

"Four."

"Did I win?"

"According to you, yes."

"I can have signed eyewitness affidavits here within the week stating that I did."

"I believe you, and I would add that part when I boasted about you to my friends."

"Well I see we've reached that point where you're all tapped out on the topic of C. J. Cavanaugh," I said bringing my chin down, looking at Destini while still holding my pose. "But I would have expected more from a keen eyed police detective such as yourself."

"Who may I remind you is off the clock."

I smiled showing my appreciation to Destini for having played along. Destini gently shook her head. "Can we eat now?" she asked. I joined her at the table.

What I wanted was for us to forget the rest of the world and enjoy each other for an evening. Destini had other things on her mind. "You're working on the Windell case?" I asked after Destini told me she had been detained questioning a suspect who confessed to killing Clinton Windell. He turned out to be just another in a string of crackpots who sprung up every time some high profile crime was committed.

"That surprises you?" Destini asked.

"Not at all," I said.

In truth, I had expected one of the senior detectives to be assigned to the Windell case. Tiptoeing around the police while doing this investigation was already going to be difficult enough. Destini's involvement was making this nearly impossible.

"So what's going on with Windell's homicide?" I asked.

"On the surface it looks pretty simple," Destini said. "Windell had just returned from an overseas business trip with a twenty-million dollars' worth of uncut gems. The thieves were lying in wait. They murder Windell and make off with the goods. End of story."

"Thieves?"

"We found enough evidence to believe two people were involved. It looked like Windell was knocked out and then dragged over to his bed where he was shot twice."

"Was it a professional hit?"

"Looks that way, no one heard a shot, not even his daughter sleeping in the next room. The shots were fired at close range, one through the heart, the other through the head. If robbery was their primary motive, they certainly knew how to kill as well. We'll know more after the M.E.'s report."

"Did they take anything else?"

"Not to our knowledge. We'll know for sure by start of business tomorrow."

We breezed through our mtori. I cleared away the dirty dishes and served the banana fritters, plantain chips, sweet potatoes, and banana and coconut beef stew.

"More wine?" I asked.

"Are you trying to get me drunk?"

"Do I need to?"

"Not tonight."

Destini gave me a sensuous smile that made me want to make love to her right then on the table. I cleared my throat after I cleared my mind of lust. Here was an opportunity to learn a wellspring of inside information about Windell's murder. Guilt crept up the back of my neck but my investigative juices had already taken over. Shame would have to wait.

"So what do you make of the Windell homicide?" I nonchalantly asked.

"No signs of forced entry," Destini said.

"Sounds like they had inside information."

Chewing on a fritter Destini answered with a nod.

"Didn't the neighbors see anything suspicious?"

"Nothing significant."

"What about the servants?"

"Their live-in butler's the only one who would've been around that time of night. He had the night off."

"Any leads?"

"Could be a number of people involved at this point. Even his wife's a suspect."

"Really?"

"According to Windell's personal attorney," Destini said, "he filed for divorce."

"That's not grounds for murder."

"It is if you've signed a prenup that would leave you penniless."

"You're kidding?" I said.

Destini was chewing a forkful of stew when she shook her head.

"Are you certain the motive wasn't robbery?"

Destini raised an eyebrow. A warning light had come on. I could see it in her eyes.

"You usually shy away when I talk shop," Destini said. "Why are you so interested in this case?"

I'm a good liar and a fair actor when I have to be, qualities which kept me alive in South America; by the same token, Destini didn't make Detective Sergeant First Class faster than anyone ever on the Portland Police force for nothing. I needed to be careful.

"This is the big time," I said. "It's not everyday a prominent citizen is robbed and murdered in his own home." Destini stared at me. She was sizing me up. Lying to her was a new experience. If she realized I wasn't telling the truth she let it pass. I needed to change the subject for a moment.

"What time are you due at the precinct?" I asked.

"Seven sharp, the chief wants closure on this case ASAP."

"You'll find the killer."

Destini thanked me for my show of confidence although her tone suggested it wasn't necessary.

"You've got to give me these recipes, C. J. And where did you find banana wine?"

"If you lived here you'd all ready know," I said.

"I would be living here if you'd marry me."

The topic of marriage was another motivation to change the subject. I had no problem with Destini and I living together but the thought of marriage made me squeamish. I've never been married. The way I felt about Destini being a homicide detective made me wonder if it could ever happen. Only last month she was involved in a shootout while working undercover. It wasn't the first time since I've known her and I'm confident it won't be her last. Knowing that Destini could one day lose her life in the line of duty scared the hell out of me. I told Destini it was the fear of her being killed that kept me from asking her to marry me. Destini argued that death could come at anytime in any form. I couldn't argue with her. All I could do was tell her how I felt. What I hadn't told her was living together was a trial run for me, a test to see if I could ever conquer that fear.

"Did you catch Farhletti with his pants down?" Destini asked.

"That and more," I said.

"Who was his mistress?"

I filled Destini in on all the sordid details.

"Why don't I ever get one of those soap opera cases?" Destini asked.

Destini wasn't fond of homicides herself. What she loved was gathering enough evidence to nail murderers of the most despicable crime she could imagine.

"You work in homicide, dear," I sarcastically said.

"I know, I know," Destini said dismissing me with a forkful of sweet potatoes. "Still you'd think every now and then I'd get a passionate homicide where the man slays the husband because it was the only way he could be with his true love."

"Sounds like someone's been reading too many romance novels," I said.

There was a long pause. For a minute we ate in comfortable silence as only two people who are satisfied with each other's company can.

"I'm sure Windell had a lot of enemies," I said.

"More than he ever realized—which brings to mind something I've wanted to discuss with you. What's going on with you and Miss Thang?"

"Pardon?"

"Your partner?"

"What about her?"

"I stopped by your office to treat you to brunch this morning and Renita was getting dressed after taking a shower."

I wondered how Destini got into the office after I had locked the door but I didn't bother to ask. Why stir the pot? "What's your point?"

"Does she always take a shower at the office?"

"Only when she rides her bike to work or exercises," I said.

"How often does she ride her bike to work or use the exercise room, C. J.?"

"Often, you know that."

"You're telling me that chick walks around the office most days wearing nothing but a towel. Well I bet you don't need a mocha java latte' to get you going?"

"Don't start Destini. Renita and I make the perfect team. I enjoy doing the legwork and most of the case files. She likes doing research, accounting and case bookings. We've been over this a dozen times. It's no big deal. I use the office shower a lot myself."

"I didn't realize P.I. work was so strenuous," Destini said not bothering to mask her mounting irritation.

"You know what I mean," I said. "After a workout you need a shower."

"I wish you'd fire that tramp."

"Renita's not a tramp. She's my associate."

"Call it what you want honey but hot is hot, and that's what that chick is for you." Destini was right. Nevertheless, Renita is to me what Liederman is to her, my partner and confidant. To find someone you can place that much faith in is rare. I trust Renita with my life.

"She's a flirtatious kid," I said trying to defuse the matter, "who likes pissing you off."

"Apparently so do you."

"You don't see me going off when someone sends you flowers or candy or ask you out on dates."

"Then who was it who threatened to rearrange Nick Traymor's face for asking me to the opera? Oh, that wasn't C. J. Cavanaugh. It must've been his jealous twin brother."

"I may have lost it on occasion."

"On a number of occasions is more like it."

I was getting disgusted both with myself for concealing my involvement with the Windell case and our conversation about Renita. My plans for the evening were being derailed by hard reality.

"Here we are," I said, "having a romantic candlelight dinner and all we can talk about is a homicide and my business partner."

"Okay let's talk about us." Destini ate the last morsel on her plate. She begged off my offer of seconds patting her tummy to indicate she was full. After a long sip of wine, Destini dabbed her berry lips with her napkin then picked up where she'd left off.

"We've been together for three years and in all of that time you've never told me how you feel. I want to hear you tell me now."

I thought about it for a moment before I realized Destini was right. I suppose I expected my actions to do my talking for me.

"You know how I feel," I said staring into her hazel eyes.

"Tell me C. J."

I squirmed in my chair. I felt like a child being asked a tough question by his grade school teacher. One of my father's expressions came to mind, "Love makes punks of us all."

"I love you," I said looking toward the fireplace where the terriers were stretched out on the Kpelle rug watching us. Andrew and Booker sat up waiting for an indication they were welcomed back into the fold.

"That will make the dogs happy," Destini said following my line of sight before looking back at me and continuing. "Look at me C. J. and say it."

After taking a moment to gather my courage, I looked at Destini and told her I loved her. She gracefully stood, walked over to me, and led me by the hand to the living room sofa. I had a fire going in the fireplace. If Destini had wanted to she could've walked the runways of New York or Paris; but her physical beauty was only one of the reasons I loved her. Destini knew who she was. Confidence, pride, wit, charm, intelligence, compassion, and commitment are characteristics that mean a great deal to me. Destini possessed all of those qualities and more. So why was I so hesitant to tell Destini I loved her? Why couldn't I come to terms with her profession and find the nerve to ask her to marry me?

CHAPTER FIVE

No greater bliss can a man and woman share than making love. Spending the night with Destini was always that pleasure. Keeping part of her wardrobe at my house made it convenient. It gave me a sense of comfort that Destini laid claim to her space. I suppose some people would have considered that a commitment but that wasn't enough for either of us. We both wanted more. Still our night together hadn't changed my mind about marriage. The onus was still on me.

After Destini left for the precinct, I called Carl Wheaton at Lunsford Insurance. Lunsford handled a wide variety of insurance needs. When it came to insuring expensive items Lunsford could be considered the Northwest's version of Lloyd's of London. I knew from my phantom source that Lunsford carried complete coverage for the Bellingham Jewelers chain and Clinton Windell. I'd done a good deal of investigative work for Lunsford on contingent claims. Carl was always impressed with my results.

Under the guise of looking for work, I asked Carl if he had anything for me. Lunsford's head investigator was very willing to help. He told me he was swamped mentioning Clinton Windell's murder being at the top of his pain-in-the-ass list. Carl offered me the case before I could even suggest it.

I called Destini after I spoke with Carl to inform her we would be working on the same case and to ask if she were up for a repeat performance of last night. She said she would get back to me on the latter. She also warned me to stay out of her way.

I felt better about what I was doing when I hung up. Working for Lunsford on the Windell case cleared me to move about freely. Flowers would be a nice gesture to let Destini know I missed her and to further ease my conscious. I called my florist and had her send Destini a bouquet of two dozen, long stemmed, pink, white, and red sweetheart roses. The card was to read, "Thinking of you, C. J.;" that done, it was time to get down to business.

Carl e-mailed me what he had on Clinton Windell. There was nothing there I hadn't already learned from my phantom clients.

I fed my finches and tropical fish, and then took Andrew and Booker with me on my run. When we got back I fed my famished terriers, showered, dressed, ate, and then checked in with Renita. She had spent all yesterday and most of the morning surfing the Web hoping to learn something about our mysterious employers. Nothing turned up. I told her what I had done to cover our tracks and that I'd fill her in when I got into the office. First, I wanted to take a trip to the crime scene to nose around. Renita said she would search the Web a while longer before moving on to her other sources.

On the way to the Windell estate, I gave some thought to my phantom employer. It's a rarity for private investigators to get involved in homicides. Primarily it's because the police are very good at their job. Secondly, few people can afford to pay an investigator what it takes to do a thorough homicide investigation. I was still puzzled why they had chosen me from all of the possible sources they could have gone to for this endeavor.

Cruising south along I-5 in my emerald Lexus, I noticed I was being tailed. A sapphire Jaguar XJS convertible with the license plate "HADES" had been following me since the I-84 on ramp. It was a safe bet my investors were keeping an eye on me just as they did Windell. I didn't like it. No one looks over my shoulder while I'm working.

I tried getting a look at who was in the vehicle but I couldn't see through the Jaguar's tinted glass. I called Renita from my car phone and asked her to run a make on the Jaguar. She came up empty. The car didn't exist according to the DMV. Renita sounded concerned. I told her of my suspicions in an attempt to calm her fears. Renita didn't sound convinced. It was the best I could do at the time.

By the time, I arrived at the Windell estate the Jaguar had vanished. They had taken the off ramp before mine. That didn't convince me they weren't still lurking.

A temporary security station detained me when I pulled into the entrance. Armed uniformed personnel were everywhere. A hive of gardeners and landscapers were working to repair damage done by the press, police, and paparazzo. The Greek God of Prophecy watched it all from the concrete fountain with indifference. A guard wearing sergeant stripes asked me my business. I explained to him who I was and why I was there. The sergeant called someone who cleared me to proceed to the house. The sergeant instructed me where to park and how to get there. I didn't smart mouth him about being in a circular driveway not leaving me much choice.

A uniformed butler answered the doorbell, a thickly muscled man, about six-foot with wide shoulders, large hands, a cleft chin, thinning brown hair, and stark blue eyes. As they say, something was amiss. Call it intuition but you get a nose for people in this field. That is how you survive. You hone your instincts until they become trustworthy allies. This man lacked the genuine charm of a gentleman's gentleman. He looked out of sorts in his butler's uniform. He inquired as to the nature of my business. I told him why I was there gave him my card and waited.

Glancing around as I waited I noticed something. It came from the tree-covered hillside to the west of where I stood. Someone was watching with binoculars. Their lenses glared like Roman candles. I pretended not to notice. The butler returned to escort me to Mrs. Windell as I started toward my car to fetch my own binoculars. I put my curiosity on hold.

People were hard at work cleaning, dusting, polishing, waxing, and repairing a house that had recently suffered an assault by the same inconsiderate forces that had trashed the gardens. Some appeared to be staff. Others were obviously outside help.

The butler led me through a large circular entrance and down a bright wide hall with large rooms on both sides. We came to a door near the right middle of the hall. The butler opened the door, announced me, and then stepped aside to allow me to enter. A woman wearing dark Armani sunglasses stood near the center of the study. Before the butler left, I asked if he would be available for questions later. He looked at the woman wearing sunglasses. She nodded her approval. He answered that he would.

From what I knew of Clinton Windell, the study struck me as having his signature. It smelled of expensive cigars. There were bell jar displays of precious stones including a piece of moon rock from the Apollo 13 mission. Ornate brass framed oil paintings decorated the walls. On the north wall nearest his eight-foot rosewood desk, were built-in dark oak bookshelves reaching to the top of the twelve-foot ceiling, stocked with books and labeled binders that Windell probably used for business and research. All along the south wall were identical bookshelves lined with antiquated books in states of disarray. Throughout the study were assorted photographs in gilded picture frames. The woman standing in the middle of the study was in most of them.

Aside from the sunglasses, Genevieve Windell looked as if she were CEO of Bellingham Jewelers. Even with a visage of grief, she was strikingly attractive with her tanned complexion, elegant features and brunette hair tied back in a lustrous ponytail. Diamond earrings, a diamond necklace, and a Rolex watch with a diamond bracelet wristband told me she was a woman comfortable with wealth.

At about five-seven and one-hundred-twenty pounds her smoke blue designer double-breasted jacket, matching skirt and black Italian leather stacked heel shoes made her appear both powerful and sensual. In the midst of what was probably the most stressful time of her life, for the moment, Genevieve Windell reigned as distinguished and in control.

We had shaken hands after the butler left. Her grip was firm. Her arms relaxed at her side. The Rolex caught daylight streaming in from draped open windows. I assumed the butler had filled her in on who I was and why I was there. I began by offering my condolences. She accepted with a curt nod. There was no place to sit aside from three leather chairs around the desk. We remained standing in the middle of the room.

***

Years ago while entrenched in my first deep cover mission, I had encountered Paulo de Tarso Celestino da Machado also known as Bebe Assassino, a ten-year old hit child for Colombian drug lord Eduardo Augusto Cardozo. Paulo's story was his mother had abandoned him. Cardozo found him and raised him as if he were his own. Rumor had it that Cardozo had actually murdered Paulo's parents and thought it would be an intriguing irony to train their child to be one of his psychotic henchmen. Cardozo had that sort of depraved sense of humor. Paulo Machado had inherited his stepfather's personality.

Once while Cardozo's top aides were away handling matters that were more pressing for their *Drogaria Senhor*, Cardozo ordered me to drive Bebe Assassino to Bogota. On the way, the pint-sized sadist cheerfully told me horror stories of torture he either witnessed or participated in. I later learned that his assignment was to execute Godofredo and Catia

Cantero. The Canteros were close friends of Alberto Acuna. Mr. Acuna once worked for Cardozo and knew a great deal about his financial empire. Word had gotten back to Cardozo that Alberto Acuna was going to broker a deal with government authorities for complete immunity in exchange for all Acuna knew about Cardozo's money laundering operations. Mr. Acuna and his family were under federal protection. Cardozo wanted Alberto Acuna to realize what lengths he would go to if Acuna did not remain silent.

About a mile northeast of Bogota, we rendezvoused with a Portuguese couple hired by Cardozo to pose as Machado's parents. The Land Rover and I remained hidden in the lush tropical forest. The couple drove Machado into town.

From my vantage point, I watched the whole thing through binoculars. There was a puppet show going on at the Porto de Graca Outdoor Theater. Machado mingled with the other children. He looked like them. Behaved like them. When the time came, from beneath his poncho, Machado produced an Ingram sub-machine gun with a silencer, given to him by the couple, and gunned down Catia and Godofredo Cantero along with their seven-year-old daughter. I saw it go down. I turned my back on the slaying I was helpless to prevent and waited for Machado in the getaway vehicle. When Bebe Assassino jumped in, he was giddy with delight.

As we maneuvered through the dense tropical forest of the Guiana Highlands to Cardozo's hideout, Bebe Assassino whistled to himself. *Duernete, Nino.* "Sleep, Little One", a Colombian lullaby.

While combating my impulse to strangle Machado, he offered me a piece of bubble gum that I refused. Bebe Assassino found it necessary to detail how easy it was for him to get those *o porcos*, confessing what joy it gave him to rid his papa of such troublesome boils. It was as if it were a game to him no different from hide-and-seek. Paulo Machado proved to me what was until then a partially accepted truth. Anyone is capable of murder. I set my sights on Genevieve Windell with Bebe Assassino in mind.

***

"How may I help you Mr. Cavanaugh?" Her voice was as commanding as her image.

"I'm sorry to trouble you at this difficult time Mrs. Windell. I'll make this as brief as possible." She nodded.

I opened by asking her ten nonthreatening questions to which I already knew the answers. Her responses were brusque but she answered each one. I observed her face and body for telltale movements and gestures right down to the slightest twitch of her mouth. She lied about her age. An involuntary tilt of her head gave her away, vanity perhaps. It was a fib I didn't judge important at the time. The second lie set off bells. It was regarding how long she had been in the United States. That was the one that made Genevieve Windell toy with her fingertips. Except for the obvious tone of annoyance, her voice never quivered or cracked nor did she sweat or stutter. Having the prelims out of the way, I began the real interrogation.

"How long were you married to Clinton Windell?"

"Twelve years."

"First marriage?"

"Only marriage."

"Do you have any children?"

"One daughter, Pamela."

"How old is Pamela?"

"Six."

"I understand Pamela was home when it happened?"

"I don't see how that is any of your business."

"At some point I'll need to speak with your daughter on this matter."

"She's just a little girl. Why would she have any bearing on an insurance investigation?"

"I'm only doing my job ma'am. Under these circumstances anyone associated with the victim has to be questioned."

"I sent her away to my parents in San Francisco. After all that's happened the poor dear is frightfully upset."

"I understand. Where exactly was Pamela when all of this happened?" Even though I knew the answer, confirmation from a party close to the source is a huge key to any investigation.

"In her bedroom, Pamela's bedroom is next to ours. Thank God she slept through this hideous ordeal." Genevieve Windell shuddered. "To think she could have discovered her father like that."

How could Pamela Windell have slept through the thunderous reports of forty-fours unless silencers were used, I thought.

"Your daughter was here alone?" I asked.

"Yes. I know what you're thinking. That was not the case. Pamela's babysitter was supposed to be here with her. I made the arrangements myself. Somehow the babysitter became confused and thought her services were needed next week."

I nodded my acquiescence allowing a quiet moment to pass before I resumed my questioning. "You're originally from Bern, Switzerland?"

"Yes."

"You met your husband in the states?"

"Don't you already have this information on file?" Genevieve Windell was starting to break. Her face quivered before she was able to regain control.

"I'm simply following procedure ma'am."

"It's irritating nonetheless."

"Yes ma'am." I watched her walk over to sit in the chair behind the desk. Her steps were shaky. The slouch in her posture suggested the weight of her grief. With her legs crossed and her arms folded across her stomach, she rocked back and forth as if trying to calm a nagging stomachache. The facade was gone revealing a woman in pain.

"Where did you and Mr. Windell meet?"

"Pardon?" Genevieve stopped rocking and looked at me as if startled by my presence. I repeated the question.

"San Francisco. I was a ballerina for the San Francisco ballet. We met at a fundraiser for the S.F.B." Genevieve stopped talking for a moment to dab her cheeks with a handkerchief. "Clinton was there with Mr. Bellingham. We fell in love and were married a year later."

"Your husband was employed by Bellingham Jewelers at the time?"

"It was simply Bellingham then a single jewelry store. Clinton made it what it is today."

"Apparently he made some lethal enemies along the way."

"People in my husband's position always have enemies."

"Any of them capable of murder?" I asked.

"The types of enemies my husband had do not have to resort to murder to destroy a person."

There was an inference in that statement I let ride. "Would any of those same people be capable of hiring someone to kill Mr. Windell?"

"How long have you been doing investigative work?" Genevieve asked annoyance turning to hostility in her voice.

"A number of years," I said.

"Isn't it customary for investigators to take notes or use a recorder when interviewing a client," Genevieve paused, "or suspect?"

"I assure you Mrs. Windell you are not a suspect."

My memory is photographic. Events I've witnessed play back totally in my mind. There are times my recollection is so vivid it feels as if I'm reliving the experience right down to how the air feels on my skin. Unfortunately, my memory isn't as selective as I would like. DEA nightmares inhabit equal space. That was the understanding behind what I told Mrs. Windell when I said to her I had an excellent memory.

"I see," Genevieve said. I wanted to see her eyes to measure the intent behind her words. Since I was a child, my parents taught me a person's true designs could be unraveled in their eyes. So far, Genevieve hadn't lied according to what I'd previously observed. Cruel as it may seem I needed to make Genevieve Windell sweat.

With Mrs. Windell's permission, I took a closer look at the books along the south wall. Collectors' items every one. Clinton Windell became a man of contradictions to me. While he clearly had the predatory instincts of a platinum card CEO, he was obviously capable of appreciating the finer things in life.

"Did Mr. Windell read all of these books?" I asked with my back to Genevieve.

"Those, no, my husband rarely touched them. Every volume is a rare edition. Clinton would stand back and admire them. They were investments to him."

"Hard to believe someone would have these treasures only for purposes of investment."

"Don't get me wrong. Clinton was a very cultured man. He'd read all of those titles just not those specific volumes. Those books," Genevieve pointed a straight forefinger, "no one was allowed near. They were capital. Something had to have value or Clinton did not believe it was worth keeping around."

"How about people?" I asked.

"What about them?"

"Did they need to have value for your husband to keep them around?"

"That depends." I waited for her to finish by reading book titles. Genevieve Windell was the sole beneficiary on Clinton Windell's life insurance policy. From the bio info, I learned Genevieve was also the sole executor to the Windell fortune.

"If you're referring to me or our daughter," Genevieve continued, "the answer is an emphatic no. Friends and family, no, business was another matter. Business is an unforgiving mistress and my husband treated her with the utmost respect."

I turned and waited a moment. I wanted to make certain I missed nothing when I asked my next question. "When was the last time you saw your husband alive?"

"We flew to Bern together to visit my grandparents," Genevieve answered without hesitation. "He stayed three days and then left for Amsterdam."

"Did he have business there?"

"He was purchasing gems for the company."

"Who else knew of this purchase?"

"The usual people: Andrea Bettencourt, Stuart Wu, Ronald Davis, Carlos Mendoza, Patrick Kemery, and Albert Taylor."

"And they are?"

"The Board of Directors of Bellingham Jewelers."

"Did you speak to your husband while he was in Amsterdam?"

"Of course."

"At any time did he sound worried?"

"Worried, *no*, he was his usual arrogant self." Genevieve used the word arrogant as if she intended it as a compliment.

"You arrived home when?"

"Around five-thirty yesterday morning."

"You drove yourself home."

"Yes."

I nonchalantly walked toward Mrs. Windell taking her in. "Why didn't your chauffeur or husband pick you up?" I asked.

"I enjoy driving Mr. Cavanaugh. It gives me an opportunity to relax."

"You discovered the body?"

"Yes," Genevieve answered sounding exhausted. "I've answered all of these questions for the police. Can't you get what you need from them?"

Destini came to mind. "Insurance investigators have to conduct independent inquiries ma'am company policy. I can come back at a later date if it's too much for you right now."

"No, no, let's be done with it."

I was standing in front of the desk by then. I looked through the window at the people working outside. Mrs. Windell began to rock again. "Did you notice anything suspicious?" I asked.

"Besides my husband's brains splattered all over our bedroom wall?"

"Yes ma'am."

"No and stop calling me ma'am. It's aggravating."

The divorce question came to mind. I decided to bypass it. I knew I'd see Genevieve Windell again and when I did, I wanted something left to throw in the mix.

"Here's my card," I said. "If anything new comes to mind please give me a call."

Genevieve Windell snatched the card from my hand and tossed it on the desk. Her hand was trembling. I asked if she minded if I saw their bedroom. She said "Fine," and mentioned that Edward would show me the way.

"Just one more question Mrs. Windell. Who is acting CEO of Bellingham?"

"I don't know and I don't care."

"Thank you," I said walking toward the study door.

"You'll find a number of people who disliked my husband," Mrs. Windell said. I stopped and turned to face her. "Some who even hated him. Not a day went by without someone making me aware of that fact. You asked me if my husband had enemies who wanted him dead. Yes he did, but this was robbery wasn't it pure and simple? I mean my husband surprised them in the act when they . . ."

Genevieve Windell's breakdown was complete. Edward rushed in to comfort her. It was as if I were watching one friend comfort another as opposed to a servant assisting his boss. I apologized for having caused her any distress and waited in the hall for the butler.

Edward emerged shortly thereafter. He closed the door behind him. When Edward turned to face me, he looked troubled in the way a person looks when the object of his affection is suffering. Did Genevieve Windell feel the same about him? Was Clinton Windell aware of Edward's feelings toward his wife? If so, how did Windell handle it?

Edward's jaw flexed as he stared at me. I could see in his eyes he wanted to hurt me. Maybe even kill me. When I didn't flinch, he reconsidered taking any action—at least for the moment. I told him what

Mrs. Windell had said about showing me the murder scene. Edward obliged.

On the way to the crime scene, the butler kept looking around attempting to appear as if he were monitoring the work-in-progress. There was a cautious bent to his observances. Edward was on the lookout for someone.

"Where were you on the night Clinton Windell was murdered?" I asked.

Edward stopped in his tracks and turned to face me. "I don't have to answer your questions."

"Suit yourself. I'll have to file your reluctance to answer questions in my report. And you know what that means?" Judging by his puzzled expression, he didn't. He started walking again and I joined him. "Lunsford won't pay off on a claim without my okay. By the way what is your last name?"

Edward grimaced, "Sutherland."

"Mr. Sutherland where were you on the night of the murder?"

"With my father."

"Can anyone else verify your whereabouts besides daddy?"

"About three thousand people, we were at The Schnitz."

"Phantom Of The Opera."

"Yes."

"Marvelous performance did you enjoy it?"

"My father did. He goes in for that Broadway stuff. I prefer sports."

"Basketball, football, that sort of thing?"

"Soccer's my game."

"What was your relationship with Mr. Windell?"

Edward grimaced again. "Amicable."

"Was there any friction between you and Mr. Windell?"

"No."

"What about Mrs. Windell and her husband?"

"What about them?"

"Did you notice any problems between them?"

"No."

"None?"

"That's what I said."

We stopped in front of a bedroom door crisscrossed with police tape. Sutherland turned to me, his eyes narrowed so he appeared to be squinting, "Genevieve—Mrs. Windell is going through hell right now. The last thing she needs is some insurance dick breathing down her neck. If anything happens to her because of your meddling, somebody's going to pay. Know what I mean?"

I paused, giving Sutherland an opportunity to see how little effect his threat had on me. Then I opened my mouth to remove all doubt.

"You're suggesting," I said tugging on a pair of latex gloves so not to spoil the crime scene, "that I might get my ass kicked for doing my job."

"You might say that."

"Let's just say I wouldn't pose that threat again if I were you."

Sutherland sneered. "You don't mind if I check with the cops to make sure you can go in there?" he asked watching me the way I had been watching Genevieve Windell.

"Be my guest," I said swallowing my amusement. Sutherland called from a cell phone he had in his breast pocket. He asked for Detective Pendleton. They spoke briefly. He relayed the message that as long as I didn't touch anything it was no problem. With that, Sutherland unlocked the bedroom door.

There was a commotion downstairs. I reached for a gun I didn't have. Sutherland had already started down the stairs to investigate. Two uniformed security guards held a thin freckle-faced redheaded man wearing a ponytail by each of his tattooed forearms. It was a scrappy newspaper reporter by the name of Shawn Calloway. Shawn had a well-deserved reputation for integrity and fact foraging. What was sometimes in question were his tactics and sincerity. I slipped inside and eased shut the door so Shawn wouldn't see me.

"Who are you?" I overheard Sutherland say.

"Shawn Calloway, The Willamette Times."

"How'd you get in here?"

"Could I have a moment of Mrs. Windell's time to ask a few simple questions?" Shawn asked.

"He disguised himself as one of the cleaning people sir," one of the guards said.

"Mrs. Windell, Mrs. Windell," Shawn yelled. "Could I please have a minute of your time?"

"Get this jerk out of here," Sutherland ordered.

"If you think you're going to stop the press think again *buddy*. I'll be back. You can bet on it!"

Shawn kept screaming about how his constitutional rights were being violated and how the real story behind Clinton Windell's murder would see the light. What story was Shawn looking for besides the obvious? My guess was Shawn was fishing with no bait.

Sutherland was waiting for me when I emerged from the murder scene. I thanked him for his cooperation with a handshake pretending I'd forgotten to shed my latex gloves. I had printed a letter from Windell's DVD dossier that I had brought along just for this purpose. It was signed D. M. I handed it to Sutherland to read leaving him with the impression I had removed it from the crime scene. The letter vaguely discussed a possible deal involving a surplus of uncut gems this D. M. had for sale. Sutherland handed the letter back to me saying, "So?" I asked if he knew what it was about.

"No," Sutherland said.

"Do you know who D. M. might be?" I asked.

"No idea."

I refolded the letter and returned it to my inside breast pocket.

"I thought you weren't supposed to touch anything in there?" Sutherland said.

"This may be evidence the police overlooked. I'll turn it over to the investigating officer." Sutherland gave me a suspicious look. I removed my gloves and shoved them into my jacket pocket ignoring his doubt.

The butler escorted me to the front door practically slamming the door behind me when I left. The Jaguar was nowhere in sight. I checked the hillside. The Roman candles were gone. These people were serious. So was I. It was time to get back in the trenches. There was only one thing troubling me when I drove away. Why did Genevieve Windell lie about how long she had been in the United States?

CHAPTER SIX

I saw enough in the bedroom to get a good picture of how the shooting went down and to agree with Destini's call that they were professionals. The only clue was their *modus operandi*. Every pro has a signature. That was all I had on one end. From the other direction if I could nail down the person who laid out the contract everything else might fall into place.

Genevieve Windell had convinced me of one thing. If she were involved in her husband's murder financial gain was not her motive. Not once did she ask about money. Her grief was genuine. In my opinion, she loved him. She was hiding something. Something that might prove valuable to the hunt.

I stopped by the rented house of Edward Sutherland to see his father. He confirmed what his son had told me about their whereabouts on the night of the homicide. After the performance, they went to the Heathman Pub for a late night snack and then returned to his son's place where they sat up most of the night having a few drinks and playing checkers. The elder Sutherland was believable. There were no holes in his story.

My gut told me my high-rolling clients were not going to respect my privacy. The soft tail was only a start in my estimation. I checked the car for bugs. It was clean. I checked my home and home phone. They were clean. Even though micro-technology allows listening devices to be smaller than ever they are still not invisible. Something disturbed cannot be returned to its original state. That fact is universal like Einstein's theory of relativity. Bearing that principle in mind along with a sharp eye one can detect any disturbance to locate hidden listening devices. Having a good bug detector didn't hurt either—last year's Christmas gift from a friend who still worked in D.C.'s DEA tech lab.

I setup simple indicators known as "exterminators" to make certain my life stayed bug free. I took my bug detector with me when I left home for the office.

Renita was upset when I got in. "Where were you?" She asked.

"Pardon?" I said as I closed the blinds. Renita stood there with her arms crossed. Her expression told me she was in no mood for games.

"I was investigating," I told Renita writing a note to her to act natural while I checked the office for bugs. She mentally stumbled for a second before resuming with her original mood.

"I'm sorry C. J. but you're going to have to keep me better informed than this," Renita said. "I'm your partner! I have a right to know what you're doing on any of our cases." I had checked her office and moved on to mine.

"You know how these things go partner," I said. "Sometimes you're caught up in the heat of the chase and you get absentminded." Renita followed me into my office continuing with what had now become a full-blown charade.

"Yeah right," Renita said, "see how you like it when I'm out on a case and you're worried about me."

Renita slammed the door behind her when she left. While her leaving took me by surprise, it turned out to be a good move. I was able to search the rest of the office and check the phones without interruption. Everything was clean. I text messaged Renita that the coast was clear. She was back in the office in no time.

I had brought in my 380 Glock from home and slipped it into my top right desk drawer. On me I had shoulder-holstered my 92F Beretta, belt-holstered my Colt 32, and calf-sheathed my stiletto switchblade. It had been a long time since I'd been packing. You don't need hardware in the insurance investigation game. Most of what's necessary is sitting on your shoulders directly behind your eyes.

I asked Renita if she still had her thirty-eight in the office. Renita said she was packing a forty-five automatic in her desk these days. I told Renita to keep it there and made her promise to carry her thirty-eight. Then I filled my partner in on what had happened to me that afternoon.

"What happens next?" Renita asked.

"We'll keep investigating; see what crawls out of the woodwork."

"What about Windell's wife?" Renita asked.

"She's clean for now," I said.

Renita nodded, "Any suspects?"

"Corny as it sounds the butler may be involved."

"Sutherland?"

She's read the bio, I thought. *Good.* "I wouldn't be surprised if he hasn't iced a few bodies in his day," I said. "I managed to lift his prints. His alibi is tight but something's not right."

I dusted the fake letter for prints. Sutherland's fingerprints were as visible as inkblots. I told Renita to check him out. She needed the practice.

Paranoia doesn't pay. It usually causes you to cut your own throat. Just ask Julius Caesar or Richard Nixon. What you want in the concrete jungle are the same instincts you'd have in the wild: keen senses, cunning, physical preparation and an evolved intellect. Renita was excited about what lay ahead. She had never been involved in anything this high stakes. We were always the hunters. Renita had never experienced being the prey. Her naiveté unnerved me a bit. If the men who killed Clinton Windell discovered we were getting close, they would not hesitate to extinguish us. Her own demise was a distant notion in Renita's mind. She wasn't acquainted with how one bullet could send you into oblivion. I needed to keep a close eye on my partner.

Renita filled me in on her day while I scanned O'Bryant Square for signs of a stakeout. The Web had turned up empty on Boswell Industries. So did her other sources.

Renita informed me that with the availability of DVD writers and writeable DVD's anyone with access to both could have burned the DVD we received. Not likely, I told her. The type of information we obtained was under strict control. They wouldn't chance a leak. Whoever created that DVD had clearance from our client. Either that or someone had enough access to pirate it. Windell's extensive dossier in combination with the money paid along with the money promised us told me we were dealing with someone near the top of the power chain.

There was one clue the DVD offered. Every magnetic disk has an alphanumeric registration number branded on it. Renita was able to trace that number back to the specific manufacturer. When she told me who it was, I gave her a thoughtful nod. Renita smiled. She walked over and put her arms around my neck whispering words to me like a lover's secret. "You heard me right honey, Brass Tacks Incorporated, a subsidiary of Diva Computer Software."

I removed Renita's arms from around my neck and walked away. Renita didn't seem surprised, disappointed, or discouraged by my action. My mind was too focused on the case to admonish Renita for her unprofessional behavior.

"Just because they manufacture DVDs doesn't mean that someone at Diva burned it," I said. "The person who copied that data could have bought writeable disks in a number of places."

"You said yourself C. J. the information on that disk had to come from someone who had high level access or something to that effect."

I was hoping she would say that, I thought. *She's been paying close attention.* "What do you think we should do next?" I asked to see if Renita had thought that far ahead.

"I think we should check out DIVA for leads. I admit it's a long shot but in my opinion it's worth pursuing."

My thoughts exactly, I thought. I stared at Renita pretending to ponder her recommendation. She toyed with her fingers that meant she was nervous. Knowing Renita as I did, I understood her uneasiness wasn't due to a lack of confidence in her suggestion. Renita was waiting to discover how her suggestion was being received. "It can't hurt," I said. "Get on it."

"Yes!" Renita said with a broad smile and an enthusiastic clap.

CHAPTER SEVEN

Nothing had changed in terms of keeping my clandestine employers from Destini; but before I ventured any further into this case, I wanted a look at the preliminary police report. I checked with the desk sergeant at the Portland Police Bureau. He said Destini and Liederman were expected back shortly from the M.E.'s. I made myself comfortable on a wooden bench outside the homicide squad room to wait.

I had been keeping an eye out for any type of surveillance since I'd spotted the soft tail. That didn't mean much. I was rusty and I knew it. The combination of luck and sloppy technique on their part allowed me to spot the Jaguar. I needed a little time to regain my edge. Time was the key ingredient. There wasn't much of that available. I only hoped spotting tails was like riding a bike once learned you never forget how to do it.

A skinny humpbacked old man was talking to the desk sergeant. He said he had just finished testimony in a homicide case. The desk sergeant kept rubbing his nose. The old man appeared shabby and dirty as if hygiene were an option and not a requirement. The desk sergeant politely listened to the man's story. Before I realized it, I was listening too.

"My neighbor shot a man last night, double barrel shotgun, both barrels right through the chest."

"Why?" The desk sergeant asked.

"Guy was breaking into his place. Top half in, bottom half out."

I studied the man: white whiskers, sun freckled skin, brown cowboy hat with a turquoise band. I would have dismissed him as a kook if he were not distressed as he spoke. His hands shook. I couldn't tell if it was due to a nervous condition or his woe at recounting the event.

"Did you see it?" The desk sergeant asked.

"I was in my backyard. Couldn't sleep, I was sitting in my lawn chair looking at the stars."

The old man looked at me as if I were someone who could help him. As if, I could save him from that agonizing memory. His eyes watered with what could have been a cold. They might as well have been tears.

"It was his ex-roommate he shot. They were arguing. Next thing I know I hear this loud crack! Crack! Double barrel shotguns makes two sounds 'cause the hammers never strike the shells at the same time. Listen close enough you can hear it. Crack! Crack! I looked over the fence and saw him on his back twitching, blood coming out his nose and mouth and ears." The old man moved his hand across each area as he mentioned it. "His eyes was wide open like he'd seen God and he scared the shit out of him."

The old man looked at his hand as if he didn't recognize them. Then his eyes dropped to his weathered cowboy boots that appeared too large for his feet.

"I called the cops. Told 'em what I saw. The bastard bragged about it. Said he did it an' he'd do it again if he got the chance; strange world."

"Yep," the desk sergeant said.

"They was best friends. 'Boys' they called each other." The old man stared at me as if expecting a response. His rheumy eyes needed a handkerchief.

"Strange world," the old man repeated before he shuffled away as if he had crushed glass in his boots. I watched him leave agreeing with his assessment of our world.

"What do we have here?" a husky voice asked. I looked up to see Jeffrey Whimple a throwback of the prehistoric waterfront cop who must have been a staple back when the City of Roses lived up to its name of Portland. Whimple was the type of cop who would have been at home in a time when white slavery was a lucrative practice and Oregon was declared a white's only state. He was the kind of man who delighted in harming others. Racism was his excuse to exercise his delight. Whimple was a good ol' boy from Butte, Montana, who had a penchant for calling black men, boys—or worse. I had matured to realize you couldn't fight every racist you encountered. Instead, I nicknamed him Schultz after the dimwitted German Sergeant from the television show Hogan's Heroes. I claimed he resembled Schultz. In actuality, he looked more like a pot bellied heavy-jowled Dennis the Menace with thinning grayish-blond hair and murky blue eyes.

***

Schultz and I had our first run-in when I was working on the Stethingson case for Lunsford Insurance. Charles Stethingson had a 2.7 million-dollar life insurance payment coming after the accidental death of his invalid father. Everything looked kosher. I was there to do a final interview with Charles Stethingson to triple check my facts against his story. Schultz was playing a dead wrong hunch that the young man was a murderer. Our paths crossed; me on the way in, Schultz on the way out. Schultz asked what I was doing there adding boy to the end of his question. His partner Weasel got a charge out of the insult. Weasel was a slender man of about six feet, dark brown hair, blue eyes, and a pitted face that didn't take kindly to shaving. His real name was Leonard Rockgarden. Destini told me they called him Weasel because it was rumored he was on the payroll of the local syndicate boss. A rat and a racist, they were the perfect pair.

We had been alone when I explained to Schultz why calling me boy was not a good idea. He led with an overhand right. I blocked it and hit him in the gut. It dropped him to his knees gasping for air. I was arrested and charged with physically assaulting a police officer.

Schultz had so many prior complaints filed against him for questionable conduct the D.A. forced him into a mutual deal. I agreed to drop my cross-complaint of racist behavior to incite violence and Schultz wouldn't be exorcised from the police force. Schultz grudgingly agreed. I walked. Politics, you've gotta love it.

***

"What cha' doin' here man?" Schultz asked in that quirky way he mistook for humor. "Come tah visit one of your bros?"

Schultz was half-a-foot shorter than me when we stood face to face. I could have sworn he'd shrunk or perhaps his girth had stolen a few inches from his height. I was certain he could feel my breath on top of his Buzz Cut. Last time I'd seen him he had his jaw wired shut. It had been broken in a fight with a patrol officer of Mexican descent. I could have guessed what precipitated that before Destini filled me in.

"Jaw's healed nicely," I said, "took you from downright gruesome to just plain ugly." Schultz threatened to lunge at me but hesitated. He looked around. I could tell he was thinking there were too many potential witnesses. I didn't say anything. I wanted what I'd said to sink into that gaseous sphere between his ears.

"Listen to me," Schultz said in a hissing whisper, "I'll book your black ass for any old trumped up charge and make it stick. By the time, anyone figures out its bogus you'll be wearing lipstick and calling yourself Yolanda. Not even your smart-ass girlfriend will be able to save your worthless butt."

The desk sergeant was staring our way. We both knew he was trying to listen. I could see Schultz's desk from where I stood. There was a framed picture of a woman and three young children. Heather Whimple was perfect for Schultz. She had a laugh that sounded like a string of hiccups, a wide behind and air for brains. Her carrot red hair perennially stuck out on the sides and her eyes bugged out behind thick eyeglasses. The Portland Police detectives had a nickname for Schultz's wife. They called her *Reina De La Gnomo*, "Queen of the Trolls."

Schultz was about to speak when I beat him to it. "How's *Reina De La Gnomo?*" For months, Schultz thought that expression meant the fairest red flower. He went ballistic when he discovered what it really meant. It was guaranteed to make him lose his cool, something I always enjoyed.

"I oughta kick your teeth in you arrogant shit," Schultz said.

"There's something I've never been able to figure out. How did two attractively-challenged people like you manage to have such adorable offspring?"

"Shut-up or I'll shut you up."

"Haven't you noticed? None of them look like you?"

Schultz glared at me. I continued. "Heaven forbid Heather would ever be unfaithful. Nevertheless, I could swear a couple of those kids have a little ash in their furnace. Know what I mean?"

Schultz grabbed me and attempted to shove me against the wall. I let him smiling at him all the while.

"Did you know when you get angry your face gets almost as red as your neck?"

Police officers come from an assortment of personalities that gelled when circumstances required them to. Even to them Schultz and Weasel were outsiders. Schultz fancied himself a maverick, a lone ranger out to correct the injustices suffered by his race by all the malcontent foreigners who should go back to from where they came. History was not his strong suit. Thinking was not even in his closet, which was why he was the only detective second class after thirty years on the force. Although that's not the way, he saw it. Affirmative action was his villain. That and all those damn laws drafted to protect people like me and put people like him at a disadvantage.

Schultz was still harassing me when the desk sergeant asked what was going on. We looked his way. Rushing our way were the ebony dick and her liberal sidekick. That was the in-precinct joke amongst some for Destini and David Liederman. Schultz released me disappearing inside the homicide squad room without uttering another word.

Destini asked what was going on. I explained. Destini and I didn't hug, kiss, or flirt. We behaved as two professionals doing our jobs without a hint of affection.

"Can I take a look at your preliminary report on the Windell murder?" I asked Destini. Police reports are not normally available for viewing by anyone outside the jurisdiction of the case. I had developed a good rapport with the PPB over the years. The top brass were aware of my DEA background and had secretly benefited from my expertise on narcotics trafficking and homicide narcotics-related cases. In exchange, I had carte blanche to all police knowledge regarding any of my private investigations—as long as I kept how I procured the information to myself.

"Sure," Destini said after a moment's hesitation that surprised me. I attempted to follow her inside the squad room. "Wait here," Destini said, shoving me away from the door. "You've already caused enough trouble." I did as instructed. Destini went inside. Liederman waited outside with me.

Destini and I were both fond of David a former linebacker at Lewis & Clark College. Six-three, muscular built, short black curly hair, large dark eyes, thick black beard, a bountiful nose, and big-hearted smile were the characteristics that embodied the man. All of his fingers had been sporadically broken during the course of his football career. Each held some crooked reminder of their misfortune. David was a soft-spoken introspective person outside of work. On the job, he was a bear.

"How's it going?" David asked.

"Okay," I said, "you?"

"About the same," David said. "Got any leads on the Windell case?"

"Nope," I said.

"Any suspects we should know about?"

"I'm merely following in your footsteps."

"Keep it that way." David was serious. I was kidding. The captain must have really turned up the heat on this one.

"If I come across anything you and Destini will be the first to know."

"To know what?" Destini asked handing me the report.

"If he finds out anything relevant on this case," David said.

"You're damn right we will," Destini said.

I had already sat down and started poring over the report. The exemplars filled in the details about what I'd already surmised. A couple of things were very useful such as the caliber and type of weapons used. The police presumed theft was the motive since it was confirmed Clinton Windell had in his possession twenty-million dollars' worth of rough-cut gems that had not been found at the crime scene. Genevieve Windell and Edward Sutherland voluntarily took gunpowder residue tests. Both came up negative, which meant nothing because the killers probably wore gloves. I asked Destini whose idea it was to test them. She said it was her idea with Genevieve Windell. Sutherland volunteered. I gave Destini back the report with a deliberate expression of disappointment.

"See anything interesting?" Destini asked.

"No," I said.

"If you ask me," David said, "the motive was robbery. The thieves got an inside tip on when Windell would return with the stones. The accomplice let them in. They killed him, took the gems, case closed."

"Give it a rest David," Destini said. "He's been pitching that line since we left the crime scene."

"Why didn't they take anything else if their main interest was property?" I asked David. "There was plenty to choose from."

"I didn't say they were greedy or stupid. Uncut gems are very, very difficult to trace. They obviously knew what they were doing."

"Who's your insider?" I asked.

"Sutherland's a good candidate," David said.

"No priors," Destini said.

"Because his sheet's clean doesn't mean he is," David said.

"What did the M.E. have to say?" I asked.

"It's official," David said. "Clinton Windell was murdered."

"Time of death?" I asked.

"Between eight-thirty and ten," Destini answered.

"They propped him up in his bed," David said, "then shot him at close range: one through the head, one through the heart."

"Weird," Destini said.

"What's weird about it?" I asked Destini.

"The M.E. said it appeared they crossed Windell's arms *after* they shot him."

"Whackos," David said.

"It was as if they were posing him, admiring him, or something," Destini said.

"Sounds like a signature," I said. Destini nodded in agreement.

"I think you're both wrong," David said.

"I hope you're right partner," Destini said, "because if these men are pros we're in for one hell of a chase."

There was a moment of silence. David got the hint and left Destini and I alone.

"What's going on C. J.?" Destini asked.

"Nothing more than a bad feeling," I said.

"My gut's running along that same line."

"They've got me worried," I said.

Destini nodded, "Me too."

"One good thing about pros," I said. "They don't do anything for free if they don't have to."

"They're probably long gone by now."

"Maybe," I said. I took a quick look around. There was still no sign of surveillance. "I didn't see anything about the board members in your report."

"We just finished questioning them. We haven't had a chance to update the prelim."

"Can I get a copy of their addresses?"

Destini handed me a computer printout. "They all had solid alibis," she said.

"Lunsford's not paying me top dollar to chew the fat. I'd better check them out."

"You're wasting your time."

"You mean Lunsford's dollar, don't you?"

"Keep me posted C. J." For a moment, I became lost in her eyes. Everyone who knew us knew Destini and I were a couple; but we had an agreement, no exhibitions of our private feelings at our public jobs.

"See you tonight?" I asked.

"If I can tear myself away," Destini said. Her eyes told me to be careful.

"Will do," I said, "you too."

"I'm with you," Destini said with a grin. "It doesn't get much more dangerous than that."

CHAPTER EIGHT

I called Renita from my car on my way to questioning the board members. All was quiet to the point Renita was bored. Sutherland's fingerprints came up empty. There was nothing new on our mystery employer. I had become less concerned about our employer and more concerned about the killers since my visit to the Windell Estate. Renita had followed up on acquiring names of people at Diva Computer Software who were capable of creating a DVD like the one we received. I asked Renita to narrow the list. That required field interviews to get a feel for motives and access. Renita was happy to do it.

On the one hand, I was glad to get Renita more involved in fieldwork. On the other hand, she was making me nervous. I'd seen what effect carrying a loaded weapon had on people. There is an anxious desire to pull that trigger. You are nagged by a twisted impulse, a morbid curiosity, to discover what it's like to shoot someone.

"Renita be careful," I said. "This is not a game. Use your gun if you have to *but* only if you have to. Is that clear?"

"I'm not a psycho C. J."

"I know. Just be careful."

"Sounds like someone's a *bit* concerned," Renita said.

"More than a bit," I said.

"I knew I was wearing you down. Don't fight it honey. Come to mama."

In my honest opinion, I didn't think Renita stood a chance if she encountered those contract killers. I wished I could have backed the whole affair up and somehow left her out of it.

"You need help," I told her. "Just make certain to keep your weapon concealed. You don't want to unnecessarily frighten anyone."

"Yes dear."

"Check in with me when you're done."

"Yes dear."

"Renita."

"Yes dear?"

"Quit calling me dear."

"Alright snookems."

This morning's Willamette Times had carried an article by Shawn Calloway. While he had taken a couple of backhanded snipes at people, surrounding Genevieve Windell there was succinct background information on the "surviving board." It proved to be a helpful introduction. My mystery source had been anemic regarding them. Whether they didn't have the information or didn't regard them as important, I couldn't answer. The revered sentiments expressed by board members in the article regarding Clinton Windell, I dismissed as bull. Between the information in the preliminary police report and The Willamette Times article, I was ready.

All of the board members lived in Southwest Hills. Albert Taylor was an affable white-haired man with graceful movements and a gentle manner. I found it difficult to believe he was capable of being tough enough to be part of an executive team. While he disliked Clinton Windell, I didn't get the impression he had anything to gain by having him murdered. There was still the question of the gems. When I asked Albert about them, he claimed full knowledge of their existence. When I asked how he knew, Albert told me it was a company purchase. Everyone on the board knew about them. The amount and cargo were itemized in the company's financial documents. Albert Taylor was scratched from my list of possible suspects. He answered every question honestly and directly. As Destini had said his alibi was solid.

Returning to my car, I noticed a hauntingly familiar sight parked in Albert's driveway that wasn't there when I arrived, a sapphire Jaguar. The license plate was different but it was the same year, make, model, and style as the one that had tailed me. I asked Mr. Taylor about the car. His wife appeared at his side. She had just returned from a visit with a friend. Mr. Taylor informed me that all of the Bellingham board members drove the same Jaguar. They were leased company cars. It was Clinton Windell's idea. He said Windell thought it would give Bellingham an image of fast track modern luxury that could translate to more business from the nouveau riche. "An exercise in excess if you ask me," Mr. Taylor went on to say.

While Carlos Mendoza and Ronald Davis clearly hated Clinton Windell for what they regarded as backstabbing undercutting methods that Windell used to keep himself on top they had no proof. I doubted those men would have hired anyone to kill Windell judging by their temperaments. They would have shot Clinton Windell themselves.

Stuart Wu was another matter. He was a smallish man of Chinese descent with clear skin, a high forehead, flat nose, and taut mouth. He had a shimmering black ponytail and his eyes were dark and calm.

"Have you spoken with Andrea yet?" Stuart asked.

"Andrea Bettencourt?" I said.

"Yes."

"Should I?"

"I think you'll find a conversation with her interesting," Stuart said.

"How so?"

"She's a widow you know."

"I didn't," I said. I did know about Andrea Bettencourt being a widow but pretended not to.

"And she places her reason for being so squarely on the shoulders of Clinton Windell," Stuart said.

"*Really*," I said feigning surprise by the news.

"Clinton would invite Harvey Bettencourt along on our once-a-month skydiving excursions," Stuart said. "Harvey had a heart condition. Both his doctor and Andrea urged him not to go. If Harvey hedged, Clinton would goad him into it by playing on his ego. 'I understand if you're not up to it Harv. Sometimes I have difficulty keeping it together when I'm up there with a strong heart. I can imagine how tough it must be for you.' It was bad enough Andrea was the more respected of the two by the board but Clinton would tweak Harvey every chance he got. It worked every time.

"Coincidentally, Harvey died two years to the day Clinton was murdered. His parachute didn't open. Investigators said his primary ripcord didn't work. Harvey panicked had a stroke and never tried his auxiliary cord."

"Sounds like an unfortunate series of events," I said.

"The investigation was closed as a skydiving accident. His parachute would have opened had Harvey pulled his auxiliary cord. He would still be alive. That's a difficult loss for a mother of three."

Wu paused to take me in. He was sizing me up to determine if I were swayed enough by his story to regard Andrea Bettencourt as a primary suspect.

"What about you?" I asked.

"What about me?"

"How did you feel about Clinton Windell?"

"I didn't *feel* anything. He was my boss. I did my job as I will continue to do now that he's deceased."

"Any gripes or unsettled scores?"

Mr. Wu smiled. "Who doesn't have such demons in their life? But I assure you there was nothing between Clinton Windell and myself that would constitute murder."

It was clear Stuart Wu was cool, evasive, and shrewd befitting his background as a corporate attorney. Useful skills in the courtroom as well as in business they also fared well for thieves and murderers. His alibi was that he attended The Phantom of the Opera with—ironically—Andrea Bettencourt the same woman he was attempting to serve up. Wu told me Bettencourt was distraught over it being the anniversary of her husband's death. Wu stayed to comfort her. When Stuart believed, Bettencourt was back to her old self he came home. How much and what kind of comfort Stuart offered I didn't inquire. Wu was smart enough not to have given me an alibi that wouldn't pan out. That made it believable.

Renita called on my way to Andrea Bettencourt's house. She had two Diva employees left to interview. I asked if she had had any problems. She said Judith Hardy had given her full run of the place. There was an anxious pause before Renita asked me, "Wasn't a sapphire Jaguar following you yesterday?"

"Yes," I said.

"License plate HADES," Renita said.

"Where are you?" I asked.

"Looking out of the Human Resources Director's office at the company parking lot," Renita answered.

"Renita —"

"I wanted to be certain before I tried getting a look at this guy."

"Stay put I'm on my way," I said.

"Am I missing something here?" Renita asked.

"What do you mean?"

"Why do I get the feeling you don't trust me to do this?"

"We're a team," I said. "This situation requires teamwork more than any we've ever encountered."

"You mean babysitting," Renita said. "I'm perfectly capable of handling myself C. J."

"I'd ask for backup if I were in your position," I said not meaning it but hoping Renita would buy it.

"Must I remind you I have a black belt in both Tae Kwon Do and Jujitsu?"

As if a bullet cares, I thought. "We'll talk about it when I get there."

"Sure," Renita said. I could tell by her tone that Renita was feeling headstrong about going through with her plan.

"Complete your interviews but for God's sake *do not* confront the driver of that car."

"Wait! Someone's heading for the Jaguar!" Renita said.

"This man is not working alone," I said. "You're going to need backup."

"I'm going to get a closer look."

"Renita stay put!" The phone went dead. I drove as fast as I could to Diva.

CHAPTER NINE

To enter the Diva complex I had to go through two armed security stations. The first cleared me to enter the grounds. The second station cleared me to enter the guest parking area. Armed uniformed security guards roamed the parking areas. Surveillance cameras were inside and out.

I surveyed the employee parking area. The Jaguar was gone. Nothing looked suspicious. I rushed inside found the Human Resources Director's office and much to my relief discovered Renita interviewing a Diva employee by the name of Benton Lawson. Could it be that same troublesome Benton Lawson, Judith Hardy had mentioned in her conversation with Antonio Farhletti? Before I could speculate further, Renita and I moved to the Human Resources Director's outer office.

My first inclination was to scold Renita for taking the risk she did. I found it difficult to settle her down when I saw how excited she was about everything. I reminded Renita a man was murdered and in all likelihood by people who made death their profession. I wanted to bring her down to earth. I hated to do it but it was for her own good.

I didn't get through to Renita at all. It was her constant reply of "You're the boss sweetie," that made me certain.

Renita told me exactly what happened as we walked to her car. The man she saw turned out to be going to a Mini Cooper. Her next interview came up so Renita never saw who was driving the Jaguar. Renita had observed from the window rather than attempting to confront a potentially dangerous suspect on her own. That showed me she was capable of using good judgment in a crucial situation. Renita told me she never intended to get any closer to the person driving the Jaguar than necessary. I stressed the not working alone portion of my argument again making it clear this was not some cozy little insurance investigation, emphasizing how these people did not value life. They mowed you down if you were in their way.

"Yes snookems," Renita replied. I gave up for the moment. I followed her back to the office at a distance keeping my eyes peeled for anything suspicious. When we arrived, I did a quick check around the office to make certain things were as we'd left them. Then we talked.

I listened to what Renita had and I agreed with her assessments. One important bit of information came out of her Benton Lawson interview. Lawson had been engaged to Roxanna Farhletti formerly Roxanna Tisdale when they were in college. Roxanna met Farhletti after she was crowned Miss Oregon. Shortly after that, Roxanna broke off her engagement to Lawson and married Farhletti. I told Renita what I had overheard—in actuality lip-read—about Benton Lawson. We speculated on what it might have meant. None of it led us to anything realistic.

"Why in the world would Lawson work for a man who stole the woman he loves?" I asked.

"It's the only company in the world involved in the type of software development he's interested in," Renita said.

"That is?"

"He wouldn't say," Renita said. "It's confidential. Apparently it's for the government."

"You believe him?"

"Yes. I also think he's doing it to stay close to Roxanna Farhletti. He's one lovesick puppy."

"What made you think he's the one who put together the DVD?" I asked.

"When I asked him about it his eyes lit up. He leaned back in his chair and grinned. He denied any knowledge of what I was talking about but his grin told a different story. That cat had swallowed the canary."

"Any idea of who he might be working with?" I asked.

"Not a clue," Renita said. "Diva provides computer software to hundreds of clients all over the world. Any number of them could be involved. For all we know it could be our government. What makes you think he's not working alone?"

"He may have generated the DVD," I said, "but he didn't compile the information that was on it. No one person could."

"What about Judith Hardy?" Renita asked.

"What about her?"

"What's your impression of her?"

"She's intelligent, aggressive, confident, a professional woman to the bone."

"Think she might be in on this?"

"I think she's clueless."

"You didn't tell anyone what was on the DVD did you?" I asked.

"Of course not I left that open for them to tell me."

"Good."

"I think Lawson's a lead worth pursuing," Renita said. "Now what do we do?"

I filled Renita in on the board members I had questioned, the Jaguars, the murder weapons, and the probable assassins' signature. I told her we still needed to check out Andrea Bettencourt and Patrick Kemery. Renita was anxious to pursue any remote lead. There was only one way I was going to keep her safe. I told Renita to meet me at the office at eight sharp. We'd finish interviewing the remaining board members and run down what we had.

"Yes dear," Renita said. I gave Renita a sideways glare. It was once again lecture time with work out of the way.

"We're professionals Renita let's conduct ourselves accordingly."

Renita said she agreed. Her coy smile said quite the opposite.

We decided to call it a day. I didn't need to tell Renita to remain cautious. Her earlier sighting of the Jaguar struck home that point. We left the office together. I walked Renita to her car and showed her how to check it for bugs. Renita learned fast. She figured out places to look I deliberately neglected to show her. Once that was done, I watched her drive away keeping a wary eye out. After Renita disappeared onto Front Street, I went to my car and drove home.

The doorbell rang about ten minutes after I'd arrived. Andrew and Booker barked at the door. I drew my Beretta looking through the peephole. It was Destini. She had a large white pizza box in her hands. I holstered my weapon then opened the door.

"Glad to see you're still in one piece," Destini said.

"Likewise," I said. Destini walked in, we kissed, and she placed the pizza on the kitchen counter.

"Just get in?" Destini asked.

"Yes," I said.

Destini kept staring at me. "Expecting a war?" Destini asked. I eventually realized what Destini was referring to. I had removed my jacket so not only was my Beretta visible but my thirty-two as well. Destini had decided not to carry her off-duty weapon in my company. The Windell case had not changed her thinking. I excused myself making a hasty retreat to my study. It's odd how quickly you can become comfortable with weapons. They grow on you. Make you feel complete.

I went to the bathroom to freshen up after disarming. When I returned Destini had already set the mood: music, candles, and a table set for two. We agreed no shoptalk. Night descended like a prowling sable. We enjoyed each other's pleasures.

I had a difficult time falling asleep. Bebe Assassino once told me: "Sleep brings with it the greatest pleasures and worst tragedies." He was referring to dreams and nightmares. I was thinking of unwelcome visitors in the dark. That was why in Colombia I never slept without a loaded gun within reach. It came in handy on more than one occasion. Destini slept soundly in my arms. I longed for a gun nearby to help protect her.

CHAPTER TEN

A certain amount of murder goes into our everyday lives. The foods we eat, liquids we consume, air we breathe. To survive we extinguish other beings. Even, sometimes, ourselves. Such is the eternal cycle of life and death. At our best, we are Gods. At our worst, we are monsters. Too often, I've seen us at our worst.

It was quiet when I walked into the office. Renita was seated behind her desk her right hand resting on her forty-five pointed in my direction. None of her excitement from the day before was present. Renita looked scared. She held up a yellow notepad. Handwritten on it was *SHOW ME HOW CHECK THE OFFICE FOR BUGS.* I nodded and motioned to Renita that we would begin in her office. Renita followed me like a curious puppy absorbing everything I did clutching the forty-five as if it were a bar of gold. There was nothing to find. We returned to her office.

Renita sat behind her desk. From the middle drawer she yanked out an envelope and handed it to me. It was addressed the same as the one before.

"Someone delivered it this morning," Renita said.

I nodded and opened the envelope.

"Personally, *here*," Renita pointed at the top of her desk. "While I was taking a shower. Along with a glass of fresh squeezed orange juice and an unfrosted cinnamon roll."

I waited. Whatever Renita was feeling she needed to let out. It would be better if it were sooner than later.

"How was your breakfast?" I asked. She ignored my sarcasm.

"It's one thing to break into a locked office when no one's around. It's something altogether different to have the audacity to do it in broad daylight while someone is in the office—and how in the hell did they know I liked fresh squeezed orange juice and unfrosted cinnamon rolls?"

"That could've been a lucky guess. Most people like fresh squeezed orange juice. The cinnamon roll, how many times have you picked up one at a bakery or coffee shop? Someone probably saw you go into one of those places. They walked in, said they were there to buy your usual. Pretended they couldn't remember what it was. The salesperson helps them out, elementary."

"I didn't *hear* anyone. I didn't *see* anyone. Whoever it was, slipped into this office without me having a clue. They could've killed me and I would've never seen it coming."

Renita was shaking. I had never seen her like that.

"What are we dealing with C. J.?"

I stared at Renita not knowing how to explain. Most people have the wrong impression about big brother. There's more than one: the CIA, NSA, FBI, Homeland Security, and Corporations, they all have different functions but often cooperate with one another. What they do have in common is that they don't regard Jill or John Doe as much of a threat. Any one of them is capable of eliminating you swiftly and silently if you become a problem. Hell, the CIA could make your mother forget she'd ever given birth to you. To drive home that point without pushing Renita over the edge was not an easy task. When I finished Renita didn't appear to be any more relaxed but she seemed to understand.

"I don't like it, C. J."

"Neither do I."

"What are we going to do?"

I thought for a moment. This was a crossroads for the investigation. I needed Renita but I needed her one hundred percent ready for anything that might arise. "What do you think we should do?" I asked.

Renita thought for a moment. She opened the top right drawer and put the forty-five inside watching the drawer slide shut.

"Read the letter," Renita said.

I let out a deep breath and read aloud. "Dear Mr. Cavanaugh: It seems you have rattled a few cages. Your progress is admirable. We see now our faith in you was well placed. As an additional incentive, we have deposited twenty-thousand of the two-hundred thousand dollars into your business account. Continue the good work!"

Renita wheeled and checked it out on her computer.

"Twenty-thousand deposited into our account today."

"Boswell Industries?" I asked.

Renita nodded again. We had learned from Windell's dossier that Boswell Industries was a dummy corporation of Clinton Windell's, one of a few associated with his Swiss Bank accounts.

"Is there anything else?" Renita asked. I read on.

"A word of caution: be careful of those who make the loudest noise. They can become your greatest distraction. Murder is only part of the puzzle. There is something much larger at stake." I paused. If there were some way to prevent Renita from discovering the remaining words on that letter I would've utilized it. Instead, I handed the letter to Renita.

"By the way," Renita read aloud, "how did Ms. Harris enjoy her treat?" Renita sounded like a grade school child speaking unfamiliar words. "We noticed she was in such a rush this morning she neglected to eat breakfast. You should inform your partner that breakfast is the most important meal of the day."

Renita stared at me. I didn't know what to say.

CHAPTER ELEVEN

We left the office at 9:53 a.m. It took that long to convince Renita there was nothing out there to fear. Our big brother—in this case our phantom employers—needed us. As long as we did our jobs and our mystery clients remained anonymous then everyone would get what they wanted. I reminded Renita about the money appealing to her sense of greed. Assuring Renita that if at anytime she believed her life was in legitimate danger say the word and we would pull the plug on the investigation. That seemed to settle Renita down enough for us to proceed. I believed what I said about our mystery employers. Whom I couldn't vouch for were their hired guns.

Renita was quiet on our way to Andrea Bettencourt's house. I had talked her into taking her thirty-eight and leaving the forty-five at the office. Renita kept looking around like a nervous drug dealer on the lookout for narcs. I tried making small talk hoping to take her mind off whatever she was thinking. Every comment garnered a startled reaction followed by a spaced-out response. I reached over and touched her hand, the one resting in her lap. Renita was trembling. Her baptism into the covert world was not as romantic as Renita may have envisioned. *Wait until the real fireworks start*, I thought.

I didn't care if we were being followed. Renita was my main concern. While it wasn't surprising to me that our phantom employer pulled such a stunt to Renita it was frightening. Her sacred space had been violated in a way unique to her. For once in a very long while, she realized she was not in control. That was something working for the DEA had taught me a long time ago.

"Renita, why don't you stay with me for a few days?" I asked.

Renita smiled. "C. J. you don't know how long I've waited for an invitation like that."

"At least until we get a firm grip on this case."

"You've got a deal."

Her trembling receded. I didn't even want to think about how I was going to explain Renita's moving in to Destini. "Will we be sharing the same bed?" Renita asked.

"No."

"Give it time."

"You'll sleep in one of the guest rooms."

"For now," she said. Renita placed her free hand atop mine and rested them all in her lap. "Thank you."

I looked into her eyes for a moment. For the first time I realized how beautiful she really was. No wonder Destini was jealous.

"You're welcome," I said. "Now can I have my hand back?"

"Think I'll hold onto it for a while." Her grip was firm but gentle. My hand was comfortable being there. I always believed Renita and I could never cross a certain physical threshold of behavior without venturing down an erotic road. Holding hands was one of those unspoken barriers. I was wrong. It was then I realized—at least under particular circumstances—men and women could be friends. I hoped that was all Renita was feeling at that moment.

CHAPTER TWELVE

Andrea Bettencourt's teenage son answered the door. He turned down the blaring rap video on TV long enough to tell us his mother was at the office. I phoned the number he'd given me from my car. Mrs. Bettencourt agreed to see us that morning. Renita and I talked about it. Renita agreed she was up to handling the Bettencourt interview.

Bellingham, Inc. is located in the KOIN building in downtown Portland. The top suite is exclusively for board members. Inside the lobby of the KOIN building, two armed uniformed security guards frisked us before they scanned our persons with metal detectors. Fortunately, we had left our hardware in the trunk of my car. One of the guards accompanied us on the elevator. Two additional armed guards were waiting when we stepped off the elevator. The guard who had accompanied us led the way while the other two brought up the rear. We were escorted down a long hallway with lush carpeting and original paintings by Grandma Moses, Monet, Picasso, Rembrandt, Collins, da Vinci, He Duoling and Ku, Fu-Sheng. We went through a pair of clear glass doors stopping in front of a receptionist desk thrice as large as my office desk. The intelligent-looking blond wearing a plain black dress smiled pleasantly and asked how she could help.

"We're here to see Andrea Bettencourt," Renita said.

"You must be Ms. Harris," the blond said to Renita. "And you're Mr. Cavanaugh?" she asked me.

Renita nodded. I politely smiled.

The accommodating tone of her voice evaporated when she spoke to the guards, "You can go now." They sauntered away without a word or gesture. The receptionist's pleasant attitude returned.

"I must apologize for these added precautions," the receptionist said. "With what happened to poor Mr. Windell, well, let's just say we can't be too careful now can we." She smiled as if appeasing children. "Follow me please." We followed. Renita readied her notepad and pen on the way.

Behind the receptionist area was a half-circle of offices each with a name plaque on their doors. All of the office doors were open. We walked into the one nearest the center. Seated behind a mahogany desk was a woman with dark curly hair scrutinizing documents.

"Pardon me Mrs. Bettencourt," the receptionist said. The woman seated behind the desk looked up. Her lips were thin and taut, her stare resolute.

"Ms. Harris and Mr. Cavanaugh are here to see you."

Andrea Bettencourt removed her glasses and eyed us for a moment. It was then you could see that her brown eyes were red and puffy. She either had a cold or had been recently crying.

"Thank you Cindy," Andrea Bettencourt said. Her voice was stern. Cindy pleasantly smiled; easing shut the door behind her as she left.

Renita handed Mrs. Bettencourt her card and then introduced me as her partner, "C. J. Cavanaugh."

"You're the principle?" Bettencourt asked me standing, a short woman, five-one to five-three, chubby build, pasty skin, Roman nose. She wore a pleated black skirt and jacket, a green jade necklace, jade earrings, jade bracelet and two gold rings on each of her doughy-fingered hands.

"We're equal partners," I said. "We haven't had a chance to update our business cards."

"Make certain he does so soon Ms. Harris," Bettencourt said to Renita. Renita smiled at me. I raised my eyebrows as a signal for Renita to continue.

"I certainly will Mrs. Bettencourt." Renita said shelving her amusement.

Renita began by explaining to Andrea Bettencourt that she was in no way obligated to answer any of our questions but it would be very helpful to our investigation if she did. I was impressed. I don't usually inform people of that stipulation because I want them to feel as if they're talking to a cop. What Renita said seemed to soften Mrs. Bettencourt's attitude. *You can catch more flies with honey than vinegar*, I thought smiling to myself.

"Who's your client Ms. Harris?" Bettencourt asked.

"Please call me Renita," Renita said. Andrea Bettencourt nodded. "Lunsford Insurance," Renita answered.

"Why are they so interested in who murdered Windell?" Bettencourt asked.

"Mr. Windell had a life insurance policy with Lunsford," Renita answered.

"So?"

"The motive behind a homicide can affect the outcome of a life insurance settlement Mrs. Bettencourt," Renita said.

"Call me Andrea." I had the feeling Andrea was extending that liberty solely to Renita.

"Lovely outfit," Renita said.

"Windell's funeral's this afternoon," Andrea said. She looked herself over. "Too good for that bastard."

Hate—like love—can be a two-way street. It was clear how Andrea felt about her deceased boss. I wondered what Windell's feelings were toward her.

"I take it you and Mr. Windell didn't get along?" Renita asked.

"Don't play coy with me Renita. I know you've spoken to the other board members. They filled you in on what I think of Clinton Windell. Especially Stuart, he loves stirring up the muck."

"Your husband died on the same day Mr. Windell was murdered?" Renita asked.

"Two years ago to the day."

"Strange coincidence," Renita said.

"More like poetic justice."

"Excuse me for saying this Andrea but it seems to me you really wanted Mr. Windell dead," Renita said.

"Dead yes, murdered no. I wanted that son-of-a-bitch to die a slow excruciating death. Cancer or AIDS are more of what I had in mind, something to make him want to call Dr. Kevorkian to finish him off."

"You were with Stuart Wu when Mr. Windell was murdered?" Renita asked.

"After The Phantom of the Opera I was feeling depressed and Stuart helped me through it, big mistake."

"Why's that?" Renita asked.

Andrea looked stunned by the question. I could only assume she thought Stuart Wu had already told us. "Because," she stumbled a moment, for the first time I noticed Andrea spoke with a lisp one she probably worked hard at controlling. "Stuart has a big mouth," she went on to say. "I should have known better than to confide in him." Andrea had answered what Stuart Wu had implied. Politics and religion weren't the only strange bedfellows.

"Is there anyone else who can vouch for your whereabouts between ten and midnight on Sunday?" Renita asked.

"Am I a suspect in Windell's murder?"

Renita was taking shorthand notes. She wrote things down without taking her eyes off Andrea. "We're simply trying to pool our facts," Renita said.

"I ran into some people I knew at the theater. I'll have my personal assistant send you there names." There was an awkward pause after Andrea answered the question. Renita and Andrea stared at one another.

"Did Stuart tell you Clinton Windell ruined Harvey's career?" Andrea asked.

"No," Renita said. Renita was correct in her answer since I was the one Stuart Wu intimated Bettencourt blamed Windell for destroying her husband's career.

"Harvey was the principle buyer for Bellingham when Clinton Windell was appointed CEO. Windell's appointment in and of itself was a huge disappointment. My husband and I were always a team.

Harvey handled the merchandise and I handled the paperwork. Harvey wasn't even considered when Windell selected his Board of Directors. He said Harvey lacked the leadership skills necessary to sit on *his board*. Already that bastard claimed the business as his. Windell vowed to keep Harvey in his current position as the principle buyer. After Geoffrey Bellingham died Windell circulated rumors about certain suspicions he had about Harvey."

"What sort of suspicions?" Renita asked.

"He claimed Harvey had been skimming a few of the best gemstones for himself to make a little extra money on the side."

"Was he?" Renita asked.

"Of course not! Harvey remained loyal to the company even after Geoff's death. Besides, Harvey had far too much integrity to become a thief. He was set up. Windell wanted the principle buyer position."

"Isn't that unusual for the CEO to also be the principle buyer?" Renita asked.

"Not really. Principle buyers often know the most about business operations, especially among family jewelry stores."

"What happened next?" Renita asked.

"Harvey was offered early retirement. If he took it then all of this theft business would be forgotten. What choice did he have?"

"But at the time of your husband's death he was the principle buyer," Renita said.

"Windell realized there was no one better and brought Harvey back into the fold."

"Why'd you stay on after your husband's initial forced retirement?" Renita asked.

"Geoff Bellingham gave us our start in this business. He cared about us when he was alive. Geoff was the best man at our wedding. He was at the christening of our children. Geoff Bellingham was like family. We love this company. We grew up here."

"Why did Mr. Windell goad Mr. Bettencourt into those parachute jumps?" Renita asked.

"Parachute jumps, poker games, dirt biking, scuba diving, it was all the same. Manipulating Harvey was Windell's way of subduing me."

"Did your husband ever dispute the theft charge?" Renita asked.

"Only in private, Harvey was more concerned about the company's reputation than his own."

"Your husband's death was a tragic accident according to authorities," Renita said.

"Accident my foot! Windell had more to do with what happened to Harvey than talking him into those stupid parachute jumps. Harvey was working on something that would have forced Windell to give him what he really wanted. A seat on Bellingham's Board of Directors."

"Could you be more specific?" Renita asked.

"Harvey never told me. Whatever it was it involved Clinton Windell."

"Who went on those parachute jumps besides Mr. Windell and your husband?" Renita asked.

"Stuart Wu, Patrick Kemery, Antonio Farhletti, Judith Hardy."

"Are you aware of anyone who might be capable of murdering Mr. Windell?" Renita asked.

"Carlos and Ron possibly, they were always pissed at Windell about something, threatened to blow his head off more than once."

"Anyone else?" Renita asked.

"I'm sure if you look hard enough you'll find a list of people as long as your arm who would want to plant Windell." The honey principle had dissolved. Andrea sounded irritated.

"Perhaps you can provide us with their names, Andrea?" Renita asked.

"You're the investigators find them yourselves."

"I gather you won't miss him," Renita said.

"Him?"

"Clinton Windell," Renita said.

"I know who you're referring to." Andrea let out a derisive laugh. "*Miss him*? Like a case of hemorrhoids."

"If you despised Mr. Windell that much why are you attending his funeral?" Renita asked.

"If nothing else I'm a professional. It's my duty as a board member to be there. Looks bad for Bellingham if I'm absent. Image is everything."

"Thanks for your time," Renita said. "We'll be on our way. It was a pleasure meeting you." Renita and Andrea shook hands.

"Wish I could say the same," Andrea said. Renita grinned. She was enjoying herself.

"Mrs. Bettencourt," I said as we shook hands before leaving.

"Mr. Cavanaugh." Her handshake was firm. Her eyes defiant. Why? I couldn't be certain. What I was sure of was Andrea Bettencourt was tough and smart. She was also our prime suspect. Renita was still grinning when we left.

"How'd I do?" Renita asked.

"Not bad."

"Any pointers?"

"Scratch the Miranda-like speech and serve up the vinegar."

CHAPTER THIRTEEN

The last couple of days had reminded me of autumn in Pittsburgh, bright colored leaves, a sharp nip in the air, sky a powdery blue and undaunted sunlight as sharp as clear crystal. Autumn was the only time I longed for home. It brought to a close a typically hot, humid summer and was the prelude to an unrelenting winter. When I visit Pittsburgh, it's always in autumn. Winter was rapidly approaching. If Renita and I could not finalize the Windell case soon this would be the first year I would not return to my native Pittsburgh since I moved away.

Renita and I stopped by her apartment. She needed to pick up a few things including her car. I followed her back to my place. The Jaguar was nowhere in sight.

I was confident we were being watched. By now a tag team umbrella system of surveillance—if it hadn't been all along—was probably being employed using a variety of vehicles and revolving stakeouts at predetermined check points such as our office, our homes, the KOIN building, the police precinct and the Windell Estate. While I disliked it, I knew how to function under that type of surveillance. When you are being watched you don't do anything that will send up a red flag. Just be yourself. Do what you'd normally do. That was why I wasn't going to share my suspicions with Renita that we were under-glass. I wasn't certain my partner was up to handling that kind of knowledge after what happened this morning.

At home, I did what had become routine and checked the house for listening devices showing Renita what to look for. The coast was clear.

Andrew and Booker were happier to see Renita than me. I let Renita decide which of the guest rooms she wanted. Once we established my bedroom was off limits, Renita chose the Scottish room. The guest bedroom closest to mine.

Renita made herself at home while I checked my phone messages. My parents called. They wanted to know when to expect me. My dry-cleaning was ready. Carl needed an update on the Windell claim and my six-year-old niece simply wanted to say "Hi" to her favorite uncle.

I phoned my parents to tell them I was on hold with a case and wasn't certain when it would be completed. They sounded disappointed. I assured them I'd do my best not to let the case interfere with my holiday plans. They said they'd pray for the best. After we exchanged our sentiments of goodwill and love, I hung up the phone feeling a little deflated. All of my family would be at my parent's house at Thanksgiving. Memories of home kept me focused and sane when I was under deep cover. While the same need was not currently necessary, my family still served as a fitting reminder to what was most important in this world.

Feeling sorry for myself wasn't going to get the job done. I shook off the iron cloak of self-pity and phoned Carl to inform him I'd e-mail him a preliminary report in the morning. In the meantime, I strongly urged Carl not to make any payments on Windell's policy until my investigation was complete. Carl agreed. I asked him about the gems. He told me they had a team of investigators working on it.

Carl wanted me to concentrate on making certain Mrs. Windell had nothing to do with her husband's murder.

I phoned Destini at home after my conversation with Carl. I didn't expect Destini to be there. What I wanted was what I got her answering machine. It was better than upsetting her at work. I expected Destini wouldn't get the message until that evening. That way when she stormed over to my place I would be ready to explain. I left a message for Destini to call me at home when she got in.

Renita had put her things away by the time I was done. Booker and Andrew were performing tricks for her in the living room. Assuming Kemery would be attending Windell's funeral I had decided to put off interviewing him until tomorrow. Based on what little we knew about the shooters I figured it was time to pay a little visit to Fullman's.

Fullman's Restaurant is a two-story establishment styled after a Spanish bordello. It also happens to be one of the finest dining experiences in the city. Waiters wear black double-breasted suits, white shirts, burgundy bow ties, and maintain a compliant manner that accentuated the old adage the customer was in charge. It was always packed for lunch and dinner and on weekends, breakfast as well. The downstairs' patrons consisted mostly of honest citizens who wined and dined on some of the best southern cuisine in Portland. The upstairs was closed off and catered more to thugs, middle management narcotics distributors, extortionists, blackmailers, players, madams, con men, burglars and thieves—a regular melting pot of criminals; those were the people I was interested in. If there was any floating information about these killers, the second floor clientele of Fullman's was the place we'd find it.

We jumped in my car and headed north to the Lombard district. If Renita were going to do more fieldwork this would be a good opportunity for her to become acquainted with some of my more credible sources. Renita's wily smile and the glint in her mischievous eyes were back. She had never been to Fullman's before in an investigative capacity so I briefed Renita on what to expect.

There was an unspoken law that nothing went down at Fullman's. You couldn't smoke a joint in a bathroom stall without finding yourself face down on the pavement with that joint shoved up your nose. Not an exaggeration but fact; that convention did not include discussing or contracting illicit deals.

At seven-three, two-hundred-eighty pounds of chiseled muscle, Ernest Fullman, the restaurant's namesake stood to the left of the door when Renita and I walked in. Ernest didn't say much. What he said was honest, direct, and sincere. That's how Ernest behaved toward people. If he liked you, you knew it. If he didn't you knew it. If he was indifferent, that didn't last long. Most people wanted Ernest to like them. I was already on that list. Ernest unfolded his arms when he saw us coming.

"What's going on Ernest?" I asked.

"C. J.," Ernest said. We shook hands. His right eyebrow raised when he saw Renita. That meant he was curious. If both eyebrows went up, he was riled. That was something no one wanted. I waited a few seconds before introducing Renita as my partner to incite the situation a bit. It fed into my untimely sense of playfulness.

"Oh!" was Ernest's response. His right eyebrow dropped. "This is the lady I've heard so much about and seen far too little of," Ernest said. "You neglected to tell a brother your partner was such a ravishing woman." Ernest took Renita's hand and kissed it. Renita was beaming.

"And such a lovely smile," Ernest said.

Ernest was charming and sophisticated. He was also the man who shoved that joint up your nose and planted you face first on the asphalt. I didn't ask Ernest anything pertinent to the case. What he knew he certainly wouldn't tell us there and he certainly wouldn't tell us now.

"May I have someone show you to a table?" Ernest asked Renita.

"If you would be so kind," I said before Renita could answer mimicking Ernest's haughty dialect despite the fact he always sounded that way. His false grin told me he was mildly amused. I asked for two seats in their second floor dining area. That clued Ernest in that we were there on business. Ernest motioned with one of his huge hands. Elma Louise Washington appeared by his side. The five-five, brown-eyed, sassy, bronze skinned body builder maitre d' had a crush on Ernest he did not reciprocate. Elma Louise had a rose pinned to her lapel, as did Ernest. Not long ago all food servers wore a red rose pinned to their lapels. One day a former waiter accidentally dropped his rose into a customer's bowl of Cajun gumbo. Unaware of his mistake the customer discovered the flower partway through her meal. The lawsuit was settled out of court. Now only management accessorized accordingly.

"Show Mr. Cavanaugh and Mrs. Harris . . . ?" Ernest awaited Renita's reaction.

"It's Ms.," Renita said. "I'm not married. But I'm working on it." Renita grabbed my arm attempting to make us appear as a couple. I offered no resistance. Ernest knew about Destini and me. His right eyebrow went up. This time he had a sly grin.

"If second best will do my dear give me a call," Ernest said. "Perhaps I can persuade you that C. J. is not the only man worth having in this town." Elma Louise's eyes narrowed on Renita. Renita didn't seem to notice.

Elma Louise led us along a carpeted aisle that separated the dining area from the bar up a circular stairway and through a pair of heavy oak doors. The mood was entirely different from the charming dining experience one would have on the first floor. The second floor was considered a private club. Smoking and after hours drinking were allowed. It offered all the downstairs' amenities. Well lit, spacious, the same layout as downstairs but with a more sinister atmosphere. Even if you knew nothing about Fullman's Restaurant and you were to enter the second floor club area, an immediate sense of wariness would envelope you.

Destini and David called it The Snake Pit. The second floor regulars called it The Lair.

Those who talk don't know, and those who know don't talk at The Lair. If the melting pot didn't know you, and what you were about, you'd have an easier time sucking golf balls through a garden hose. Keeping that in mind during your dialogues with the melting pot crowd allowed you to siphon fact from fiction.

We had missed the lunch crowd. The afternoon regulars were out in full force. Elma Louise knew why we were there as well. She sat us at a table behind a pillar obscuring our view to the bar. Elma Louise only seated me then went to inform Ernest's partner we were waiting. That didn't set well with Renita.

"Seven Steps To Heaven" was playing low throughout The Lair. Jazz, blues, old standards, and the best of contemporaries were all you heard at Fullman's. There was nothing else on the jukebox. KMHD was the only radio station allowed. "All jazz, all day." Newspapers and magazines were available upon request. If they didn't have what you were looking for and you were a valued customer, it was placed on a list and would be waiting for you the next day.

Monty Holbrook is a short powerful man with aubergine skin and an incredible smile who told prison stories as if they were nostalgia. It appeared that was what he was doing when I looked around the pillar and saw him talking to a couple of avid listeners at the bar.

Monty was clean even if the majority of his second floor clientele were not. The only reason Monty wasn't incarcerated was due to a promise he had made his mother before she died to stay free and stay straight. While he kept his promise, Monty still found the company of the nefarious types preferable to the straight set. That was how we met.

Monty came into my office the first week I hung out my shingle. He was nervous and agitated. He had a serious problem he needed fixed quickly before it escalated beyond his control. I took care of it for him. I got him through it unsullied, which helped him keep his promise to his mother. He's been my most reliable source ever since.

Ernest had never been in any trouble with the law as far as I knew which made being business partners with a known felon a curious marriage, one I hadn't gotten around to discovering more about. Emma interrupted Monty to point us out. Monty nodded toward us. He told his fans he'd finish his story later. Monty put out his cigarette and headed our way.

If you want to know about criminal activities go to criminals. The police are usually good for after-the-fact information. Monty gets the word on many villainous ventures up-front.

"You remember Renita Harris," I said to Monty when he stood beside our table. Renita nodded. Monty tipped his derby to Renita then sat across from me.

"A couple of days before Windell got it there was a dude in here buzz cut, blue eyes, lean and mean," Monty began in answer to my question of whether there were any new faces at The Lair recently. "Never seen him before, he looked like he was waiting on somebody. He had a drink, bourbon and soda, then dinner, the Creole chicken, another drink, then left. All in all, I'd say he was here 'bout an hour-and-a-half. I haven't seen him since."

"The other party ever show?" I asked.

"Nope; Ham might know more. He tried running some scam on the dude. The dude leaned over and whispered something in Ham's ear. Sent Ham scurrying away like a scared rabbit."

"Anything else?" I asked.

Monty thought for a moment. "I seem to remember Clinton Windell showing his face in The Lair more than once."

Renita and I looked at each other in mild surprise.

"After that man died in a parachuting accident I saw him talking to some dude. Overheard a little of their conversation. They were in the Navy together."

"What did the other man look like?" I asked.

"White dude, thick built, had on a wig and phony beard. Was probably wearing color contacts. That man was definitely on the down low."

Windell having been to The Lair did not appear on his dossier. I had a feeling Clinton Windell was aware of his unsolicited biographers and dodged them when necessary. Either that or his visits to Fullman's were deliberately omitted.

"Anything else?" I asked.

"The man who died in the parachuting accident—what's his name?" Monty said.

"Harvey Bettencourt?" I said.

"That's him. I heard his name mentioned a couple of times, something about Bettencourt finding out something about them."

"You're telling me Bettencourt's death was no accident?" I said.

Monty nodded. "That'd be my guess." Monty and I both knew a chute packed to fail was nearly impossible to prove.

"Did you overhear exactly what it was Bettencourt had on them?" I asked.

"Nah," Monty said.

"Why didn't you tell the police?" Renita asked.

"None of my business, C. J.'s like family. That's the only reason I give it up to him." Monty paused for a moment. "Anyway nobody asked, nothing but trouble for me dropping a dime on someone like Windell. Why bother?"

"How is it you get all the dope in this city nobody else can dig up?" Renita asked.

"Eyes, ears, nose, Ms. Harris," Monty pointed to each one as he mentioned it. "People come here to relax. They have a couple of drinks and a good meal. They get comfortable and let things drop. When the fruit falls I'm simply fortunate enough to be there to gather it."

Renita appeared perturbed. I reminded Renita with a look that this was my show and that she was there to watch, listen, and learn. Renita appeared to get the message. I decided to fill her in later on some of the silent codes of The Lair one of which was to take no unnecessary risks.

"Anything else?" I asked.

"Nothing comes to mind," Monty said.

"Thanks," I said.

"No problem." Monty stood. "I've got to get back to the books."

"The usual payment plan?" I asked. That meant leaving a cash tip with Elma Louise. This information was easily worth five hundred.

"Yep," Monty said. "Nice meeting you Miss Harris." Monty tipped his hat. He was a gentleman, well mannered and considerate. Renita was unimpressed.

"I'll send Ham over," Monty said. "Get him to keep it down. We got a couple of press moles in here trying to get the 4-1-1 on this Windell thing."

I looked around. Monty leaned into my ear. "The black dude looks like Richard Roundtree and the dough boy at the bar." I saw them and nodded.

"Calloway been here?" I asked.

"Left about an hour ago," Monty said.

I was glad. If I had to deal with Calloway, I preferred it to be on my own terms. There was more assurance we'd both get what we wanted that way.

"No cops?" Renita asked.

"Nah, Destini knows better," Monty said. Monty and I smiled. Renita was not amused.

"One other thing," I said to Monty as he was about to walk away. "Did anybody see a Jaguar with the license plate HADES?"

"Don't know. Check with Ernest. He might have spotted it on his rounds."

Monty went over to Ham and whispered something to him before Monty disappeared into his office. Ham sat down a couple of minutes later like a man who didn't want to be there. Monty had probably ordered him to tell us what he knew.

Tyrone Hamson was the kind of man who would smile in your face while taking your wallet, sleeping with your wife, and selling crack to your children. He had an insincere laugh and dark soulless eyes that were absent of genuine emotion. All he was usually worth was information. I needed a tip. In Portland, Ham was as good as the FBI.

Ham pulled the glass ashtray on our table toward him and tapped his cigar ashes into it. He was a beige man with a pencil mustache, large eyes, and fat cheeks to match his fat body. He wore an earring in each ear and expensive rings on every finger as well as his thumbs. A dark green suit, avocado colored shirt, alligator shoes and celery colored silk tie rounded out that day's ensemble. It was typical attire for a man who had his fingers in every dirty pie he could reach. I wasn't concerned about him packing. No weapons were allowed in Fullman's. Once again, Renita and I had left our hardware in the car. Ham glared at Renita. Renita stared back. Ham was sizing her up. Renita didn't give him anything to nibble on. Tough kid, I was proud of her.

It was said Ham was a different man before his first stint in the state pen. He was supposedly a good-natured hustler who didn't take advantage of those who couldn't afford it. He had ethics and compassion but came out a bitter, sadistic, violent man. It made no difference to me. I dealt with the man in front of me. The man I saw deserved no pity.

I was working on a missing person's case for Lunsford when Ham and I first met. I suppose I asked one too many tough questions about his involvement because with a jerk of his head he sicced one of his bully-guards on me. My attacker's name—I later learned—was Alan Biggs. I broke Alan's collarbone. Ham thought better of sending another. It turned out Ham was innocent of any wrongdoing that time.

"Clubbing alone?" I asked.

"I have assistants nearby if needed."

I looked around the pillar and saw his bully-guards seated near the middle of the bar. "How's Alan?" I asked. I wanted to remind Ham I was still capable of causing him distress in case he wanted to get physical.

"Retired," Ham said.

"Too bad," I said.

"It happens," Ham said.

"Any thoughts," I said.

"*About what*," Ham snapped. I leaned in close.

"Keep your voice down or I'll break your fat jaw," I said.

"Then how would I answer your questions," Ham mused, "with my jaw wired shut?"

I took out a pen and notepad and shoved them across the table at Ham. "Get the picture?"

"You should have been a gangster," Ham said with a surly grin.

"I am what I should be," I said.

"As am I," Ham said.

"That's not saying much," I said.

"What'd I ever do to you?" The grin vanished with Ham's question.

"Nothing, what have you ever done *for* me?" I said.

"Not a damn thing," Ham said. "I'd like to keep it that way."

I sat back and eyed Ham for a moment. He took a long draw on his cigar. Ham wasn't scared just anxious. He exhaled toward the ceiling. The pale smoke mushroomed above his head for a moment before dispersing. Robert Cray made the musical statement:

Everybody likes them folding bills,
And you might need them little white pills,
Fast little cars give some people chills.

"Did you talk to a white man with a buzz cut a couple of nights ago?" I asked under the high voltage blues of Robert Cray.

"Yeah," Ham said.

"What about?" I asked.

Ham rolled his eyes toward Renita. Renita was holding her own. Ham took a deep draw on his cigar and nonchalantly exhaled blowing the smoke away from us. He knew that if he didn't I'd grind that cigar out on his face.

"I'd acquired some property," Ham said. "I thought a prosperous looking dude like him might be interested. He wasn't. End of story."

"Did you get a name?" I asked.

"Nope," Ham said.

"Notice anything distinctive about him?" I asked.

"Nope," Ham said.

"You don't remember *anything* about this man?" I asked.

"Only that he told me if I didn't get the hell away from him he'd rip my heart out and show it to me before I died."

"And you believed him," I said. Ham looked cautiously around. People who are intimate with dispensing death seldom joke about it. Whatever he saw in that man's eyes shook him like a near death experience. Ham licked his lips and leaned toward the middle of the table. Renita and I joined him.

"I've seen some bad dudes in my day, looked the devil in the eyes a couple of times and managed not to blink. I know the difference between some fool talking shit and a maniac. Whether he could do it or not wasn't the question. That fool *believed* he could. I wasn't about to stick around as a test subject."

"Why didn't you have some of your muscle take care of him?" I asked.

"Contrary to popular belief I'm a business man. Wasting my time on silly personal beefs ain't my style. Now are we through?"

"For now," I said. Ham left scowling.

Renita and I were famished. We ordered a late lunch that we ate downstairs. It was the middle of the afternoon so we had most of the place to ourselves. A sweet dusting of vibraphone jazz floated down from the speakers. Ernest paid us a visit. He offered to pay for Renita's meal. Renita accepted. When I asked Ernest about mine, he told me I was working and that I could pay for my own. Renita asked Ernest about the Jaguar before I had the chance. He had seen it parked in their parking lot the same night that Ham was scared away by Buzz Cut. Ernest said he didn't see the driver. He confirmed it was the only time he ever saw the vehicle. Ernest gave Renita his business card with his private phone number written on the back before we left. Renita wouldn't admit it but I believed she liked Ernest. God, I hoped so.

The Jaguar was possibly tied to a man who could turn out to be one of our shooters. It would also make sense that the driver of the Jaguar wasn't connected to our phantom clients. I was still convinced we should go after the person who hired the assassins but I couldn't ignore the evidence before us. I asked Renita to follow up on Patrick Kemery. I felt confident letting her interview Kemery alone after the way she handled Andrea Bettencourt. I was going after the man with the Buzz Cut and I knew just where to start.

Something kept gnawing at me on the way back to my place. A feeling I couldn't shake. There was a man seated in the restaurant I noticed as we were leaving. Something about him had struck me as familiar. While opening my front door it dawned on me like a Hawaiian sunrise. It was his eyes. His eyes were clear that time but he was the same old man I saw telling his eyewitness homicide account to the precinct desk sergeant. He was tidy and well dressed but I was certain it was him. I was about to relay that fact to Renita when the sight of Destini sitting cross-legged on the sofa with a thirty-two resting in her lap distracted me.

CHAPTER FOURTEEN

After seeing Renita's car in my driveway, her bike in my garage, and her clothes in the Scottish bedroom, it only took Destini half a minute to piece together that something was awry. The bigger problem was what was going to prevent Destini from using her weapon? Pissed off would have been a step up from the expression on her face.

"Officer Pendleton," Renita said. "What a nice surprise!" Renita was enjoying herself too much. The more I squirmed the better Renita seemed to like it. I asked Renita if she could leave us alone. Renita did so after kissing me on the cheek and thanking me for lunch.

Destini glared at me. She didn't need the gun. I was already a dead man in her eyes. It was a good thing I'd stashed the Windell DVD and printed bio in the basement in a secret cubbyhole behind the dryer.

"Renita's being stalked," I told Destini. "We don't know by whom. I thought it would be prudent for her to stay with me until we got a better handle on things." It was a small lie but I hated telling it.

"That a fact," Destini sarcastically said.

I nodded.

"Sounds like a police matter."

"Normally I would agree but Renita's my partner. I'm ultimately responsible for her safety."

"Are you saying the Portland Police are incapable of protecting your *partner* from a stalker?"

"Not at all."

"Then what are you saying?"

"Renita is my responsibility. Now I know what you're thinking but you're wrong. There has never been—nor will there ever be—anything romantic between Renita and myself."

Destini stood. She pointed the weapon toward my aquarium. The look in her eyes had not changed. I was geared to move.

"Your precious *Miss Harris* can stay with me until her little stalking problem blows over. I'll make certain nothing happens to her."

"This is our problem. She's staying here. You're just going to have to trust me."

"I see," Destini said.

Destini aimed her off duty thirty-two at me. I rose on the balls of my feet ready to make a dash for the door. I flashed back to when Cardozo was prepared to shred me with a Coonan 357 Magnum for being a suspected CIA spy. I remained calm and was able to talk my way out of it. I said all of the right things and made all of the right moves. I wanted to tell Destini the truth, clear my conscience, and give Destini some insight into the full scope her homicide case had taken. If I could have trusted Destini not to be a cop first, I would have taken her into my confidence. Destini was a duty bound professional. Asking her to keep quiet on vital information to a homicide investigation would have been like asking a dentist to ignore a cavity.

Renita walked in. Andrew and Booker were with her. Renita tossed their giant gumball toward Destini. The terriers chased after it. Andrew retrieved it at Destini's feet. They eagerly circled Destini trying to induce her to play. Destini picked up the toy and tossed it toward the study. The terriers chased after it. Renita had her thirty-eight pointed at Destini.

I rushed between them waving a hand at both in surrender. "Don't shoot," was all I could think of saying. My being shot didn't frighten me. Seeing either of them hurt did.

"As long as she's here I'm here," Destini said.

"No problem," I said keeping my hands where Destini could see them. I had been trying to get Destini to move in with me for ages. If I'd known jealousy would work, I would have had Renita for a roommate a long time ago.

***

Cardozo's Yari operation was hit by *los federals*. They had burned his marijuana and coco crops, confiscated equipment, product, facilities, and captured over one hundred men and women vital to his narcotics empire. A few of his people managed to slip through the snare. One of the men made his way to Cardozo. He was tortured for his efforts. Bebe Assassino invited me along to witness how they handled traitors to his lord.

Bebe Assassino and I stood by as Cardozo supervised. His own sons had refused to be party to it and they were by no means saints. They believed in dispensing with their problems swiftly, which usually meant beheading a person with a machete or a bullet through their brain.

That poor man was subjected to a harrowing variety of brutalities, the worst of which was the "Dragon's Chair." The victim was forced to sit in what resembled a barber's chair. He was restrained by leather straps covered with foam rubber. His tormentors tied his toes and fingers with electric wires. While one torturer administered a series of electric shocks, another shocked him with an electric rod between his legs and on his penis. Cardozo and Bebe Assassino gleamed at his suffering.

There is little more unsettling to me than a terrorized human being. I'll never forget the nauseating mixture of his burning hair and flesh, urine, feces, fear and contorted expressions. The wrenching sounds of broken bones, ripped ligaments, and tormented screams. The more he agonized, the brighter Cardozo and Bebe Assassino glowed.

The victim confessed to having been the informant who cost Cardozo millions after nearly three hours of anguished denials. He told a disjointed story about how he managed to slip covert information to an agent of the state. This agent supposedly coordinated with him when, and how, to take Yari down. It got so it was no longer him speaking but his tormentors who dominated and possessed him. How could a man become a whole person again after such demoralization?

When I asked the man why, he stuttered an explanation that wouldn't have convinced a grade school teacher. Cardozo seemed satisfied. Bebe Assassino put the man out of his misery. He shot him through the back of his head. I knew that man wasn't the leak. I was.

***

I stared off into the fire. Andrew and Booker rested near my feet. Destini was in the shower. Renita walked into the living room wearing a guest cotton robe that was too large for her. She sat beside me. I would be a liar if I said I minded. We discussed her pulling a gun on Destini. I told her I didn't want her ever to do that again. Renita told me she wouldn't as long as Destini gave her no reason. I reminded Renita, Destini was not only a police officer but also the woman I loved. That didn't seem to faze

Renita. I realized there was only one way this conflict would be resolved and that was to remove Renita from my premises as soon as possible.

"Don't you have any Terry McMillan or Walter Mosley?" Renita asked. I assumed the Scottish literature in her bedroom was not to her liking.

"Check the study," I said. "I want to congratulate you on how you handled yourself today – except for your pulling a gun on Destini."

"Thanks," Renita said with a weary smile. We were both tired.

"Where'd you learn that stuff?" I asked.

"What stuff?"

"The way you questioned Andrea Bettencourt that wasn't amateur hour."

"From you of course."

"When?"

"Writing your reports," Renita said.

"And?"

"I have to organize your facts."

"So?"

"You pass along the details to me." Renita yawned. "And I put them into a comprehensive chronological form for everyone involved to understand."

"You have to know how I acquired the information in order to do that," I said, "and by what methods."

"Now you're catching on," Renita said.

"I'm impressed."

"In case you haven't noticed I'm more than just another pretty face with a great body."

I ignored Renita's flirtatious advance. "As of today Andrea Bettencourt is our number one suspect," I said.

"Sure looks that way. How do we tie her in with the hit men?"

"We'll have to track down the assassins first. Then we can make a connection. Let's see what turns up tomorrow."

"What about tonight?" Renita allowed her robe to fall open showing a great deal of her sleek athletic legs.

"Goodnight Renita," I said.

"Everything doesn't have to do with love, C. J. Sometimes it's about the simple act of satisfying a lustful urge. What's wrong with that?"

"Nothing, as long as both parties agree."

Renita leaned forward. I gently grabbed her by her shoulders and held her back. Her smile was sensual. Renita delicately traced my lips with her forefinger.

"I'm only playing with you, C. J. I wouldn't seduce you with your lady in the next room. When I get you and I will, I want you all to myself."

With that, Renita returned to her bedroom.

***

Trust is like a leather strap, if well oiled it will serve you for a lifetime. If neglected or abused, it cracks and weakens. Abused for too long and it snaps. You can mend it, make it stronger than before, but it's not the same.

Destini and I calmed down enough to try to sleep. Destini told me she didn't believe my stalking story. I stuck to my guns. Destini said she didn't know what was going on with me but she was certain it had a lot to do with the Windell case. I tried persuading Destini she was hallucinating. Of course that didn't fly. Her silence told me she had her teeth in this one and wasn't about to let go. I changed the subject. I asked Destini how the Windell case was going. She said there were no new leads. No firm suspects.

There was a pause. Destini rolled over resting her head on my shoulder. I felt her smooth hand rub my abs. One silky leg rested across my thighs. It was then Destini confided in me. Destini said it wasn't me she distrusted it was Renita. Destini pointed to the fact Renita pulled a gun on her. I reminded Destini that Renita was my partner. She was trying to protect me. Renita reacted no differently than David would have had I pulled a gun on her. Destini said Renita was going to shoot her not because we were partners but because Destini was threatening the life of the man Renita loved.

Destini said I underestimated what a woman in love would do. I half expected Barbra Streisand to start singing. Destini had no doubt Renita would have shot her. I told Destini, I had no doubt she would have shot me. Destini assured me she would not have. She said I wasn't getting off the hook that easily. I said I felt the whole situation had gotten out of hand. Destini blamed me for that. Somehow I kept missing the point because we went around and around about that scene. I was just thankful no one got hurt.

CHAPTER FIFTEEN

The house was quiet on the cusp of dawn when I awoke. Renita and Destini were sound asleep. Andrew, Booker, and I went for our morning run under an overcast sky that threatened rain. It was chilly and still damp from earlier rainfall. It was good thinking weather. The morning route I had chosen was 39th to Glisan to 82nd to Halsey back to 39th and home, all and all about six miles. Booker and Andrew stayed with me stride for stride.

A principle key to being a solid investigator is being alert to all possibilities. Things don't typically fall in line up front in our business. Sometimes you must rise up on your toes to see what's in the back. You have to learn to trust your instincts. Mine were screaming we were on the right track.

Danger aside I was feeling good about how this case was progressing. So good in fact, I added an extra spin around Laurelhurst Park to our run. Wish I could say I felt as good about my personal life.

When I returned home, Renita had taken care of the finches. Destini had seen to my tropical fish. We all pitched in on an uneasy affair known as breakfast. Renita's ill-fated attempts at humor were met with disdainful stares or blank looks. I tried keeping those deadly women in sight whenever fate brought them together. Mercifully, Renita left to interview Kemery and Destini left shortly after that for work.

That gave me an opportunity to write my Lunsford report omitting everything about our visit to Fullman's and of course our phantom employers. I e-mailed Carl his copy of my report before I left for the office.

***

From mid-morning to late afternoon, when the weather was decent, Smoky and Winston could be found downtown on the Morrison and Broadway corner of Pioneer Courthouse Square playing chess on a black-and-white marble chessboard. They'd have coffee, crumb cake and a serious match going. They were my eyes and ears to downtown Portland. If a visitor stayed downtown, he or she had probably passed by or through Pioneer Courthouse Square. If Buzz Cut had been around Courthouse Square, Winston and Smoky would have seen him.

Rain had come in the form of a light drizzle. Winston and Smoky moved their match to Metro on Broadway when the weather became a nuisance. The Metro is an old-fashioned restaurant complex with a communal dining area where you find college students eating pizza alongside business suits, maintenance workers devouring gyros next to engineers, medical doctors slurping soup across from subcontractors, or sales clerks nibbling elephant ears at close quarters to stockbrokers. They gossiped about coworkers, family and friends, debated gender and race relations as well as politics and the environment. They discussed sports, fashions, television shows, films, the theater, dance, art and books, expressing themselves and gaining different perspectives on their lives. Common ground was tread if only for a few moments before each returned to the deluge of their unique and structured worlds.

I found the dueling duo at Metro on Broadway. They were seated on the far right, at a table near the window in the section by the bar. From there you could see north to Pioneer Courthouse Square one block east to sixth and most of the Taylor and Broadway intersection. They had polished off their crumb cake and their cups were empty. I arrived bearing gifts of cheesecake and black coffee. They nodded their thanks, keeping their attention on their chess match.

"Shit man!" Winston said, "I hated that job. It was like being at a Republican convention with Rush Limbaugh as the guest speaker. Only reason I showed up was to do the time to get the dime they paid me."

"It couldn't have been all that bad," Smoky said.

"Are you kidding, urban redneck count in double digits," Winston said.

"Life's too short to play silly games with foolish people," Smoky said.

"I've never worked with a bigger group of pricks in all my life," Winston said. "You hear all the talk about quotas. I'll tell you about quotas."

"Do you have to?" Smoky asked. Winston ignored him.

"There should be a quota on how many fools are allowed in this world. Once it's reached you've got to wait until a few of them drop dead before any more can get in."

"Why didn't you get another job?" Smoky asked.

"There some place out here better for a black man you know about?"

"Not offhand."

Smoky and Winston reminded me of my deaf Uncle Kellar and his best friend Mr. Stringer. Except with Uncle Kellar and Mr. Stringer, it was checkers, hot chocolate, sweet rolls and cigars. Smoky would comment on Winston fussing for a while. I had to be patient. They would get to me when they were ready. Until their chess match was finished, they wouldn't be much good for information. I pulled up a chair to watch the game and bide my time.

"You C. J.," Winston asked in reference to his question about a better place for a black man.

"Make of it what you will," I said. "We're all branded."

"Now what the hell is that supposed to mean?" Winston said.

"Do something about it," I said.

"Like what?" Winston said.

"Whatever you think will make a difference," I said.

"Bust a cap smooth off in their ass," Winston said. "That'll make a difference."

"For prisons and cemeteries," I said.

"See that's what I don't like about your bourgeois ass. You think you know it all. You need to read "Faces At The Bottom Of The Well" to get your head on straight."

"Read it," I said.

"Apparently it didn't sink in," Winston said.

"My enemies are black, white, red, yellow, brown, gay, bi and straight," I said. "And so are my friends."

When I was a young man running the streets of Pittsburgh, I learned a lot about life. I enjoyed talking to older folks. Those who had danced to music I had yet to hear and now recognized the songs before they were played. My parents were a source of that wisdom when I listened. So was my Uncle Kellar. He was a surly man who had gone deaf by age seven. He told me there were some white people who believed the only thing they had going for them in this world was the color of their skin. It was what kept them believing they were one-step above us so called "minority" people. Without that belief, they would be nothing in their own minds even less than a nigger. Schultz and Weasel are the type of white people my uncle spoke of. He also warned me not to be blind to good people no matter their skin color. Like his friend Mr. Stringer, a white man he considered his brother. Content of character is all that matters about a person my Uncle Kellar said quoting Dr. King. That was why I said what I said.

"You should be concentrating on playing chess," Smoky said to Winston.

"Man you ain't got nothing I ain't seen before," Winston said.

"Yadda, yadda, yadda, you always do most of your talking when I'm about to polish you off *Mr. Davis*."

During down times I do impromptu pro bono investigations to keep my skills honed. Smoky's real name is Holland Jenkins, Marylhurst music grad and self-taught philosopher; a mocha skinned man with a white beard who always wore a baseball cap.

His musicianship was smooth and lilting, which was how he got his nickname. He made a run on the jazz scene for a while. Cut a few records. He wore himself down trying to keep up the high level of performance he was noted for. Smoky collapsed on stage from exhaustion in the middle of a sixty city international tour. That was fifteen years ago. He never returned to the music scene. Never married, no children, he lived with his oldest sister and her family in a large modern house in northwest Portland. His paternal grandparents had left him, his two sisters, and older brother small fortunes. Between his inheritance and the money he had saved from his professional music career, Smoky wasn't hurting for funds.

Winston Davis lived in a small one-bedroom apartment in northeast Portland. He was a decorated Korean War veteran. His deadpan expression and fervid eyes masked his passion and sensitivity. To Winston there were no small injustices. He managed to scrape by on a VA pension and short-lived night jobs. He had been married and divorced twice and had four children in all. He didn't know where any of them were and he didn't seem to care.

Winston was also a musician albeit self-taught. Winston and Smoky occasionally performed street corner concerts near Pioneer Courthouse Square. There wasn't an instrument they couldn't play well. Large crowds always formed forcing the police to break up their extemporaneous concerts. Smoky and Winston used a large can or instrument case for donations, which they promptly turned over to the Rescue Mission on Burnside Avenue.

"You hear all this noise about affirmative action," Winston said. "Hell, racism been affirmative action for white folks long as I can remember. Now they want to take away what few chances we got under the guise of some bullshit about equal opportunity for all. Why don't they call it what it really is, Jim Crow coming home to roost. Some of them crackers been looking for a way to get at us for a long time. They just used that reverse discrimination bullshit, as an excuse to make enough of them believe we getting away with something. Give them a chance to say what's really in they's heart. We got no more use for your black asses is what they really saying. So get to gettin' on back wherever it is we dragged you from."

"You get no argument from me," Smoky said. "I got through Korea without a scratch, suffered a broken leg down in Selma during The March. That says it all about America and me. What say you C.J.?"

I knew exactly what they meant. Rumor had it that Reagan gave black people another twenty-five years before their right to vote would be rescinded when he was in office. It wouldn't surprise me if the current Supreme Court didn't help fulfill that prophecy.

"There certainly is a white supremacist movement resurfacing but I'm not going anywhere. I'll fight the wheels of constructive progress from being halted with everything I've got," I said.

"Halted!" Winston said. "Son the train's been thrown in reverse."

"Not long ago a man in Texas was dragged to death behind a pickup because of the color of his skin," Smoky said.

"Then it's time we tear up the tracks behind that train so we can't go back," I said.

"Sounds good," Smoky said, "how?"

"Quoting The Last Poets," Winston said, "The revolution will not be televised."

The PGE antique streetcar coming to a stop made sounds identical to the pulse-pounding music of when Norman Bates psychotic personality was on the prowl in the movie "Psycho." A man as thin as the smoldering cigarette dangling from his lips rode by on his bicycle. Across the street, a homeless man ran his fingers through his disheveled hair using a window of the Downtown Hilton as his mirror.

"Life's too short to be on lock down anyway," Winston said, "pain in the ass job with pain in the ass people."

"Think you can stop bitching long enough to move?" Smoky asked.

"There you go." Winston moved his queen's knight to queen's file five threatening Smoky's queen and leaving Winston's king vulnerable.

"Do something with that," Winston said.

"When what we trust dissolves we turn to faith," Smoky said as he made the first of his three moves to checkmate. "When what we believe is crushed we are no more."

"Here we go. Mahatma Jenkins," Winston said. "Shouldn't you be fasting? Let me help you out. Slide what's left of that cheesecake over here so I can eliminate temptation of the taste buds."

"I'm sure you'd like that," Smoky said.

"It's a sacrifice I'm willing to make," Winston said.

"Just trying to lay a little wisdom on you my brother," Smoky said.

"Well peep this *smart-ass*." Winston captured Smoky's queen's bishop's pawn with his king's rook, "Now what you going do with that?" Winston asked.

"Smart, hell, I'm intelligent," Smoky said. "You're confusing my I.Q. with your attitude."

"Attitude is just another word for confidence as in I'm about to wallop you *Mr. Jenkins*."

"What is victory without understanding defeat?" Smoky asked.

"Sweet," Winston said.

"Well it won't be yours today my friend," Smoky said. "Checkmate."

Winston was stunned. "Shit! C. J. move over here and get you some of this," Winston said.

"Mind if I ask a few questions?" I asked.

"Put your rusty behind in that chair and maybe you'll get some answers," Winston said.

Smoky and I switched places.

"What's it going to cost me?"

"Fifty dollars," Winston said.

"Let's make it five hundred. I feel lucky today," I said.

"*Five hundred*, I can't cover that," Winston said.

"I've got your back partner," Smoky said.

"Five hundred it is for the lucky man," Winston said.

I showed them the color of my money. Although Winston had white, he allowed me to move first.

Like Winston told Smoky, he didn't have anything I hadn't seen before. Smoky didn't need money. Winston would never accept what he regarded as charity despite the fact I considered it payment on services rendered. I made it a habit to lose. The trick was making Winston believed he had won.

"Have either of you seen anyone new in downtown lately?" I asked.

"All the time," Winston said.

"Like that homeless man across the street a minute ago," Smoky said.

"Yeah," I said.

"Never seen him before," Smoky said. "Matter of fact I don't think he's a street person."

I glanced around. The transient was nowhere in sight.

"Bet he's an undercover cop trying to bust some of them drug dealing punks been hanging around here lately," Winston said.

"Could be," I said. He wasn't a cop. He was in all likelihood one of a few people tailing me I chose to ignore.

"What you packing C. J.?" Winston asked.

"A licensed gun," I said.

"No doubt of that, just wondering why."

"It's dangerous out here. I know it's time to break out the hardware when people like the Windells aren't safe in their own home."

"If you say so," Smoky said not masking his skepticism to my answer.

"The man I'm looking for has blue eyes and a military cut, lean built, kind of mean looking."

"Yeah we saw him," Winston said.

"Four times in all," Smoky said. "He was wearing combat boots and fatigues the first time we saw him. We thought he was a skinhead."

"Dude looked like he was straight out of boot camp," Winston said. "I wanted that wool field jacket. It was dope."

"The only thing dope around here is you," Smoky said.

"I got your dope and your sister's too," Winston said.

"And then you woke up."

"Gentleman can I get a word in," I said.

"What are you working on C. J.?" Smoky asked.

"Insurance investigation for the Windell homicide," I said.

"Me and Smoky got a bet. I say his wife did him. Smoky thinks it was one of the board members looking to get his job. What's your take on it?"

"You two have too much time on your hands."

"Nobody has too much time," Smoky said.

"This dude got anything to do with who shot Windell?" Winston asked.

"Maybe," I said.

"Well anyway," Winston said. "First time we saw him was about a week before Windell got it."

"We saw him come and go out of the Heathman a couple of times," Smoky said.

"Was he staying there?" I asked.

"Doubt it," Smoky said.

"He never came out with a change of clothes or nothing," Winston said.

"We think he was visiting somebody," Smoky said.

"Did you see him with anybody?" I asked.

"Nope," Winston said, "he was always alone."

"You two should have been private investigators," I said. "You're good at this."

"And put you out of business," Winston said with a wry smile.

"We wouldn't think of it," Smoky added smiling as well.

"Then I wouldn't get the chance to spank you like *this*," Winston said. "*Check* and *mate*."

Winston was as ungracious a winner as he was a loser. I did my best to appear stunned. I doubt anyone was genuinely fooled. It was the game outside the match we played. All of us seemed pleased with that arrangement. I thanked them for their help, paid Winston and left. Winston invited me back for a rematch anytime I felt lucky. I promised Winston I'd take him up on that invitation vowing the next time the outcome would be different.

CHAPTER SIXTEEN

Two desk clerks at the Heathman remembered seeing a man fitting Buzz Cut's description. "I called to the man you're asking about," the young woman said, "but he ignored me making a beeline for the elevator." The young woman recalled seeing Buzz Cut on two separate occasions, once on the day before the Windell slaying and again the next evening. Neither of them knew whom Buzz Cut went upstairs to see.

I checked other hotels and motels in the area for additional leads no luck with any of them.

Renita was there when I entered the office. "Scone?" I asked.

"Yes," Renita said. That was our code as to whether our office had been checked for bugs. It was something we came up with that morning when Destini was out of earshot.

Renita gave me an overview of her interview with Patrick Kemery. She described him as a helpful, gracious individual who answered every question she put to him to her satisfaction. Renita said Kemery was at a fundraiser on the night Windell was murdered. She rattled off the names of a dozen people who could vouch for his whereabouts. Kemery did mention one thing of interest Renita said. Come next board election Andrea Bettencourt would have been voted out of the Board of Directors.

I mentioned to Renita that Kemery's alibi was immaterial. I was confident professionals were hired to do the job. Renita agreed. From what she had learned from Kemery, he had no motive. We both agreed that left Andrea Bettencourt as our prime suspect. Mrs. Bettencourt had motive and financial means. Now all that remained was to prove opportunity.

There was an e-mail message to Renita from Benton Lawson. He needed to meet Renita to discuss something he claimed was critically important. Renita called his work number. There was no answer. She tried his home number and got the same result. We decided to take a trip out to the Beaverton Research Complex to see if we could catch up with Lawson. "Why don't you go ahead," I told Renita. "I've got a stop to make. I'll meet you there."

"Will do," Renita said.

"Are you packing?" I asked. Renita opened her cranberry blazer to show me a new leather shoulder holster with the black handle of her thirty-eight peeking out.

***

It was a gamble. I was taking a chance on making matters worse. From the dozen tulips, box of See's chocolates and card in my hands, the desk sergeant correctly guessed when he said Destini and I had an argument. Before he could pursue my personal shortcomings any further, I asked the sergeant about the old man who talked to him the last time I was there.

"Funny thing about that guy," the desk sergeant said. "There was a case like the one he mentioned on the docket that day, The Elledge shooting. The old man had the details right and everything but he was never a witness. The real eyewitness to the shooting was a thirty-nine-year old transportation engineer. He's the one who gave the testimony that old guy claimed. I'm guessing the old guy listened to testimony from the real eyewitness and repeated it back to me; strange huh?"

"Have you seen him since?" I asked.

"Nah, I figured the old man was lonely and needed somebody to talk to so he made up that cock-and-bull story." Destini walked up to me before I could respond.

"C. J.," she said in a matter of fact tone. Destini was none too happy to see me. I handed her my peace offerings. Her expression never changed but her eyes showed an appreciation that belied her.

"Thank you," Destini said. I asked her if there were some place, we could talk in private. Destini led me to an empty interrogation room after I waited for her to drop off her gifts at her desk.

"I realize my behavior the past couple of weeks has been unusual," I said. "Allow me to explain."

I filled Destini in on everything that happened including the incident involving Renita at the office. I twisted the details as necessary leaving out any information about my sources and making no mention of my phantom employers.

Destini was angry that I didn't come to her sooner. Most of her questions centered on what I knew about Buzz Cut. Her line of query suggested she was looking to connect Buzz Cut to Genevieve Windell. I didn't try to dissuade her. For all I new Destini could be right.

When Destini asked why they would go after Renita and not me, I responded: "They may have thought Renita would be easier to frighten. Maybe they thought they could scare me off through her."

"Obviously they don't know your partner," Destini said.

"Obviously."

"You realize from what you've told me, I could detain you for willfully withholding evidence?"

"I only substantiated Buzz Cut today. He's purely circumstantial at this point."

"Not to mention what's happened to Renita. That incident places her square in the jurisdiction of my case."

"I realize that and I'm asking you to let me handle it."

"And if I don't?"

"You've known me long enough to know my answer."

"I could bring you in. Hold you long enough that I might be able to wring it out of your partner."

"Do you really think Renita would talk?"

Destini gave serious consideration to the matter. "I don't believe she would," Destini said.

I knew I was playing it close but I had to find a way to get out of there. The armistice I'd hoped for hadn't materialized. We were both headstrong professionals bent on doing our jobs. Love was not the issue.

We came to an understanding that once Destini was confident Renita was out of danger Renita was to get out of my house. I agreed. We sealed the deal with a kiss.

"And one other thing," Destini said while we stood with our arms around each other. "If that chick ever pulls a gun on me again she's going to be looking out from the business side of a set of bars. And that's on a good day."

Not to mention what you'd do to me if you found out everything I was keeping from you, I thought. Destini and I kissed again before I left to meet Renita.

***

I parked next to Renita in the visitor's section of the Beaverton Research Complex. Lawson was coming out of his office building as we approached. Benton was a pale, lanky, slightly slumped-shouldered man with a scraggly goatee who probably wore thick eyeglasses when he wasn't wearing contacts. Slung over Lawson's shoulder was a black shoulder case that caused him to lean away from it so he wouldn't topple over. Lawson told us it contained his laptop, portable printer, and peripherals as well as assorted work-related items he always kept with him.

So this was the person giving Judith Hardy so much trouble, I thought. Benton appeared on edge. I couldn't tell if he was always that way or if this was something new. Renita's expression suggested the latter.

Renita introduced me. My presence didn't seem to throw him. Whatever made Lawson fidgety wasn't me. Maybe he knew more about our phantom employer than we did. Maybe he was the contact for our phantom employer. I suggested taking a ride in my car that way we could talk. Lawson leapt at the opportunity.

We drove through some of the scenic wine country of Yamhill County. It looked like a surreal tapestry of sedentary life this time of year.

"Can we get some music in here?" Lawson asked. He kept looking around as if expecting the world to collapse on him. I turned on the radio. KMHD came to life.

"Jazz, good," Lawson said, "my favorite music, its art, man, pure and simple. Have you ever listened to Wynton Marsalis's *Blood On The Fields*?" Lawson asked both of us.

"If we say yes will you tell us what we're doing here?" I asked.

"The same men who killed Clinton Windell are after me," Lawson blurted out.

"What makes you think so?" I asked.

"I work a lot of late nights. Everything seemed normal. On the way to my car, I passed a blue Jaguar sitting in the parking lot. It was easy to notice. There aren't many cars in the parking lot at that time of night. At first I didn't think much about the Jag until it followed me home."

"There are a number of Jaguars in Beaverton," I said. "That person could have simply been an employee or visiting someone."

"Not just anyone can park in the VIP parking section and I know every car that can. You've seen how tight security is at The Cage. It's like being under house arrest. I have to account for practically every move I make inside that complex. Outside the complex I'm being followed half the time by the FBI who don't think I know they're there."

Then it wouldn't surprise Lawson to know a two-tone brown Ford Explorer was tailing us, I thought.

"I got laid last week." Benton went on to say. "And I'll bet they've got that on video somewhere. The FBI I've gotten used to, this Jaguar business—it's not the same. There's something eerie about this whole situation."

"Is there more?" I asked.

"I told myself Benton you're being paranoid. Settle down. It's only a coincidence. I didn't turn on the lights right away when I got inside. I sneaked a peek out of the living room window to see if the Jag was still there. There it was parked down the street a little ways."

"Did you get a look at the license plate?" Renita asked.

"HADES," Lawson said. "Who comes up with this nonsense?"

Renita and I kept quiet about the Jaguar. The coincidence was startling. I resisted the temptation to look at Renita. Instead, I stared at Benton Lawson in my rearview mirror. He wasn't making this up.

One thing about Lawson made me suspicious. From what Renita had told me Lawson knew about the DVD. What was his involvement? Either Lawson was trying to be coy or he knew very little about our phantom employers. Now was the time to squeeze it out of him.

"For that you called us?" I asked.

"HADES?" Renita asked.

"Yes," Lawson replied in answer to both of our questions.

"What do you know about a DVD we received?" I asked.

"All I know is Andrew Tollman came to me with a hush-hush project he needed done in a hurry. I took some encrypted data he had on a flash drive, decoded it, then transferred the decoded data onto a DVD and gave Tollman back the flash drive and the newly burned DVD."

"Do you know where Tollman got his information?" I asked.

"No and don't bother trying to find him. Tollman disappeared shortly after they fired him."

"You didn't make a copy for yourself?" I asked.

"I didn't have a chance. Tollman stayed with me the entire time. What was on that DVD anyway?"

"That's not your concern," I said. "What's your involvement with Clinton Windell?"

"Absolutely nothing, all I know about Clinton Windell is what I've heard or read in the newspaper."

"Why would anyone be after you?" Renita asked.

Benton Lawson paused as if he had stopped breathing for a moment. I would have sworn he was about to cry.

"Both of you must swear to me that what I'm about to say will not go any further than this car."

Renita and I agreed.

"Have either of you ever heard of a program called the Universal Translator?"

Renita and I both answered no.

"It's top-secret. What this program allows anyone to do is have computer programs talk to each another. Even programs that are specialized or customized by individuals. No matter what platform this software can enable the user to get inside any program and communicate with it as if they speak the same language. Imagine if you will having the ability to go to any country in the world, and, with the use of a device be able to understand the language of another culture. Read, write, speak and comprehend Spanish, French, Swahili, Gaelic, Japanese, and Russian. All because of software, you could load onto any PC or laptop. Not only comprehend another language but also have them completely understand you. That's what the Universal Translator is to computers. Any computer system in the world, any program, any routine, you can communicate with as we are doing right now."

"The applications would be endless," Renita said.

"Infinite," Lawson said.

"In today's world nothing would be secure," Renita said.

"*Precisely*," Lawson said. "We're under contract by the Pentagon for exclusive rights to U.T. Imagine what a program like this would be worth on the black market."

"What do you know about the black market?" I asked.

"Only that it exists and that's all I want to know."

"Do you have it with you?" I asked.

"No. I'm taking a big risk telling you two. If I'm found out getting fired will be the least of my problems."

"If you've got something to say Lawson say it," I said.

Lawson sighed. "Here goes. I've been snooping around some of Diva's highly classified files—"

"How are you able to do that?" Renita asked.

"Are you kidding? It's a no brainer. Half of the software I wrote myself."

Renita appeared impressed. I despise that expression "It's a no brainer." There's no such thing.

"Why didn't you use U.T. to get what you needed?" I asked.

"Why don't I paint a big red bull's-eye on my chest," Lawson sarcastically said. "I couldn't take the chance some two bit network manager didn't get lucky and spot it piggy backing in on another program. Network security at DIVA is tighter than the NSA's. Believe me I know."

I let Lawson's inference of breaking into the NSA's computer system slide. I was only interested in information Lawson had that could help us solve the case.

"Besides, I didn't need U.T.," Lawson said.

"I see," I said itching for Lawson to pick up the pace on his melodrama.

"As I was saying," Lawson went on to say, "I've been snooping around some of DIVA's highly classified files and from what I could piece together Antonio Farhletti has plans for U.T. the Pentagon doesn't know about."

A project this valuable was being overseen. If the Pentagon had missed some treachery, you can bet the NSA or Homeland Security hadn't. "Are you sure you're on the up and up?" I asked.

"What do you mean?" Lawson asked.

"We know about you and Roxanna Farhletti," Renita said.

"I've made no secret about how I feel about Roxanna."

"So how do we know this isn't some convoluted scheme of yours to get back at Antonio Farhletti?" I asked.

"One thing has nothing to do with the other. Besides, everyone knows Roxanna has filed for divorce. Based on your work from what I hear Cavanaugh."

"That's all well and good," I said. "But what does any of this have to do with Clinton Windell?"

"I'm getting to that. Windell's name appeared on a couple of files."

"In reference to what specifically?" I asked.

"Buying gems."

"And you find that odd?" I asked.

"Don't you?"

"I hate to break this to you, Lawson," I said, "but that's part of what the man did for a living."

"Don't you find it strange his name was mentioned at all?" Lawson said.

I did but I wouldn't share that with Lawson. "I'm missing your point," I said.

"One of those memos made mention of a particular overseas business transaction, a recent Amsterdam purchase to be exact," Lawson said.

"Go on," I said.

"It detailed Windell's trip, lodging, times and dates of his appointments. It looked to me as though someone were tracking Windell's entire overseas itinerary."

"If you say so," I said.

"What else could it be?"

"Were Farhletti and Windell friends?" Renita asked.

"To my knowledge they knew each other but I wouldn't call them friends."

"You're suggesting Farhletti may have been tied into Clinton Windell's death?" Renita asked.

"Possibly," Lawson said.

"Why?" I asked.

"I don't know. Maybe Farhletti and Windell had some sort of deal that went sour. Farhletti wanted to get back at him and this was his way. He's capable of that type of thing you know. I suspect he's literally knocked off some of his stiffer competition along the way to get to where he is now."

"If I were you Lawson," I said. "I wouldn't repeat those sorts of accusations to anyone without hard and fast evidence and lots of it."

"What I'm getting at is Farhletti is capable of a lot of things. Being involved in something like murder wouldn't surprise me."

"Antonio Farhletti is a successful wealthy man," I said. "From what you've told us about this Universal Translator he's about to become even richer. What possible motive could he have to murder Clinton Windell?"

"That's a question you should ask Farhletti."

"Any mention of an Andrea Bettencourt while you were snooping around?" I asked.

"No."

"Are you certain?" I asked.

"Positive."

"What about Harvey Bettencourt?" Renita asked.

"No," Lawson said.

"What is it you think we can do for you Lawson?" I asked.

"Protect me."

"From who?" I said.

"Windell's killers."

"Why us?" I said.

"I've asked around," Lawson said. "You come highly recommended."

"We're not bodyguards," I said. "You should take your story to the police."

"And tell them what? The same men who killed Clinton Windell are following me; and when they ask why that is I'll simply tell them I happened to be illegally sniffing around highly classified files that detailed the movements of Clinton Windell before he was murdered. Oh and by the way, I also stumbled upon bits and pieces of information that may implicate the president of Diva Computer Software in a possible scheme to make illegal gains from a top-secret program we developed for the Pentagon.

"I don't know what world you're living in Cavanaugh but something as crucial as the Universal Translator would be—to any nation—given top priority over anyone."

I did believe Benton Lawson. Being an ex-DEA agent and ex-service man did not make me naive. Our country was capable of doing many things to protect its way of life some of which I did not agree with; but those were battles to be fought when they presented themselves. This was not the matter at hand.

"I suggest you take a little vacation Lawson," I said. "Go to Europe or South America. Get away for a while."

"You think I'm paranoid. Just making all this shit up," Lawson said to me. "What about you Renita? Do you think this is all nonsense?"

"I think you're overreacting a little," Renita said.

"I was followed by a blue Jaguar *damn it*; and someone is trying to kill me! The same people who killed Clinton Windell!"

"Then we suggest you go to the police and tell them what you've told us," I said.

"Take me back," Lawson said in a deflated voice. "Take me back to The Cage."

On the way back to the research complex, I occasioned a glance in Renita's direction. I could tell she was mulling over these developments. Benton Lawson sat slouched down in the back seat looking like a trapped man seeking a way out.

Lawson made a last ditch effort to convince us of his plight before he left. While I wanted to help Benton, I had my hands full watching Renita's back and protecting myself. Lawson was going to have to find his own safety net.

I told Benton we would investigate what we could and that we would be in touch. I told him if he had any information essential to the Windell case to call us.

"I would simply disappear if I were you," was the advice I gave Lawson in parting. "Drop everything, don't pack, get as much cash as you can get your hands on and simply drop out of sight. Because if half of what you said is true then you're in way over your head with people who play for keeps."

"What about Roxanna?" Benton asked.

"What about her?" I said.

"Who's going to be there to catch her when Farhletti falls?"

"Good luck Mr. Lawson," I said with curt exasperation. Lawson turned and stormed away. Renita was right. He was one lovesick puppy. I waited for Lawson to be out of earshot before I spoke to Renita.

"I want you to follow-up on what Lawson told us."

"Do you believe him?"

"Yes. Check with the security guards on duty to see if any of them saw a sapphire, black, or blue Jaguar over the last few days with the license plate HADES. Also, see if you can get a look at last night's surveillance video. That car and one of our shadows may be on it."

"What are you going to be doing?"

"I'm taking a trip to the Windell Estate. There are a few questions I have to ask Mrs. Windell and her daughter."

"That reminds me," Renita said. "I sent Sutherland's prints to your man at the DEA. He was able to go back as you requested."

I was playing a hunch. Sutherland didn't strike me as a gentleman's gentleman. According to current fingerprint records Sutherland was who he said he was. I asked Renita to ask one of my DEA contacts to run Sutherland's prints against computer files dated before 1999. That would have been before the dance club fire.

"Got the info this morning," Renita said.

"It's about time. What took so long?"

"Your contact was on vacation."

"If you would have told me sooner I know half a dozen other people we could have used."

"Sorry," Renita said.

"Does he have a record?"

"Edward Sutherland is not who he says he is."

CHAPTER SEVENTEEN

The hordes of gardeners and cleaning people were gone. Armed security personnel were still in place. I was surprised when Sutherland did not answer the door. The new gentlemen's gentleman led me to the study where he notified me that Mrs. Windell would join me shortly. I quietly waited trying to still my mind in the pale light of the room.

"Mr. Cavanaugh," Genevieve Windell said after entering the study. This time her brunette hair fell loosely onto her shoulders. She wore only enough makeup to accent her positives and soften her look. The designer sky blue dress didn't hurt with a diamond necklace dipping into its jewel neckline.

Beside her was a child no more than six, clutching a doll. The child was the spitting image of her mother. They both stood erect. Genevieve Windell was a great deal more composed than on my first visit. "This is my daughter Pamela," Mrs. Windell said. "Say hello to Mr. Cavanaugh," Genevieve added with a graceful wave of her arm reminding me of a stage performer gratefully accepting enthusiastic applause from a doting audience.

Mrs. Windell led Pamela toward me by her shoulders. They stopped directly in front of me. Pamela extended her tiny right hand. Her arm was stiff as a plank. Her face was sad. Her eyes were a mystery. I shook her hand. It felt as though it had no bones.

"Pleased to meet you Mr. Cavanaugh," Pamela said sounding rehearsed.

"Likewise Pamela," I replied.

"You said on the phone you wanted to speak to my daughter," Genevieve said. The tone of Genevieve Windell's voice was sharp almost threatening. Mrs. Windell took her daughter's left hand in her right.

Holding it firmly but gently I imagined. One false move on my part and Genevieve Windell was ready to take off my head.

I squatted so Pamela and I could see eye-to-eye. "Thank you for seeing me Pamela," I said.

"You're welcome," Pamela said with a jittery smile.

This was tougher than I had imagined. Pamela was no Bebe Assassino. I didn't have contempt working for me. How was I going to question this child about the night of her father's homicide without triggering the memory?

"That's a very pretty doll you have Pamela," I said.

"Thank you," Pamela said.

"Does she have a name?"

"Yes."

"Would you share it with me?"

"Her name is Claire."

"Did you give Claire her name?"

Pamela nodded in that vigorous way children will sometimes do.

"Did you know Claire means bright or shining?" A lingering fact I picked up while researching perspective baby names for nieces and nephews. Pamela shook her head in wide-eyed wonder. "Well it does. That says an awful lot about a person who could select such a wise and precious name. It says to me that person is warm and caring and pretty and very, very smart."

Pamela looked up at her mom. Genevieve Windell smiled down at her daughter. Pamela grinned at her mom minus the nervous edge. Maybe it was because the butterflies had fluttered from her stomach into mine.

"Was Claire a gift Pamela?" I asked.

Pamela nodded. "My daddy gave her to me. He always brought me a doll when he went someplace far away."

"Do you remember when your daddy gave you Claire?"

"I was asleep when Claire came," Pamela said. "When I woke up she was sitting on my dresser."

"Pamela what's the last thing you remember about that night?"

"Having milk and cookies with Uncle Eddie and watching The Wizard of Oz." Pamela looked up at her mother. "I'm sorry mom. I know you told me not to have any snacks before bedtime but Uncle Eddie said it would be okay just this once. He said it would be our little secret. I didn't know daddy would get hurt."

"It's all right baby. It's not your fault." Genevieve Windell looked at me. "Uncle Eddie is what Pamela called our butler."

"I didn't know I'd never see daddy again," Pamela said. "I wouldn't have snacked if I knew daddy would get hurt. I wouldn't have fallen asleep."

"It's okay honey." Mrs. Windell knelt to comfort her daughter. I stood and took a step back. Pamela's face was trembling. Genevieve Windell held her daughter close while Pamela did the same for Claire. Pamela had told me what I needed to know. Genevieve Windell led her daughter away notifying me that she would return shortly.

***

When Mrs. Windell returned, I noticed for the first time her clear blue eyes. Strangely, behind them she looked at peace. Genevieve walked to within one pace of me folded her hands congenially before her and waited.

"Your daughter is precious," I said.

"She misses her father."

"Were you and your husband having marital problems Mrs. Windell?"

"No."

"Then why did your husband file for divorce; a divorce that could have left you without any visible means of support?"

"We'd worked all of that out. That was part of the reason we went to Bern. To remove ourselves from the pressures of our everyday lives and spend some quality time together. It had not been that way with us for some time. Clinton was a romantic, sensitive man in the early years. We had forgotten how to love each other. Our trip granted us an opportunity to reacquaint ourselves with ourselves. We were actually planning to renew our vows before he was killed." After a heavy sigh Genevieve continued.

"Yes I knew Clinton was considering a divorce. I am also well aware of the pre-nuptial agreement I willingly signed that would have left me empty-handed. You are mistaken about my financial condition. Just as you are wrong in suggesting, I may have had a hand in murdering my husband. By the time, we had decided to move to Oregon I had already retired from the ballet. Teaching did not interest me so I chose another direction. A number of years back I earned a degree in Investment

Finance. If you will do a little background research on our financial portfolios, you will discover that I handled all of our investments. My husband paid me a handsome salary as our personal investment counselor. With that money, I established my own portfolio that has grown quite plump over the years. I am far from a pauper Mr. Cavanaugh with or without my husband's money. So you see justice is my only interest concerning my husband's death."

"On what grounds was your husband requesting a divorce?"

"Adultery, I was having an affair."

"With who?"

"Does that matter now? It's over. I put an end to it after Clinton and I reaffirmed our commitment to one another."

"It could be important. If your ex-lover was the jealous type, who might do anything to keep you. Or he may have wanted to avenge his being dumped."

"I can assure you he is not the jealous type, and that he moved on without resentment. I believe he was as relieved about ending our affair as I was. If not more so."

"If you insist; what brought you to San Francisco in the first place?"

"My attorney has informed me that I am in no way obligated to answer any of your questions."

"I believe I stated something to that effect during our first meeting Mrs. Windell."

"Just so you are aware I am volunteering this information."

"Duly noted," I said. Mrs. Windell confirmed my affirmation with an easy nod of her head. I continued. "When did you arrive in this country?"

"2002."

"That was well before your mother received her appointment as director of the San Francisco ballet."

"Yes," Genevieve said clearly taken aback that I knew that.

"You were friendless in America."

"Not entirely I had made a few acquaintances prior to coming to the states."

"Did you stay with anyone?"

"For a couple of months I stayed with an artist friend Joyce Caldwell. Eventually I was able to earn enough money to move into a modest studio apartment."

"How did you do that? Earn enough money I mean?"

"Doing odd jobs, I also landed a teaching job at a ballet school in the Tenderloin District. It wasn't necessary for long. Six weeks later I became a *bébé cygne* of the San Francisco ballet." Genevieve Windell glowed when she spoke that French phrase. Her appointment to the ballet was no doubt one of her proudest moments.

"Teaching and odd jobs were how you initially supported yourself?" I asked.

"Primarily, yes—where is this leading to Mr. Cavanaugh?"

"I'm getting to that. Were your parents able to offer any financial assistance?"

"They did what they could. No need to tell you they were very upset with me for leaving home and coming to America to perform."

"I can imagine their displeasure but I can't imagine a storefront teaching job paying anyone enough to live on."

"Like I said I had help when I needed it."

"Why?"

"I don't follow you."

"According to your insurance records you were educated in some of the finest schools in Switzerland. You were performing in a country, on a continent, that has a history of immense appreciation for the arts. Even I know the arts here do not receive the level of recognition they do in Europe. Why come here at all to dance? Why not stay where you would be infinitely more supported and respected?"

"I wanted to make my own mark. My parents were highly regarded throughout Europe for their dance artistry. Everywhere I went, I was known as Katherine and Johannes Wissmann's darling little ballerina. I needed new frontier to prove myself. America was that place."

I paused to take in Mrs. Windell. She patiently watched me as if awaiting her cue to go on stage. "What else can I do for you Mr. Cavanaugh?" Genevieve asked.

"Help me find your husband's killers."

"I'll do all I can."

"How long have you known Edward Sutherland?"

"For as long as he has been our butler about twelve years," Genevieve said.

"You never met him while you lived in the Bay area?"

"No."

"How about while you lived in Bern, did you meet him then?"

"What are you talking about?"

"I know about Mark Strait."

"Who?" Mrs. Windell wasn't convincing. The second fingerprint check I had ordered on Edward Sutherland had turned up the fact his real name was Mark Strait. I recognized it immediately from Windell's dossier. The background check my DEA connection ran on Strait revealed some interesting and saucy details including: he served six months in a Lebanon, Tennessee prison for drunk and disorderly conduct; he was associated with a strip club in San Francisco's red light district, and, he had been under investigation for being a suspected smuggler while in the Navy.

"Mark Strait a.k.a. Edward Sutherland," I said, "the same Mark Strait who served with your husband aboard the George Clymer back in his navy days."

"I haven't the foggiest idea of what you're referring to."

"Your butler—"

"First of all my husband hired Edward Sutherland. I had nothing to do with his selection. Secondly, Edward Sutherland resigned."

"Where is he now?"

"I don't know."

"There was a fire in the red light district of San Francisco involving a Mark Strait. A strip club called the Tulip Room burned down. Mark Strait was part owner. He was the only person reported to have escaped alive."

"Meaning?"

"Let's suppose Mark Strait wasn't the only person who escaped that fire. Let's suppose there was at least one other person, someone Strait himself believed dead. Strait has a chance meeting with this person. She has a new life—a life that would suffer if a seedy little fact got out about what she'd done at one time to earn money."

"Please get to the point Mr. Cavanaugh."

"I believe one other person escaped those flames alive, an exotic dancer who once worked for Mark Strait; a woman whose life had taken an incredible uphill swing and could not afford her scandalous past to surface. You wouldn't happen to know who that exotic dancer might be."

"Why would I?"

"Somehow you were connected with Mark Strait. Perhaps you two met when he was ashore in Europe. Maybe you two became lovers then pen pals. Maybe he was in love with you. Maybe he said he could get you on with a prestigious ballet company. Maybe he said he knew people, had connections, pushing whatever buttons he thought would lure you to San Francisco to be with him and you seized it.

Here was an opportunity to get away from the suffocating shadow of your parents' good fortune and engrave your mark in the community of dance. Except things weren't how he painted them out to be. His connections were non-existent. The only thing he had going was the Tulip Room and for a minute that was all you had going as well."

"You're being crude and absurd."

"It's not unusual for a young woman to turn to exotic dancing to make ends meet, particularly aspiring dancers."

"You're insane!"

"Am I?"

"Absolutely!"

"Being a sailor Mark Strait had an opportunity to travel the world. I'll bet that if I check his naval records I'll find that he made more than one port-of-call to France or Italy. Perhaps he made a few junkets to Bern while he was in the area."

"Your point being?"

"I believe you've known Mark Strait a good deal longer than you're letting on."

"And just what are you basing all of this nonsense on?"

"Mostly conjecture but with a little digging I'll bet I could unearth some very supportive facts."

"You are insane."

"Did you tell your parents you were moving to America? Or did you simply take flight expecting to inform them of your whereabouts once you found fame?"

"So what if I did? When one is dedicated to one's art there is no compromise. I was young and justifiably believed that—if necessary—I could always return to Bern. What I wanted most was to dance with a major American company. Joyce believed that opportunity was in San Francisco. She turned out to be correct."

The tranquility in Genevieve Windell's eyes had clouded with caution. Her voice did not waiver. Her neck tensed. She squeezed her hands but did not budge. Genevieve remained poised.

"How dare you come into my home fomenting wild accusations? If you had done your job properly, you would have discovered I danced for five years with the San Francisco Ballet prior to my mother becoming director. It was shortly thereafter that I retired so as not to compromise my mother's position. By then I was engaged to Clinton. My priorities had changed. That pretty much summarizes my Bay area experience."

"That's not quite everything," I said.

"What do you mean?"

"I had a reliable source do a general background check on you and she uncovered an interesting fact," I said not allowing the amusement of referring to Renita as some clandestine source to show in my eyes. "According to my source you arrived on these shores in 2000, not 2002 as you previously stated."

"So what if I did," Genevieve said without missing a beat. "It was an honest mistake."

"How do you account for the two-year gap?" I asked.

"I've already explained."

"Odd jobs and storefront teaching," I said.

"Exactly," Genevieve said.

"Your artist's friend's name was what again?"

"Joyce Caldwell."

"That name turned up as one of the people killed in the Tulip Room fire."

"If Joyce was an exotic dancer I knew nothing about it."

"Do you think the police would buy that?"

"I've had enough of your innuendoes. I want you to leave my home at once."

"If I were in your shoes Mrs. Windell I'd want every ally I could muster."

"Get out of my house!"

"In parting I must tell you it won't be difficult for the police to exhume the same information I have."

"Get out!"

"One more thing before I go. Would you be kind enough to supply me with Bellingham's car lease records for the past year specifically the Jaguars?"

"Andrea Bettencourt handles the paperwork for vehicle leasing company wide. Now get out of my house! And don't come back without a court order!"

"Thanks for your cooperation Mrs. Windell. I'll be seeing you soon."

I walked past Genevieve Windell showing myself to the front door. I glanced up from the circular entrance. Pamela Windell was staring down at me. Pamela managed a weak smile. I waved. Pamela waved back. I left vowing to find her father's murderers. I hoped for her sake that her mother wasn't involved.

CHAPTER EIGHTEEN

On the way back to my office, I saw Shawn Calloway coming right toward me a short block and a half away conversing with two of his colleagues at *The Willamette Times*. I ducked into Rich's Cigar store before Shawn noticed me. I'd been following Calloway's articles in *The Willamette Times*. Nothing substantial just basic P.R. updates on how the case was progressing. There were no mentions of suspects and only speculative motives, the usual tap dance when the facts were not in evidence. Calloway was tenacious. He also had an itch for news. All I knew was he wasn't going to ferret any information out of me.

One thing I hadn't been able to establish was the motive for Clinton Windell's murder. Destini was still of the belief Genevieve Windell did it for the money. Her partner, David, held fast to the theory it was no more than a robbery. I saw two—conceivably three—other reasons why Clinton Windell was murdered.

My primary suspect remained Andrea Bettencourt. Her motive, the obvious, revenge for her husband's death along with the possibility of her losing her job. Mark Strait was definitely involved. Could be revenge was on his mind as well. From what I'd learned about Clinton Windell's character, I wouldn't be at all surprised if he didn't have something to do with Strait's stint in prison. Genevieve Windell may have needed to protect herself from potential financial ruin. Although if her story checked out about her personal finances that would still leave her exotic past to sift through for clues.

Things were percolating. Mark Strait's fingerprints brought what was cloudy speculation into the light. Mrs. Windell's association with Mark Strait was a certainty as far as I was concerned. Was he blackmailing her? Did he persuade her to aide in her husband's murder? Who had the gems? Was either of them connected with Andrea Bettencourt in a way that would produce an allegiance to murder? In addition who at the Beaverton Research Complex had their mitts in this and why?

As I leafed through a copy of Soldier of Fortune, Calloway and his colleagues stopped on the S.W. Park side of Rich's. Calloway and the man wearing glasses and a blond ponytail were having a disagreement. The man with the ponytail was the Editor-in-Chief of The Willamette Times.

From what I could make out from my lip-reading, Calloway had something he wanted to go to print. His boss's back was to me so I couldn't get his response. Calloway became agitated. Calloway said he could substantiate the Windell piece if given time. Gauging from Calloway's reaction his boss must have said his time was up or something to that effect. The third party excused herself saying she had to get back to the office. Calloway and his boss argued back and forth about Calloway's unsubstantiated piece. Calloway threw his hands into the air in exasperation and stormed off. His boss calmly followed.

I made my way back to the office without incident. There was a woman following me wearing a blue jeans outfit and Trailblazers' jacket. I ignored her as I did the man nonchalantly reading a magazine in a white Dodge Taurus staking out our office building.

Renita wasn't in the office. I didn't bother checking for bugs there would be nothing to hear. Renita had left an e-mail message saying she would meet me at home. The "darling" part as usual was uncalled for. The message also went on to say there were no signs of the Jaguar on the surveillance footage but two security guards were willing to swear they saw a dark blue Jaguar with the license plate HADES last night. Both guards confirmed it had a special Diva VIP parking permit. Neither of the security guards had seen the driver. Renita's message concluded by saying she took the liberty to update our report files on the Windell case.

No sooner had I finished reading Renita's e-mail than an Internet e-mail came through.

Dear Mr. Cavanaugh:

We are impressed with your progress. Since our last correspondence, there has been a change in plans. The time originally believed available for resolution of this situation has been reduced by three weeks. Due to this unforeseeable inconvenience, we have increased your fee to $500,000.00 that will be paid in full upon completion of this case. As before, if within that time you fail to complete this mission our relationship will be terminated and the $500,000.00 will remain ours.

We would also like to take this opportunity to offer our sincerest apologies at having frightened Ms. Harris. That was not our intention. You and your colleague are as much aware of us as we are of you. Our presence exists as a protective force for the two of you as much as it is an informative one for us. While we can sympathize with your feelings regarding this annoyance, it cannot be helped for what is at stake. Be warned Mr. Cavanaugh your foes are mighty and prepared to do anything to meet their goals.

Please e-mail a copy of your most recent report to boswell@burn.com as soon as possible. If we can be of service, leave any questions or messages at the above-mentioned address. We will assist in any way we can."

It went on to say, "We have made an incentive deposit into your agency's account as a show of good faith. It is yours for services rendered. Once again, do not trouble yourself attempting to trace the bank deposit. Not even Benton Lawson could discover its source. Our previous arrangement is still in effect. Should any of our stipulations be violated this relationship will be immediately terminated. Good hunting."

I printed out a copy of the e-mail to show Renita in the morning. Perhaps its contents would relax her in regards to our clients whoever they were. One thing had become clear. We had nothing to fear from our phantom employers for the moment. If they intended to eradicate us, they'd have no difficulty doing so.

I read Renita's updated report, made a few revisions, and added what I had learned before sending it down the I-way. I wondered if Renita could trace the e-mail address. I bet Benton Lawson could. No matter I verified the deposit, one-hundred-thousand dollars. This had turned out to be a decent day after all.

CHAPTER NINETEEN

Destini's car was parked in the driveway. That meant Renita was the first home and had parked in the garage. I parked on the street.

The twin terriers greeted me when I entered through the front door. Renita and Destini were talking in the kitchen while preparing dinner. I had to admit any man would be incredibly lucky to have either of these women in their life. For whatever reason, I had been twice blessed. It did my heart good to see neither of them packing.

When I walked within earshot of Renita and Destini's conversation, they stopped. Both of them stared at me as if I were an alien intruder. I said hello to which they coolly responded. "Can I help with anything?" I asked.

"We've got it under control," Renita said before Destini could reply. I asked if they minded if I took a quick shower before dinner. Destini said, "It's your house." I could see a mischievous glint in Renita's eyes along the lines of wanting to wash my back an offer she'd made repeatedly at the office. I gave them each a curious glance before retreating to the bathroom.

Earlier in the day I had warned Renita I wanted no more gunslinging in my home. Renita said, "If Destini don't start no mess, won't be no mess." I emphasized for her to chill. If she didn't she was out. "All right honey I'll do it for you," Renita said. Rather than argue I accepted that as the best of possible agreements I could get from Renita.

My mom is fond of saying that in life, sometimes you get what you want, and other times you get what you deserve. She means that of course in reference to one's own actions or inactions to any given situation. Whether Renita and Destini both living in my house was something I wanted or deserved only a shrink could answer. All I knew was I needed one and the other needed me. Put that into any category you want.

Habits are like self-induced hypnotic suggestions. You're unconscious of their existence until someone brings them to light. The presence of Renita was a bright and shiny beacon upon one of my private pleasures.

I was accustomed to parading around my house nude. When I stepped out of the shower, I dried myself off and deposited the damp towel in the dirty clothes' hamper. I'll admit I was distracted by thoughts of the Windell case, which was why I was halfway to my bedroom before I realized I was naked. It was the sound of Renita and Destini's conversation that awoke that realization in me.

They were in the living room. I had no qualms with Destini seeing me *au naturel*. There was no way I was going to parade by Renita without any clothes.

I'd forgotten my bathrobe in the bedroom. To get to my bedroom I needed to pass within plain sight of the living room. Maybe I meant to eavesdrop or maybe it was pure chance. As I was about to double back to grab a clean bath towel from the utility closet to cover myself, I overheard the ladies discussing what was a monumental turning point in our current living arrangement.

"I love C. J.," Destini said.

"So do I," Renita said.

"You know how he feels about me," Destini said.

"Of course, if he felt that way about me we wouldn't be having this discussion," Renita said.

"So why are you so damned determined to destroy what we have?"

"It won't be my doing."

"Pardon?" Destini said.

"If you and C. J. don't click it won't be my fault," Renita said.

"Whose fault will it be?"

"Take a guess."

"Mine?"

"You've got it sister."

"Now how do you figure that?" Destini said.

"Who else can tarnish a relationship but the two people themselves? Nobody can take what isn't theirs."

"I see. Did you learn that dime store philosophy from Sesame Street or a fortune cookie?"

"Dis' me all you want," Renita said. "The bottom line is if you drop C. J., I'll be there to catch him. And I won't let go."

I knew how tough Destini was but Renita was continuously surprising me. There was a moment of silence. Andrew and Booker had sniffed me out. I petted them and then ordered them away with a hand signal. The ladies hadn't noticed the terriers were gone.

"Were you really going to shoot me?" I overheard Destini ask.

"Were you going to shoot C. J.?" Renita said.

"Maybe," Destini said.

"If you would've shot C. J., I would have shot you."

"You love him that much?"

"Yes. I know he thinks it's nothing more than a schoolgirl crush but I'd go through hell for that man."

"How do you think I feel?" Destini said.

"Then why were you going to shoot him?"

"How would you react if you came to your man's house and found another woman had moved in?"

"Been there done that," Renita said referring to the cheating ways of her ex-fiancé.

There was a short pause. At that time, I was caught between staying to listen or tiptoeing back to the utility closet. I elected to stay.

"I'll admit," Destini said, "I do get a little jealous of C. J. sometimes."

"Tell me about it," Renita said.

There was another pause.

"I realize C. J.'s nose is wide open for you," Renita said. "But the fact is I don't know why you two aren't married."

"It's complicated," Destini said.

"I'll make you a deal," Renita said. "I'll back off C. J. for now. Because the truth is all I care about is his happiness."

"I can't believe you're telling me this," Destini said.

"Just being honest, deal?"

There was a long pause before Destini said, "Deal."

A temporary peace accord had been reached. A gentlewoman's agreement. I doubled back to the utility closet and grabbed a towel making it to the bedroom without being spotted.

I entered the living room wearing my pajamas and bathrobe behaving as if nothing had happened. Renita gave me a great big smile. Destini walked over put her arms around me and kissed me as if we hadn't seen each other for weeks. "Dinner is just about ready," Destini said, turned, and sashayed into the kitchen leaving me spellbound. There is nothing more powerful than a sensual woman. The look in Destini's eyes told me what she had in mind for dessert. Renita went into the dining area and checked the place settings. I was indeed a lucky man.

CHAPTER TWENTY

I gave Renita my impression of what we were dealing with after Renita read the e-mail I printed out for her.

"We are caught in a covert operation involving major league players," I said, "judging by the resources and manpower being used to keep us under twenty-four hour surveillance. Although I don't believe the FBI, NSA, CIA, Homeland Security or DEA are directly involved there may be ties to any one or more of those organizations. Whatever they're after has to be more than a satchel of stolen gems. There's something we're missing."

"What about the stuff Benton Lawson told us?" Renita said.

"I believe him. The problem is aside from the presence of the Jaguar the rest is unsubstantiated. I will say this someone at Diva is involved in this mess. It's worth investigating, leave Lawson to me."

"I wish we could get our hands on those killers," Renita said.

"Amen to that but I wouldn't be so anxious if I were you. The kinds of people we're after make murder a business. They are lethal and ruthless. Which brings me to today's agenda. We need to get Bellingham's car lease records from Andrea Bettencourt. Why don't you handle that?" Renita nodded. "While you're at it run a background check on Mrs. Bettencourt's finances since the death of her husband."

"Who should I use?" Renita asked.

"Have Carl Wheaton put one of his people on the financial records. Make certain to tell him to be discreet. We don't want to alarm anyone."

"What if Carl wants justification? You know he needs an explanation for everything."

"Good point," I said. "Make it financial background checks on the entire Bellingham board and Mrs. Windell. He'll assume its routine."

Renita picked up the phone. "Mrs. Bettencourt please," Renita said into the mouthpiece, "Renita Harris with the Cavanaugh Detective Agency."

"That's Cavanaugh Investigation Agency," I whispered to Renita. Renita winked at me. All I could do was smile.

"Yes I'll hold."

Renita covered the mouthpiece with her hand. "I'm assuming she has all of her lease records on a computer," Renita whispered. "She can e-mail the information to us. It'll make the HADES search a whole lot easier."

"Hello Mrs. Bettencourt this is Renita Harris with the Cavanaugh *Investigation* Agency." Renita listened. "Yes I'm still working for that jar head."

"I'm not a jar head," I mouthed to Renita. "That's the Marines." Renita grinned.

"Fine thanks," Renita responded to an obvious question. I signaled Renita that I would leave her to her work. I had other matters to attend. For starters, I needed to find Mark Strait.

I called Mark Strait's home from my office. There was no answer. From what I gathered from my earlier conversation with his father, Frank Strait—a.k.a. Frank Sutherland—Frank planned to stay with his son through the New Year. It was worth a trip to the home rented by Edward Sutherland to see if his father had stuck around.

I grabbed my trench coat and wool hat. A cold, steady drizzle made them necessities. I looked in on Renita to see how it was going. Renita gave me a thumb's up. I whispered to her to call me once she had something. Renita nodded. I left feeling proud about how my partner was handling herself.

***

Frank Strait did his best not to help. He claimed not to know where his son was. When I asked him why he and his son changed their last name, Frank Strait calmly told me it was none of my damn business. He disavowed his son being involved in anything remotely illegal or unethical. I suspected Frank was acting as some sort of lookout for his son. When I asked him why he went along with the Edward Sutherland charade, Frank Strait denied ever having done any such thing. He said I must have been mistaken. Since it wasn't vital to the investigation, I didn't pursue the matter any further.

Frank Strait was experienced at being evasive judging by the ease which he dodged most of my questions. Whether it was due to his or his son's mishaps was not important. My only concern was the here and now. Between Frank Strait and a couple of dollars, I could have gotten more information about his son from a daily newspaper.

There was one bit of information Frank Strait let slip. When I mentioned his son's place in Klamath Falls, Frank Strait said he'd only been to his son's fishing cabin in Detroit, a small town just southeast of Salem. Mark Strait didn't have a place in Klamath Falls as far as I knew. Frank Strait never realized his mistake. I kept the conversation going to make certain that he wouldn't. When I left twenty minutes later, I was confident Frank Strait called his son to inform him I had been there and to assure him that everything was fine. That deception would buy me enough time to make a beeline to Detroit and possibly get at the truth.

***

Detroit was about a two-hour drive from Portland. I phoned Renita to let her know of my plans and to find out how it went with Andrea Bettencourt.

"Scone?" Renita said. I told Renita there would be no further need to check for bugs. I believed what the e-mail from our phantom employers had said. That didn't mean we were going to stop packing. Not because of our clients capabilities but as a response to where our case was leading us which in my estimation was into the jaws of cold-blooded killers.

"How did it go with Mrs. Bettencourt?" I asked.

"She wanted to know why we wanted the lease records. I told her that according to the police the same make Jaguar the board members of her company drove was probably the same type of car the murderers used. She got quiet. You would've enjoyed that. She e-mailed them to me as we spoke."

"That's shaking the trees," I said. "Now let's see what falls out."

"The lease records only go back for the past four years," Renita said.

"Why four years?" I asked.

"That's when Andrea Bettencourt took over that segment of the company."

"Who handled it before?"

"Patrick Kemery. According to Bettencourt, the whole Jaguar leasing idea was Kemery's. He only allowed Windell to take credit for the idea because he thought it would score him brownie points."

"Any luck?"

"A big fat zero according to Bettencourt," Renita said.

"I meant with the Jaguars," I said.

"I've cross-checked for a sapphire, blue and black Jaguar with the license plate HADES in her records. Same results as the DMV search nothing."

"Sounds like our murderers have a phony plate or Mrs. Bettencourt deliberately omitted it," I said.

"Now how do we track them?" Renita asked.

"Let's keep doing what we're doing. I have a hunch they'll find us. Are you ready?"

"Got my sidewinder right here under my new burgundy blazer," Renita said.

"Fly and lethal."

"You know it."

"I don't expect any trouble just yet but keep it close just in case."

"How long do you think you'll be?"

"That depends on Strait."

"Be careful," Renita said.

"There is no luck except where there is discipline," I said.

"Meaning," Renita said.

"I'm always careful."

CHAPTER TWENTY-ONE

I kept an eye out for who was tailing me on my drive to Detroit. The weather cleared around Woodburn, pale blue skies spotted by a few gray clouds. There was a variety of vehicles with a variety of drivers. None of the vehicles was a sapphire Jaguar. None of the drivers was Buzz Cut.

After I decided how I was going to handle Mark Strait once I found him, I concentrated on summarizing the details of this bizarre case. Clinton Windell was murdered in his home, robbed of an estimated twenty-million dollars of uncut stones, with his daughter asleep in the next room, professional, clean, and clueless. Enter Genevieve Windell: wife, mother, and artist, an independent and strong-willed woman with a scandalous secret. Mark Strait a.k.a. Edward Sutherland, former exotic dance club owner and ex-shipmate of Clinton Windell, investigated for smuggling while in the Navy, probable romantic involvement with Genevieve Windell at some time. Pamela Windell an innocent. Benton Lawson, the programming genius behind the Universal Translator and Roxanna Farhletti's ex-lover, a man who was still head over heels for his ex-flame.

I theorized that Antonio Farhletti was somehow involved in Clinton Windell's murder. Renita confirmed the sapphire Jaguar had visited the Beaverton Research Complex but it was unconfirmed that the Jaguar had followed Lawson. Andrea Bettencourt, prime suspect. Andrea had means and motive but so far no opportunity. If a link could be established between her and Buzz Cut, or the sapphire Jaguar with the license plate HADES, that might do it. Mark Strait might have some answers. End of summary.

I made a quick stop at the Marion County Clerk's Office in Salem and discovered that Mark Strait had purchased a hideaway under his real name.

Just north of Detroit, I found the dirt road the county clerk told me about and drove until I reached a small boulder shaped like a beaver, a landmark indicating I was within a mile of Mark Strait's place. There was a small clearing to the right of the beaver. It was the perfect place to stash my Lexus. I tucked my car into the clearing and got to work.

I pulled out a gym bag from the trunk of my car. In it, I had camouflage fatigues and lightweight hiking boots. The boy scouts aren't the only ones whose motto is be prepared. With my binoculars and weaponry, I took the high road to Mark Strait's place.

At about a quarter-mile from Strait's hideaway, I found a vantage point that allowed me to observe his place through my binoculars. It was a two-story log house in a secluded wooded area facing Detroit. I couldn't see inside. All of the windows were blinded by closed shades. A green Chevy Suburban was parked out front. On the west side was a twenty-three-foot Boston Whaler nestled in its trailer hitch. The north side faced a panoramic wealth of hibernating forest and plucky pines. As my gaze shifted to the east side of the house, I saw Mark Strait step out of a Jacuzzi onto a wooden deck. Strait wrapped his wide body in a snug-fitting terry cloth bathrobe, forced his fat feet into a pair of flip-flops, picked up a Mitchell semiautomatic carbine, and disappeared inside the cabin through a sliding glass door.

I jogged the remainder of the way navigating as carefully as a field mouse through the autumn forest and being almost as quiet. I made it to the Chevy without incident. From behind the Suburban, I couldn't see Strait. I crept around to the wooden deck. A quick peek inside revealed Mark Strait settled into a chair with his feet propped up on an ottoman and a can of beer in his hand watching TV. I rolled a pebble in the direction of the Jacuzzi and waited off to the side of the sliding glass doors. My Beretta was familiar and steady in my right hand. I heard Strait come to the door. I could hear that he was wearing those flip-flops. A few moments later the glass door slowly slid open. The first thing I saw was the barrel of a 12-gauge pump action shotgun. I waited. Soon enough Strait's head was in full view. I pressed the barrel of my Beretta to his temple and cocked the hammer. Strait froze. I'm not afraid of death and I'm not too righteous to kill. The latter I have done. The previous was still pending. If Strait had made one suspicious move, I would have shot him.

"Remove your finger from the trigger," I ordered. Strait did as instructed. "Slowly, carefully, place the shotgun on the deck." I could tell Strait had other ideas. I grabbed his ear with my left hand and pressed the barrel a little harder into his sweating temple. It must have dissuaded him from trying anything for the moment. Strait did as I said.

I made Strait go back inside with my gun pressed to the back of his head leaving his shotgun on the deck. I ordered Strait to stand in the middle of the living room while I had a quick look around.

On the west wall was a wooden gun rack holding five weapons: two deer hunting rifles with scopes, a Colt semiautomatic rifle, the Mitchell semiautomatic carbine, an M-16, and an empty spot were I guessed the shotgun had been. I would have been willing to bet if I had done a casual search of the log house, I would have found half a dozen handguns stashed in a variety of unlikely places. A camelback sofa looked to be the best place for Strait while I questioned him. Once I was satisfied the sofa and the area around it were weapons free zones, I ordered him to sit in the middle of the sofa and to keep his hands in his lap.

I sat cross-legged on the hardwood floor across from him. Strait and I eyed each other for a few moments. He looked exhausted. His double-bagged bloodshot eyes told me he was hiding all right but it wasn't from me and it wasn't from the police. Strait was ready for war with all of that artillery.

"My father had nothing to do with this," Strait said. "Going to The Phantom of the Opera *was* his idea. I wanted to show him a good time and it gave me an alibi."

"Like I care," I said.

"How'd you find me?" Strait asked.

"That's not important."

"You don't need the gun you know."

"Let's just say I'm keeping it aimed at your heart as a motivational tool," I said.

"You won't shoot," Strait said.

"Believe me when I tell you that I will."

Strait fixed his stare deep into my eyes. He was trying to discern if I was bluffing. I wasn't.

"Why should I tell you anything?" Strait said.

"Because I have the gun," I said.

"Somehow I don't see an insurance investigator killing someone in cold blood."

"They do when it comes to self defense."

Strait's eyebrows raised a little.

"Picture this," I went on to say. "In an effort to discover what involvement Mr. Strait a.k.a. Edward Sutherland had regarding the Windell homicide, I tracked him to this hideaway. He was hostile. I drew my weapon in order to restrain him. He attacked me. The next thing I knew he was shot, dead."

"It won't fly," Strait said.

"Maybe it will, maybe it won't. All I know is fugitives who use aliases don't receive a great deal in the credibility department particularly when they're not around to defend themselves."

"Last I heard the police weren't looking for me," Strait said.

"Not yet," I said. "They will be a little curious as to why you disappeared especially if someone drops your name in the investigating detective's ear."

"Son-of-a-bitch."

"Hardly, now let's get down to it. What's your involvement with the Windell murder?"

"Before I say anything," Strait said, "I want your word what I tell you stays between us."

"I'll do what I can."

"That ain't good enough."

"It's the best I'm offering."

"What do you want to know?"

"Let's start with why you drugged Pamela Windell?"

"Who says I did?" Strait said.

"Milk and cookies with Uncle Eddie says so to me."

"All right I slipped the kid a Mickey so what?"

"The *so what* makes you an accessory to murder," I said.

"Wait a minute! I had nothing to do with Windell's murder, not intentionally anyway."

"Convince me."

Strait shifted his bulk to one side. While I was confident he had no access to any weapons, I kept an eye on his hands. To be on the safe side I slightly lowered my aim. That way if he made any sudden moves my first shot would punch a hole through the trunk of his body.

"Let me start at the beginning," Strait said.

CHAPTER TWENTY-TWO

Strait hesitated a moment. He was frazzled. He was probably wondering how much he could trust me. How much he could get by with not saying. I waited. My patience paid off.

"Windell and me knew a couple of people down at FBI records," Strait said. "Let's just say we had done business together in the Navy. I had one of the guys do the switch with my prints, clean-up my record, and doctor my past."

"You and Windell served together aboard the George Clymer?" I asked to keep the ball rolling.

"That's how we met," Strait said.

"When did the smuggling start?" I asked.

"You know about that huh?" Strait said. "Early in our naval careers we started what you might call a little specialty items business."

"You were smugglers," I said.

"If you like, it was easy money with minimum risk Windell's favorite arrangement. Can't say I minded it much either. Once Windell set things in motion, made the connections and laid out the overall plan, it was up to me to handle the details. It was the equivalent of Windell being the captain and me the commander. He was even generous about it. Windell took forty percent, I got fifty, and the other ten percent went for operating expenses. Supposedly, mine was the greater risk so I got the larger share. Windell kept the books though. I'll bet if I was to take a close look at those books, it worked out Windell got a bigger slice of the pie than me. He was crafty like that."

"How did you manage to smuggle things past naval security?"

"We didn't. First off, we never smuggled anything into the U.S. We employed the don't shit where you live principle. We used a third and sometimes a fourth party to do the actual pickups and deliveries."

"Mules," I said.

"Exactly, once I told them what we wanted and where and who it was to be delivered to the mules handled it from there. Wasn't any skin off our backs if they got caught. As long as they kept their mouths shut nobody aboard the George Clymer took the fall."

"Anyone ever blow the whistle?"

"Nope, Windell was a genius at reading people and figuring out the best ways to set things up. He sure had me pegged. Did you know Windell had a special courier's license? It gave him clearance to bring just about anything he wanted back in that little gem bag of his. As long as he had the proper paperwork to back up his declaration. Can you believe it? I couldn't, a man like him. He could've transported contraband into the U.S. as a legitimate businessman if he wanted to."

"That's nice," I said even though I was aware of that fact. "Let's get back to Windell's homicide?" My statement visibly irritated Strait. I could care less. "How were payments handled on your shipments?" I asked.

"Deposits were made to three separate Swiss bank accounts, fifty percent in mine, forty in Windell's, and ten percent in a phony account under the fictitious name of Duncan Minor. Of course our accounts were under phony names too."

"Is that how you met Genevieve Windell?"

"Yeah, she was Genevieve Wissmann then. It was during one of my frequent shore leaves to check on my bounty. I was having a bite at a sidewalk café when Genevieve walked by. She was the most beautiful woman I had ever seen. I knew I was in love. I rushed over and somehow managed to convince Genevieve to have a cup of coffee with me. Every chance I got after that I went to Bern. We got to know each other. I told Windell I didn't trust the Swiss bankers so I was keeping close tabs on my money. He didn't believe me but what the hell; as long as I did my job who cared?"

"Windell never found out about you and his wife?"

"I didn't see any reason to tell him and neither did Genevieve."

"Why didn't you marry her?"

"Genevieve never loved me. She cares about me but that's the extent of it."

"Is that why you lured her to America?"

"I knew she wanted to branch out on her own as a ballerina. I figured if I got her to the U.S., I could change her heart. There was nothing sexual between us during all the time we spent together in Bern. It was only after she moved to the U.S. that we became lovers. You could say I used the situation to coerce her into it. Genevieve wouldn't marry me even to hasten her citizenship.

Strait looked dejected. My compassion started to well up. I thought about Pamela Windell to put a cork in it. Feeling sorry for Strait wasn't going to get me any closer to her father's murderers. Besides, he wasn't exactly a victim in this whole ordeal.

"Back to Windell, when did you and Windell part company?"

"The how's more important than the when, let me give you an idea of what kind of man Clinton Windell really was. You know anything about an assault charge in West Virginia that was later dropped?"

I nodded.

"Windell told me about that when we were in the Navy. Bragged about how he beat up this girl's father."

"Why?"

"Because Windell thought he was in love with the girl and she asked him to. According to Windell, the man had been molesting her anyway so it served him right. Windell convinced the girl's father that if he didn't drop the charge against him his daughter would accuse her father of rape. One of the girl's brothers wound up doing the old man. Windell was especially proud of the whole ugly mess because he set it up. Manipulated the girl's brother into killing her father by getting the boy to believe his daddy's molestation wouldn't stop with his sister. He bragged about how it was the first time he had ever done such a thing. The end of the story always brought a smile to Windell's face. It was as if he relished the moment. Man, I hated that bastard."

"Where's this going Strait?"

"We had our Swiss accounts dissolved and the funds transferred to banks of our own choosing under phony names. We decided on small town banks. Windell said small town banks would arouse less suspicion. Our plan was to let the money sit tight in the banks for a few months then disperse it into a variety of banks throughout the U.S. I have to give Windell credit it worked like a charm.

Windell and I were celebrating our honorable discharges from the Navy in a Lebanon, Tennessee bar. We got drunk and got into a fistfight with some of the locals. Police came to break it up. Somehow, Windell managed to escape. I wasn't so lucky, did six months for drunk and disorderly conduct. Windell never lifted a finger to help. I went looking for him when I got out after I checked on my money. Every dime was still there.

I would've let it go at that except for what happened while I was in the brig. It turned out Windell contacted my family. He told them I was missing and he was trying to locate me. What he was really after was information about my bank account. I suppose he figured if I told anyone about it, my family would be the ones. He was right in his thinking but his timing was way off. I just hadn't gotten around to it. That's not the kind of thing you talk about over the phone.

During my incarceration, my younger sister killed herself by overdosing on sleeping pills. Turns out, she was pregnant at the time. My mother told me she suspected Windell and my sister had relations. She believed Windell was the father. So did I.

Windell always told me nobody got in the way of his dreams. He'd do whatever it took to see to that. I saw him do some horrendous shit, man. He could kill you as quick as turning off a light but only if he regarded it as a last resort. I have to admit you didn't want to see the dark side of that man. As CEO of Bellingham, he was just as ruthless. Man had no respect for women. They were pleasure toys to him. Once he got bored with them, he'd throw them away and get another. From what I knew about Windell, I knew my sister and her baby were just things that would get in his way. He may not have shoved those pills down her throat but he knew which buttons to push to send her there. My sister's death sent my mother to an early grave and nearly killed my father."

"Was he that manipulative with Genevieve and Pamela Windell?"

"The bastard actually loved Genevieve and his daughter. He never messed around on Genevieve or nothing like that. If he had believe me, I would've added that to the blackmail list, cleaned him out, and then spilled my guts to Genevieve. I mean I would have told Genevieve everything. About the smuggling, my sister and any other dirty secret I could remember about Clinton Windell."

"You were blackmailing Windell?"

"I'll get to that. After things settled down with my family, I tried a few legitimate business ventures. All of them went belly up."

"Including the Tulip Room?"

"Yeah."

"Did you start the fire that destroyed it?"

"Hell no! I just wanted to sell and cut our losses. My business partner said we could make a killing on the insurance if the place burned down. Torching the place was his idea. We never intended for anyone to get hurt. Somehow, the man my partner hired to do the job got his times mixed up. Instead of the place going up at four-thirty the next morning, it flamed up at ten-thirty that night. The Tulip Room was packed. There was what sounded like a small explosion and then the place went up in a ball of flames like somebody dropped a bomb on it. Those poor people never had a chance. I was outside having a quick smoke and second thoughts. I didn't know Genevieve had skipped out early."

Strait paused. His puffy face became pale. His eyes became misty.

"My partner was inside when it went up. After the police cleared me, I took off leaving behind the insurance money and everything."

"Did you know your partner was connected to organized crime?"

"My partner had Mafia affiliations. I never did. What he did aside from the business was none of my business. He did a good job managing the club. That was all I cared about."

"Understood," I said.

"A few years after that tragedy, I wound up back in Baghdad by the Sea where I ran into Genevieve. She tried pretending she didn't know me but I wouldn't play along. How could I walk away from the woman I loved come back from the dead? I did a little spying and found out she was married to my old buddy Clinton Windell. I got in touch with Windell right away.

That's when I found out Windell was some big mucky-muck with Bellingham Jewelers. Can you imagine scum like Windell rubbing elbows with the big brass? When I caught up with him, I confronted Windell about what he'd done to my sister. He said he was as upset about it as I was. Windell tried convincing me he didn't know anything about her being pregnant and couldn't imagine what had made her do such a thing. He swore the baby wasn't his. Windell let slip that my sister asked him to buy her those sleeping pills because she was suffering from a bout with insomnia. He didn't know she was planning to commit suicide. *Lying bastard*, he knew exactly what he was doing."

"How could you work for a man like that?"

"At first I wanted revenge in the worst way. I plotted on how I was going to kill him—until I saw how much Genevieve actually loved that asshole. Snuffing him would've been like killing my sister all over again."

"Didn't Genevieve have a problem with you being there?"

"At first she did. But once I convinced her that I'd keep our shared past a secret she relaxed and went with the flow."

"What about your father?"

"What about him?"

"Did he know about Windell and your sister?"

"No. My dad was working at a Texas oil field the entire time. My mother never told him. Neither did I. He's in the dark about it. I'm going to keep him that way. He don't have but a few years left. No sense dredging up the worst time of his life."

"What happened next?" I asked.

"I was down on my luck. All the money I made smuggling while in the Navy was gone. I was never good at business." Strait paused for a moment as if to reflect on what he had just said. "I told Windell I'd spill the beans about our smuggling days if he didn't let me in on some of his action. He said he couldn't do it without directing attention to himself, so we went back and forth about it for a while until he devised a scheme to bring me into the fold without raising an eyebrow. His regular butler was retiring and they would be looking to replace him. Edward Sutherland was born. Windell sent me to a butler school. I had a crash course in the profession. Windell fixed me up with fake references and credentials in time for the interview process. After that, it was a slam-dunk. I received my payments regularly, got a chance to be close to Genevieve, and could keep an eye on Windell. It was a sweet deal."

I'm sure it also gave Windell a chance to keep an eye on you, I thought. "In essence blackmail," I said.

"I'd call it restitution," Strait said. "How else could I afford this little getaway? Or that boat out there, all courtesy of the deceased."

"Mrs. Windell went along with this?"

"You've got it all wrong Cavanaugh. I never told Genevieve anything about Windell. He never told her anything about me. There was no way for her to make the connection. Windell no more wanted her to know that we served together than I did. Are you getting the picture?"

Reflecting briefly on my last dialogue with Mrs. Windell, *She hadn't known about your naval years together until recently*, I thought. I nodded in response to his question.

"Did you ever tell Windell about Genevieve working for you at the Tulip Room?"

"Not a word—or anybody else for that matter. I love Genevieve. I wouldn't do anything to harm her; including shattering her belief that her husband was the upstanding gentleman, she made him out to be. I'd take my own life rather than hurt her like that."

"Where were you when Windell was murdered?" I asked.

"Like I told you with my father, I gave Pamela a mild sedative in her milk just like you said. Nothing lethal just something, to make sure she'd be asleep when the robbery went down. I watched The Wizard of Oz with her until she fell asleep. Then I left to be with my father. If I knew, Windell was going to get hurt, I would have put a stop it. I was only interested in the gems."

"Wasn't there supposed to be a babysitter staying with Pamela Windell that night?"

"I took care of the babysitter. I sent her a text message from Genevieve's PC that she wouldn't be needed until the following weekend."

"At about what time did you leave the Windell mansion?"

"Between six-thirty and seven, I needed to pick up my father from my house for the eight o'clock performance."

"Are you certain the gems were the only thing you were after?" I asked.

"That and a little revenge over my sister's death," Strait said.

"You thought if you had enough money then maybe Genevieve might consider you over Windell didn't you?"

"Something like that. I got a quarter of what was in that gem bag."

"Five-million dollars?"

"Cash delivered to my doorstep in Portland the day after Windell was killed."

If what Strait said was true the thieves must have had a buyer lined up before they committed the crime. Those gems could be spread all over the world by now.

"Who are your partners?" I asked.

"I never met them," Strait said. "Some woman arranged a meeting with me over the phone."

"Did you recognize her voice?"

"No. She told me what she wanted. We met at Fullman's parking lot to work out the details. A week later, a key was left in my mailbox to a blue Jaguar that was parked in Fullman's parking lot. I showed up, got in and my connection was hiding in the back seat."

"Did she ever say why she chose you?"

"No and I didn't care. I was just glad for the opportunity."

"What was the plate number?"

"I remember because it was so weird. HADES. Where do people come up with that crap?"

"Didn't it strike you as strange that this woman was using the same type and color car that all of Bellingham board members leased?"

"Yes and no. It suggested to me that either one or more of the board members were involved or someone had done their homework. Either way it didn't matter to me."

"Did you get a look at the other party?" I asked.

"She held a gun to the back of my head to make certain I wouldn't. Told me if I moved she'd use it. It had a silencer. I know that sensation from experience. She had even covered the rearview and side mirrors so I couldn't see anything. She instructed me on what to do, made me hand over the Jaguar key and then she forced me to put on a blindfold and count to twenty. When I removed the blindfold, she was gone. I got in my car and left."

"Would you recognize this woman's voice if you heard it again?"

"Doubtful. I was nervous and she was obviously disguising it."

"When was this?"

"A couple of days before the robbery."

That's how it worked. Buzz Cut showed up at Fullman's driving the sapphire Jaguar. While he waited inside for someone he was supposed to meet, this mystery woman got into the Jaguar and waited for Strait. She gave Strait his instructions. They both left and Buzz Cut was none the wiser. This Windell conspiracy was getting interesting. How many players were involved?

"Were you the man Genevieve Windell was having an affair with?" I asked.

"I wish," Strait said.

"Who was?"

"If Genevieve didn't tell you then it's none of your business."

Chivalrous to the end, I thought. *Maybe he did learn something from butler school.*

"The man Genevieve was having an affair with could be involved in Clinton Windell's murder," I said.

"So?"

"Aren't you concerned the same people that murdered Clinton Windell are looking to air condition you?"

"Don't you think I know that? I'm not waiting around to have my ticket punched. Look Cavanaugh, I'm a hustler. Killing for me is a final resort. If it weren't Windell would've been dead long before now after what he did to my family."

"What about that threat you made to me back at the Windell estate?"

"That was to warn you off Genevieve. I get a little crazy when she's involved."

"Why are you worried if the thieves kept their end of the bargain?"

"I recognize a setup when I see it. The police find me dead with five-million dollars in my house. After a deep background check, they find out I'm not who I say I am and then they link me to Clinton Windell. See we had some bad blood between us. Case closed."

"Sounds like a plan," I said.

"No honor among thieves especially those who kill," Strait said.

"Are you sure Windell didn't do something to his wife to make you crazy?"

"If he had and I found out about it there would be no question who pulled the trigger."

"What about Diva Computer Software?" I asked.

"What about them?" Strait said.

"How do they fit into all this?"

"I have no idea what you're talking about."

"Any idea about how Harvey Bettencourt died?"

"A parachuting accident."

"From what I hear a convenient accident arranged by Clinton Windell."

"Wouldn't surprise me if it was."

"Did you meet with Windell at Fullman's wearing a disguise to discuss that same accident?"

"How are you finding out this stuff?"

"Just answer the question," I said. Strait's eyes narrowed on my Beretta. If he believed things had changed regarding whether I'd use it, one look at my face discarded the thought.

"Yeah I met with him to discuss Harvey Bettencourt's accident. I was actually recording the conversation trying to get Windell to admit to having rigged it so I could add it to my blackmail list, up the ante so to speak."

"Why?"

"Why what?"

"Why'd you meet at Fullman's? What was wrong with talking at Windell's house?"

"It was Windell's idea to meet at Fullman's. Maybe he was trying to set me up somehow. Who knows?"

"Did you relay any of your inklings to Mrs. Bettencourt?"

"There was nothing to pass on. Even if there were I'd be taking a chance at blowing my cover if I did."

"Did the Bettencourts have anything on Windell or his wife?"

"Nothing I'm aware of."

"What about you?"

"Meaning?"

"Did the Bettencourts know you were Mark Strait? Did they know anything about your past sins?"

"If they did they kept it to themselves."

My opinion about Strait had changed from when we first met. He was a lot smarter than I'd given him credit. I could see why Clinton Windell trusted him as his commander. "You had no idea Windell was going to be killed?" I asked.

"I swear to you, it was supposed to be a simple robbery that's all. I hated that bastard but he was much more valuable to me alive than dead."

"I'm surprised you're not sticking around to protect Genevieve Windell and make with the romance."

"Get real Cavanaugh. The last person Genevieve needs in her life right now is a target like me. Besides, Windell's death didn't make a damn bit of difference about how she felt about me."

"Did you ever stop to think that the people who are looking for you might use Genevieve and her daughter to flush you out?"

"No chance."

"And why's that?"

"Look Cavanaugh, I don't know what you used to do before this insurance investigation game but it sure as hell wasn't selling used cars. Whatever connections you have are long and deep. You know who I am.

My background and my associations. That kind of information doesn't grow on trees. The people that are after me believe I'm Edward Sutherland, a butler who wanted a little more out of life. As long as that's all they know then Genevieve and Pamela are safe."

"They won't hear differently from me."

"I appreciate that."

"What about your father? He's in danger too you know."

"These people—whoever the hell they are—want to keep this thing quiet. They're smart enough to realize that if anything happens to my father they can't be sure what I'll do. If the cops get wind of any of this it'll be like raiding a whorehouse. No telling who's going to come running out of those rooms when the whistles blow. The killers want me."

"How can they be so sure you haven't told someone?"

"Besides you, you mean? If I had the cops would already be shining bright lights down some dark alleys."

"Why are you still in Oregon if you're so confident everyone you love is safe from these murderers except you?"

"The last place people will look for a fugitive is in their own backyard," Strait said.

"Where'd you hear that?" I asked.

"Homegrown."

I tried convincing Strait to tell his story to the police. From what I had learned, divulging this information would in no way jeopardize my clients' interest. Strait was convinced he wouldn't last five minutes if he surfaced. My mind was made up, I was going directly to Destini with what I knew, and that included Strait's whereabouts. If I had found Strait, I was certain it wouldn't take long for Windell's killers to do the same.

Strait said there would be no sense telling anyone where he was because he would be long gone before then. He asked about Genevieve Windell. I told him she was fine. Strait wanted me to tell Genevieve that he always loved her when I saw her again. I told him to tell her himself. He gave a snort of a laugh before warning me, "Sound general quarters Cavanaugh. You're in harm's way." I left without another word.

When I left Mark Strait, I could've sworn I saw something, a sunburst, for just a moment amongst the dark shadows of Douglas firs. I jogged away from the cabin and found a place behind some brushwood to observe. Nothing happened. Mark Strait remained inside. *Probably just my client's people catching up*, I thought. If that's what I believed then why were my knuckles tingling?

CHAPTER TWENTY-THREE

While I changed back into my civvies I wrestled with my concerns governing what I saw when I left Mark Strait. Someone had been watching. Had I led them to Strait? My instincts told me yes just as they had prompted me to stick around to find out more. I doubted it was one of my constant shadows. Without previous knowledge of where I was going, there was no way they could have been prepared to follow me under those conditions. I had a choice. Should I leave my partner alone while I staked out Strait's log house or return to Portland to watch Renita's back and have Strait fend for himself? My decision was obvious.

On the way back to Portland, I recognized six people in four of the vehicles who had followed me to Detroit. My little excursion into the woods threw them for a loop. They maintained tight tails all the way to my office.

I did not see one vehicle tailing me north. It was a pine green Ford pickup that had trailed me from the time I left Frank Strait until the time I entered the Marion County Clerk's Office. He used his cell phone more than the others. I assumed he was the flagship of the whole operation coordinating vehicle switches and the like. The driver of the pickup managed to keep distance enough so I couldn't get a good look at him. A precaution the others apparently did not find necessary. If he wasn't one of my phantom employers' agents then who was he? Maybe he was the sunburst at the Windell mansion. What did he want?

On my final deep cover mission in South America, being an outsider my room was constantly searched. I kept my field journal in one of the few places no one ever rifled. In Bebe Assassino's room beneath a loose floorboard in his closet. One day I was jotting down an entry when I heard Bebe Assassino approaching. He was talking to one of his bodyguards. I wasn't expecting his return for another hour. Bebe

Assassino had been checking the cocaine packaging process in the southwest quadrant at Cardozo's insistence. I slid the closet door nearly shut leaving enough of a crack to see through, put back my field journal and silently replaced the floorboard.

Bebe Assassino walked in wearing all white. A uniform of affluence around those parts. He was smoking a cigar. Bebe Assassino removed his Panama hat and laid it on his dresser. With a large bandanna, he wiped his face and neck. He walked around the room and closed all of the drapes grinding out his cigar in an ashtray atop the dresser. For a moment, Bebe Assassino sat on the edge of the bed staring listlessly out into space. He looked like a child then, dreaming, pondering, and not at all grown-up. When he walked my way, I moved away from the crack. I listened as his footsteps came closer. I readied myself to attack. My plan would be to knock him unconscious but kill him only if I had to.

Bebe Assassino never opened the closet. I heard sounds similar to the ones I made when working free the floorboard I used to hide my field journal. There was a moment of silence. Bebe Assassino walked away from the closet. I peered back through the crack. He sat on the bed with his back to me. Beside him he'd set a padlocked black metal box. It was badly dented and slightly rusted. He set it in his lap, opened it and spent the next half-hour looking at its contents. I couldn't see what he was looking at but my guess was it was cash, mad money if you will. I waited, sweating, suffocating in that stifling closet until he was done. About fifteen minutes after Bebe Assassino left, I was able to slip out unnoticed.

***

Like a cold dark liquid curtain, the rain returned with a fury around Newberg. It was a pelting reminder from the heavens of what it took to wash away our sins. I called the office. "Cavanaugh Detective Agency," Renita answered.

"That's *Investigation* Agency," I said.

"Hey C. J.! How'd it go?" Renita said.

I filled Renita in what Strait told me.

"Sounds like he could be our man," Renita said.

"I don't think so," I said. "I believed his story."

"Carl was able to obtain the financial records for the Bellingham Board Members including Andrea Bettencourt," Renita said. "He e-mailed us a copy."

"Anything noteworthy?"

"It appears that Harvey Bettencourt was not only reinstated but he received a twenty-five thousand-dollar fee every month from Bellingham for miscellaneous services. A fee approved exclusively by Clinton Windell. When Harvey Bettencourt died those fee payments were doubled and directly deposited to Andrea Bettencourt's personal checking account. No one else on the board had that sort of special allowance or showed any conspicuous leap in income."

"Interesting," I said.

"Blackmail," Renita said.

"Probably but for what," I said.

"Maybe Andrea Bettencourt knew about the smuggling?"

"Strait didn't mention anyone else being aware of that."

"Sounds as if there were several people involved in their operation someone else could have popped up."

"It's worth looking into," I said. "There's a DEA agent by the name of Jon Adams who works out of the San Francisco office. Ask him to get all of the information he can on a San Francisco strip club called the Tulip Room that burned down back in around 2000. We're looking for anything he can drum up on the former owners of the Tulip Room and any employees—particularly dancers who were working there at the time."

"C. J., I didn't know you were into exotic dancing. You know I do a mean—never mind." Renita was being true to her word. Maybe this Three's Company living arrangement wasn't such a bad deal after all.

"While he's at it have him see what he can find out about Buzz Cut," I said. "Give him the details on how Windell was murdered and see if he can match anyone to that particular M.O."

"He'll do this for us why?" Renita asked.

"Because he owes me a few favors," I said. "We go way back."

"I'll get right on it," Renita said. "How is a DEA agent going to get that kind of information without arousing unwarranted suspicion?"

"Tell him to keep a low profile," I said. "He'll know what to do."

"Anything else?"

"That should do it for now. Call me if you need anything."

"You're what I—forget I said that," Renita said.

"Done," I said.

"When will you be back in the office?" Renita asked.

I glanced at my car clock. "About three," I said.

"I was thinking of leaving early," Renita said. "I need to go by my place and grab a few things."

"Wouldn't you rather wait and have me escort you?" I asked.

"I can handle it," Renita said.

"How about giving Ernest a call?" I said. "I'm certain he wouldn't have a problem seeing a lady home."

"An interesting thought," Renita said, "but I'll save the vulnerable female bit for a more appropriate time."

"Don't forget your weapon or your caution."

"Not a chance," Renita said. "I'll head directly to your place when I'm done."

"See you at home," I said adding, "Renita! You're doing an excellent job."

"Thanks C. J.," Renita said. "Be careful."

That was advice Mark Strait needed more than me, I thought. "Right back at you," I said.

CHAPTER TWENTY-FOUR

Renita had posted the "OUT TO LUNCH" sign on the doorknob. I assumed she meant it as some sort of joke. I unlocked the office and went inside. Everything appeared normal. After a quick shower and a fresh change of clothes, I made myself comfortable, switched on my computer, and began writing an update file about what I had learned.

Renita had left me an e-mail. It said that Shawn Calloway had been by the office. Calloway wanted to talk to me regarding the Windell investigation. Renita stated she had played dumb. Since Renita had never been more than a computer-jock-office-clerk in his eyes I could believe Calloway bought it. Calloway didn't seem to know much according to Renita. Her assessment of Calloway was that he was fishing.

I was two-thirds through my update file when Destini called. "Where have you been? All your partner would tell me was you were checking out a lead."

"Detroit," I said.

"Michigan?"

"Of course not."

"What's in Detroit, Oregon?"

"More like who," I said. "Mark Strait. At least he was when I left."

"The butler," Destini said.

"You know his real name," I said.

"Found out a week after the homicide," Destini said. "Know all about his connection with that fire in San Francisco, too. We've been looking all over for him."

"Thanks for sharing," I said.

"What have you got C. J.?"

I filled Destini in on everything Mark Strait told me omitting only the information involving Genevieve Windell. Destini found most of what I had to say about Clinton Windell interesting. I know because she used that word repeatedly as her only comment.

"Detroit's out of my jurisdiction," Destini said. "I'll have the locals pick him up."

"You may want to get the Troopers involved," I said.

"I'll let the locals make that call," Destini said. "Expecting trouble?"

"Trouble may have already come and gone," I said.

"Then I'd better stop wasting time talking to you."

"Did I tell you how much I miss you?" I said.

"Save it C. J. Do you know who Strait's partner was?"

"Yes," I said.

"Knudsen Costello a small time hood with peripheral connections to organized crime," Destini said.

"What difference does it make? Knudsen's a corpse."

"This is how I see it," Destini said. "Clinton Windell was going to divorce his wife. Maybe he told his wife or maybe she found out about it through word of mouth. The wife realized a divorce might cost her everything especially if she were discovered having an affair. An affair I've gotten wind of from a couple of Windell's domestics. The homes, the cars, the checkbook, she could kiss them all goodbye. So she looks for another way to end it while keeping her lifestyle intact."

"Are you still on that dead-end road?" I said. "You told me before you thought the butler did it."

"I said I thought the butler was in on it," Destini said. "From what you've told me he was. He used his old time affiliations with organized crime; got somebody to call up a couple of professionals and the rest is as they say history."

"Where's your proof?" I said.

"I'm working on it. Did Strait say anything that might incriminate Genevieve Windell?"

"You should talk to him yourself."

"You can count on it," Destini said. "One good turn deserves another. You already know Clinton Windell filed for divorce."

"I also know Windell changed his mind after their Switzerland trip."

"If he did he forgot to inform his attorney. According to Windell's personal legal council the divorce was very much in progress when his client was killed."

"What's her motive?" I said.

"Weren't you listening, m-o-n-e-y."

"According to Genevieve Windell she has money."

"She has a few bucks. She stood to lose over one-hundred-million dollars if Windell could prove his wife was having an affair. I don't suppose Strait had anything to say to that effect?"

"He shut down whenever I questioned him about Genevieve Windell," I said. "He's in love with her."

"What's your theory?" Destini asked.

"Unsubstantiated hunches aren't worth telling you about darling," I said.

"Nothing but the facts huh," Destini said.

"Something like that," I said.

"Might that unsubstantiated hunch be Andrea Bettencourt?" Destini said.

"How'd you guess?" I said.

"I know you C. J."

"Bettencourt has the oldest motive in the book revenge."

"It doesn't pan out," Destini said. "Why would she wait so long?"

"Good question," I said. "I'll ask her before I bring her in."

"You just remember whose investigation this is hotshot. All roads to its resolution go through me. Am I making myself clear?"

"As a refined diamond."

"Good and one other thing."

"Yes?"

"Don't call me darling when I'm working."

"Yes detective."

"That's more like it. Where can I find Mr. Strait?"

I filled Destini in on Strait's location. Destini volunteered that she would keep my name out of it. I gave Destini the details on how I tracked Strait down. That way if it were necessary Destini could answer any questions regarding Strait's apprehension.

"What are we doing for dinner tonight?" Destini asked.

"I thought I'd whip up some stir-fry," I said.

"Sounds good I've got to run," Destini said. "See you this evening."

"That won't be soon enough," I said.

"I'm beginning to enjoy having Renita around. She makes you more amorous."

"If you think I'm being attentive now wait until tonight detective."

CHAPTER TWENTY-FIVE

Someone came in just as I was about to wrap it up for the day. I eased open my top right desk drawer where I kept my loaded 380 Glock. After having been with Mark Strait I wasn't taking any chances.

"Mr. Cavanaugh!" It was a woman's voice.

"In here!" I yelled moving a step to my left so that I would not be where she had just heard my voice.

She walked into my office with all the swagger and confidence of a top-drawer attorney. Her hands were in plain view at her sides. She was wearing an Armani trench coat and three inch red high heels. When she removed the trench coat, I saw the reason she wore those Armani shoes. A red Armani dress that looked painted onto her slender figure. The whole facade put me on alert.

After a slow pirouette to convince me she was unarmed, I relaxed. I was ready to put down my weapon once I saw her but why spoil the show.

"I'm Judith Hardy, Mr. Cavanaugh. You probably recognize me from those compromising photos you took of Antonio Farhletti and me."

I put away the Glock then shook her extended right hand. "Would you like a seat?" I said.

"Thank you," Hardy said. Judith Hardy sat crossing her legs. "Do you always greet people with a gun?"

"I'm working on a special case, one that requires unique precautions. How may I help you Ms. Hardy?"

"I've come to ask you to forgo your testimony on behalf of Roxanna Farhletti's divorce petition," Hardy said.

"Did Mrs. Farhletti send you?" I asked.

"No," Hardy said.

"Then why would I do such a thing?" I said.

"As an act of decency," Hardy said.

"Adultery is not a decent act."

"Mr. Farhletti loves his wife," Hardy said. "What you witnessed was a one-time fling for both of us, a minor indiscretion that I initiated. I hate to see a good man ruined because of one moment of vulnerability. As someone who works closely with Mr. Farhletti, I can assure you he is a devoted husband, who would like nothing more than to have the opportunity to reaffirm his love for his wife."

"That may be," I said, "but on that night Mr. Farhletti was an adulterer. I will not withdraw my testimony. Even if I wanted to Mrs. Farhletti's attorney need only subpoena me."

"Suppose you stated the reason for your change of heart was due to a firm belief Mrs. Farhletti was making a mistake throwing away years of marriage based upon one paltry imprudence. What divorce attorney would want to put a reluctant witness on the stand who would issue such detrimental testimony?"

"How would this change of heart be substantiated?"

"By the fact you followed Mr. Farhletti for weeks and at no time found him to behave in any fashion that suggested illicit behavior prior to that one brief encounter of regrettable indulgence."

I couldn't believe Judith Hardy expected me to buy any of that bunk. Hardy could possibly have answers to some questions I had so I willingly played along. I was also curious to see how far Hardy would go.

"From what I witnessed," I said, "Mr. Farhletti was not a man inflamed by a spark of lust. The pictures bear that out."

"The photographs," Hardy smiled like a child savoring the last piece of candy that every child wanted. "We can arrange for your so-called evidence to disappear. We will compensate you of course with a generous token of our appreciation for your cooperation in this bothersome matter."

"By we, I presume you're speaking of yourself and Mr. Farhletti?"

"You're allowed that presumption."

"Perhaps we can negotiate," I said.

"What did you have in mind?" Hardy crossed and uncrossed her legs taking her time enjoying the act of seductive persuasion.

"Answer a few questions and I'll consider it," I said.

"How do I know you will respond in good faith?" Hardy said.

"I give you my word."

"You seem like a trustworthy man. Ask your questions."

"Why didn't Farhletti come himself?"

"He wanted to," Hardy said. "I insisted he let me speak with you instead since I'm the cause of his recent misfortune."

"A woman's touch," I said.

"More like a genuine effort to help Mr. Farhletti restore his good name," Hardy said.

"Let's turn our attention toward the Clinton Windell homicide."

"I can't help you there," Hardy said.

"Maybe you can," I said. "There was a sapphire Jaguar with the license plate HADES parked in the VIP section at your Beaverton Research Complex the other night. Do you have any idea whose it was or why they were there?"

"None," Hardy said.

"Could they have been there illegally?"

"I don't get involved with matters that small," Hardy said. "Did you check with security?"

"Two of the guards swore they saw the car that night but when they checked the security footage there was no sign of it."

"That is unusual," Hardy said. "I'll look into it."

"Who do you know on Bellingham's Board of Directors?" I asked.

"Everyone we travel in the same circles," Hardy said.

"Are you closer to some than others?" I asked.

"I'm not close to any of them," Hardy said.

"What about Antonio Farhletti?"

"What about Mr. Farhletti?" Hardy said.

"Does he have a closer rapport with some members of the board than others?" I asked.

"Not to my knowledge," Hardy said.

"Then why would Mr. Farhletti have a complete itinerary of Mr. Windell's last business trip in his personal computer files?"

"Who told you that?"

"That doesn't answer my question," I said.

"How in the world could you know what Mr. Farhletti has in his personal computer files?" Hardy asked.

"That still doesn't answer my question," I said.

"If such an itinerary did exist," Hardy said, "I would know about it. I don't know where you're getting your information but I'm putting a stop to it right now. Mr. Farhletti's personal computer files are classified. No one is allowed in without Mr. Farhletti's expressed permission."

"I don't imagine it would be much of a problem for the Universal Translator," I said.

Judith Hardy's eyes narrowed in the same way they did when she told Farhletti that Benton Lawson would be taken care of. Hardy slowly rose not taking her eyes away from mine.

"I can see we are not going to be able to reach an agreement," Hardy said. "I'll be on my way." Hardy turned and walked away.

"I'll leave you with this to think about," Hardy said over her shoulder with her hand resting on the doorknob. "Roxanna Farhletti is a delicate woman with a fragile psyche who does not fare well under duress. A woman who still boasts she was once the most desirable woman in all of Oregon. You've met her. What do you think Mr. Farhletti's attorney will do to her on the witness stand during divorce proceedings? It won't be pretty. Consider having a talk with your client."

"I believe you underestimate Mrs. Farhletti," I said before Hardy could exit.

"That very well may be," Hardy said. "It seems I've underestimated a number of people lately. Goodbye Mr. Cavanaugh."

"Ms. Hardy," I said with a nod wondering if I had been premature in playing my trump card.

When the door snapped shut, it made the same sound as an ammunition clip being shoved into an automatic rifle. I called Benton Lawson. He wasn't in. I left a message on Lawson's machine for him to contact me as soon as possible. I was concerned that after Judith Hardy told Farhletti what just happened, Farhletti might take some drastic measures against Benton Lawson. I wanted to get to Lawson first.

CHAPTER TWENTY-SIX

Dinner had become a pleasant affair for two reasons: Destini and Renita's gentlewoman's agreement regarding yours truly and a pact the three of us willingly made to leave the Windell case outside. Destini would not have volunteered information regarding her investigations in Renita's presence anyway. If Destini were going to try to get information from Renita, she'd make her move when she and Renita were alone. I based my conjecture on what I know of my sweet Destini and what I would do if I were in her shoes.

I had instructed Renita not to share critical information with Destini if the Windell topic came up. That was not much of a stretch for Renita especially when it came to Detective Pendleton. Renita's pat answer was to be that she only knew what I told her and that was that our case was moving along at a good clip and the details were none of Renita's concern. Destini would not believe Renita of course. However, Destini would realize that Renita and I had discussed the possibility of the detective's subtle inquires.

Conversation was mostly polite small talk at dinner. My Chinese stir-fry went over well. Renita and Destini cleaned up while I drafted up a report for Carl. After both ladies had showered, we savored German chocolate cake that Destini had brought home from Rose's bakery washing it down with a spot of Amaretto tea. The ladies complained about what the cake would do to their figures. I let them know their concerns were unwarranted. As for me, a little self-indulgence was long overdue. None of us left more than a few crumbs on our plates.

Destini had placed two years running in the Miss USA Fitness pageant before we met. When Destini came to bed wearing only her natural braids that reached to the small of her bare back, I was reminded of why she had managed to do so well. At thirty-six Destini could have passed for a toned twenty-five with her full face and even skin. With all of the stress law enforcement can burden one with I was amazed at Destini's ability to maintain her youthful appearance. Some people have a singular idea of feminine beauty that sweet illusion known as perfection. I was blessed with the presence of mine.

I had made a backhanded promise on the phone earlier. I'm not a man who exudes passion but I am passionate. I had no trouble living up to my promise with Destini as my inspiration.

It had only been a few days but closet space was at a premium. Destini and I shared a master bedroom closet. Destini also had an additional closet all too herself in the unused guest bedroom. That closet was full too. Renita had her bedroom closet stuffed with just "a few things" she couldn't do without.

Neither of the guest bedroom closets were very large in fairness to the women. I asked Renita not to bring anything else unless it was absolutely necessary. Renita agreed. Destini had free reign. For her my closets could overflow. Other than that and getting into the bathroom in the morning, things were working out fine. Fortunately, for me they were usually finished with the bathroom by the time I returned from my morning run.

It snowed the next morning. Nothing devastating but enough of a dusting to remind me of Pittsburgh. I took a little time after my morning jog to appreciate the glory of the large white powdery flakes descending from the heavens. A boy no older than thirteen showed his little sister – who was no older than five—what happened to snowflakes when she caught them in her hand. The girl's wide eyes revealed her astonishment at the results.

My father used to say snow was dandruff from when God scratched his head. I was a child again for an inexplicable moment. I stuck out my tongue to capture a few dandruff flakes. They tasted like cold drops of clear clean water, cooling my face. I closed my eyes. My breathing slowed absorbing the breath of winter come early. I remembered how my mother would sometimes catch snow in a pot add vanilla extract place it in the freezer and we'd have snow cream as a winter treat. The first snow was best, the sweetest cream. Magic is not often the spectacular but the simplest experiences in life. I was enjoying one of those moments. I wanted it to last long after the snow had melted into my memory. The most I could do to suspend that moment, to relish those hushed minutes of unheralded serenity, was to take the scenic route to the office that morning. And to try to block out the fact all the while I was being watched by two men in a van parked across the street from my house.

I phoned Calloway from the office first thing to follow-up on what he wanted. The Willamette news reporter asked me what the butler heard. Apparently, Strait had his ear pressed to the study door the entire time I was in there with Mrs. Windell. I hadn't been aware Calloway had seen me at all. I told Calloway a boring tale of insurance investigatory dribble. Calloway asked if that was why the butler burst into the study and Mrs. Windell came out crying. I explained Mrs. Windell's tears as a result of her being distraught at her husband's murder—which was true. The butler I said did what we all do from time to time. He was eavesdropping. The butler probably could not stand hearing the lady of the house suffer any longer and burst in to comfort her. Being a gentleman, I said to Calloway you could understand that. Calloway ignored my prompting and continued with his questions.

I'd been following Calloway's articles in The Willamette Times, nothing substantial, basic updates on how the case was progressing with no mention of suspects or motives. Calloway was doing the usual speculative tap dance when the facts were not in evidence. In a nutshell, it had become back page news but Calloway was tenacious. He sounded desperate to save his story.

We bandied about a few items Calloway wanted confirmation or clarification. I offered him neither. Calloway persisted with an adroit question here and there. I answered each firmly and directly and without a drop of substance. Calloway asked if I thought Genevieve Windell did it. I told him flat out, "No." I went on to say that as far as I was concerned Genevieve Windell was clean. When Calloway asked about what the police thought, I remarked I couldn't speak for the police. Of course, Mrs. Windell was my first focus of investigation I said in conclusion.

Calloway's most interesting questions addressed what he regarded as the suspect background of Edward Sutherland. I would have helped Calloway in most cases. What I knew in this case was off limits to him. Calloway must have gotten a strong sense that I was a much bigger part of the Windell investigation than I let on. Being in the newspaper game gave Calloway assurance if nothing else. Calloway could become a problem if he remained persistent. I hoped that all of his queries led him down the path to nowhere where I had just taken him. If not, I would be forced to find a way to use his bosses' desire to crush the story to my advantage. We were done for the moment but I knew Calloway and I were not finished.

CHAPTER TWENTY-SEVEN

Not much happened for the next few days. Strait was true to his word. He had managed to disappear and so had his father. My phantom employers were getting antsy. There remained less than twenty-one days before their deadline. Time was drawing short. Carl Wheaton wanted closure as well. I told Carl he could issue a check to Mrs. Windell stating, "I was confident she had absolutely nothing to do with her husband's murder." Carl wanted to wait a little longer to see whom the police arrested. He said it would look better to his superiors if he did. Carl also said he couldn't pay me until such time. That was expected. I told Carl I would keep the case open in any event. Carl had no objections. My front remained in place.

The Straits disappearances left Destini in a crisis. Destini had a truckload of second hand information from a confidential informant— yours truly—regarding the Straits' involvement in the Windell murder case and no one—but yours truly—to corroborate it. If that weren't enough Destini was getting pressure from her superiors as well, the usual snowball rolling downhill effect. The mayor, who was being hounded by Southwest Hills' residents, pressured the Chief of Police who in turn vented on the Chief of Detectives who demanded immediate results from Destini and David. As if that were all it took to solve a crime.

I volunteered to come forward and give eyewitness testimony on what Mark and Frank Strait had told me. As far as I could see not only would that help Destini it would in no way jeopardize my agreement with my clandestine clients. Destini refused my offer. When I asked Destini why she said she didn't see the point. Translation: I don't need your help. I backed off. The most I could do to help Destini for the moment was to be her eye in the storm. Renita and I kept busy following up on information Jon Adams had e-mailed us. It substantiated what we had already uncovered or suspected with no new information about Windell's assassins.

Jon had been good enough to look into the Lotus Room arson case. There were no records of a Genevieve Wissmann having worked at the Lotus Room. Neither was her name listed among the unfortunate dead. Joyce Caldwell, Genevieve's artist friend did work at the Lotus Room and was one of the people who died in the flames. Jon was able to confirm Genevieve Wissmann had roomed with Joyce Caldwell not for two months as Mrs. Windell had claimed but two years. The landlord recognized Mark Strait from a recent digital photograph we had sent Jon. The landlord recollected Strait frequently visited their apartment.

I had an eyewitness who placed Genevieve Wissmann now Genevieve Windell in the San Francisco Bay area in the company of Mark Strait around the time the Lotus Room was torched. Proving my assumption Genevieve danced at the Lotus Room would be near impossible especially with Mark Strait out of the picture.

The lives of Genevieve and Clinton Windell were coming into focus. How did their separate pasts fit into her husband's murder if at all? The questions were growing faster than weeds in an open field. The stock curse of investigative work. Clues were at a premium. Riddles were easy to come by.

I checked in with Ernest, Monty, Smoky, and Winston. None of them had seen or heard anything more about Buzz Cut. There was no sign of the sapphire Jaguar. If Buzz Cut had vamoosed, so had our chances of catching the killers. Even with a sworn confession in hand by whoever hired them that would not guarantee their apprehension. Professional assassins know how to vanish.

As party to my follow-ups, I visited Diva to question Judith Hardy. Hardy was none too hospitable. My free pass had been revoked. I was escorted to Hardy's office by armed uniformed security. Five minutes of her valuable time was all I was allotted. Hardy denied Windell's itinerary ever existed in her boss's personal computer files. She hadn't looked into the Jaguar incident. Too busy, Hardy said. Ms. Hardy was all business in attire and manner.

When I asked to see Mr. Farhletti, Ms. Hardy coolly informed me his attorney had a restraining order issued to keep me away from him. No doubt, a good idea. It would help to villainy me at the divorce proceedings. Farhletti did not have legitimate grounds to acquire a restraining order. What he had was money and powerful associations. It was of no consequence. Anything I needed to know about Mr. Farhletti I could learn from the people around him hospitable or not.

Hardy did not know where Benton Lawson was and she was furious about his mysterious disappearance. Without him, "The Project," as she referred to the Universal Translator could not proceed. Lawson had been missing since the day after our car pool conference. I only hoped that Lawson had taken my advice and left the country.

I knew Judith Hardy had pieced together who had leaked the information to me about the itinerary and the Universal Translator. Benton Lawson had gone from the doghouse to the outhouse in her mind. If Hardy didn't need Lawson, he'd be out on the street in a grocery cart. After precisely five minutes the armed security guards who had escorted me in escorted me back to my car and made certain I was on my way. People were getting nervous. That was a good sign. Nervous people make mistakes. If there were any ties between Antonio Farhletti and the person responsible for the murder of Clinton Windell, it could have a ripple effect that might centrifuge the culprits. It wasn't as rewarding as rattling Andrea Bettencourt was but for the moment, I'd take what I could get.

***

I paid Stuart Wu a visit. Mr. Wu proved more of an ally than I would have believed after our first meeting. He was happy to give me a rundown on all of the board members not excluding himself. Nothing Wu told me incriminated any of them including Andrea Bettencourt. When I asked Wu if he thought Mrs. Bettencourt capable of murder his reply was typical for Mr. Wu: "Aren't we all? If you're asking if she's responsible for Mr. Windell's murder I don't believe so." That was how we left it.

There was one clear advantage I still had going for me. I had the immense dossier on Clinton Windell. All the information and events surrounding the life of Clifton Windell were fresh in my mind. According to my phantom sources, Clinton Windell's mentor Geoffrey Bellingham was a man who did whatever it took to get what he wanted. Since I believed what Mark Strait had told me, his deceased employer proved to be no different from his mentor possibly taking it to the extreme. No wonder a number of people hated Clinton Windell. With Mark Strait no longer a suspect the sole heir to the Windell murder became Andrea Bettencourt.

I had to admit Destini had gotten to me with her comment about Andrea Bettencourt. Bettencourt didn't strike me as patient or reserved. She would have had to show a great deal of restraint to lie in wait long enough to hatch a plan to avenge her husband's death. I still didn't believe Genevieve Windell was behind it. That left me rustling for plausible leads or fresh suspects.

I sent an e-mail soliciting assistance to the Internet address my phantom employers had given me. A one-sentence reply came back almost instantly: "Mr. Cavanaugh: let Mrs. Bettencourt go."

While I disliked living in a fishbowl, I had come to respect my employers. They managed to give Renita and me enough space to do our jobs while keeping a taut line of surveillance on us and who knows whom else. I decided to take a different approach to the Windell case. It was time to confront my prime suspect.

CHAPTER TWENTY-EIGHT

"Cavanaugh," Bettencourt said with her hand extended. Her greeting was as cool as her expression and handshake. Andrea Bettencourt was not pleased to see me. She had gotten a slight tan since the last time I saw her and her hair and nails had been recently done. Bettencourt was wearing a gray gabardine suit with a pink rose pinned to the lapel. The rose suited the color in her cheeks. I made a mental note of the changes. We sat across from each other. Bristling with confidence from behind her desk, Andrea Bettencourt attempted to stare me down.

"Where is Ms. Harris?" Bettencourt asked with a smug tone in her voice.

"Her whereabouts are none of your concern," I said.

I didn't tell Renita I was visiting Andrea Bettencourt. The last thing I wanted was to disappoint my partner but there are some battles one must go at alone. Andrea Bettencourt liked Renita. She resented me. I didn't care why. Her resentment played in my favor. Bettencourt had no choice but to deal directly with me without Renita to bounce off her quips. Bettencourt was accustomed to fastballs. She would not be prepared for a slow curve.

"Have you found our gems?" Bettencourt asked.

There was no need to inform Bettencourt their gems were in all likelihood history. I decided it would be wiser to let Carl deliver that news. "I haven't," I answered.

"Find the gems you'll find the killer," Bettencourt said.

"Killers, two bullets, different guns," I said.

Andrea smiled as if pleased by the thought. Her smile vanished just as quickly. "What is it you want Cavanaugh? I'm busy."

"Who's responsible for your courier services?" I asked.

"For the purchasing and transporting of uncut gems you mean?"

"Yes."

"We have a short list of authorized elite professionals who select gems and negotiate price on our behalf," Bettencourt said. "Windell was making an unscheduled buy in an effort to prove to the board he had not lost his touch."

"Do any of your couriers have the initials D.M.?"

"Should they?" Bettencourt asked raising a curious eyebrow.

"Guess not," I said.

Bettencourt thought for a moment. "No," she answered. I paused for an instant as if pondering her answer.

"Do you know anyone with those initials?" I asked.

"No. What is this about?"

"Just fishing," I said. The letter I had printed from Windell's dossier to get Strait's fingerprints had come to mind. For some reason it had become important although I couldn't quite distinguish why.

"Do you handle procuring couriers?" I asked.

"I never did."

"Who does?"

"Patrick Kemery, mostly, I see no reason to alter that arrangement. Except for his dealings with Windell, he's been doing an admirable job." Andrea Bettencourt spoke as if the mantle of leadership was already hers. I suppose in a way it was. Nice turnaround for someone who was almost out of a job.

"How did Mr. Kemery feel about having his responsibilities undermined?" I asked.

"I imagine he felt about the same as he will if I become the new CEO. He was not pleased. Patrick has a difficult time dealing with these sorts of issues. Even I realized what Windell was doing was not personal. It was simply business."

I've come to understand what is truly meant by nothing personal just business. Loosely translated if I screw you it's just business. If you screw me then it's personal.

"Why did Mr. Windell find it necessary to handle this purchase?" I asked.

"As I said before, Windell was attempting to prove to the board he had not lost touch with the heartbeat of our business. For the last couple of years several of his authorized purchases were of subpar quality."

"Wouldn't Patrick Kemery ultimately be responsible?"

"Kemery makes the arrangements. He gives the stones a glancing seal of acceptance. The CEO makes final approval. Windell had been slipping. The quality of uncut gems he was letting by was getting worse with each successive purchase over the last year in particular. His track record was in serious jeopardy. Windell was on the verge of being ousted."

"I heard if anyone was going to be ousted it would be you," I said.

"Where'd you hear that?"

"From a reliable source."

"By reliable source you mean a board member I take it."

"Could be."

"Don't believe everything you hear Cavanaugh. If rumors were true, I would have been gone a long time ago. But I'm still here."

"Are you the CEO of Bellingham Jewelers?"

"Not officially," Bettencourt said. "I'm currently handling all CEO duties. Only the board and stockholders can say. However, I would expect so. I have the experience, intelligence, and savvy to keep Bellingham at the forefront of the jewelry business."

"I'm not a stockholder," I said. "You don't have to sell me."

"I wasn't trying to."

"Why do you think Mr. Windell started botching purchases?"

"It's no secret my husband was the one who did the final review of the gem stones Cavanaugh. He had an eye like no other. He could hold a stone in his hand and tell from its feel what it was worth and how its beauty could best be brought to light. Once Harvey died, Windell had to do the job himself. That was when his incompetence showed."

"Was it necessary for the CEO to sanction every gem purchase?"

"It's a mandate of the position. Set down by Geoff Bellingham himself."

"Back to your husband, you believe Mr. Windell murdered him?"

"I know he did."

"How?"

"What?"

"How do you know?"

"Because I knew what kind of man Windell was."

"Careful you don't become that which you despise."

"A private dick and tea leaf philosopher. How quaint. Do you read palms as well?"

I had that coming. I let it go and pressed on. "If Mr. Windell relied so heavily on your husband why would he kill him?"

"What's your point?"

"Why kill someone who is so valuable to you? It doesn't make sense."

Bettencourt shrugged her shoulders. "Who knows why Windell did half the things he did."

"Did Mr. Windell strike you as irrational or impulsive?" I asked.

"He did not strike me at all but to answer your question no."

"Was he the type of man who was prone to bad judgment or poor intuition?"

"I can't honestly say he was."

"I never met Mr. Windell. Yet from what I know of him he didn't seem the sort of man who would murder someone without what he would have regarded as ample provocation, particularly someone who was as necessary to him as your husband, someone who was already under his thumb according to you and everyone else I've spoken to regarding Mr. Bettencourt."

"What are you driving at?"

"If your husband was murdered by Mr. Windell what was his motive?"

"I don't know jealousy of my husband's abilities. Fear Harvey might expose him for the fraud he really was."

I had her oh and two. Bettencourt had taken great swings at a couple of pitches but she couldn't keep the ball in the playing field. The setup was in place. It was time for my slow curve.

"Or blackmail," I said.

Andrea Bettencourt leaned in close. She wanted the ultimatum in her hushed voice not to be mistaken for anything other than it sounded, "If you have something to say Cavanaugh say it. Otherwise get out of my office."

"Let's suppose your husband was blackmailing Mr. Windell," I said. "That would explain the exorbitant consulting fee deposited into his personal checking account each month exclusively endorsed by Mr. Windell."

"That proves nothing," Bettencourt said.

"That would also explain why you received a consultant fee of twice that amount deposited into your personal checking account after your husband's death."

"Windell paid me a consultant fee outside of my regular job requirements. So what that isn't uncommon for a person in my position."

"What did you consult Mr. Windell on?"

"A variety of company matters."

"Name a few."

"You have no authority to question me like this."

"You're right," I said. "These questions will be elementary compared to what my law enforcement colleagues will ask once they get wind of those suspicious deposits."

"Your law enforcement colleagues are already aware of my consultant fees and are fully convinced they are legitimate sources of income."

"I'm certain the police are not aware of the coincidence that your consulting fees were double those of your husband's. Just as I am certain they were unaware your husband received an exclusive consulting fee from Mr. Windell."

"Are you threatening me?"

"I'm simply pointing out the advantages of cooperating with me."

Andrea Bettencourt hesitated for a moment. She was trying to determine if I was bluffing. I wasn't. Bettencourt walked over and opened the door. She peered out. I assumed to see who might be within earshot. Satisfied, she gently closed the door and returned to her seat. I watched her every move.

"About three years before Harvey's death," Bettencourt said, "my husband came upon a man who was in the Navy with Windell. They got to talking over a few drinks. The man told Harvey about a smuggling operation Windell was reputed to have run while they served together in the Navy."

"Who was this man?"

"I don't know. Harvey never told me. Harvey hired private investigators to look into what the man had told him. His investigators were competent—unlike you. They dug up enough circumstantial evidence to make the man's claims feasible. Harvey never acquired any hard evidence mind you but he had enough to make Windell squeamish."

"That was why Windell gave your husband back his job."

"Adding on the consultant fee."

"Why do you think Windell decided to end that arrangement?"

"I warned Harvey not to push it. He thought Windell was not giving him the recognition he deserved. Harvey was still working in the shadows while Windell basked in the glory of Harvey's efforts. Harvey threatened to go public with what he had learned if Windell did not make him a full-fledged executive board member. Windell realized he couldn't do that without bringing a good deal of attention upon himself. He was already showing favoritism toward me because of what Harvey knew. Meeting Harvey's demand would have prompted a full-blown executive inquiry. Either way Windell was in deep trouble. I suppose that's when Windell elected to take his chances by eliminating my husband."

"How did you get involved?"

"While Harvey was alive I knew nothing about the details of what Harvey had on Windell. Harvey said it was for my own safety. After my husband's death a package arrived that contained everything. There was a letter explaining Harvey's arrangement with Windell. Along with a flash drive containing copies of scanned documents showing information about dates, times, doctored manifests and suspicious payments that indirectly linked Windell to naval smuggling operations."

"Why didn't you go to the police or naval authorities with this information?"

"None of the documents had Windell's name on them. Most were signed by some numbskull named Mark Strait. Windell was the officer in charge of what Strait did. On the whole Windell was lastly responsible."

"How do you know Mark Strait wasn't operating on his own?"

"Because when I confronted Windell with what I had his eyes told me the truth. You don't work with someone for years and not recognize his poker face. Windell knew all about it."

"What about Mark Strait?"

"What about him?"

"Did you talk to him?"

"I never met the man. There was no need. Windell was the one I wanted. I cared nothing about Mark Strait."

There was a lull in our banter. Two gunslingers sizing each other up.

"So where do we go from here?" Bettencourt asked.

I stood and walked to the door satisfied I had gotten a strikeout. Before I opened the door, I looked into Bettencourt's eyes. I could see she was nervous even through her poker face. Bettencourt wasn't writhing with remorse for what she had done. She sat erect behind her mahogany desk staring back at me.

"I'm going back to work Mrs. Bettencourt," I said. "If I were you I'd get rid of any physical evidence you have on the matter we just discussed."

"I'm way ahead of you Cavanaugh."

"Of that I have no doubt."

"One final question," I said placing a hand on the doorknob. Bettencourt nodded. "Did you arrange for the murder of Clinton Windell?"

Without hesitation she answered, "I did not." She paused for a moment before continuing. "For once in his paltry life Windell was as precious to me as platinum. With that scum breathing I was assured the CEO charge not that I won't get the appointment anyway."

Andrea Bettencourt was a blackmailer but she wasn't the brains behind the murder. On the other hand, she had been the second person to say Windell was a more valuable asset than liability alive. Someone thought the opposite. I needed something tangible to lead me to them— and fast.

"Any idea of who might have set this whole thing up?" I asked.

"I thought you asked your final question."

"Sometimes one question automatically leads to another."

"I wouldn't tell if I had any idea."

"Me?"

"Or anyone else. If you should capture—"

"When Mrs. Bettencourt, it's only a matter of time."

"When you *capture* the people responsible for killing Windell tell them I said thanks."

"Mrs. Bettencourt," I said opening the door to leave, "that is something you will have to do yourself."

CHAPTER TWENTY-NINE

One week had gone by and all that had changed was the weather. Rain was a constant joined by lower temperatures and shorter days. Renita and I beat our heads against the wall hoping to discover something we missed. Destini and David were not faring any better.

Eliminating Andrea Bettencourt as my prime suspect did more good than harm. I had so convinced myself of her guilt that every road I traveled I sought the paths leading back to her. The ones that did delivered unexpected and disappointing results.

One of the most elementary questions any investigator should ask oneself had gone by the wayside. Who had the most to gain from Clinton Windell's death? I suppose I could blame it on the unusual way this case came about. If I found the answer to that question, it would in all likelihood be the key to enlightenment.

So far, not Genevieve Windell, Mark Strait or the executive board of Bellingham Jewelers fit that description. Everyone Renita and I talked to had more to lose—or nothing at all to gain—from Clinton Windell's demise. Even The Willamette Times had dropped the story.

Perhaps that meant robbery was the primary goal of the intruders. The murder was additional insurance of escape. The gems still had not surfaced. From what we had learned so far, they probably wouldn't. Why did the murderers go to Windell's home? What was the significance? There had to be at least a dozen places from the time Windell took possession of the stones to the time he arrived home they could have successfully robbed and murdered him. Mark Strait might have indirectly answered that question. Maybe it didn't have any special significance except that it was controlled, isolated and a place the victim would let down his guard. The setup had all the earmarks of professional robbers.

The murder had all the earmarks of professional assassins. A lethal combination but not unheard of.

It was three-thirty-seven when the phone rang. I know because I looked at my computer clock when it did.

"Mark Strait is dead." It was Destini.

"M.O.?" I asked.

"Shotgun blast through the back of his head."

Whoever did it probably used Strait's shotgun, I thought.

"The call came in from the Troopers when I got into the office this morning," Destini said. "David and I took the police chopper down to the scene."

"PPB's own version of Air Force One, I'm impressed."

"Kiss my keister C. J." This case must have been more of a strain on Destini than I realized. She was in no mood for jokes. It didn't mean I wouldn't stop trying to cheer her up.

"The Troopers hadn't disturbed anything," Destini said. "From the looks of the murder scene it went down like this: Strait dug his own grave. An open body bag was laid in the grave. Strait kneeled at one end of the body bag. His head was down judging by the direction of the entry wound. I'm guessing he was forced to bow his head so the shot would propel his body into the bag."

"Maybe he was praying," I said.

"Amen," Destini said without missing a beat. "Strait toppled forward into the grave after the killer shot him. The killer zipped up the bag, filled in the grave and left Strait to rot. Some hikers stumbled onto the body about a mile from Strait's hideaway."

I couldn't say I was surprised. Disappointed, yes, I halfheartedly hoped Strait had gotten away. "Sounds like the killer wanted the body found," I said.

"What makes you say that?"

"Body bag, shallow grave."

"Or the killer could've been in a hurry. A body bag would keep the corpse from decomposing as fast. Animals wouldn't find it as easily."

"I disagree," I said, "any clues?"

"None yet, if there had been any they were trampled by animals and human traffic that's been through here lately. What do you mean you disagree?"

"Think it's the same killers?" I asked wanting to find out as much as I could before Destini turned the tables.

"Of course Strait's murder could be linked to Windell's. Right now there's no evidence to suggest that."

"Good answer. Save that one for the press."

"There was one positive thing that came out of this ugly affair," Destini said.

"What?"

"Going through Strait's pants' pockets I found a key."

"That's why I keep my eye on you. Turn my back for one minute and you're rummaging through another man's pants."

"That's sick C. J. even for you. You're lucky I'm not there. I'd club you for that one."

"That's why I said it over the phone."

"You and your tired jokes. Don't try making it a career."

"I'm keeping my day job."

"Are you listening C. J.?" Destini's irritation was unmistakable. My lame gallows humor would have to wait another day.

"Yes detective," I said in answer to her question.

"The key was an easy trace. We found papers in Strait's cabin that led us right to it. It belonged to a safe deposit box in Vancouver, Washington under the name of Duncan Minor. You wouldn't believe what was in it.

"Astound me."

"Detailed information on the smuggling operations Windell and Strait ran while they were in the Navy. Letters, documents, copies of naval manifests, Swiss Bank account numbers, money transfers to the U.S., and last, but certainly not least, a handwritten outline of Clinton Windell's robbery and murder. Right down to getting Strait to give Pamela Windell sleeping pills. You told me Strait and Windell were into smuggling but you would be amazed to what extent. It's a good thing they're already dead. With the evidence we currently have in our possession Strait and Windell would be put away for life."

"Who's behind all of this?" I asked.

"I'm getting to that," Destini said. "It seems Genevieve Windell and Mark Strait go back a ways. They wrote love letters to each other while she was a young, impressionable resident of Switzerland. They were still in love according to what we found in Strait's deposit box. There was a covenant—albeit written by Strait—for them to be together for life. And guess who Strait named as the brains behind it all?"

"Genevieve Windell," I said in disbelief.

"Bingo," Destini said.

I was startled, not in the fact Strait had a safe deposit box but that he would incriminate Genevieve Windell. It made no sense.

"Too clean, too coincidental," I said.

"Pardon?"

"Have you talked to the widow Windell about this?"

"At length," Destini said. "We have her in lockup."

"It's a setup," I said.

"We've got her dead to rights."

"I still believe she's innocent."

"As sin maybe," Destini said.

I had no response.

"There are love letters in Strait's safe deposit box addressed to him from a Genevieve Wissmann talking about her intimate feelings and their lifelong friendship. There are explicit entries in Strait's diary—"

"*Diary?*"

"His *diary.*"

"Strait kept a diary?"

"Apparently," Destini said.

Strait didn't strike me as the type of man prone to chronicling his life's experiences.

"In his diary," Destini went on to say, "Strait talked about the Lotus Room fire and how each thought the other dead. It was shortly after the fire Genevieve Wissmann met her husband. After Genevieve discovered Mark Strait was alive, she wanted to be with him but she also wanted to keep her husband's money. Genevieve talked Windell into arranging things so that Strait could become their butler. Strait having blackmail information didn't hurt. Did you know Strait and Genevieve Windell were lovers?"

"I didn't know because it wasn't true," I said. "Strait told me so himself."

"What Strait told you doesn't correspond with what he's written in his diary. Mark Strait was the man Genevieve Windell was having an affair with and there's a lot more. According to Strait, Genevieve Windell was a part of their smuggling operation—and, oh yeah—there are pictures too. Of Ms. Wissmann when she was, let's just say free of spirit."

"You can't be buying this?"

"Do you have hard evidence to dispute it?"

"It's still one person's word against another."

"What we have is the equivalent of a dying man's confession."

"You've charged her?"

"You better believe it, first degree murder."

"This is all wrong."

"Genevieve Windell has been formally charged with the murder of her husband. If you can disprove the charges, I suggest you do it. If not back off because as far as I'm concerned this case is rock solid."

"Have you talked to Frank Strait?" I asked.

"Are you trying to tell me how to do my job?" Destini said.

"No detective."

There was a disquieting pause. "We haven't been able to locate Frank Strait," Destini said.

Try dragging the Willamette River, I thought. "Something in my gut tells me she's innocent," I said.

"Indigestion get an antacid."

"Could be," I said. I didn't want to provoke an argument. Destini didn't need the aggravation and I needed information.

"Some of our evidence is in Genevieve Windell's own handwriting," Destini said. "We've had a handwriting expert verify hers, Mark Strait's and Clinton Windell's. He's willing to testify in court that Genevieve Windell did the handwritten blueprints outlining the Windell murder. I thought you'd like to know if his *opinion* means anything to you."

"What's a frame without an expert testimony to support it?" I said.

"Or evidence Genevieve Windell thought Strait had destroyed."

"Fairly stupid for a mastermind don't you think?"

"Being a bit facetious aren't we?"

"Suspicious of false evidence."

"You and I usually see eye-to-eye on most cases," Destini said. "What's got you so bugged about Genevieve Windell setting up the whole thing?"

"It's too pat. She loved her husband. She loves her daughter and wouldn't deprive her of her father. She's not a greedy person, and no means, no motive, no opportunity."

"Obviously you're not listening because I've been pointing out motive long before this. Now we've added means and opportunity."

"Maybe it's only my intuition," I said.

"You're willing to toss everything out the window because none of the hard evidence we have matches your gut feelings?" Destini said.

"Works for me," I said.

"It doesn't for me—or my partner—or my captain, which is why Genevieve Windell is in custody."

"What else did you find in Strait's safe deposit box?"

"Nothing."

Mark Strait had probably turned over most of the money he made from the robbery to his father for safekeeping. There was no need to tell anyone about it until this case was over.

"What about the gems?" I asked.

"They weren't there."

"Did the plan say where they would be?"

"No."

"Don't you find that odd?"

"Yes and no," Destini said. "They probably met someplace and decided what to do with them afterwards."

"Where?"

"I don't know."

"The plan didn't say?"

"C. J. this has become tiresome. If you come up with some hard evidence let me know. In the meantime stay out of my way."

"Can I talk to Genevieve Windell?" I asked.

"About what," Destini said.

"To hear her side of the story," I said.

"I know you're not going to try to spring this woman."

"I need to get all of the facts consolidated for my insurance report. You know Carl everything above board. He wants firsthand testimony from the would-be benefactor even if she is a murderer."

"What I *know* is you've been handing me a line of bull since this case began." Destini sighed. She really was getting fried. "If you hurry you should be able to get in a few words before her attorney arrives to arrange bail."

"I'm on my way," I said.

"No congratulations?"

"In due time detective, we have yet to travel that final mile."

"See you when you get here."

Renita had been standing in the doorway listening to my end of the conversation. I gave her the edited version of recent events. Renita wanted to come with me to the precinct. I asked her to run a check on guests who stayed at the Heathman Hotel the week of Clinton Windell's murder instead. "Concentrate on people who paid cash," I said. "Also see what you can find out about twenty-million dollars in cash being withdrawn from any of the local banks during that same dark week." Renita wasn't happy about—what she regarded as—being left behind. I managed to convince Renita of how important it was to both finding the killers and Genevieve Windell's freedom. Renita reluctantly gave in. My knuckles were tingling. This was the beginning of something huge.

CHAPTER THIRTY

The death of Mark Strait turned out to be a break in the Windell case. It verified the killers were still about if nothing else. Unless I missed my guess, they would stick around long enough to make certain their plan to frame Genevieve Windell had worked.

I jogged to the downtown precinct where they were holding Genevieve Windell. The lobby was chock full of newspaper and television reporters. Word of Mrs. Windell's arrest had obviously leaked. The sharks smelled blood and were circling for the kill.

David met me by the front entrance. He ushered me to an interrogation room where Destini was waiting. I heard someone call my name on the way. It was Shawn Calloway. I chose to ignore him. Shawn could wait. Genevieve Windell could not.

David and I remained quiet after a handshake and quick greeting. For an investigator who was half of the team who collared the brains behind Portland's biggest homicide case David didn't seem pleased. Neither did Destini when David opened the door to the interrogation room. I soon discovered our last conversation was at the forefront of her displeasure.

The IR smelled of cheap cigarettes. Two beat-up chairs and a battered wooden table that wouldn't get five bucks at a flea market was the only furniture in the room. The walls were scarred from physical confrontations and vented frustrations. To my right was a two-way mirror. I doubted anyone was on the other side. In many ways this was more personal than business. It was between Destini and me.

Destini looked tired. The Windell case had taken its toil. "Have a seat." I did as the detective ordered. This was her house. I sat at one end of the table and folded my hands before me. Destini remained standing at the other end. "Before I let you see Genevieve Windell, I want some straight answers." I nodded. "Who are you working for?"

"Carl Wheaton at Lunsford Insurance," I answered.

"Wheaton's your only client?"

"Yes," I said.

Lying to Destini wasn't getting any easier. It was the facade that was becoming more proficient. Destini stared into my eyes. She was checking for that glint of deception. In my head I recited The United States Declaration of Independence: *THE UNANIMOUS DECLARATION OF THE THIRTEEN UNITED STATES OF AMERICA, WHEN in the Course of human events, it becomes necessary for one people to dissolve the political bands which have connected them with another, and to assume among the powers of earth, the separate and equal station to which the Laws of Nature and of Nature's God entitle them, a decent respect to the opinions of mankind requires that they should declare the causes which impel them to the separation—We hold these truths to be self-evident, that all men are created equal, that they are endowed by their Creator with certain unalienable Rights, that among these are Life, Liberty and the pursuit of Happiness.*

"We'll let that slide for now," Destini said about my response to her client question. "Why is Renita living in your house?"

"It was like I told you before. A stalker—"

"Don't give me that shit. I didn't buy it then and I'm not buying it now." Destini waited for a response. I stoically sat knowing anything I'd say would be a lie.

"So that's your story and you're sticking to it," Destini said.

"I've told you all I can," I said.

"That's not good enough," Destini said. "Don't forget I'm the officer in charge of a murder investigation."

"Being a fellow investigator I hope you'll understand the necessity for certain confidentialities."

"What I understand is up until now your secrecy has been tolerable. We've gone our separate ways on this case, which has worked so far. We have a prime suspect with a mountain of evidence against her and you're seeking ways to discredit it. I want to know everything Strait told you and everything you saw and heard when you were with him in Detroit."

I filled Destini in on most of the details. Most of it was a reiteration of what I'd previously told her. As strongly as I believed Genevieve Windell was innocent withholding information from Destini that she was bound to uncover did Mrs. Windell no good. Destini asked why I neglected to mention Genevieve Windell's past as a stripper. I told her I didn't think it was relevant. Destini believed me probably because I was telling the truth. The only thing I didn't tell Destini about was my phantom employer and their involvement in this case.

"We're both after the same thing," I said, "the truth."

"I suppose some people merit more convincing than others in that area," Destini said.

"What's gotten into you?" I asked. "You're the one who's normally the skeptic. Evidence like this would typically make all sorts of bells go off."

"This case isn't typical now is it? In answer to your first question, you're what's gotten into me C. J. And I don't mind saying I'm disappointed in you."

"In what?" I asked as if I didn't already know.

"You're lying to me," Destini said.

"I'm doing my job."

"So am I," Destini said. "You know as well as I do that the last thing we wanted to do was arrest Genevieve Windell for the murder of her husband but all of the facts point to her; her affair with Mark Strait, Clinton Windell filing for a divorce that included full custody of their daughter. Their prenuptial agreement left her out of her husband's millions. Genevieve Windell had enough personal resources to pay a couple of axes to do the job. Her association with Mark Strait landed her inroads into organized crime, an organization notorious for—if I haven't missed a news flash to the contrary—supplying murderers for hires. What else do you need videotape?"

"That would help," I said. "You've checked Genevieve Windell's financial records. She's hardly penniless. Her husband was rescinding his divorce decree, and even if he wasn't there's no way any judge would declare her an unfit mother. According to Mrs. Windell she broke off her affair—and it wasn't with Mark Strait."

"Who was it then?" Destini asked.

"I don't know."

"You don't know. Maybe I can help. According to Mrs. Windell she was having an affair with Patrick Kemery."

"The same Patrick Kemery who sits on the board of Bellingham Jewelers?"

"None other," Destini said.

"Did you check him out?"

"There you go again telling me how to do my job."

"Sorry," I said.

"Kemery denies the whole thing."

"Do you believe him?"

"On the night of the murder," Destini said, "Patrick Kemery was at a benefit party for muscular dystrophy. There are at least twenty people ready to sign sworn affidavits to that effect. Kemery has no connections with known felons in his background. His sheet's so clean its blank."

"There's always a first time," I said.

"Today won't be his."

"Why would she lie? Particularly about something you'd have no trouble checking out?"

"She's desperate," Destini said. "Which is another reason I don't want you involved. In her situation she'll say anything to get off."

"I'm not gullible."

"But you're stubborn. Remember the Bronski case?"

The Bronski case was my personal Waterloo. I wasn't long retired from the DEA and I needed something to believe in again. Larry Bronski was strangled and robbed of $472.73 while walking home from work late one night through Laurelhurst Park. Destini and David had found the murder weapon in Gene Pringle's basement. Forensics found hair and blood samples on the scene that matched Pringle's. They also found footprints that were exact impressions of a pair of shoes Pringle owned with soil from the crime scene still embedded in their soles. Fibers found at the scene were a precise match to clothes Pringle had recently worn. Add to that the ME's findings of skin underneath Bronski's fingernails that matched Pringle's and the case was a lock.

The only loophole was Pringle's eight-year-old son. Jay backed his father's story he was home with him all night on the night of Bronski's murder. I believed Jay and worked feverishly to prove his father's alibi. I was made the fool in the end. It turned out Jay was asleep when Gene Pringle murdered and robbed Larry Bronski. Destini proved it. Jay didn't know. Destini wouldn't have brought that up had she not felt the necessity to bring me to my senses.

"This case is different," I said. "I've drawn my conclusions based solely on the facts. Not from the dreamy-eyed face of a child."

"Don't you see the similarities?" Destini said.

"I was wrong about Pringle."

"You believed Pringle though didn't you?"

"Yes," I said.

"Why?"

"Where's this going detective?"

"It's Pamela Windell isn't it? She's the reason you're so set on proving Genevieve Windell innocent."

"Pamela Windell has nothing to do with it," I said. Destini was right. Pamela Windell had a good deal to do with it. While I believed Genevieve Windell innocent before I met her daughter, I knew there would be no chance of convincing Destini without concrete proof.

"Yeah it's her alright," Destini said. "You have a weakness for children. You can't let that blind you to the evidence."

Bebe Assassino came to mind. "Not all children."

"I know Pamela Windell makes you want to believe her mother is innocent. She's not."

"You've got the wrong person."

"Is that your expert opinion? Or are you speaking from your heart?"

"That and the facts."

"If Genevieve Windell was childless would you still believe in her innocence?" Destini asked.

"Let's just say witnessing life through the eyes of a young child is like seeing the world through the eyes of the universe."

"*Bravo* a Cavanaugh original?"

"I take the blame," I said.

"Impressive, now back to the case."

"Detective we merely interpret the so-called evidence differently. I believed what Mark Strait told me not what was found in his safe deposit box."

Destini was searching for answers to some of the moves I was making. Besides not buying the story about Renita, she was suspicious about the extent of my involvement in this case. My weakness for children would have been a plausible explanation.

"Possibly," Destini said. "One thing's for certain. Your recent behavior has been irrational."

"You know how I am when I'm focused on a case," I said.

"In that regard you're no different from me. Which is why I know there are things you haven't been telling me."

"Specifics, Destini."

"What good would it do C. J.? You'd only come up with another tall tale. I don't mind telling you I'm disappointed. I never thought you would lie to me."

"You'll have to trust me when I tell you Genevieve Windell is innocent."

"What I trust are solid facts. All of which say Genevieve Windell is responsible for her husband's murder."

"Can I speak to her?"

"Were you like this in the DEA?"

"Compared to my work in the DEA this is child's play."

"It's not to me," Destini said. "This is very, *very* serious. I want to know everything Genevieve Windell tells you in there. And I mean everything."

"Yes detective," I said.

Destini gave me her don't mess with me glare. "Don't hold out on me C. J. You do and I'll have you in a cell right next to the widow Windell. That'll give you all the time you'll need to get your head straight. Do I make myself clear?"

"Yes detective."

Destini gave me that look again. She knew me well enough to know I would do whatever I deemed necessary to prove Genevieve Windell innocent. Just as I realized Destini would be tugging relentlessly on the other end of that rope.

"Let's go," Destini said escorting me out of IR. Destini led the way to the detention area. Her silence was the only indication I needed of her mood. I questioned if this was worth it. Was anything worth risking losing the woman I loved? Stubbornness can be a curse as much as a blessing.

Staring into Destini's eyes before we left the IR, I did not see my love but an obstacle. Destini was another person who was to be left out of the loop. I had made the leap backwards, returned to the credo of my covert days. Trust only those you must. Emotion is your enemy, intuition your ally. Let your intellect rule. It had happened without my ever realizing it. I was lost in the fray.

Destini had the jailer unlock the cell. At that point, I wouldn't have been surprised if Destini didn't regard me as a criminal. My only hope was she would understand in the end or at least find enough forgiveness for me to continue our relationship. "Fifteen minutes," Destini said. "When you're done, show yourself out." With those words, Destini left me alone with Genevieve Windell.

CHAPTER THIRTY-ONE

Few people belong in a prison cell. Genevieve Windell was standing staring out of her cell window. She looked completely out of place wearing her own version of prison blues. Only hers was a tailor made wool double-breasted shell gray suit with matching Italian Loafers. Genevieve wore no jewelry. Even knowing why, I found it odd seeing her without any. One aspect still measured up. Her poise, distinction, and dignity held fast. You could see it in her upright posture and firm gaze. How long would they last under the onslaught she was about to encounter was the question? If there are times which try women's souls, this was one of them.

"We don't have much time so let me get right to it," I said. Ammonia cleaner only intensified the stench of urine in the cell. Genevieve didn't let on if she noticed.

"Is this your doing?" Genevieve Windell asked coming toward me. She stood before me as if expecting me to cower. I would have supposed she knew better by now.

"I don't believe you had anything to do with your husband's murder," I said.

"Then why am I here?"

"I'm an independent investigator. The Portland Police are a law enforcement agency. We operate under different principles. My clients are my major concern. The PPB's quest is strictly for justice."

"You call this justice?" Genevieve said.

"There is considerable evidence mounted against you," I said.

"Fabrications," Genevieve said.

"Do you have any idea how the handwritten plans outlining your husband's execution and robbery got into Strait's safe deposit box?"

"They are obviously forgeries."

"Not according to a handwriting expert for the police."

"Are you saying the police believe I orchestrated my husband's execution?"

"Unless you have another explanation of how they got there."

"I don't know," Genevieve said. "But I can assure you I didn't write them."

"What about the love letters?"

"They weren't love letters. They were more like correspondence between friends."

"Friends who became lovers."

"You've spoken to Mark."

"Yes."

"I suppose he told you about the Tulip Room?"

"He confirmed it," I said.

"Why doesn't Mark come forward with the truth?"

"He's dead," I said. Genevieve Windell was dumbfounded. She stumbled backwards falling onto her bunk.

"When?" Genevieve asked.

"The body was found this morning. They didn't tell you?"

"No."

Low blow Destini, I thought.

"Oh my God!" Mrs. Windell said. "Whose going to dispute what's in Mark's safe deposit box? There's no one to come forward with the truth!"

"I wouldn't go that far," I said.

"The police said Mark was blackmailing Clinton. Is that true?"

"I'm afraid so."

"They were smugglers in the Navy?" Genevieve said.

"Yes."

Genevieve Windell looked defeated for the first time since I entered the cell. I felt sorry for her. She had come to realize the man she loved and another she cared for were not at all the men she envisioned them to be.

"Mrs. Windell—"

"Genevieve, call me Genevieve, please."

"All right Genevieve. I need your help. Tell me everything you can about your husband and Mark Strait."

"Obviously that isn't much." Genevieve gave me the overview of her relationships with both her husband and Strait. She was definitely in the dark about their shared past.

"Is it true that Clinton may have been mixed up in murder as well?" Genevieve asked.

"I'm afraid so," I said.

"What a fool I've been. I knew Clinton wasn't a saint but," Genevieve sighed and then slid further back onto the bunk. Her eyes were disbelieving and distant. "I never imagined he would be mixed up in murder."

"Didn't you?" It came out harsh which was what I intended. Genevieve stared at me in shock. This was no time to screw around. If she knew something, it was time for her to spill it. Her life was literally on the line. Nice guys don't get that type of information.

"I should say not!" Genevieve said.

"In all of the years you've been with that man you've never come across evidence of his slimy secrets?"

"No!"

"Maybe you turned your back on what was there because you didn't want to know?" Genevieve Windell's stare shifted to the floor. She stood and walked back to the window. Genevieve looked back and forth out of the window and at me several times before she spoke again.

"I did ignore Clinton's past and many of his more current dealings. It was for Pamela's sake. She adored her father. I suppose I did not want to know. How does that saying go, ignorance is bliss? The more I allowed myself to live in the dark the less likely I was to leave Clinton."

"You were thinking of leaving your husband?"

"Yes." Genevieve walked toward me stopping halfway. Her face appeared drawn in the bland prison light. Her eyes were dim. Melancholy will do that to a person as well as numbing pain. Which Genevieve was experiencing was not clear.

"The intention behind my affair was to force Clinton to file for divorce. Guilt got the better of me. That and the fact no matter what I was in love with Clinton Windell. Before I could call it off Clinton found out about the affair. He filed for divorce without hesitation. I asked for another chance. Clinton was willing to grant me that opportunity before he was killed but that is another story."

"One day I'd like to hear it."

"I hope not to tell it to you from inside a prison cell." I nodded. Genevieve continued.

"Some time ago I accidentally came across another set of books my husband was keeping aside from our regular accounts. Clinton became furious when I asked him about them. He snatched the ledgers from me and locked them in his desk. I was stunned. I went into shock when he violently shook me by the shoulders. He ordered me not to ever breathe a word to anyone about them. I agreed of course. I was so frightened I would have agreed to anything at the time. Clinton had never lost his temper with me. The anger on his face. The fury in his eyes. It was as though he was a different person. I did as he ordered. At least I led Clinton to believe that was the case."

"You investigated?"

"I did," Genevieve said. "I made some discreet telephone inquiries under assumed identities. Asked several innocent sounding questions, got a number of startling answers. No one was the wiser."

"What did you find out?"

"Clinton had been skimming a few rough cut gems for himself from Bellingham purchases and selling them through third parties overseas."

"How long had this been going on?"

"According to the set of books I found for at least four years."

"How did he keep the extra income from surfacing?"

"A phony Swiss account."

"The name on the account wouldn't be Duncan Minor by any chance?"

"How did you know?"

"You can't teach an old dog new tricks; anything else?"

"I stopped looking after that. I was afraid of what else I might find."

"Did you know about the relationship your husband had with Mark Strait?"

"Not until you brought it up at our last meeting. I went to see Frank Strait after you left hoping he might tell me where his son had disappeared to so we could clear up what I was certain was a mistake. Mark's father said he had no idea where his son was. Another liar, like son, like father I suppose. How did I manage to make such terrible choices in men?"

"I had presumed you knew all along what your husband and Strait were involved in. I apologize. Have you seen Frank Strait since?"

"No he's probably in hiding by now."

I'll bet he's a lot closer than you know, I thought. My mind detoured toward Destini. How was I going to right things with her? When this case concluded Destini would recover but would our relationship?

Genevieve attempted a smile that failed miserably. I thought of Pamela Windell. I imagined Genevieve was much like her daughter at that age. I wanted to hug Genevieve, to reassure her she was not alone in this fight. To make her that fate-filled promise we all say to people in times of crises, "Everything will be all right." I didn't know that any more than Genevieve did. How could I? How could anyone?

"How's Pamela?" I asked.

"I haven't spoken to her since my arrest. I told my staff to tell her mommy needed time alone. She has already lost her father. Now she may lose her mother falsely accused or not. Detective Pendleton was kind enough to allow me to send her to my parents in San Francisco. At least there Pamela will be well cared for and hopefully sheltered from this madness."

"Is there anything else you can tell me that might help?" I asked.

"Nothing comes to mind," Genevieve answered. I walked up to her. "One other thing," I said almost as an afterthought. "Who were you having an affair with?" This was my test question. If she lied, I was walking away from her for good. I was not going to be made the fool again. "Patrick Kemery," she answered after a moment's hesitation. There was no involuntary tilt of her head. No toying with her fingertips. Genevieve Windell was telling the truth.

"Did Strait know it was Kemery?" I asked.

"Until Clinton found out Mark was the only one who did. Mark became furious when he found out. He threatened to expose my flirt with exotic dancing if I did not stop seeing Patrick. I refused. Fortunately, for me Mark never made good on his threat, which is why I can't believe he would set me up with the safe deposit box. How could he leave me such a legacy?"

Exotic dancing of itself is no big deal these days. For a woman of Genevieve Windell's stature it would make titillating press. Judging by what I had observed of Genevieve it would be a monumental embarrassment as well. "How did your husband find out about your affair?" I asked.

"I don't know," Genevieve said. My suspicion was that Strait told Clinton Windell. All was fair in love and war. After all, Strait did lure Genevieve to the States in an effort to trap her into falling in love with him. A man like that wouldn't think twice about taking advantage of an opportunity to win her hand. Strait may not have been as chivalrous as I thought.

"Did Kemery know about any of this?" I asked.

"Any of what?"

"Any of the things the police found in Strait's safe deposit box?"

"Not to my knowledge," Genevieve said.

"Have the police spoken to Kemery?"

"I don't know. To think I talked Clinton out of firing Kemery."

"Why was your husband going to fire Patrick Kemery?"

"As retaliation for the affair. If I knew then what I know now. Kemery and I would have never happened. I don't know what I ever saw in that man."

"You mean you wouldn't have had an affair?"

"I would have had the affair alright just with a better choice of lovers."

Some of the old fire was returning. Genevieve Windell would need every ember to survive the storm front ahead. My father has a saying, "Do nothing in the dark that cannot stand the light." Genevieve was living proof.

"Did Kemery know your husband's itinerary?" I asked.

"Time's up! Let's go." It was the jailer. He opened the cell door and stood off to the side.

"All of the board members did," Genevieve answered.

"Don't worry," I said. "Your attorney will be here shortly to get you out."

"It won't be soon enough," Genevieve said. After a heavy sigh, which sounded more like relief than sorrow, she said, "I didn't kill my husband Mr. Cavanaugh."

"I know," I said. Someone had managed to scratch out in the stone beneath the window a phrase I could just make out: "YOU HAVE THE GOD GIVEN RIGHT TO BURN IN HELL." I handed Genevieve one of my business cards.

"Call me if you think of anything else—or if you just need to talk."

"Thank you," she said. It was barely audible.

"Let's go Cavanaugh," the jailer said with an impatient edge. I walked out. The jailer slammed the cell door shut. You could hear the lock bang into place. What an awful sound, a reverberation of hopelessness resonating in your soul. I refused to look back at Genevieve Windell. I did not want to bear witness to justice detained.

CHAPTER THIRTY-TWO

Genevieve Windell was innocent. Andrea Bettencourt was a blackmailer but innocent of conspiracy to commit murder. Patrick Kemery had emerged as a player. Where did Kemery fit in? Why was he involved? More questions without answers.

Mark Strait had referred to the person in the back seat of the sapphire Jaguar as "she." Andrea Bettencourt had the chutzpah but not the expertise. Bettencourt despised guns according to our research. There was no other woman to suspect besides Genevieve Windell. That led to Mark and Frank Strait. One of which was dead. The other—I suspected—was fish food. I was missing someone, someone obvious. I didn't have a chance to pursue that line of thinking before Shawn Calloway caught up to me.

I had made my way out of a side exit to elude the press. No sooner had the door closed behind me when Shawn Calloway called my name. I turned to see Calloway a few yards away. He must have been waiting for me there. I wasn't going to avoid him any longer. What I didn't want him to know he wouldn't. It was as simple as that.

"What can I do for you Calloway?" I asked.

"You can start by telling me what you and Genevieve Windell discussed in there." Calloway had a digital recorder shoved under my nose.

"Who's to say I was having a discussion with Genevieve Windell?"

"Come off it Cavanaugh. Genevieve Windell's brought in for questioning. You show up and Liederman escorts you back toward the interrogation area. Next thing I know you're trying to sneak out of the precinct without as much as a hello. What did the widow have to say?"

"You know that's privileged information—and I wasn't sneaking anywhere."

"Since when did you become an attorney?"

"The same rules apply between an investigator and those involved in the investigation as far as I'm concerned."

"Why are you still investigating Genevieve Windell? Does she have anything to do with her husband's murder?"

"Those are not questions for me to answer," I said.

"You must suspect something," Calloway said. "Otherwise you would've given Lunsford Insurance the okay to issue the widow a check by now."

"The Windell insurance investigation is still pending. Mrs. Windell is only a part of that investigation."

"Who else is involved in your investigation?"

"Again privileged information," I said.

"Did Genevieve Windell confess to the murder of her husband?"

"Is that the word on the grapevine?"

"Did she?" Calloway asked.

"How many times must I tell you? My involvement in this case is strictly from an insurance investigation standpoint. Homicide is a police matter," I said walking away. Calloway followed attempting to keep his recorder under my nose. In his effort to keep pace Calloway dropped a manila folder he was holding under his left arm spilling its contents onto the ground. I helped Calloway scoop up the 8x10 color glossies.

"Isn't this a group photo of Bellingham's board members?" I asked about one of the photos.

"Yes what about it?" Calloway felt compelled to shove his recorder under my nose again. I wanted to shove it up his ass.

"Where'd you get this?" I asked studying the photograph.

"They're publicity shots. Bellingham's public relations people hand them out all the time. Have you got something Cavanaugh?"

"Only a case of stupidity," I said walking away. Calloway attempted to follow. "You'd better head back inside or you'll be the only reporter in this hemisphere who misses the police announcement on Mrs. Windell's situation and what precipitated it."

Calloway quickly considered what I said. "We're not through Cavanaugh," Calloway said rushing back toward the precinct.

I must have seen that photograph a half dozen times, in the Windell study, at the homes of various board members, in the newspapers and now from the armpit of Shawn Calloway. The only board member I had not personally questioned, the same man I saw meet Antonio Farhletti and Judith Hardy on the night Farhletti was so photogenic. Patrick Kemery. The what, who and why were no longer in question. Shoring my deductions with facts was another matter.

My first instinct was to have a talk with Kemery. I suppressed that impulse. It would be better if I kept that information to myself. Not even Renita could know. This was an ace up my sleeve. There was no need to sound the alarm. That might make the rats go underground. I needed to make certain they would continue to scavenge in the light. With Genevieve as good as convicted and Mark Strait dead, the person behind it all had to be feeling good about themselves. There was more here than gems and vendettas. This was shaping up to be full-scale international theft.

While helping Calloway recover his photos I noticed three people watching me: a man pretending to read a newspaper in a gray Toyota, a gaunt woman strolling near the south side of the precinct, and lastly an old man. The old man was across the street at a bus stop making his best effort to fit in amongst the five people waiting at the stop with him.

Calloway disappeared inside along with the rest of the reporters. I made a beeline for the old man. *Who knows?* I thought. *Maybe I could get the old man to tell me something important about this bizarre case.* All I knew is it was worth a try.

A bus pulled up. The old man was gone when it rolled away. He wasn't getting away that easily. Every bus stops at every other block in downtown Portland. I took off for the bus the old man had boarded knowing ahead of time where it would dock. I got there in time to board behind a teenager blaring Hip Hop music from the headphones of his smartphone. To make certain the old man hadn't disembarked through the back door, I kept an eye out for everyone and anything that moved. The old man wasn't amongst the previous group that disembarked. I had seen the bus the whole time.

There were only a handful of people on the bus. I strolled to the back keeping both eyes peeled for the old man. By the time the bus traveled a block, I'd realized I'd been duped. The old man wasn't on-board. He never was. I got off at the next stop and made my way to my car. I needed to see someone, a man who could unlock the final door to this mystery.

CHAPTER THIRTY-THREE

I parked catty-corner to Benton Lawson's house. Drawn drapes prevented me from seeing inside. There wasn't any mail or newspapers piled on the front porch. The place looked lived in but deserted, like a vacation home people visit only a few weeks out of a year. It was difficult for me to believe Lawson would have taken my advice. He didn't strike me as the type of man I would call a survivor. Lawson was anal, repressed and in love, not a person with keen instincts, daring and cunning. While Lawson wouldn't rush in to save Roxanna Farhletti from a burning building, he would sound the alarm. Something was wrong with his disappearance. I waited hoping to find out if my hunch was right.

Thirty-five minutes and nothing, I couldn't tell if anything was going on inside that house. I took a quick look around. The house was locked tight. I could see part of the living room and loft through the kitchen curtains. One of Lawson's computer monitors faced me from the loft. It had a screen saver of little Einstein busts floating across it. Everything seemed in order. I flirted with the idea of breaking in. Destini's face popped into my head like a warning sign not to do it. I was certain Lawson wasn't there. What I was looking for wasn't either. They had him. They'd probably had him all along.

I returned to the front of the house. Standing on the porch, I took a quick look around. The usual trackers were following me of course. I slipped a business card through Lawson's mail slot with my personal numbers and a written message on the back: "Need to talk ASAP about U-T."

I had made too many mistakes on this case. Even the obvious had rushed by me like a child on an amusement park ride. I should have picked up immediately on Andrea Bettencourt's blackmail scheme; been quicker to piece together Mark Strait and Clinton Windell's linked past;

smoked out Genevieve Windell, and recognized a connection between Patrick Kemery and Antonio Farhletti. My retirement from the DEA had clearly tarnished my skills. With time being at a premium, I wouldn't have an opportunity to work my way back into top shape. I would have to proceed believing things would continue to click as needed. Besides, I had guardian angels or at least watchdogs.

Before I headed back to the office, I decided to check in on Genevieve Windell. The Windell estate was swarming with all sorts of media people. Rent-a-cop security had barricaded the place making it inaccessible except for a temporary metal gate. I identified myself to the sergeant over the din of reporters barking at him. The sergeant telephoned the house. I was cleared to go in.

Genevieve was collapsed on the living room sofa. She appeared casual in her blue jeans, slippers, and pink cashmere sweater even if her mood wasn't. Genevieve was wearing a gold necklace. Dangling from it was a gold heart with a heart shape cut out of its center. I found that appropriate for her current situation. The first things Genevieve said she did when she got home were to take a shower then a bubble bath. Prison stench soils more than your clothes. It grates its way into your skin until it seems to permeate through your pores. Prolonged freedom is the only cleanser. Knowing you won't go back the only cure.

Genevieve had spoken to Pamela not long before. Her daughter had heard the report of her arrest on television. Genevieve said it took her nearly an hour to calm Pamela down. Trying to convince Pamela that her mommy didn't kill her daddy and would not go to jail were not easy tasks. Genevieve's attorney assured Genevieve that her chances for an acquittal were good. How he was going to discredit a mountain of dead man's evidence against his client was what I wanted to know. While I was there, I'd thought I'd see if I could help her attorney and me out.

"Do you mind if I question your household staff?" I asked.

"Regarding what?" Genevieve's response was reflexively. There was no bite to her curiosity.

"A variety of issues surrounding the week of your husband's…"

"Certainly," Genevieve said without resistance. "You may use the study."

I asked her not to get up. My advice to Genevieve was to put on good music, have a glass of wine, and let the day pass on its own accord. "Peace will come in its own time," I said.

"Thank you Mr. Cavanaugh but it's going to take more than encouraging words to get me out of this mess." Her voice was barely above a whisper.

"My friends call me C. J."

"You know the way to the study C. J.?"

"I do."

"The run of the house is yours. It doesn't feel like home anymore. It's as much a prison as that cell I was in earlier."

"I'll make this as brief as possible," I said. "Then I'll be on my way." Genevieve nodded, or rather she let her head fall forward then found only enough strength to bring it up halfway.

I independently questioned each member of the household staff. I asked them about Edward Sutherland a.k.a. Mark Strait, Clinton Windell, Antonio Farhletti, and Patrick Kemery. Besides unsubstantiated gossip, no one knew much. Most damaging was no one knew anything about an affair between Patrick Kemery and Genevieve Windell. That was until word had leaked about their affair to the media. Kemery had unequivocally denied it. He even suggested that the whole matter was fabricated to avert suspicion from Genevieve for her husband's murder. The sheer implication would poison any jury's opinion of her as if the affair itself were not enough believed or not.

As I was leaving, I wanted to stop in to wish Genevieve a good night. The door was closed. I heard the music from Swan Lake coming from within. I showed myself out.

When I returned to the office, Renita was leaving for the day. Renita had gotten the information I requested regarding reservations at the Heathman Hotel. During the week of Windell's murder, four people had paid in cash for their rooms. Only one of them rang a bell. Antonio Farhletti. Paying cash for a room was unusual in a business sense but befitting the scheme of this case. The twenty-million dollars in cash quest came up empty. That meant nothing. There were dozens of ways an influential person could come up with that kind of money not including illegal means.

I decided to stay a little longer at the office. I wasn't anxious to face Destini and it would give me an opportunity to plan how I was going to handle Kemery. I escorted Renita to her car filling her in on everything I learned that I wanted her to know. After a little serious badgering from me, Renita agreed to call me once she got home. My home, I had become so accustomed to the idea of her being there I had to remind myself of that fact. I felt the heat was off for the moment but if I had any say in the matter, it would soon be hotter than ever. I needed to make certain Renita remained alert.

CHAPTER THIRTY-FOUR

Most of us can't see beyond the nose on our face. I had omitted Kemery from my report. He wasn't vital to the adultery case against Antonio Farhletti. In what did Antonio Farhletti and Patrick Kemery have a shared interest? Whatever it was, I was certain it was illegal and mutually profitable. I didn't know much about Kemery but Farhletti never made moves that weren't geared toward profit. I needed hard facts. Questioning Kemery might get a few. More likely, it would do more harm than good. Whatever they had cooking, Farhletti would probably put a tight lid on it if he felt their plan was compromised. I needed a leak and I knew just who. Where to find him was still in question. Lawson didn't call. Judith Hardy did shortly after Renita had phoned to say she was home safe.

"I looked into that unusual incident you told me about the other day," Hardy said.

"Involving the Jaguar?" I asked.

"Yes," Hardy said, "it turns out the guards on duty that night were shirking their responsibilities. They had a poker game going in one of the back rooms. The two who said they saw the Jaguar skipped out on their rounds because they didn't want to leave the game. They weren't aware those back rooms have hidden surveillance cameras. It's all right here on this flash drive. Needless to say all four of those security people have been dismissed."

"Thanks for your assistance Ms. Hardy," I said.

"Not a problem," Hardy said. "I don't suppose you've changed your mind about what we discussed?"

"No I haven't."

"If you do you know where to reach me."

No sooner had I hung up the phone than I heard the door open. I quietly slid open my top right drawer and extracted my Glock. Roxanna Farhletti walked in. I hadn't seen her since I closed her adultery case. I managed to put my weapon away before she saw it. Mrs. Farhletti looked antsy. Dressed in a black satin gown, pearl necklace, pearl earrings, and a sable jacket Roxanna Farhletti marched into my office with all the stilted bearing they teach in beauty academies. Her brunette hair was a product of a top of the line hair salon. Her make-up was so deftly applied it hid any negatives and accented all of her positives including a small birthmark on her right cheek. Her medium brown eyes were as excitable as a child's. Except for a few womanly pounds, Roxanna Farhletti appeared ready to walk the runway for the Miss Oregon pageant again.

"I must speak with you," Roxanna said in that same urgent voice she used when we first met. I offered her a seat. She quickly sat then continued. In a nutshell, Roxanna explained that she and Lawson were having an affair.

"When did you and Lawson begin this affair?"

Mrs. Farhletti told me the tale of how Lawson was comforting her after she had confronted her husband about one of his flings. One thing led to another. The next thing she knew they were lovers again. Roxanna said they were still lovers when Lawson inexplicably disappeared. Mrs. Farhletti was confident Benton Lawson would not have vanished without letting her know why and to where. Roxanna Farhletti believed her husband found out about their affair and had Lawson murdered.

"Do you really think your husband is capable of such a thing?" I asked.

"It wouldn't surprise me," Roxanna said. "My husband is capable of anything Mr. Cavanaugh."

None of what I already knew was worth sharing with Roxanna Farhletti. My belief was Lawson was in danger. I expected he wasn't dead yet, and with a little luck I could keep it that way. I assured Mrs. Farhletti I'd look into the matter. It seemed to settle her down.

We left the office together. Her chauffeur was waiting. Roxanna Farhletti was on her way to the opera. Antonio Farhletti would be meeting her there. Roxanna offered me a ride. I politely refused. My car was parked only a few blocks away. The walk would give me time to finalize my plans. I only hoped I wasn't too late.

With Lawson out of the way, Strait dead, and Genevieve Windell a shoe-in for the conviction of the murder of her husband, there would be no need for Buzz Cut and his partner to stick around. I needed to give them a new target. How do I serve myself up to them? Then it dawned on me: Those who have one foot in the canoe and one foot in the boat are going to fall into the river. It was time to make my move.

CHAPTER THIRTY-FIVE

A visit to Patrick Kemery was in order. I was wrong to call them rats. The people involved in these crimes were more like quail. It was time to flush them out.

Destini had cracked the case. Not in the way she may have imagined but her arrest of Genevieve Windell based on evidence found in a safe deposit box of Mark Strait, a.k.a. Duncan Minor, brought forward a revelation of sorts, one that would take a little time to bring to light.

What would convince the killers to doubt their plan had succeeded in framing Genevieve Windell and that somehow, the finger of suspicion could point right at them?

The butler answered. I asked to see Patrick Kemery. His face twitched. The butler wasn't comfortable lying. "Mr. Kemery is attending the opera tonight," the butler said with a slight quiver in his voice.

"May I give him a message—when he returns?" If I had forced the issue, the distinguished gentleman would have folded easier than wet cardboard. It wasn't necessary to place him in that predicament.

I handed the butler one of my business cards that I had prepared especially for that situation. I had written on the back, "I know what you're up to. Call me."

To stir the brooding embers a bit I stressed to the butler it was imperative Mr. Kemery get in touch with me immediately. He inquired as to my reasons for such an urgent response. I told him it was regarding the Windell case. I made it clear there were a number of questions I had for Mr. Kemery including questions regarding his meeting with Judith Hardy and Antonio Farhletti at the Tea Room in the Heathman Hotel on the night of Clinton Windell's murder. The butler agreed to give Kemery the message. I went to my car and waited keeping an eye on the house.

A light came on in the study. A silhouette of the butler appeared from behind the closed curtains. A figure was seated behind what appeared to be a desk. The butler handed the figure something, my card I presumed. The seated figure erupted from his seat. His body language suggested he was irate. The butler was dismissed. The lone silhouette paced. The light went out. I waited a few minutes longer then left. My work there was done.

CHAPTER THIRTY-SIX

It was a gamble. If someone didn't shake the trees, the people behind this plot would get away with murder, international theft, and large-scale blackmail. Not to mention that an innocent woman could be convicted of a crime she didn't commit. Motives, opportunities and means, I had it all figured out. I hadn't a clue about how I was going to convince Destini to trust me again. That's what I was thinking about on the way home when my car phone rang.

It was Lawson. He sounded scared. He wanted to meet me at his house right away.

"It's crucial," Lawson said. "Mrs. Farhletti could be in danger."

When I tried to get him to elaborate Lawson kept stating he couldn't go into it over the phone, insisting all along that Mrs. Farhletti's life was at risk if I didn't come. I told Lawson I was on my way. My hope was I wouldn't be too late.

Lawson wasn't alone when he telephoned. The tip was his reference to Roxanna Farhletti. He kept calling her "Mrs. Farhletti." A man fearing for the love of his life tended to use the familiar. In short, why didn't he refer to Mrs. Farhletti as Roxanna? Maybe I was paranoid. Chasing murderers will do that to a person. Make you start eyeing shadows crawling along walls as would-be assassins. If I were paranoid, so be it, better paranoid than caught off guard.

I parked my car a block from Lawson's house and jogged the rest of the way. The street lighting was dim against the pitch black and steady drizzle. They provided perfect urban cover. Lawson's neighborhood was quiet and still. I approached the house from the front so I wouldn't be seen making my way to the back.

Peering through the kitchen window, I couldn't see much. Only a faint light was on. It was coming from the living room. Einstein was gone. I took my stiletto out of its sheath and put it in my left trench coat pocket. Thank God, I'm ambidextrous. Besides being a close fighting weapon it was a good throwing knife. I wanted to be prepared for anything. The back door was unlocked. My Beretta was at the ready. I didn't survive DEA assignments by having a death wish. They were going to have to do better if this was a trap.

I stood to the side, turned the knob, and pushed the door open. Nothing happened. I entered ready to riddle anything that moved. The place was in a shambles. Where was Lawson?

I waded through the debris that was Lawson's home remaining alert. The kitchen and dining areas held no surprises. The living room set me aback. A bed sheet was secured at one end to the oak railing of the loft. Dangling from the other end was the lifeless body of Benton Lawson. A gooseneck lamp pointed directly at him like a spotlight, casting an ominous shadow on the flat white wall. That was meant for me a clear and present message of my possible fate if I didn't back off. The psychos had gone to the extreme.

Say what you will about how peaceful a person looks after death. From my experience that's the undertaker's doing. Of the fresh corpses I've seen, not one looked at peace. A general sense of agony, terror, and deep wrenching pain was projected on their faces and twisted throughout their limbs. Lawson was no exception.

I brought Lawson down. Laying his body on the floor I could tell his neck was broken. My guess was before he was hung. The smell of death was fresh upon him. I searched Lawson's person. Stuffed in his jacket pocket was a handwritten suicide note. No doubt planted by his killers. It said he was distraught over his lost love and his inability to take the U-T project to completion. According to the letter, ending it all was his only way out. I pocketed the letter.

Someone had ransacked the place. All of Lawson's computer equipment and peripherals were gone. His laptop was missing too. I had no way of knowing if anything else was taken. How could they have possibly expected the police to ignore a looted home to buy suicide? What were they really trying to accomplish here? Everything still appeared to be in Lawson's wallet. I jotted down his credit and banking card numbers for the chance Renita could track his movements since last we saw him.

Where were the FBI Lawson said constantly dogged him? I could only surmise they had lost Lawson a long time before tonight. What were the people who did this looking for? What would I be looking for from Benton Lawson? Information? Secrets? Secrets kept on electronic media. Did they find it? Maybe they found what Lawson wanted them to find. What if my hunch was right? Where would I hide U-T if I were Lawson?

There were musical CDs scattered all over the place. I took a quick look at some of the CDs assuming whoever did this would not have missed something so obvious. I will say this for Lawson, his music collection was a regular jazz smorgasbord: Dizzy Gillespie, Count Basie, Sidney Bechet, Art Blakely, Sonny Rollins, Ella Fitzgerald, Max Roach, Weather Report, Archie Shepp, Benny Goodman, Django Reinhardt, Art Pepper, Tito Puente, Duke Ellington, Wynton Marsalis, Billie Holiday, Louis Armstrong, Al Jarreau, Jean Luc Ponty, Herbie Hancock, Charlie Parker, Clifford Brown, Ramsey Lewis, the list of jazz luminaries went on and on. A lyric from a Duke Ellington classic came to mind: "It don't mean a thing, if it ain't got that swing!" Cruel thought under those circumstances, gallows humor. I didn't know I still had it in me. I was puzzled how I should feel about that revelation. Time was a-wastin'. I moved on.

I was about to toss a couple of Lawson's music CD's back amongst the plunder when it occurred to me. Lawson had mentioned his love for jazz during our car conference. If I wanted to hide something from someone, where would I put it? Lawson was the man who put together the Windell DVD. He had access to labeling and packaging as well. I commandeered one of Lawson's shoulder bags. I gathered up all of his music CD's and put them in it.

I took the sheet Lawson hung from into the basement and mixed it in with a stack of dirty laundry. That way the police wouldn't suspect suicide for an instant. They would be looking for a murder suspect from the start. That would keep the heat on Lawson, Clinton Windell and Mark Strait's killers since I believed they were one in the same.

After taking a last look around to see if I missed any clues I used Lawson's phone to call 9-1-1 disguising my voice. My fingerprints weren't a concern. I was wearing gloves the entire time. On my way out, I took a final look at Lawson. His eyes were filled with stark terror. I slipped out through the back way after covering his face with a towel.

CHAPTER THIRTY-SEVEN

The twins were the first to greet me when I got home. Destini and Renita were sitting like college roomies on the couch in their bathrobes watching TV. The eleven o'clock news was winding down. Renita appeared relieved to see me. Destini looked suspicious.

"It's about time somebody found their way home," Renita said with a genuine smile. Her eyes sparkled with a joy that can't be manufactured. The smell of fresh basil, oregano, and warm bread lingered in the air. They probably had spaghetti for dinner. Destini looked hungry for a meal of a different sort. She wanted a bite out of me. Destini had questions gnawing at her that I knew she would wait until we were alone to ask.

"Are you hungry?" Destini asked.

I was. "Not really," I said.

"I'm glad you're okay," Destini said. Her words were sincere. Right then Destini was combating mixed emotions. The role of Destini my lover was reaping havoc on the role of Destini the police detective.

"Goodnight C. J.," Renita said still smiling as she headed off to bed. "See you both in the morning." The twins followed Renita. They had done that a lot lately. I assumed it was because Renita played with them more than Destini and me.

Destini's stare hardened. The detective had taken control. I got out of my trench coat, hat and gloves and put them away in the living room closet. The stiletto remained in my trench coat pocket. I could get it later. I had my suit jacket buttoned so Destini couldn't see my guns. She had become accustomed to me carrying them. She was almost as inured to them as my lies.

My life was moving backwards all because of this lousy case. As good as I was at walking the tightrope my balance was starting to stray. It was time to get my priorities back in line. I made a quick mental adjustment in that department. Destini came first then Renita then the case. When I went to the study to put my firearms away, Destini followed me.

"Working late on the Windell case?" Destini asked.

"Yep," I said.

"Anything you'd care to share?"

"Renita didn't tell you?" I wasn't being sarcastic. I expected Destini had been grilling Renita. From the tilt of her head and the crossing of her arms, Renita hadn't told Destini anything useful. Then there were key elements I was keeping even from Renita.

"I want to know what's going on," Destini said.

"I thought we worked that out," I said.

"Worked what out?"

"Renita, you, and me," I said. Destini was not amused.

"I'm over that," Destini said. "I'm talking about the Windell case and you know it. Why does Genevieve Windell put so much faith in you?"

"Who says she does?"

"I do."

"Genevieve Windell knows I'm involved in her insurance investigation."

"Go on."

"And most of that involves looking into who murdered Clinton Windell."

"Go on."

"I guess she figures I might have enough information to clear her."

"More information than the police?"

I locked away my firearms in my oak gun cabinet and turned to face Destini.

"She's been charged with the murder of her husband," I said. "The police aren't exactly the people she's going to look to for help."

"We're still poring over the evidence," Destini said. "There's still a chance the charge could be lifted."

"Not likely."

"Just so I have this straight. You're telling me that our prime suspect believes you can do what we can't?"

"It certainly looks that way."

"Is this some sort of maverick DEA thing or are we just that incompetent?"

Destini was venting from what I had said to her earlier over the phone. After the way I teed off on her about investigative work who could blame her? Add to that my lying and the covert activities, and I was looking at being handed my walking papers.

"I can't speak for Mrs. Windell," I said.

"Are you ever going to be honest with me?" Destini sincerely asked.

Honest? The word struck my ear like a sour note in a Wynton Marsalis rhapsody. "About what?" I said feigning ignorance.

"Everything regarding this case?"

"I thought we agreed to leave our work outside."

"Where were you tonight?" That question had the double inclination of sounding as though it were coming from a police officer and a jealous wife.

"At the Windell estate," I said.

"You've been with Genevieve Windell all of this time?"

"Most of it, I tried to see Patrick Kemery but missed him. He was at the opera." These had become what I was telling myself were necessary lies. Each one I told Destini was like a punch to my heart. I couldn't imagine how it must have felt to her.

"You're not going to let it go are you?" Destini said. "You're so convinced this woman's innocent—despite all of the evidence against her—you're willing to go to the mat for her."

"There's something you're overlooking," I said.

"What's that?"

"Two people shot Clinton Windell."

"Her and Mark Strait."

"Does it say that in the evidence that you found in Strait's safe deposit box?"

"Not that it's any of your business but Strait does imply that's what happened. Strait admits doing it for Genevieve Windell—or as he refers to her, Genevieve Wissmann. He never says who pulled the other trigger. It doesn't take a genius to put it together."

"You don't have the murder weapons," I said.

"They'll turn up soon enough," Destini said.

"I know she's innocent."

"I hope that's you're gut talking."

"What's that supposed to mean?"

"Beautiful widow, rich, vulnerable and in dire need to be rescued, you put it together," Destini said.

"Pardon," I said.

Destini got in my face. "Are you certain you don't have feelings for this woman?"

Staring back into Destini's eyes, I wanted to tell her everything, about the anonymous letter, U-T, the CD's, Windell, Lawson, Strait, my phantom employers, the people following me. Not because Detective Pendleton intimidated me but to mollify the heart and mind of the woman I loved.

"If Genevieve Windell was a poor, wart-faced, toothless, scraggly, crack dealing skinhead, I'd still believe her innocent of this crime," I said.

"That's your gut talking?" Destini said.

"Yes," I said.

Destini was trying to stare me down. It was late for us working folks. She was tired. So was I. Her eyes kept giving away her feelings in spite of her efforts to hide them. Destini was angry, yes. She was also hurt, confused and frustrated. Flowers weren't going to fix what I was doing. Even a full-blown confession would require time for the wounds to heal.

When Destini kissed me, I was stunned. I put my arms around her before she could pull away. Our kiss was long and passionate. I could feel the heat from her naked body coming through her cotton robe. It had been the most honest I had been with Destini all day.

"You're a lousy liar Cedric Joseph Cavanaugh," Destini said when we came up for air, "but a great kisser." Destini pressed her forefinger to my lips before I could say anything.

"We left you a plate in the refrigerator," Destini said.

"Spaghetti," I said.

"How'd you know?" Her question was flavored with amusement. It made me wonder if I wasn't the one taking the Windell case too personally. It had been a long time since I'd been involved in a case this convoluted and complex. The green space between personal versus professional had become grayed.

"Lucky guess," I said in response to Destini's question.

"I'm exhausted," Destini said. "I'm going to bed. Join me when you're ready."

Destini slipped out of my arms and walked away. I followed holding her hand. I mentioned I was taking a shower and then maybe I'd have a little something to eat. That seemed to please her. Destini went to bed without another word.

A hot shower and warm meal did a great deal to clear my mind from the day's events. There was nothing more I could do until the Lawson news hit the fan.

I made it to bed at close to one. Destini was sound asleep. Her face was relaxed, satiny smooth and lovely as a Jamaican sunset, sweet as strawberry jam. Destini sighed when I settled in beside her. She rolled onto her side and placed her head and hand on my bare chest. Her soft hair tickled a bit. The balmy fragrance of her moisturizing lotion filled my lungs. I put my arm around her then pulled the top sheet and blanket up to her neck. I could feel her warm breath near my heart. We nestled one another. What we did we did out of quiet reflex, an impulse. It was conditioning we were as helpless to prevent as Pavlov's dog, habitual, ritualistic, a cozy solace. I regretted not having told Destini I loved her before sleep invited her in.

A thunderstorm pounced on us during the night. Its tumultuous hammering cracked my comfort dome. The outside world raged like ravaged locust streaming through serrated fissures devouring my hard-earned tranquility and bringing with them that disquieting edge that I had recently become reacquainted. Bebe Assassino crossed my mind. "*Olha bem, meu amigo. A luz e a obscuridade sao bobas aparentadas. Ambas sao igualmente enganadas. Só as sombras compartilham cada um dos seus segredos. E elas os cochicham somente para Deus*," he once said to me. "Look well my friend. Light and darkness are kindred fools both are equally deceived. Only shadows share each of their secrets. And they whisper them solely to God." With all that had recently transpired I would have been more at ease if I had my Beretta within reach.

CHAPTER THIRTY-EIGHT

On my way home from discovering Lawson dead I had stopped by Renita's house. I needed a place to stash Lawson's CDs, a place Renita could work undisturbed. I still had the key Renita had given me to her place the day after she moved in with me. Our original arrangement was I would pick up from her home anything she needed. That agreement disintegrated into one in which Renita went accompanied by someone of my choosing. Ernest was always glad to join her on those errands. Of late, Renita had been making solo trips. I could tell by the sudden appearance of her things at my place. Carrying a firearm can give one a false sense of security. Your wits remain your greatest mechanism of defense. Renita may have forgotten that. She had obviously all but forgotten that unnerving office incident. It was up to me to ensure Renita did not become complacent.

I slipped in through the front door, waited about a minute, and turned on a lamp in the living room. Renita's blinds were closed. I'd told her to keep them closed while she was away to discourage riffraff. At least she had listened to something I'd said.

My guardians couldn't see my silhouette through the dense blinds. I wasn't taking any chances. I took my time going upstairs to Renita's bedroom. After waiting another minute, I turned on the light. The blinds in the bedroom were closed. I walked over to her bedroom closet opened it and looked around inside. There was opportunity. I set Lawson's shoulder bag on the floor beside me and opened it. There was a gym bag on the closet floor already open. I casually bent over and looked inside the gym bag. It was empty. I took the CDs out of the shoulder bag and placed them into Renita's gym bag. From her closet, I grabbed two pairs of jeans, a couple of sweatshirts and an old pair of athletic shoes and stuffed them into Lawson's shoulder bag. I picked up the gym bag and shoulder bag then walked to the light switch. I waited about fifteen seconds to give my observers the continuing impression of unfamiliarity with my surroundings.

After I turned out the bedroom light, I made a mad dash for the back door dropping the shoulder bag at the foot of the stairs. After unlocking the back door, I darted to the basement. There was just enough light streaming in from the basement window for me to make out everything. I opened the dryer and tossed in Renita's gym bag. If my watchers came into Renita's house to check on my actions, they would not check the dryer even if they looked in the basement. They might notice some of her clothes missing and would assume that was the reason I was there. Though I'm certain what I took from Lawson's house had aroused some curiosity it was not to the extent they would find it necessary to pursue. They would have a difficult time pinpointing what I had in the bag even if they did.

I slammed shut the dryer and rushed upstairs. Grabbing the shoulder bag, I made a casual walk across the living room to turn off the lamp. They saw me leave with the same bag I went in with. I only needed to buy Renita enough time to uncover what Lawson's murderers were after.

CHAPTER THIRTY-NINE

Renita and I took my car to work in the morning. That's when I told her Lawson was dead. I left out the details. Renita didn't ask and I saw no reason to tell her. Renita appeared dismayed by the news. She was asking herself the same question I had. Could I have done something to prevent Lawson's death?

Lawson's murder was preordained from the way I figured it. If anything, our intervention extended his life. Windell and Lawson's murders were part of a plan. Strait's was not. Strait was originally supposed to be the patsy for Windell's murder along with Genevieve Windell. Lawson's homicide was to appear to be a suicide. To paraphrase the suicide note I'd stolen Lawson was distraught over his lost love and his inability to take the Universal Translator project to completion.

The bigger lie was Lawson had completed the Universal Translator project. Someone on the inside kept him from realizing it probably by sabotaging the software just enough to make his tests come up short. With the creator of the Universal Translator deceased, it could take years to digest what Lawson had compiled unless someone had procured a working copy of U-T. The murder of Benton Lawson in my mind gave credence to Lawson's claim of a Farhletti connection.

Our involvement threw a wrench in the works. Lawson's death was supposed to occur a lot closer to Windell's; within a couple of weeks was my guess. His meeting with us delayed that from happening. If they had killed Lawson then it might arouse an undesirable connection between the Windell murder and his apparent suicide. Without us the plan would have worked. It still might if Renita and I couldn't get some quick hard evidence.

I asked Renita if she needed time to herself when we arrived at the office. Renita said she'd be fine. I knew she would. This was her first direct connection to a homicide. Feeling responsible for another person's life—justifiable or not—is a heavy burden. I only hoped it would be her last.

Renita changed into a heather gray cotton sweat suit she kept at the office. The next thing I knew, I heard her kicking and punching the heavy bag we had in the exercise room. This continued – off and on—for close to a half-hour. After a shower and change of dress, Renita emerged not quite herself but ready to go.

I told Renita about the CDs I had taken from Lawson's home and where to find them. Renita asked whether the police would be looking for them. I told Renita that in all likelihood they would. Only they would be looking for data CDs not music ones. They would be operating under the assumption the same people who stole Lawson's computer equipment took the CDs. What I needed from Renita was for her to check each compact disc for anything that shouldn't be there primarily software programs. When Renita asked if I had anything specific in mind I told her.

"U-T?" Renita said startled.

"None other, do you have at home what you need to do the job?" I asked.

"*Definitely* code breaking is my hobby."

"What we're looking for won't be difficult to identify. Sifting through the gravel for the gold involves most of the labor."

"How many CDs are we talking about?"

"Easily over a hundred," I said.

"That may take some time," Renita said. "Why can't I do it here?"

"I have a feeling things are going to be hopping around here. It'll be easier for you to work at home fewer distractions."

Renita looked hesitant. "Are you alright?" I asked. Renita said she was fine but she wasn't. Her spirit was deflated. It would take time for her to put Lawson out of her mind. The same amount of time it would require for her to realize there was nothing she could have done to save him.

"I want you to take your bike and head away from the office for a few miles," I said. "Make it appear as though you're out for a joy ride. That'll be enough to make your tail break off."

"What are you going to do?" Renita asked.

"I'm going to drive over to the Beaverton Research Complex to have a talk with Farhletti."

"Won't our employer still be watching both of us?" Renita asked.

"Trust me," I said. "When pursuing what are regarded as false leads even professionals get bored, make assumptions and take shortcuts. They'll probably break off and wait for you to come back to the office. That's why it's important to make absolutely certain your house appears no different from the outside. When you don't show back at the office, your place will be the second place they'll look. Mine will be the first."

Renita nodded.

"Are you ready?" I asked.

"Ready as I'm going to be."

"I've asked Winston and Smoky to stay with you. They're waiting for you at your place."

"Why?"

"As an added precaution plus they're good company," I said with a smile. Renita half grinned.

"Don't get me wrong C. J. I like Smoky and Winston a lot. But what are a couple of old men going to do if trouble comes?"

"Don't ever underestimate the wiles of combat veterans. I'd trust them with my life. Now I'm entrusting them with yours."

The night before when I left Renita, I called Winston from my car. There was some Ellington playing in the background. Winston was not happy to hear from me. A woman's giddy beckoning in the background to hurry before it got cold was obviously the reason. I was confident she wasn't referring to his coffee. I made it brief. I asked Winston to get Smoky early tomorrow morning and slip through the unlocked back door of Renita's house. Make certain no one sees you I emphasized. Do it before daylight. Bring small firearms. There's a thousand dollars a piece in it for you and Smoky. They would've done it for free. Why should they when I could afford to pay? Winston didn't ask any questions. I needed him. That was all that was required. I knew Smoky would feel the same.

"If you say so," Renita said in response to my answer to her question. Renita wasn't convinced. "Think there'll be any trouble?" Renita asked.

"Just lay low and everything will be fine," I said.

I was being completely honest with Renita. No one would suspect Renita was at home if she kept a low profile. If anyone was a target right now, it was me. I asked Renita to call once she settled in. I was stunned when Renita kissed me. It was only a peck on the cheek but I enjoyed it too much, just as I was enjoying having Renita in my home too much. This whole thing had gotten out of hand.

"Thank you," Renita said.

"For what," I said.

"For trusting me to handle something this important," Renita said.

"You're my partner. Who else should I trust?"

Her smile was faint. There was a soft glimmer in her eyes. When Renita wasn't trying to be Ms. All That, she was frightfully alluring.

"Go on," I said. "We don't have much time."

I held the door open for Renita as she carted her bike out. "One last bit of advice," I said. Renita paused long enough to listen. "Start with the Wynton Marsalis CDs. Lawson said something about being a big fan of his in the car." Renita nodded. "Be careful," I said. This time her smile was brighter. Whether it was due to my concern or a reason only her gray cells had access to I couldn't say. One thing her reaction did tell me. Renita was getting back in the fray.

CHAPTER FORTY

I stood at the office window and watched Renita ride along S.W. Washington for as far as I could see. A green Chevy Suburban followed her. The office door burst open. I swiveled on the balls of my feet whipped out my Beretta and was ready to shoot. Destini closed the door then boldly strode toward me. "What's your story this time?" Destini said ignoring my weapon. Destini stopped just inside my office door her fist on her hips, trench coat open, revealing the twill navy blue suit that fit her so well.

"What do you mean?" I asked holstering my weapon.

"What the hell were you doing at Benton Lawson's?" Destini asked. I sat behind my desk hoping to entice Destini to take the chair across from me. She didn't.

"I don't know what you're talking about," I said.

"Don't give me that shit! Ever since you've been on the Windell investigation, you've been holding out on me. I want to know what's going on and I want to know now. Or God help me if you and *Ms.* Harris won't be doing a little time in some of our first class detention facilities."

Destini was angrier than I had ever seen her. "What about Lawson?" I said adding fuel to the fire. Destini stepped forward stopping at my desk. It symbolized our barrier, our divide. This was as far as we would go on this case. The closest we would come to meeting in the middle.

"Lawson's dead! You were there! I want to know what you saw!"

"I can't help you," I said.

"Can't, or won't," Destini said.

"Both," I said.

"I'll bet if I took the shoes you were wearing last night to the lab soil samples from them would match the soil found around Lawson's house."

Destini was bluffing. I stayed on the concrete path careful not to step any place that might leave a footprint. On the floor, just inside the kitchen door was a throw rug. I immediately wiped my feet. I checked before I left for any dried footprints where I'd been throughout the house. There was none. The last thing I did was toss the throw rug into the back lawn. There was nothing useful that throw rug could tell them with the thunderstorm last night.

"Be my guest," I said. I put my feet up on the desk. I wasn't wearing the shoes I had on last night but I doubted Destini realized it.

"I may just do that." Destini was serious. Proving me innocent would be a snap but the time it would take to do so could be enough to make me miss my deadline, a deadline that I suspected was tied to the killers. I put my feet down.

"I'm waiting," Destini said. I pondered my options for a moment. There was too much on the line to go for broke. I decided to relent a bit on the Lawson issue.

"I did visit Lawson last night," I said. "I needed to speak to him."

"Regarding what?" Destini asked.

"The matter he'd brought up before," I said. "The one I told you about where he thought he was being followed."

"Again with the stalking," Destini said, "do you realize you've reported more stalkings in the last few weeks than we've had in the last six months?"

"Blame it on bad karma," I said.

"Don't be cute," Destini said. "I'm not playing with you." I gave Destini an obsequious nod. She continued. "Was he being followed?" Destini was a good detective. She rarely allowed any possibility to slip by unchecked.

"I didn't find any evidence of it," I said.

"You're lying again."

"Detective the man was a little loose in the noggin. He was under the impression the same people who killed Clinton Windell were after him," I said still trying to throw Destini off my scent.

"Why would he think that?" Destini asked.

"He'd mentioned—in my first and only meeting with him—that he'd stumbled upon some high security interoffice memos from Antonio Farhletti that linked Farhletti with the Windell homicide." There was no love lost between Farhletti and myself. While I did not dislike the man, I could care less if the police went after him. "I stopped by to reassure Lawson nothing was going on."

"Antonio Farhletti involved in the Windell murder," Destini said. I could see the wheels turning. Destini was hashing over that slim prospect in her mind. I wasn't naive enough to believe Destini would go after Farhletti on hearsay. There was the slight chance she could be misled long enough for a few hours peace.

"Lawson wanted my protection," I said hoping to seal the deal.

"First Genevieve Windell now Benton Lawson," Destini said. "Why don't we get you a pair of blue tights and a cape?"

"I told Lawson to take his story to the police but he wouldn't listen. He didn't think anyone would believe him. I know I didn't." I was lying about the last part. I believed Lawson was in trouble. I didn't realize just how deep until it was too late.

"He was right," Destini said. "I wouldn't have believed him any more than I believe you right now."

"Now do you see why I didn't say anything? The only reason I was there was because Lawson called me frantic about some vital information he supposedly found to prove his rants."

"Thoughtful and considerate that's my C. J."

"Thank you," I said with equal sarcasm.

"What time did Lawson phone you?" Destini asked.

"Between eight and nine," I said. We both realized that would be a cinch to verify.

"Hand it over," Destini said.

"Hand what over?"

"Whatever you found," Destini said.

"Detective I would hand *it* over if I had an *it* to hand over. I rang the doorbell. No one answered. I left."

"I suppose you don't have any idea who the anonymous caller was?"

"Anonymous caller?"

"Someone called 9-1-1 from Lawson's place. I'll bet you an Alaskan cruise for two if we do a voice analysis comparing that person's voice to yours we'd get a match."

They'd be lucky to get close to a match. I was brief. They didn't have enough of a sample. I needed to give Destini something soon. Her obsession with my involvement on the Windell case was doing neither of us any good. I would have to remain strong and focused. Destini would have to keep the faith.

"You're mistaken if you think it was me detective," I said.

"Thanks for nothing," Destini said.

"Sorry I couldn't be of more help," I said.

Destini slammed her hands against my desk. Something clicked inside me. In a flood my training, my field experience all came back on how to handle hostile situations. I also remembered last night the part about me possibly being the one taking this personally. At that moment, I knew it was true. Even now, Destini was only doing her job. She couldn't respect herself if she didn't. What troubled her most was why I was lying. Destini knew something was awry, something she couldn't share with me or her partner or her captain. Whatever suspicions Destini had, she believed I held the key. For the first time I saw an aspect of my deception I had not realized earlier. I wasn't the only one who knew a good deal more than they were telling about these recent homicide cases.

"Allow me to let you in on a little something," Destini said. "It seems the uniforms that checked out the Lawson house didn't notice anything bizarre and wrote your call off as a crank. The chief got word of it and asked me to take a quick look. Seems a Judith Hardy had filed a missing person's report on behalf of Diva Computer Software. David and I were the first detectives on the crime scene."

"That's what you get for being first in the office," I said. Destini didn't find my comment amusing. On second thought neither did I.

"I'll have you know it's those early office arrivals and late office nights that earned me Detective Sergeant first class faster than any other Portland Police officer," Destini said. "It might do you some good to shut up and listen for a change. Maybe you'll learn something."

I nodded.

"I found this in Lawson's wallet." Destini pulled an evidence bag with a business card inside out of her coat pocket and slid it face down across my desk to me. It was mine. That wasn't there when I rifled Lawson. I had looked for it. Someone had planted it after I left. They probably switched off the light too making it seem as if no one was home. Why? What were they expecting to happen?

"Notice the bloody smudge on the right side," Destini said. I had. Destini pointed to it with her right index finger to make certain I didn't miss it. I nodded.

"Looks like a fingerprint doesn't it?"

I nodded again.

"Suppose for the sake of argument that fingerprint belongs to you? What would one conclude from finding such evidence?"

The presumption was obvious. I would become a murder suspect. Destini and I stared each other down. Neither of us blinked. Neither of us ever would. I wasn't looking into the eyes of my lover. Those were the eyes of an adversary. One who was intelligent, resourceful, and relentless. I was going to play this one to the hilt. Destini had never seen me do this. It was something an experienced covert agent is capable of doing. My only hope was that Destini would still be there when the work was done. I remained silent.

"Any idea how it got there?" Destini asked.

"It must be the card I gave Lawson when I saw him last," I said. "I told you about that."

"Last as in aside from last night?"

"I didn't see him last night."

"Are you certain?"

"Yes." Destini made a dramatic pause. She looked me over debating her next move.

"No one but you and I and possibly Renita knows this card exists. Although after questioning Renita last night I suspect I'm not the only one in the dark about some of your crucial information."

"Your point," I said.

"My deduction—for what it's worth—is you'd already looked through Lawson's wallet. Probably jotted down his credit card numbers, bankcard number and anything else you thought could help track Lawson's movements for the last few weeks. Am I warm?"

I had decided to do the background search on the card numbers myself. That left Renita free to concentrate on the more valuable work of checking Lawson's CDs. If Destini had searched me, she would have found Lawson's card numbers on a slip of paper in my wallet.

"Cold as ice," I said. My lie told her exactly what she needed to know. Destini grinned for a moment. She was the cat and I was the canary. All she had to do was grab me and I was lunch.

"I suspect you wouldn't have missed so obvious a clue pointing toward you as a homicide suspect," Destini said.

"No motive, no opportunity, no means," I said.

"Means and opportunity you certainly had, motive none that I'm aware of. Then I don't know much about that mysterious DEA past of yours." Destini paused, straightened, and then said, "Who knows what demons lurk there?"

Destini snatched the card from my hand. "Maybe I should let Rockgarden have a crack at you—or better yet—Whimple? After all Whimple's been handed this case."

That was all I needed Schultz and Weasel in my way. With only seven days left, there wasn't time to outwit those stooges. If they got in my way, I'd use the direct approach. Any assault issues that might arise would hopefully be postponed until after resolution of my clients' case.

"Be my guest," I said. This conflict had become a test of wills. I hadn't wanted that. I'm certain Destini didn't either. If I didn't watch my step, I could find myself too far out on a limb to recover.

Destini gave a heavy sigh. "Man you are lucky I love you." Destini sounded exasperated as if speaking to a child who had driven her to her wits end. "Tell me about it," I said.

"That's your story," Destini said.

"Yes," I said.

"I'm not buying it. You're going to have to do better."

"I don't understand." I did but we both needed to play this charade out.

"You don't tell me something feasible right this instant I'm turning this evidence over to Schultz and Weasel."

"You wouldn't," I said.

"In a heartbeat," Destini said.

I sighed as I briefly weighed my options. Destini was serious. It was time to institute my backup plan. "I went to see Benton Lawson to ask him more questions about what he found in Farhletti's e-mail connecting Clinton Windell to Antonio Farhletti."

"Why didn't you stick around?"

"Who needs the grief? Besides, there was nothing to tell."

"That's it," Destini said.

"That's it," I said.

"You left the scene of a capital crime," Destini said. "I don't have to lecture you on what that means."

"Was it a crime?" I asked knowing full well that it was.

"You weren't the only one who didn't buy that suicide note balled up in Lawson's hand." I had taken the suicide note I found on Lawson with me. Someone must have written another and placed it in Lawson's hand no doubt the same person who murdered him.

"That note was bogus," I said hoping to learn more. Destini ignored my statement as if it was ludicrous.

"You found the place ransacked?" Destini asked.

"Of course," I said.

"You weren't looking for anything?"

"No."

"Lawson was dead when you got there?"

"Yes," I said. "I checked his vitals then immediately called 9-1-1."

Destini couldn't be implying that I murdered Lawson. She knew me better than that at least the part not associated with the DEA. If my lying had steered her to accepting the prospect I had something to do with Lawson's murder perhaps it didn't stop there. Maybe she thought I had something to do with Strait's homicide as well.

"Are you insinuating something detective?" I asked.

"Should I be?" Destini asked.

I sighed. "Lawson was dead when I got there."

"Were you the one who brought him down?"

"Brought him down from what?"

"You may not have noticed," Destini said, "but the wood railing of the loft was varnished. It made any markings show up like a candle in the dark. Slight abrasions on the loft's railing suggested something heavy had recently hung from it. The forensic team found traces of cotton in the abrasions that matched cotton fibers found on Lawson's neck. Add to that the chaffing around Lawson's neck similar to rope burns. We looked around. Found a bed sheet among Lawson's dirty clothes that matched the pattern. Blood, hair, saliva and skin tissue on the sheet matched the victim's. He was hung from that railing. Someone brought him down then stashed evidence thinking we incompetent cops wouldn't find it. Was that you?"

"Yes," I said.

Destini was in my face again. She was all detective now. Her eyes were gouging mine for the truth. She was tuned in. She recognized the truth. It excited her in a way I would rather not experience again.

"Why?" Destini asked.

"Because he was murdered," I said.

"That's for us to decide."

"It was a matter of brevity. If the police waste time suspecting suicide they'll have less chance of nailing the guilty."

"Mr. C. J. Cavanaugh looking out for us Keystone Cops thanks so very much. We might not have decided his neck was broken before he was hung without your interference."

"I was only trying to help."

"If you really want to help you can do two things: stay out of my way and tell me the whole god-damn truth!"

A moment of primitive silence passed that might have existed upon the banks of time before the emergence of humans. We waited and then waited some more.

"You always did have an attitude," Destini said.

I nodded.

"Let's do lunch real soon shall we?" Destini said with a smug smile. She was enjoying herself too much for my taste. My deserved humiliation was a small price to pay to remain free to roam the plains of this case. I would have thanked Destini but that would have spoiled her fun. I moved toward Destini to walk her out. Destini put her hand up to stop me.

"Don't bother I know the way. See you this evening," Destini said over her shoulder as she walked away. "That is if you can stay out of trouble until then?"

Before leaving Destini turned to me with her hand on the doorknob and said, "C. J. I love you with all of my being but if you can't tell me the absolute truth about your involvement on the Windell case then we have very little to say to one another." Her smile vanished. With that, Destini left. That woman was all business. Love would have to wait.

After the door closed, I breathed a sigh of relief. An e-mail from our phantom employers had arrived requesting a progress report. I had used the time Renita was in the exercise room to write one. When Renita left, I was three-quarters finished. Had Destini stepped around the desk shortly after she arrived she would have seen the report I was composing to send to my phantom employers. Thankfully, my haunted house screen saver had kicked in for most of her visit.

I was grateful to Destini for more than she knew. Returning my incriminating business card was one thing. It kept me out of the loop of suspicion. An action if leaked could prove damaging to her career. I would never jeopardize her career. I would deny Destiny had ever done anything unlawful, unethical, or unprofessional. Genevieve Windell wasn't the only person for who I would go to the mat. For Destini Pendleton I would sacrifice it all. Her behavior suggested that in spite of all of the deceit that Destini still believed in me, believed in us.

CHAPTER FORTY-ONE

I had told Destini the truth. The card she returned to me was blank on the back. The card I had given Lawson had my handwritten message on the back. The fact Destini found one of my cards at the crime scene at all confirmed my suspicion. The killers wanted to keep the existence of U-T under wraps. I burned the card with the bloody fingerprint; blood I assumed had belonged to Benton Lawson. There was no sense in leaving incriminating physical evidence lying around.

Renita phoned to say she was settled in. I asked Renita what Destini questioned her about last night. From what Renita told me there wasn't any reason for alarm. To make certain Renita was loose I told her what Destini said regarding my attitude. Renita laughed and then said she agreed. I told her I took that as a compliment coming from her. Smoky got on the phone for a minute. He wanted to know if I needed one of them to guard my back. I assured him I'd be okay. He assured me Renita would be as well. What I didn't admit to any of them was how deeply I was concerned. Someone was cleaning house. From what I could determine, I would be next. Once I was out of the way, not knowing what Renita knew the killers might dispose of her as an added precaution against further interference. None of which would occur if my plan worked.

Lawson was correct. Antonio Farhletti was up to his neck in it, which was why I phoned Judith Hardy. Hardy sounded a bit shaken about what had happened to Benton Lawson until I brought up the topic of U-T. Her voice went from dazed to intense. I asked if it would be possible to speak with Farhletti. Hardy said she would try to arrange it.

***

Four armed uniformed security guards greeted me outside the metal gates of Diva's Beaverton Research Complex. One got in the passenger side of my car. The other sat in the back. The last two got into a security vehicle and closely followed us inside. I noticed each of them had the leather safety strap undone on their holsters. Their instructions were clear. Take me to their leader, no detours, no conversation.

We were quite a sight marching through the lobby, two guards abreast in front, two bringing up to the rear. Each guard kept a hand on his service revolver. I imagined I looked like a dangerous criminal being paraded to the gas chamber or an important dignitary being escorted to an imperative meeting. I pretended I was the latter.

I was escorted to Judith Hardy's office and frisked. I'd expected as much. They were checking me for a wire as well as weapons. I had put most of my hardware in the trunk of my car before I left the parking garage.

Hardy had a corner penthouse office. The area behind Hardy had drawn vertical blinds that reached from ceiling to floor. From behind the blinds, the faint light from a large picture window doubled as a wall. To my left was a quaint, stylish, fully furnished, stocked wet bar. To my right, a cozy sitting area and what appeared to be the doorway to a private bath. Strategically placed about the office were prints by Rembrandt, Dali, Cezanne, Monet, Smibert, and Chagall. Directly ahead, a modern cherry wood desk formed a daunting semicircle. An imposing Judith Hardy stood in the heart of that semicircle. Her desk was as spotless as the sinfully soft carpet beneath our feet. This was where Hardy conducted business, her domain, her rules.

Hardy remained behind her desk. The guard who searched me told Hardy I was clean. He missed my insurance, a stiletto strapped to my forearm hidden by my cuff-linked shirtsleeve. Once I undid the cufflink, a downward flick of my right arm would drop the stiletto into my palm. I could've cut his throat and taken his revolver before any of the other guards cleared their holsters. Hardy nodded and then waited. She wanted no doubt in my mind that she was in charge. After a few mute moments, Hardy dismissed the guards. They left without a word. Farhletti had refused to see me. Judith Hardy didn't have that luxury.

"A while back I had a meeting with Benton Lawson about a personal matter," I said walking forward stopping directly in front of Hardy's desk. "After the meeting Lawson gave me a package. Lawson instructed me not to open it unless he died. Weird huh, how someone can be here one minute then gone the next?" It was pure fabrication on my part. A lie I expected interested Hardy. A fib she could not afford to dismiss. Hardy's eyes narrowed. "Go on," she said.

"I opened it. There was a letter saying these flash drives—there were flash drives in the package—contain a copy of the Universal Translator. That was it. Do you know anything about that?" I knew Hardy was aware Benton Lawson carried flash drives with him constantly. That would make it a conceivable possibility in her mind.

"Where's the package?" Hardy asked.

"Safe," I said. "Whoever killed Lawson ransacked his place. They took all of his computer stuff. They must have been looking for what Lawson gave me. I thought I'd take it to the police and then it dawned on me. Maybe this really belongs to Mr. Farhletti. I mean Lawson was working on a hush-hush project for Diva and all."

"That package is the property of Diva Computer Software," Hardy said. "I demand you hand it over to me at once."

"*Property*," I said, "not any more. It's part of a homicide investigation now."

"*Homicide*," Hardy said.

"Didn't the police tell you?" I said. "How silly of me, of course they wouldn't have. Lawson's neck was broken *before* he was hung. That makes it murder."

"How did you come by so much inside information?" Hardy asked.

"I have a couple of inside connections with the Portland PB, asked a few questions you know the routine." Hardy didn't respond. I continued. "Lawson believed your boss had more than a friendly connection with Clinton Windell. There's a copy of an e-mail referencing Windell's movements before his murder that makes it appear as though the two of them may have been brewing something." The e-mail thing was a gamble. I was relying on Hardy knowing more about it than Lawson did.

"You looked at the drives?" Hardy asked.

"Of course," I said, "wouldn't you? I couldn't make out any of that Universal Translator stuff but the e-mail files were easy pickings."

"It sounds preposterous." Her denial was very convincing. Only Hardy had to know about Farhletti's e-mail. Being head of security having crucial information about all activities in your jurisdiction is central to your job.

"I'm just trying to play the hand dealt me," I said.

"You're doing a poor job," Hardy said.

I shrugged my shoulders. "My best is all I can do."

"Benton Lawson was a programming genius," Hardy said. "Finding another one like him will be difficult enough. But do you realize how long it will take to bring another programmer up to speed on U-T before he could proceed with it?" Before I could respond, Hardy answered for me, "Too long."

"Not my problem," I said.

"What would it take to convince you to return to us what is rightfully ours?" Hardy asked.

"Are you offering me a bribe?"

"Call it a reward," Hardy said. "We lost something. You found it. It happens all of the time in this great land of ours."

"I'll give it to Farhletti," I said, "no one else." Hardy gave me her coldest glare. After my morning with Destini, it was like warm milk on a sleepless night. "As an added bonus I'll even throw in the divorce testimony we previously discussed." Hardy's eyes brightened. They were still as keen as ever behind her brief smile.

"I'll arrange it," Hardy said. "Just make certain you don't lose those drives."

"What is this Universal Translator?" I asked. Since I already knew, I was testing Hardy to see how forthcoming she would be. Judith Hardy stared at me. True power is not intimidated by courage and intelligence it respects them. I could see a grudging respect brooding in Hardy's eyes probably brought on by the way I was using my advantage.

"That's none of your concern," Hardy said. "Is there anything else I can pass along to Mr. Farhletti?"

"Have a nice day," I waggishly said cognizant of Hardy's proverbial daggers. I had played the part of the shady detective and computer dud. Hardy may not have bought all of it but she was desperate to get her hands on the Lawson copy of the Universal Translator. The seed had been planted, watered, and nurtured. It was ready to sprout. The next move was theirs.

Hardy pressed a button on her phone. I had clandestinely unfastened my right cufflink. The four guards who escorted me in returned. I kept both hands in my trench coat pockets ready to strike if need be. The guards saw to it I knew my way out.

CHAPTER FORTY-TWO

The killers could not afford to call my bluff. The very fact I knew about the Universal Translator was bad enough. The possibility of me having a copy was not worth risking. If they had any doubts about what needed to be done, my last move dismissed them.

I checked in with Renita. She had nothing to report. It was going to be a lengthy task to find anything on the 127 CDs. For Renita to be certain Lawson hadn't dispersed the information throughout a series of unrelated CDs, she literally had to play each one through. The music of Wynton Marsalis had come up empty. With Smoky and Winston's help, Renita had alphabetized the CDs and was working her way through the rest from A to Z. I told her to do what she needed to do mentioning for her not to return to the office.

"Bike home at about five," I said.

"Why?" Renita asked.

"We've got to make it seem like a regular work day. I guarantee your disappearance has sparked an interest from our watchdogs. They're going to be wondering where you've been all day."

"Won't that make their surveillance on me tighter from here on out?" Renita asked. It was a good question. The answer of which I had already taken into account.

"Probably," I said. In fact, I was betting on it. I was using our employers as a backup security blanket for Renita in case the killers found where Renita was and what she was doing. My hope was they would intervene if something went down.

"What are we going to do about my shadows?" Renita asked.

"Leave them to me," I said.

"What about Destini?" Renita asked.

"She'll be after me for a while," I said. Destini doesn't think I'm telling you everything."

"Are you?"

"Not you too," I said. Renita sighed.

"Sorry," Renita said. "Guess I'm a little edgy after what happened to Lawson." I indulged that feeling to avoid answering Renita about withholding information from her.

"I understand," I said. "You can't blame yourself. There was nothing we could do."

"I know," Renita said. "You still can't help but wonder."

I filled Renita in on my visit with Judith Hardy. Renita thought the flash drives were a nice touch. "That throws them off a CD trail," Renita said.

"My thinking exactly," I said.

"What's next?" Renita asked.

"I'm heading home to write an update for our insurance investigation report, and to check on Lawson's credit cards and bank card activities. That's about it." What I didn't tell Renita that I was awaiting the killers' next move.

"Think there'll be some action soon?" Renita asked.

"Yes," I said.

"I'm ready," Renita said. The measure of courage is not always in the action but overcoming the fear that would strangle it. Renita was doing that.

"I'm proud of you," I said. It came out like a father to his child. There was a quiet pause before Renita spoke.

"Thanks, C. J."

"Now get back to work," I said.

"It's like that?" I could hear the sass in her voice. Renita really was ready. She wouldn't have to be if my plan worked.

"Always," I said in answer to her question.

"Okay boss," Renita said.

"Call me if you need me," I said.

"Right," Renita said.

"Stay low, stay cool."

"Don't worry C. J. We've got it covered."

"Good. I'd hate to hear Winston had to put you over his knee to get you to behave."

Renita laughed. "He'd like that."

"You bet he would."

"I'll behave."

"I've got to go. We'll talk soon."

The afternoon was quiet. Lawson's bankcard and credit cards came up empty. There had been no activity on them since the day we had met with Lawson. I settled in and wrote, then e-mailed my insurance report to Carl, played with the twins, visited with my finches and tropical fish, and enjoyed having the house to myself. At four-thirty-two, the phone rang. Patrick Kemery had gotten my message. He wanted to meet in Pioneer Courthouse Square at five-thirty. I told him I'd be there.

Six-thirteen and still no Kemery, I called his house. The butler said Kemery wasn't there. I waited another ten minutes then headed home.

No one was home when I got there. There were a few messages on my voice mail. Destini said she would be working late and did not know what time she would be home. My little sister was hopeful I would make it to our parents' for Thanksgiving. Carl wanted further justification regarding my proclamation of Genevieve Windell's innocence. Winston said the day went without a hitch informing me that he and Smoky would report for duty again bright and early tomorrow morning. Ernest wanted to know if I was playing basketball Saturday afternoon and if Renita was free for breakfast this weekend.

I erased all of the messages. I would have to warn Winston about leaving any messages regarding the Windell case on my home voice mail. It was pure luck Destini hadn't been home to listen to Winston's message. Our cover would have been blown right out of the water.

Renita had been there. Her bike was in the garage. I didn't like Renita not letting me know of her whereabouts. I liked it less when I found out where she was.

The phone rang just as I was about to call Winston. "C. J. this is Monty." From the muffled background noise, it sounded as though Monty was in his office at Fullman's. "You'd better move. Buzz Cut's here."

"Is he alone?" I asked.

"Far as I can tell," Monty said.

"If he tries to leave, stall him."

"I'll do what I can. There's something else."

"What?"

"Your partner's here," Monty said.

"Renita," I said.

"In the flesh; how long has she been at this detective game, C. J.?"

"Not long enough."

"Who you telling. I'm pretty sure Buzz Cut's on to her."

"Keep an eye on her for me," I said. "Don't let her get in over her head."

"Right," Monty said.

"And whatever happens don't let Renita leave with Buzz Cut."

"You got it."

CHAPTER FORTY-THREE

A big reason the killers may not have come for me at my home was because Destini was there. They needed to minimize police involvement. Killing me was one thing. Killing me, right under the nose of a homicide police detective was another.

Renita on the other hand was supposed to remain clear of any peril. When it went down Renita was supposed to be involved in checking CDs, or enjoying a meal, or a book, or a movie, or television, surfing the web, anything but in the throes of this dangerous mess. All I could think of on my drive over to Fullman's was Renita. If any harm came to her those responsible, the murderers I expected to be lying in wait for me would become my vindictive example of urban justice.

I pulled into a well-lit asphalt parking lot thirty feet east from the blind side of Fullman's. Renita roamed near the first row of parallel-parked cars searching for something or someone. I parked as quickly as possible and ran toward Renita. Renita turned and saw me. She smiled. Anyone watching us would have thought I was her lover rushing into her arms. Within a couple of steps of reaching Renita, something whizzed past my head. It sounded like a high velocity mosquito. I grabbed Renita, lifted her off her feet, and dropped us both to the ground landing on my back with her on top.

"C. J. this is so sudden and in the parking lot," Renita said.

"We're being shot at," I said.

We scrambled to squatting positions behind a deep brown vintage '83 Cutlass Supreme. Renita pulled out her forty-five and maneuvered herself into a crouched position. I ignored the fact I had specifically asked Renita to carry her thirty-eight. Renita looked ready. I gave her ten for style points. I knelt on one knee.

"What are you doing out here?" I asked.

"Keeping an eye on Buzz Cut," Renita said.

"Where is he?"

Renita looked around. She was embarrassed when she said, "I kind of lost him."

"Have you ever been shot at before?"

"No," Renita said. That told me all I needed to know. Renita had to be removed from this situation as quickly as possible.

"Monty was supposed to keep you inside," I said.

"He tried," Renita said. "I noticed Buzz Cut leaving so I excused myself to use the ladies' room and slipped out. Somehow, I missed Buzz Cut. I was looking for him when you showed up."

"Renita what are you doing here?" I said.

"Smoky said he would call home—your place that is—to make sure I got in okay. When the phone rang, I thought it was Smoky. Some spooky dude on the other end said: 'I hear you're looking for me. Meet me at Fullman's at seven if you're still interested. This will be your last chance.' Then he hung up."

"Why didn't you call me?"

"I tried your car phone," Renita said, "then the office. I didn't know what else to do. It could've been our last chance to nail Buzz Cut."

"I don't care if it's our last shot at preventing a nuclear holocaust next time you wait for me."

Renita nodded. She was doing the same thing I was looking around for the shooter. "Where is he?" Renita asked rising up to get a better look. I forced her down by her shoulder.

"Are you sure we're being shot at?" Renita said. "I didn't hear anything."

"He's using a silencer," I said. "That's what the hit men used who killed Windell. That's why nobody heard a shot."

"How are we going to smoke him out?" Renita asked.

"That's *flush* him out," I said.

"Smoke, flush, what's the difference?"

Neither of us had time for this. "I want you to stay put. I'm going to draw his fire. When he goes for me make your way back to Fullman's and stay there until I come for you."

"I'm not leaving you," Renita said.

"This is no time for heroes," I said thinking *is there ever a good time.* "Go inside and wait."

"C. J.—"

"I don't have time to argue with you," I said not holding back my fury. "You're going back inside Fullman's *now*."

Renita looked stunned. I had rarely had occasion to be cross with Renita but this wasn't kid's play. It was time to let a professional handle this. I'd apologize later.

"Here's how it works," I said. "I'm going to draw his fire. When I give you the signal, I want you to make your way back to Fullman's. Stay low. Once you're at the edge of the parking lot make a mad dash for the door. Don't look back and don't slow down. Are we clear on this?"

Renita nodded.

"And keep your mouth shut. I want some private time with Buzz Cut. Understand?" Renita nodded again. Renita looked hurt. Like a child denied her favorite toy. Maybe that meant she'd listen for a change. "I'll join you inside as soon as possible."

I duck-walked to the rear quarter panel of the Cutlass. On the count of two, I moved swift and low the length of three vehicles away straightening only enough to give the shooter a good look at who was on the move. Nothing happened. I signaled Renita to get moving.

"What was that?" Renita asked looking around as if she'd heard something.

"Nothing," I said. Renita looked scared. I winked at her to let her know everything would be fine. It seemed to help. I popped my head up for a quick peek. Again, nothing happened. This time when I gave Renita the signal she hesitated. Her weapon was still drawn. I don't think Renita was certain what she was going to do. Then she took off. Renita moved like a cat. She was quick and agile even in the crouched position. Renita made her way across the open area between the parking lot and Fullman's without a problem. At the door, she paused long enough to wave before going inside. It was just as I suspected. Renita was the bait. I was the prey. Renita was safely out of the way. Now it was my turn to do a little hunting.

The first thing I did was remove my trench coat. It would only slow me down. I rolled it up and tossed it over the bed of the pickup I was crouched beside. My trench took two bullets. The next thing I got rid of was my suit jacket. It only took one. On the count of two, I bolted toward a Jeep Cherokee five cars over. Three bullets missed me, one near my head, one near my right leg, one across my back lodging themselves with dull thuds in vehicles around me. The one across my back came from a different direction. I had two shooters gunning for me. My Beretta was at the ready to return fire, but only if necessary. I wanted to keep this battle as quiet as possible.

I was able to locate one shooter behind a silver Mercedes 200XL. The other I was uncertain. I duck-walked my way through the maze of cars closer to the Benz, popping up occasionally to make certain the one shooter stayed put. Two more shots were fired. Both came from the direction of the Mercedes. The shooter never moved from that spot. He was the bait. The other was the hunter.

I continued to snake my way toward the bait from his left occasionally giving them something to see. When I was close enough, I changed direction approaching my bait from the opposite side. I stayed low weaving my way through parked cars making my way stealthily toward him. Since no shots were fired, I assumed the hunter nor did the bait have any better vantage point than I did.

I took him by surprise. I plowed into him before he could turn and fire leveling him on the pavement with me on top. I could hear his forty-four skittering away across the blacktop. He went for my eyes with his thumbs. I wiped away his attempt with a sweeping forearm block, followed by a left to his nose and the butt of my Beretta to his chin. It dazed him. Before he could recover, I holstered my Beretta then drove a straight right into his solar plexus. As he was gasping for air, I flipped him over onto his stomach and cuffed him. He was wearing a ski mask. When I ripped off his ski mask, I was surprised to learn it wasn't Buzz Cut.

A man with clear blue eyes, shaved eyebrows, long dirty blond hair, square jaw and chin with a few days unruly growth wavered between consciousness and unconsciousness.

"Who are you?" I asked yanking him up by his shirt collar. He grinned. Blood trickled from his nose meandering across his upper lip staining his teeth. I heard someone rushing toward us. Buzz Cut no doubt. I released my grip. Even dazed my prisoner knew how to land pressing his chin to his chest so his back struck the pavement first, absorbing the brunt of his fall.

I yanked my Beretta out of its holster and threw myself against the Mercedes for cover. For a moment the footsteps stopped. Suddenly they were moving away. I stood to see a man dressed in black with a gun wearing a ski mask running away from Fullman's toward Riddle Avenue.

Looking toward Fullman's I could see why. Led by Ernest, Monty, and Renita, half the second floor crowd had rushed out brandishing weapons. It didn't take a genius to figure out Renita wasn't able to keep quiet. Maybe it was for the best. If Buzz Cut were foolish enough to fire a shot now, he would have been bum rushed by a hard-nosed posse of gunslingers. Not to mention the police were probably on their way.

I glanced over at the one who didn't get away. He had rolled onto his stomach and was struggling to get to his feet. A hard kick to his rear-end put him flat on his stomach.

"C. J.! C. J.!" Renita's voice resounded through the parking lot. I stood and waved my arms. "Over here!" I was prepared to take cover in case some of the posse decided to shoot first. They had me and my captive surrounded in less than a minute.

I didn't have an opportunity to question my mystery prisoner. I was too busy trying to convince some of the Fullman crowd not to kill him or rough him up a little to teach him a lesson as Elma Louise suggested.

The police arrived and took charge. My story was Renita and I were leaving the club after having dinner and this man starting shooting at us. Renita, Ernest and Monty backed my story about dinner. The shooter kept his mouth shut. He hadn't said anything. It didn't appear that he would.

When two officers returned from a search of the grounds with a man dressed in black, I knew immediately who it was. Buzz Cut had not gotten away. I read one of the officers' lips when he told the sergeant in charge that they found him unconscious draped over a blue Jaguar. He showed the officer in charge an evidence bag with a small dart in it. Someone had shot Buzz Cut with a tranquilizer dart.

After the commotion died down was when I saw him. As Renita and I were getting into my car, I caught a glimpse of the old man in the back seat of a black Seville stealthily pulling away. His window was rolled down. Our eyes met. He gave me a nod and a wink. I returned the gestures. A mutual respect passed between us. In that moment I realized the old man was the one who bagged Buzz Cut, the brains behind our watchers, the eyes, and ears of our phantom employers. I also knew our chess match was not over.

CHAPTER FORTY-FOUR

Renita and I were questioned by a uniformed officer then released. That same officer inadvertently told us the names of Buzz Cut and his shooter pal when he asked if we knew Samuel or Steven Horrock. Buzz Cut was Steven. The rest I learned from the wallet I pinched from Samuel Horrock before the posse descended upon us. Aside from Samuel Horrock's driver's license, there was a bankcard, charge cards, an insurance card, eight-hundred-nine dollars, a photograph, and a folded piece of white paper with a telephone number on it. The photograph showed two smiling Marines wearing military fatigues. Each man had an M-16 propped on his hip. On the back of the photograph was a handwritten note: "Together in death as in life always." A close look at the photograph revealed they were twins.

We were also able to uncover additional information from that same officer. I pretended to make a big deal about locking up the Horrocks out of concern for Renita's safety and mine. The officer assured us the Horrocks would be taken to Bess Kaiser Medical Center for any necessary medical treatment. Upon doctor's approval, they would be placed in a holding cell pending formal charges. Those conditions the officer spoke of were Steven being found unconscious and Samuel still bleeding and woozy. The police had to make certain both men were physically fit for trial not because the officers were concerned for their well-being. It was their job and it helped to avoid lawsuits.

Renita and I left Fullman's in my car. Ernest volunteered to drop Renita's car at my place in the morning. I wanted Renita along to keep an eye on her. Her adrenaline was out of control. Not uncommon for rookies involved in their first firefight. Renita was a chatterbox of excitement the whole way. I had to take her forty-five away to prevent her from waving it around as if it were a toy while she expounded on the gunplay we'd just experienced. I was concerned Renita might shoot something or someone by accident mainly me.

I tried telephoning the number I found in Samuel Horrock's wallet. No one answered. Since my car number was unlisted, I didn't worry about caller ID. There was no pickup from an answering machine or service. We didn't have time to trace the number. Time was paramount.

Renita and I waited in the hospital parking lot until the police cleared out. I'd kept my DEA credentials as a sort of a gag retirement gift. They were no longer valid but you wouldn't know that unless you closely checked.

I flashed my DEA badge and ID to the desk nurse who immediately summoned the doctor in charge. The doctor informed us that Samuel Horrock was fine and resting comfortably. It turned out my love tap with the Beretta required a few stitches to Samuel's chin. He had also suffered a mild concussion and a broken nose. The doctor wanted to keep him overnight for observation. His brother on the other hand would be unconscious for the remainder of the night. He had enough amobarbital to sleep through the apocalypse.

The uniformed police officer posted outside Samuel Horrock's room was new. That worked in my favor. It didn't take much to convince him of Horrock's affiliation with major drug smuggling. He gladly stepped aside to let us in. I told Renita to wait for me in the car. I was still concerned about her adrenaline. Renita was not happy about being left behind. Fortunately, she saw the wisdom in not airing her grievance in front of the officer. That was what I had hoped. It was also, why I hadn't asked her earlier. I went in alone.

Horrock was awake resting in an upright position in the quiet of his sanitary room. I stood by his bedside. He was handcuffed to the bed. The black seam of stitches seemed appropriate across his chin. His left cheek was bruised and swollen to the size of a golf ball. His left eye was blackened and his nose was black-and-blue and swollen. I didn't realize I'd hit him that hard. It didn't mean I was sorry about it.

"Here's your wallet." I tossed Horrock his wallet. It landed on his chest. Horrock leafed through it. I didn't need his wallet anymore. I had memorized the information in it.

"Looks like everything's where I left it," Horrock said.

"Glad to hear it," I said and then got right to it. "Your brother's been shot." I flashed my DEA badge and stared into his eyes. The white of his left eye was blood red. His right eye was clear blue.

"You're lying," Horrock said. I wasn't. Steven Horrock had been shot only it was with a tranquilizer dart. Let Samuel assume the worst.

"Didn't they tell you?" I asked. "Of course they wouldn't. Not until they questioned you. They found your brother draped over a sapphire Jaguar with the license plate HADES."

"If anything happened to Steve I would've felt it," Horrock said.

"Felt it?"

"We're identical twins. Can't you tell?"

The two of them working together explained the two shooters tonight and unless I missed my guess who murdered Clinton Windell. Horrock continued.

"My brother's a long way from here. Steve was in Utah last I heard from him."

"Who hired you to kill Clinton Windell?" I asked.

"Nobody hired me to kill anybody," Horrock said.

"Why were you shooting at me and my partner tonight?"

"I don't know what you're talking about."

"The police have your weapon," I said. "They've dug bullets out of the vehicles you sharpshooters hit when you missed." Horrock's right jaw tightened. His eyes became laser dots. If he were in pain, it didn't show.

"I was having a little target practice and didn't see you. My mistake," Horrock dryly said. I ignored his attempt at what could've been humor.

"Bet they'll match the bullets from your weapon with slugs dug out of Clinton Windell," I said.

"Clinton who," Horrock said.

"Clinton Windell," I said.

"Is he that rich dude who got whacked a while back?"

"One in the same," I said.

Horrock started to roll over on his right side. He changed his mind after a grimace of discomfort crossed his face. "Shame," Horrock said slowly shaking his head. An act that at full health I'm certain he would've done a lot faster. "Never heard of the sucker except for on the news. Didn't the police arrest his wife for icing him?"

"She didn't do it," I said.

"You don't say?"

"No matter the cops will nail your ass," I said. "We're after your boss."

"You're losing me," Horrock said.

"You're already lost," I said. "You must be a fool if you think someone would hire you boneheads to do what you did and let you live to tell about it. I'm looking at chewing gum that's lost its flavor."

"What are you talking about?"

"Have you or Steve ever met the person behind this?"

"Behind what?—Mr. D-E-A."

"The homicides," I said, "the Windell robbery not to mention the attempted murder of a DEA agent."

"Man you've been standing too close to the coke."

"Dead men don't tell tales, Horrock. The two of you are the only living connection to the brains behind all of this. Once you numbskulls disposed of me what would stop your boss from disposing of you and your brother. What would you do if you were in her shoes?"

"Her," Horrock said.

"Judith Hardy," I said.

"What's DEA got to do with this?"

I gambled on throwing a name out there. Horrock didn't look the least bit surprised when I mentioned Judith Hardy. That was confirmation as far as I was concerned but I wanted to hear Horrock spell it out. I fabricated a story about Hardy having a history of erasing her tracks. Horrock wanted to know more.

"Let's just say Hardy's big time. You help us hang her; we pull a few strings who knows. You and brother Steve could wind up doing as little as seven years—if you behave yourselves."

Horrock glared at me for a moment. I didn't know whether Hardy would come after them or not. I had tried to scare him to get him to crack. It wasn't working. Samuel Horrock wasn't a man prone to fear. The light was on. He was trying to assure himself a good bargaining position. Bargaining didn't matter to me. I did not intend to help him or his brother in any way. I was no longer DEA. There was no necessity to play by any sort of rules. I wanted to nail Hardy for her involvement in this case. Let Samuel and Steven Horrock fry for the murders they committed. If they didn't like it, sue me.

"That bitch," Horrock said without warning. I couldn't tell if he believed what I told him about Hardy cleaning house. I decided to go with it.

"Judith Hardy?" I said.

"Yeah how'd you know?"

"We've had this puzzle figured out for some time," I said. "You and your brother were the only missing pieces. Did she hire you and Steve to kill Clinton Windell?"

"How do I know I can trust you?"

"Do you have a choice?"

"I can keep my mouth shut and take my chances," Horrock said.

"Suit yourself," I said as I turned to leave.

"Wait!" Horrock yelled. I looked over my shoulder visibly annoyed. Horrock grimaced.

"What do you want to know?" he asked. I returned to Horrock's bedside.

"Did Judith Hardy hire you and Steven Horrock to murder Clinton Windell?"

"Yep."

"Mark Strait?"

"Not originally," Horrock said.

"Who did?"

"Clinton Windell."

Even in death, Windell managed to squeeze another evil skeleton in that crowded cesspool closet of his. "Clinton Windell hired you to kill Mark Strait?"

"Yep that's how we met Hardy. My brother and me met Windell at a bed and breakfast to discuss the arrangements for exterminating Mark Strait. Strait had become too much of a liability and Windell wanted him smoked. Hardy was leaving with some dude. They saw us with Windell and came over. Windell was forced to introduce us."

"Can you describe the man Hardy was with?" I asked.

"I'll do better than that," Horrock said. "His tag was Patrick Kemery."

"The same Patrick Kemery who's a member of the Bellingham board-of-directors."

"One in the same. I remember Windell mentioning a board meeting being canceled until Windell got back from Europe. Kemery didn't like it none. Little did Windell know he'd be the one being canceled." Horrock grinned from ear-to-ear. "That must have hurt." He loved digging up dirt and burying corpses. This was one demented puppy. When I didn't grin back, his disappeared.

"Windell introduced us as old Navy buddies. Hardy must have done some checking because she found out differently. Anyway, my brother got a call from this Hardy the next day. She wanted to hire us. We told her we didn't do business over the phone. We met. Hardy told us she wanted Windell whacked. Told us half the diamonds were ours if we did the job. Sweet deal, we took it—you got a cigarette?"

"No," I said. Horrock made an expression as if he had a bad taste in his mouth.

"Did you ever see Kemery again?" I asked.

"Only on the exchange. We divided the diamonds. Kemery took the gem bag we took from Windell and gave us a gym bag to put our stuff in."

That explained it. Hardy was using Windell as a mule and he never knew it. There was more in that gem bag than twenty-million dollars' worth of uncut gems.

"So you did Windell and took the diamonds as payment?" I asked.

Horrock nodded.

"You still have the diamonds?"

"Spent them," Horrock grinned. A sarcastic lie and we both knew it. He was looking to get a rise out of me. When it didn't work, Horrock stopped grinning and waited for my next question.

"Why did you kill Strait?"

"Strait was nosy," Horrock said. "He kept fishing around. Strait wasn't satisfied getting a cut of the action. He needed to know the whole story."

"Strait thought he was being set up as the fall guy for the Windell murder," I said.

"You could be right," Horrock said. "I don't know nothing about that."

"Did Hardy order a hit on Strait?"

"Doing Strait was more of a mutual agreement. An insurance policy if you will."

"What about Benton Lawson?" I asked.

"Who?"

"The man you and your brother hung," I said.

"We didn't hang anybody. We never heard of Benton Lawson." Horrock looked confused. So was I. That left Hardy, Farhletti, or Kemery. What was I missing? I made a mental note to be especially careful. Lethal and intelligent adversaries are the worst.

"Why did you come after me and my partner?" I asked.

"Your partner *please*," Horrock said. "If we wanted her dead it would've happened a long time ago. You were the one we were after. Maybe next time we won't miss *Mr. D-E-A*."

"Is that a threat," I said.

"Not at all," Horrock said not masking his sarcasm before he squirmed for a moment as he settled in.

"Maybe next time I'll shoot back," I said. Horrock seemed pleased by the thought.

"Did Hardy order the hit on me?" I asked.

"We didn't know you were DEA."

"And that makes it alright?"

Horrock glanced away as if to think it over. Before he spoke again, he looked back at me with the same hard stare he had before his conscience pondered my statement, "Yep."

"She ordered the hit on me?"

Horrock nodded. He looked drowsy. Suffering from a mild concussion, I doubted it was caused from any medication. The most he probably received was something for the pain. He was probably exhausted. Maybe I'd get lucky and he'd slip into a coma.

"One other thing," I said.

Horrock looked leery. "You are going to honor your end of the bargain right? This ain't no shyster deal?"

"I'll do all I can," I said. That was an honest answer; nothing was what he and his brother were going to get from me.

"Did I lead you to Mark Strait?"

Horrock grinned. "Like a dog on a leash. We followed some people who were following you. Once we saw you go into Detroit's Public Records office we pieced the rest together ourselves."

I could've killed him and left without a twinge of guilt. Then what would separate me from people like him? I was leaving when Horrock said after me, "What about our deal?" I grinned. "Make a deal with the devil you take what you get."

CHAPTER FORTY-FIVE

None of what Samuel Horrock told me was admissible in court. It was obtained under duress and false pretenses on my part. I had impersonated a DEA agent and could be prosecuted because of it. Those were not my main concerns. What I needed was enough enticing information to convince Destini to look elsewhere for the murderers. I had it. Judith Hardy was a sharp resourceful adversary. My deepest hope was that I wasn't too late.

The telephone number I found in Horrock's wallet was no doubt a contact number to let Hardy know everything went according to plan. If Hardy hadn't heard from her hired guns, she would assume things went sour. That meant instituting a back-up plan one that would require Hardy take flight—expectedly out of the country. I had one shot at intercepting her. If my hunch were wrong, Judith Hardy would be long gone.

Renita had calmed down. The wait in the car cooled her engines to where she could sit still. I filled her in on what Samuel Horrock told me while I drove to DIVA. I explained to Renita that Judith Hardy was the only common denominator throughout this case from the Kemery exchange of vital information to the Benton Lawson murder. I had only wished I realized it sooner.

Renita was surprised Judith Hardy was behind it all. She tried disguising her initial reaction by saying Hardy was on her short list of suspects. I played along as if I believed her and then tried the contact number I found in Horrock's wallet. There was still no answer. I made one other call to someone who was not at all happy to hear from me.

I noticed an area of access that was unguarded at the Beaverton Research Complex. A small grassy knoll led down to a wooded section along the westerly backside of Parking Lot C. On the other side of the wooded section was a two-lane asphalt road. My guess was Judith Hardy was in her office at DIVA. What better place to hide a working copy of the Universal Translator than right under everyone's nose.

Renita didn't like it but I made her take the car and leave. The spindly denuded trees were dark silhouettes dripping from the last drizzle. Night provided a dense black cover that even the luminous parking lot lights had difficulty penetrating. Except for my shoes I didn't waste time changing into the gear I kept in my trunk. I was armed and ready as I made my way through that small patch of woods.

When I reached the edge of the west parking lot, I noticed two uniformed security guards patrolling near the building. They were not a problem. The security cameras were. I needed a diversion. As I was deciding on how to proceed, the security guards received a call. They ran around toward the front of the building. I trusted the guards watching the surveillance monitors had responded in kind. Now was my chance. As I ran across the parking lot, I could see the lights in Judith Hardy's office. She was there all right.

Security was lax inside the building. Running across the wide lobby, I was able to catch a glimpse of a chaotic scene. Someone had crashed through the front gate. It was Renita. I paused for a moment to make certain Renita would be all right. She had gotten out of my damaged car with her hands in the air. Renita staggered and then fell. I suspected she might have struck her head from the impact of the car with the gate. Two guards helped Renita to her feet. Those same two guards draped an arm over their shoulders and began to help Renita walk. They were coming my way. I was torn between aiding Renita and pursuing Judith Hardy. Then something happened to help with my decision.

Renita spotted me. She shoved the guards helping her away yelling at them: "Don't be trying to feel me up! I ain't that drunk!" Renita was faking the whole thing. God bless that woman for being hardheaded. Renita was the diversion I needed. I didn't know how she was going to pull it off without reeking of alcohol but so be it. The security guards had Renita in custody. The whole security force must have converged on her. I only wondered if it had been her car would she have shown such zeal. Renita would be safe with DIVA security. I had to believe that in order to do what I needed to do. I slipped onto a penthouse elevator unnoticed.

I ran off the elevator with my Beretta at the ready. Hardy's office was at the west end. Farhletti's was at the east. They were the only offices on the top floor. I assumed Hardy heard the elevator arrive. I had pressed

"L" to return it to the lobby in case Hardy made it past me and was looking to escape.

The lights were out when I burst into Hardy's office. Those few seconds of blindness were all she needed. The feel of cold steel pressed against the back of my head, followed by that familiar sound of a cocked gun hammer locking in place made me freeze. She took my Beretta from me without a word and shoved me in my back. When she turned on the lights the person holding me at gunpoint was not who I expected.

CHAPTER FORTY-SIX

"Surprised Mr. Cavanaugh?"

"Stunned is more like it. What are you doing here?" I took a step forward. Roxanna Farhletti raised her weapon a little higher. I froze.

"Don't let the innocent demeanor fool you. I know how to use this. Now step back before I put a hole through you."

"You're the cold-hearted murdering thief," I said.

"Tsk tsk I'm no such thing."

"You hired the Horrocks to kill Windell and Strait. Tonight you tried to have me killed."

"Correction had you killed," Roxanna said. "This is a forty-four Smith & Wesson with a silencer. Same make and model as the ones the Horrocks used."

"Dead in Hardy's office well after the Horrocks have been taken into custody. It won't fly."

"You're right," Roxanna said. "It's the best I could do on such short notice. In any event I'll be a continent away by the time they cut you open."

"Was I part of your plan all along?" I asked stepping backward.

"*Absolutely not*," Roxanna said. "You were hired to do the job you did so well. I didn't expect you to be involved in the Windell case. That turned out to be our misfortune."

"Our?"

"Judith and mine we're partners."

"You sent Hardy to see me not your husband."

Roxanna nodded. "I couldn't chance going to you myself. We needed to know what you knew about the Windell murder and U-T. Judith was perfect. She doled out a seductive pretense. Your libido should have done the rest. You are to be commended for resisting her charms.

Most men would have taken Judith up on her sensuous offer. My husband certainly did."

"Are you telling me catching Hardy and your husband fooling around was a setup?"

"Something like that," Roxanna said. "You see nailing my husband in the act of adultery naturally led to my filing for divorce. The outcome of the trail could prove very costly to Tony in terms of an extremely generous settlement awarded to his wife, yours truly. With that on his mind, Tony's attention wasn't one-hundred-percent where it should have been."

"On what was going on with U-T," I said.

"Correct."

"Now I get the picture."

"Judith and I are partners—not lovers. Men can be such one-dimensional jerks at times. Thinking with the tingle in their balls instead of the gray matter between their ears."

"That's not what I meant," I said, "but thanks for clearing that up. Why are you so desperate to have U-T?"

"You haven't ventured a guess?"

"Only you know for certain," I said.

"What is your conjecture?"

"Blackmail."

"My dear Mr. Cavanaugh you are amazing," Roxanna said as if I had just won first prize on a game show.

"Not as amazing as you," I said not sharing her enthusiasm.

"Flattery won't stop me from killing you."

"Humor me for a minute," I said. Roxanna checked her watch.

"I have a little time to kill. No pun intended." I grinned while considering going for my stiletto. With my hands at my sides, it would take too long. Roxanna could fire two shots before I'd be able to throw my blade. I would never see the knife hit its target. The same held true for the thirty-two that she was unaware I had.

Why hadn't the guards called? They had to know someone was in Hardy's office or maybe they didn't. Maybe the penthouse lights were on all of the time. It would make sense. That way Hardy or Roxanna could come and go as they pleased and no one would be the wiser. Hardy probably set up the security system. Which meant she knew all of the security codes and how to override them. What about my shadows where were they? I needed to buy time. There was still an ace I had up my sleeve and it wasn't my stiletto.

"You needed a virgin copy of U-T," I said, "unsullied by limitations that will be placed on commercial copies released to the public. The same program only our government and big money would have at full strength."

"You make it sound like a detergent," Roxanna said. "Go on."

"U-T at its ultimate capacity can decipher anything written in any language or code that exists on an electronic medium."

Roxanna nodded.

"Suppose someone had in mind a plan—oh let's just say blackmail."

"You've already said that."

"Not penny ante extortion such as making people pay to keep quiet about their past sins but something more substantial, more profitable." Roxanna smiled. She was thoroughly enjoying witnessing her genius come to light.

"How about blackmailing people with secret Swiss Bank accounts?" I said. Roxanna's smile brightened. I paused for effect and to squeeze every second I could in hopes that the cavalry would arrive at any moment.

"Continue," Roxanna said with a nod.

"U-T could crack anything the programming community could come up with to stop it. It would be a cinch for you to obtain names, account numbers, balances, passwords, ID's, etcetera. With all of that clandestine money at your fingertips you would contact a few high-end clients with copies of their financial records as proof and they will listen."

"Yes they will," Roxanna said. "Now answer me this. Why not simply open false accounts all over the world? Why take a chance on blackmail?"

"Phony bank accounts are too easy to uncover. You have to create personal histories with each financial institution, keep the amounts small enough so not to attract attention, remain vigilant of constantly changing security codes. The list of obstacles goes on and on. The money you receive from blackmail clients is yours. You can handle it any way you wish with a lot less hassle. As long as your victims kept their mouths shut. Especially if you have Swiss bank accounts of your own to deposit your payments into."

Roxanna gave me a knowing nod. "How do I piece together a client list from so many worthy candidates? Can you answer me that?" Roxanna was still smiling. She wanted me to continue feeding her ego. I obliged.

I thought about my phantom employer. The necessary secrecy and large sums of money at their disposal. Windell's gem buying trip to Switzerland. It all fit. The Swiss banking community was bankrolling my investigation.

"There was only one thing missing," I said. "You still needed electronic files of the accounts to translate. Enter Clinton Windell. Windell had a special courier's license as an international jewelry buyer. His gem bag was never checked. Not long before Windell made his final trip to Amsterdam you arranged for his old gem bag to disappear replacing it with a new gem bag with a false bottom."

"How did I manage to accomplish that?" Roxanna asked.

"Patrick Kemery took care of that," I said.

"Mr. Cavanaugh you are very good," Roxanna said. "Very good indeed! Judith, you and I would've made an incredible team. Pity I have to kill you. Nothing personal please continue. I'd like to hear how you think Windell contributed to our little ruse."

"While in Europe your inside source to the Swiss Banking Consortium managed to get his hands on copies of the latest top secret programs used by the Swiss Banks."

"My contact was a woman," Roxanna said.

"My apologies," I said.

"Apology accepted continue."

"*She* placed the information in the false bottom of Windell's gem bag at some time before Windell purchased the Bellingham gems. Windell would not have been as vigilant of his gem bag prior to that. When Windell returned to the U.S., he not only had the gems but valuable information for you."

"Go on."

"The Horrocks never knew what else was in that bag. They were being paid handsomely on the spot for a job they had committed and that's all they cared about. At the Benson Hotel, Kemery met with the Horrocks to finalize the deal. The divide was made and Kemery took the gem bag so the Horrocks couldn't be tied to the murder. The Horrocks never guessed what else that gem bag contained. Patrick Kemery knew—and so did Farhletti. At least they thought they did. Farhletti and Kemery thought it contained illegal inside market information on China and the dispersed Soviet Union, information that would give Diva and Bellingham Jewelers a clear edge over other free world competitors. Only you knew otherwise."

"Judith and I knew otherwise," Roxanna said.

"How did you make the switch?" I asked.

"Come now Mr. Cavanaugh surely you know?"

"I have no idea," I said. I'd made a presumption on the topic but I needed to buy time.

"I can't take credit for the switch," Roxanna said. "It was Judith's idea. Judith already had the market information. She simply exchanged the appropriate flash drives with the ones Kemery gave her on the night you revealed my husband's adulterous affair."

"Of course," I said. My presumption was correct big deal for a dead man.

"I must say Mr. Cavanaugh—may I call you C. J.?"

"Please do. You're the one with the gun."

"I am, aren't I. C. J. you're almost as brilliant as I."

"If this Universal Translator is so great why not just steal the money?"

"U-T may be the greatest thing since the microchip but it's not invisible. Eventually it would be detected. From what I know about it, U-T can be traced. Once it's traced who knows where it might lead. Why take that risk?"

"And blackmailing's safer," I said.

"As you stated earlier," Roxanna said, "the source of the money will be cleaner."

"If none of your blackmail victims talk."

"They won't," Roxanna said. "If they did they could stand to lose a great deal of their squirreled away tax hidden fortune."

"You're banking on your victims' silence."

"Exactly," Roxanna said.

"And the Swiss wouldn't think anything was wrong?" I asked.

"Why would they. They handle hundreds of multimillion-dollar transactions every day. A few million more electronic dollar transfers from one verifiable legitimate source to another won't raise an eyebrow. Especially since we're only asking a few million per client from people who consider that pocket change."

Roxanna had it all figured out. To be honest I couldn't see a hole in her plan. My immediate concern was how to prevent her from putting a hole in me. "How do you know your plan will work?" I asked.

"Field tested and mother approved," Roxanna said.

"You've already tried U-T on the Swiss?"

"Yes and with wonderful results," Roxanna said. "I all ready have all the information I need from the Swiss for the time being to make a sizeable profit with a few wealthy test cases to boot. My focus is now on my recalcitrant benefactors."

Roxanna Farhletti had implied what the Swiss could not state for security purposes. One of her blackmail victims must have talked. Like all big institutions, the Swiss Banks have abundant resources at their disposal. What they lacked was exactly where to point those lumbering resources and time to uncover the blackmailer. I suppose they thought Clinton Windell was behind it since they probably discovered he carried copies of their stolen programs back to the U.S. Unfortunately, for them their discovery probably came after Windell was dead. In any case, Windell was their link to the blackmailer. The problem for the Swiss was, Windell was used and never realized it. Lawson's meddling must have forced Roxanna to move up her timetable, which forced the Swiss to move up mine. Roxanna couldn't be sure to whom Lawson told what.

"What I don't understand is why kill Windell at all," I said.

"We didn't kill Windell," Roxanna said. "We *had* Windell killed. It was part of our agreement with Kemery. Kemery believed with Windell out of the way he would be a shoe-in for the CEO spot."

Man was Kemery ever wrong, I thought.

"As CEO of Bellingham Jewelers," Roxanna said, "and having at his disposal the advantage of inside market information Kemery would become a very wealthy man. Although personally I think Andrea Bettencourt is better suited for the position. All I wanted was to use Windell as a courier. We could have gotten the information from the gem bag a dozen ways without harming him. It turned out robbing and killing Windell in his home directed all of the attention toward the people around him. No one would think to look elsewhere. No one except you, that is."

"Are you certain you can trust Kemery?" I asked.

"Trust has no bearing on it," Roxanna said. "Kemery has no proof. The calfskin gem bag has been destroyed. It would be his word against Judith's."

"Kemery never knew you were involved did he?"

"I'm as silent as silent partners come."

"Why kill Mark Strait? He did what you wanted."

"Strait was a toxic liability. He was blackmailing Windell. What was to stop Strait from blackmailing us if he found out what we were up to?"

"The Lawson phone call?" I asked. I knew the frantic call from Benton Lawson was staged. Judith Hardy probably held a gun to his head and forced him to read something she had written. As added incentive, I'm certain she threatened to kill Roxanna Farhletti if he didn't comply. Hardy already had the Universal Translator. Trashing the place only gave more credence to her story that Lawson never completed it.

"That was a little red herring to keep your detective girlfriend moving in the wrong direction," Roxanna said not really answering my question. Roxanna and Hardy had expected me to call in Lawson's murder as an upstanding citizen would do, not disturb anything and somehow become woven into this tapestry of deceit. Having ties to Benton Lawson the police would have checked Renita and me out making certain we were clear of any wrongdoing regarding his death. The Pentagon, NSA, Homeland Security and the FBI would be interested as well. That would have given Roxanna and Hardy enough time to complete their plans unobstructed.

"You handed the police Genevieve Windell?" I asked.

"On a platinum platter forged documents and all," Roxanna said with pride.

"Why?"

"It wasn't personal simply business," Roxanna said. "Adding her to the fire surrounding Clinton Windell's murder helped detract attention away from the robbery. The less thought people gave to the robbery the better our chances they would overlook any clues pointing in our direction. Not to mention upsetting your lady friend even more with you for not telling her everything."

"You know about me and Destini," I said.

"Who doesn't?" Roxanna said. "Hell hath no fury like a woman scorned. I know."

Or like an egotistical bitch with a forty-four pointed at you," I thought. "Why kill Lawson?" I asked.

"What makes you think I killed Benton?"

"I've spoken to Steve Horrock."

"Ah," Roxanna said with a nod. "Since they didn't do it you assumed it was me."

"Something like that," I said.

"Good assumption," Roxanna said. "Benton was a genius. He perfected the Universal Translator months ago although he never realized it."

"Hardy kept bugging it enough to keep him off balance," I said.

"Actually," Roxanna said, "I tampered with the results not the program. You didn't know I was a Computer Science major. That's how Benton and I met. I currently have my doctorates in the same field. I've written several original software packages for Diva. Bet you didn't know that either? That was another time and another person. Clandestinely bugging U-T's output was challenging but with Benton's unwitting assistance it became a lot easier."

"Why did you kill Lawson when you already had U-T?"

"So did Benton. U-T was his baby. He'd made a copy of it without our knowledge. The smart little shit had been e-mailing himself the program all along bit by bit. I didn't discover he had smuggled a full working copy of U-T until after Windell was killed. Over the last two months, he'd been running tests on U-T at home. Of course, he was getting much different results than the ones I doctored. His detection could have disrupted my plans. Fortunately, for me I had used my husband's security clearances as my scouting grounds for U-T and a seeding area to create the false errors in U-T's output. Benton assumed it was Antonio who was sabotaging the results."

"Was that also how Clinton Windell's itinerary got into your husband's files?"

"I knew Benton liked to snoop where he didn't belong," Roxanna said. "Judith got a copy of Windell's itinerary from Kemery and I planted it amongst my husband's personal computer files, a bone for Benton to gnaw on."

"Lawson came to you when he discovered the sabotaged results?"

"He went to Judith. As head of security Benton assumed her first allegiance would be to the project, silly boy."

"That and the fact he was still in love with you."

"Yes he was," Roxanna said with a tinge of melancholy. "Benton visited me the first day he came to work here. We talked for hours about old times. Antonio was nowhere to be found. I believe my husband was screwing his vice-president of Marketing on that particular evening. I was feeling amorous so I talked Benton into showing me his place. We made love. It wouldn't be the last time. While I lay snuggled in Benton's arms, he told me all about the Universal Translator. That was when my plan began to hatch."

"You were the mastermind all along," I said.

"Shocking isn't it," Roxanna said. "You don't know how difficult it is to be constantly portrayed as the victimized wife who loves her unfaithful husband to pieces. Even before Benton arrived on the scene, I was no saint. I had a small stable of virile studs who are better than Antonio ever was."

Roxanna checked her watch. "Judith should be on foreign soil by now. I'll be joining her shortly."

"How'd you get Hardy wrapped up in this?"

"It was easy. Judith Hardy is a stone cold businessperson. Like most ruthless business people, she has no morals or ethics. Judith saw a great profit opportunity and leapt at it. I on the other hand obtain independent wealth and get back at Antonio at the same time."

"You do resent his womanizing," I said.

"I despise him for it," Roxanna hissed.

"The divorce would make you independently wealthy," I said.

"That isn't enough," Roxanna said. "I want him to experience the anguish I felt every time I knew he was in the arms of one of his sluts."

"You admitted to having affairs yourself," I said.

"That was after the fact," Roxanna said. "To give me satisfaction I wasn't getting at home."

"Benton Lawson loved you and you murdered him," I said. "If that's the price for loving you it's too high." Roxanna's face drew taut. Her lips tightened. Her eyes expressed searing rage. I had definitely said the wrong thing.

"You've got it all figured out," Roxanna said not the least bit amused.

"Not all of it," I said.

"Well it's too little too late."

"I've got Lawson's copy of U-T," I calmly said coolly staring Roxanna in the eye.

"Maybe you do. Maybe you don't. At this point it doesn't matter."

"You still haven't said why you killed Benton Lawson."

"He was dead the moment U-T worked," Roxanna said. "I couldn't have the most knowledgeable person about the most powerful program in the world running around. He might come up with a way to defuse it before I could amass my fortune."

"You are one fine piece of work," I said.

"Ain't I though," Roxanna said as if accepting a compliment.

Roxanna took careful aim. I was about to make a desperate move for the stiletto when the door burst open. My ace had come through. Antonio Farhletti rushed inside with three uniformed security guards. Roxanna whirled and aimed her weapon at the middle guard. The guards looked nervous. If I were to bet on the outcome of a shootout, I'd pick Roxanna to win. Roxanna calmly pointed her weapon back at me.

"I was on my way to see you dear," she said to Farhletti, "when I heard something coming out of Judith's office. I looked in and found this man rummaging through her things. Look!" Roxanna said adding panic to her voice.

Farhletti looked at me. He seemed disappointed I was still alive. It was late and Farhletti was dressed as if he were attending an important business meeting. Roxanna and I both knew he had plans to meet another woman. Sleaze ball or not he was my life jacket.

Farhletti turned his attention to his wife. "Rox, Cavanaugh called me earlier tonight. He said Judith Hardy would be here. He also said Judith would be stealing the only working copy of the Universal Translator we had."

"That's why he's here," Roxanna said. "Cavanaugh and Hardy are in this together. He had this when I caught him." Roxanna kicked a beige traveling bag at her feet. Farhletti picked it up and looked through it. Farhletti took the travel bag then stepped away from Roxanna standing near the door. Farhletti pulled out a hand full of flash drives. The guards turned their weapons on me.

"What are these?" Farhletti asked Roxanna.

"I don't know." Roxanna jerked her forty-four toward me. "Ask him."

Farhletti pulled out his smartphone. "What are you doing?" Roxanna asked her husband.

"Calling the police," Farhletti said. "We'll let them sort this out."

"Tony you don't want the police involved," Roxanne said. "We can handle this. Think of the negative publicity something like this will cause." Roxanna's tone had gone from feigned panic to mild desperation.

"It's too late for that now," Farhletti said. "Yes I'd like to report a break-in."

"Put down that phone!" Roxanna said pointing her weapon at Farhletti's heart. Farhletti was so stunned he dropped his phone. The guards trained their weapons on Roxanna.

"Tell them to drop their weapons," Roxanna said to her husband. The guards' eyes darted between Roxanna and Farhletti. I used the moment to get at my thirty-two. With my thirty-two aimed at her mid-section, I ordered Roxanna to drop her weapon.

"Put down the gun Rox," Farhletti said trying to disguise his fear.

"Get real you two-timing male slut," Roxanna said.

There is a moment of sharp clarity when the eyes of people like Roxanna and me meet. We had no doubt, what the other was capable of doing. Roxanna wasn't concerned about being shot even less about dying. Her only issue was whether it was her most feasible option at the moment. My biggest concern wasn't Roxanna Farhletti. It was those three nervous security guards who had not lowered their weapons.

"For the last time," I said, "drop your weapon."

"Why not?" Roxanna said with a droll smile. Roxanna turned the forty-four over in her hand and offered it to Farhletti. Farhletti ordered one of the guards to take it from her. After one of the guards took Roxanna's weapon two of them managed to handcuff her. I put my thirty-two away. Farhletti walked over to the desk and telephoned the police forgetting his smartphone on the floor. I retrieved my Beretta from Roxanna's coat pocket and then stood at arms' length away from her. Roxanna appeared more amused than anything.

"What do you suppose happens now C. J.?" Roxanna asked.

"You'll be charged on a variety of counts ranging from first degree homicide to theft of government property," I said.

"Really," Roxanna said.

"Yes ma'am," I said.

Roxanna stepped closer. She was wearing Cerruti 1881. "What sort of deal do you think our government will make to obtain the Universal Translator?"

"I'll give it to the government free of charge," I said. Bluffing and hoping. Bluffing because I didn't have U-T. Hoping U-T was on the CDs I took from Lawson's home. Roxanna smiled.

"Those flash drives hold only one tenth the software needed to compile the Universal Translator. For the past six months, I've been siphoning tenths of U-T to nine other parties throughout the world. Not one of them knows about the other. They each think they have the other half. All of their names are kept in one place. Inside my head. Not even Judith knows who they are. If our government wants U-T, they'll have to cut a deal. It may not be the profit I had in mind but sometimes you have to take what the market will allow. In addition, of course, I won't do a day of time. This will never make it to trail. My arrest will vanish. Just like the security footage of the Jaguar you were after, gone in the twinkling of an eye."

Roxanna was right. I knew my government would do what every government in the world would do under those circumstances cut a deal. Roxanna Farhletti would serve no time and make a healthy profit. That's the thing about justice. It's always a matter of perspective.

"Now you say you have a working copy of U-T," Roxanna went on to say. "I find that difficult to believe. I may be wrong but I'm willing to take that gamble. You see I found a working copy of U-T on one of Benton's PCs and literally incinerated it. You can't be too careful these days."

Farhletti stood next to me. "The police are on their way," Farhletti said to me. He turned to Roxanna. "Why Rox, why'd you do this?"

"You can ask me that after the years of humiliation you have put me through," Roxanna said. "Sleeping around at every opportunity you get. How do you think that makes me feel Tony? It was time to cut the cord. Divorcing you wouldn't be enough. I didn't want your alimony. I wanted nothing more to do with you. I simply wanted to take a chunk of you with me when I left. U-T was your megastar. Now that security has been breached and you haven't been able to deliver the goods, no government is ever going to trust you with a contract again. As for me, I saw a lucrative business opportunity and went for it."

I would have left to check on Renita but I thought I'd better stay to keep an eye on Roxanna. Even handcuffed, she seemed a threat to the fidgety security guards and a visibly shaken Antonio Farhletti. My latest concern was how I was going to explain all of what transpired to Destini—and live.

CHAPTER FORTY-SEVEN

I pounded on his bedroom door. Identifying myself as D-E-A, I ordered Bebe Assassino to surrender or die. A gunshot from inside caused my raiding party and me to slam our backs against the wall. It took only an instant to realize what had happened. I kicked in the door and led the assault. Most of Bebe Assassino's head had been blown away. His body shook violently with spasmodic contractions atop his bed. I was angry with that little bastard. Angry he had denied me the satisfaction of arresting him. So angry in fact I aimed my weapon at his convulsing chest and was ready to squeeze the trigger when something distracted me. On the floor next to the bed was my field journal. Beside my field journal was the battered metal box I had seen Bebe Assassino with on the day he almost caught me in his room.

The box was open. I looked inside. On top were two weather beaten black-and-white photographs. One was of a smiling Portuguese couple proudly posing in their traditional wedding clothes. The other was of the bride dressed in casual wear gleefully displaying an infant wrapped in a brightly colored blanket whose face you could barely see. Underneath the photographs were orphaned sheets of paper that appeared ripped from a spiral notebook. I lifted out the paper along with the photographs only to discover a scattering of items I would later learn were cherished mementos from Bebe Assassino's biological family.

There was writing on the notebook's disemboweled pages. Though poorly penned Portuguese they were painful in content. Bebe Assassino's words began by explaining how he learned the truth of his heritage. A little less than two years before my arrival Bebe Assassino met a man who proved to be his uncle. His father's brother told him of his past and about the merciless execution of his family at the hands of Cardoza and his men. The uncle who told Bebe Assassino those things had given him the battered metal box filled with the precious pearls of his ancestry. It was then Bebe Assassino began plotting his revenge.

Those same writings also pointed out the various bank records of money Bebe Assassino had squirreled away from his association with Cardoza. He asked that the money be distributed amongst the neediest of his people. Bebe Assassino expressed his shame and deep regrets for the lives he had taken and those he ruined from his association with illicit drugs.

The pictures were those of Bebe Assassino's parents. He was christened Federico Bernardo Vicente Cortez. There was disclosure of an older sister and brother killed by Cardozo's men. Bebe Assassino repeatedly referred to that fateful day when he would exact revenge upon the man who murdered the family he never knew. In detail, Bebe Assassino outlined how he had undermined a number of Cardoza's operations. He believed the discovery of my field journal was a blessing from God. He had kept quiet about it because he saw it as a great opportunity. When Bebe Assassino saw the entry in my journal mentioning the upcoming DEA raid he knew precisely what to do.

"This is my chance," he wrote, "perhaps my last to take from Cardoza that which he has taken from me from the start. His sons and their families will pay the price for what he did to my family. Cardoza will face American justice and I will go to hell for what I have done. I can only hope those who I made suffer in this life found peace and abundance in the next. Forgive me for I cannot forgive myself."

There was a sidebar near the end of Bebe Assassino's writings that I found surprising. "My dear DEA agent I know you hated me," Bebe Assassino wrote. "The fire of hatred burned bright in your eyes. It is good that you did. Had you shown a taste for our butchery, that would have made you no better than us. Had that been the case I would have killed you myself and found another way to avenge the slaying of my family. As it is, you should thank your lucky stars for me. Cardoza would have killed you at least a dozen times had I not been there. I was the one who kept convincing him that you were not DEA or CIA. How did I know you were DEA? A number of ways but first and foremost one should never hide one's diary in the room of one's enemy.

"Cardozo is alone now. By the time you read this, Cardozo should be in the hands of your U.S. government. Do not fail me. For if you do I promise I will rise from the dead to introduce you and Cardozo to the distasteful discomforts of the Dragon's Chair. Take care of yourself my avenger. May God be with you. I must go now. It is time to pay for my sins." It was signed Federico Bernardo Vicente Cortez.

Our surprise raid on Cardoza was very successful. We suffered only a few casualties during his capture. We found Cardoza's wife, sons and grandchildren dead, shot at close range by an Ingram sub-machine gun the type of weapon Bebe Assassino favored. To this day, I have Bebe Assassino's writings to serve as a reminder not to judge a book by its cover. Roxanna Farhletti made me realize it was a lesson I had not fully absorbed.

***

Only a fraction of U-T was on the CDs I confiscated from Lawson's home. Some of the CDs were blank. Renita found portions of the U-T program early on sandwiched between music tracks. More U-T and less music was found the further Renita investigated. Lawson probably realized he was running out of time and needed to speed up the process. I speculated his motive for copying U-T was one of two: He was attempting to safeguard his creation from the suspected clutches of Antonio Farhletti who Lawson had been misled to believe was behind the sabotaging of U-T's output; and, or, he wanted an all-powerful copy of the Universal Translator for his personal use. I asked Renita if she could piece together U-T from what she had. Renita laughed. According to my partner, "By the time I become familiar with the inner workings of the program enough to even know what I had you'll be able to pick up a copy of U-T at your local computer store." In any case, it left Roxanna Farhletti holding all the chips.

A week had gone by since the capture of Roxanna Farhletti. Renita and I had successfully faded into the gray of anonymity. News reports bristled with the arrests of the Horrock twins and Patrick Kemery. Destini and David were credited with their collars. The Horrock twins were charged with the murderers of Clinton Windell and Edward Sutherland. Robbery was given as the motive behind the murder of Clinton Windell. Sutherland—the inside source for the thieves according to the press—was characterized as the partner who became greedy and was dispensed with by the Horrocks. Patrick Kemery was thrust into the role of Roxanna Farhletti, the mastermind who saw murder as his means of acquiring the CEO position he felt he rightfully deserved. There was no mention of Roxanna Farhletti, Judith Hardy, Benton Lawson, Edward Sutherland's real name, or past life, the Universal Translator, Swiss Bank Accounts, or Diva Computer Software. As far as the public was concerned, the Windell incident was simply another tale of greed and twisted ambition gone berserk. Even Calloway bought that story, hook, line and sinker.

Word on the inside was Roxanna Farhletti had cut herself a sweet deal. In exchange for a full working copy of the Universal Translator, the stolen Swiss software programs and the name of her associates, Roxanna was granted full immunity, given a new identity and a tidy sum to boot. To top it off the Federal Government canceled all Diva Computer Software contracts. Roxanna had maintained her freedom made a sizable profit and still managed to dig a proverbial knife into the ribs of her adulterous husband. Roxanna Farhletti had it more together than any of us. I was lucky to finish in a dead heat with her.

Roxanna Farhletti may have overlooked one lethal problem. From what little I knew about Judith Hardy she struck me as a vindictive person who did not forgive or forget. Hardy probably bolted when Roxanna did not show at their proposed rendezvous point. Hardy would immediately blame Roxanna Farhletti when Hardy discovered the authorities were after her. Navigating her way through the underworld would not be difficult for a person like Hardy. Roxanna Farhletti had better pray the authorities found Judith Hardy before Hardy found her. As for Renita and me, I believed Hardy a true business professional. She would write us off as doing the job we were hired to do. At least that was my hope.

On the up side, I received an evite to Pamela Windell's seventh birthday party. The last time I saw Pamela she wanted to thank me for my part in freeing her mother by offering me Claire as a gift. I explained to Pamela while I appreciated her generosity I was simply doing my job. I suggested she might want to keep Claire claiming her doll might miss her home and the love that only Pamela could give her. I'm not certain but I believe Pamela comprehended the underlying reason for my discouraging her gift. Someday Claire would be one of many unique reminders she would have of her father. I'm basing this on no experience or insight into the mind of Pamela but just a certain glint in her eyes that suggested to me she understood. Genevieve insisted I have dinner with them soon. I accepted. Some time in December, I'll take them up on that offer.

Carl Wheaton was pleased. So he told me were his superiors. Lunsford Insurance immediately issued a beneficiary check to Genevieve Windell once she was cleared of any wrongdoing. Add to that the fact that half of the diamonds were recovered and Carl was on Cloud Nine. Carl had not expected any of the diamonds to turn up. The Horrocks had stashed their cuts in separate safe deposit boxes in two central Oregon banks. They weren't very bright about it. They had used their real names. It was good news for the Cavanaugh Investigation Agency as well. Not only did Lunsford Insurance pay us handsomely for services rendered we also shared in a finder's fee for the diamonds.

There was one thing puzzling me about the diamonds. If Mark Strait received one quarter of their worth and fifty percent of them were recovered, where did the other quarter disappear? Patrick Kemery didn't have them. Roxanna Farhletti didn't have them. Frank Strait—who I was convinced was dead did not have them. That left Judith Hardy. It was probably her cut for helping coordinate the entire scenario. That woman didn't miss an opportunity as far as I could see. With that kind of collateral if I were she I'd bury myself so deep you'd have to go through hell to find me.

My phantom employers were no longer a mystery as their last e-mail went on to explain although I never discovered who vouched for my services in the first place.

Bravo Mr. Cavanaugh! We knew we could rely on you to ferret out the villains behind this international blackmail scheme. As promised the remainder of your fee has been posted to your private business account along with a sizable bonus for a job well done. Have no fear of how you will explain your sudden growth in income. We will provide you with all the cover information you will need to justify any of this to anyone including the IRS.

By now, you have some notion of who we really are and why we had such an interest in the Clinton Windell homicide. We ask one other favor. Would you be so kind as to keep this little venture confidential? Should news of our security breach leak the reputation of the Swiss banking community would be forever tarnished. The work on your end has helped us plug the leak on ours compliments of Roxanna Farhletti.

There is one last matter that I expect your partner will be most pleased to hear. We have called off our troops. It would seem you had very little use for them in the first place. Perhaps one day we will meet under more mutually advantageous circumstances. If you should like to build a nest egg, give us a ring. We would only be too happy to accommodate you. That offer extends to Ms. Harris as well.

Thank you again and goodbye.

Between the money, we received from our Swiss employers and Lunsford Insurance—even after expenses—Renita and I could settle into a comfortable early retirement. On the other hand, if wealth were my primary objective I would have never chosen this profession in the first place. The nest egg idea was one I would salt away for serious consideration.

CHAPTER FORTY-EIGHT

Renita was running me out of closet space faster than the dogs at Multnomah Greyhound Park. Not to mention she wasn't the tidiest person in the world. Even the twins had started avoiding her bedroom after a while. It took Destini, Renita, and me almost six hours with three cars to move Renita out of my place. Renita had entrenched herself in my home without my ever noticing. I blamed my preoccupation on the Windell case with my lack of observance. Destini probably was of a different opinion one that I might never hear since she wasn't speaking to me these days.

The day after Renita moved out, I told Destini everything about the unusual circumstances regarding the Windell investigation. We had just enjoyed a leisurely continental breakfast—whipped together by yours truly—when I eased my confession into the conversation. I had hoped the food, relaxed atmosphere, and Renita's eviction would help smooth matters over. It didn't.

Destini was furious with me for not having faith enough in her to respect my situation and make the right choice. My explanation of not wanting to put her in a position where she would have to compromise her duty as a police officer didn't fly albeit true. Destini dressed, packed, and stormed out refusing to listen to anymore of my "bullshit explanations." My hope was Destini and I would one-day leap past the Windell case to find ourselves stronger for the experience. Stronger how, I couldn't say.

Destini did not share in my prospective. The only saving grace was she had left some of her personal belongings behind. They numbered fewer than the time prior to Renita's moving in but it kept a floundering hope alive that our relationship might survive my debacle. Flowers, candy, amusing and romantic gifts did not soothe her. Even promises of an Alaskan cruise or African safari didn't coax a smile. What was most disheartening was Destini would not be joining me for Thanksgiving in Pittsburgh.

I was exhausted. The case had taken a lot more out of me than I had realized. The time away would do me good. I had made a number of mistakes on the Windell case. Some of which may have cost lives, which was why I felt guilty about mulling over my personal problems with that sort of flotsam in my wake.

Alone with my family of pets my home felt different. Destini and Renita living with me had expanded my definition of what a home could—and perhaps—should be. Like my family, it was their presence, not the walls, artifacts, or furnishings that made my parent's house a home. It was the memories and feelings, the love and the anger, the sentiments and regrets, a sharing of hearts, souls and minds that elevated a place, a dwelling, a residence to an abode of warmth, safety and love. Home *is* what you make it. Destini and Renita had made it special for me in the last few weeks for different reasons. Destini as my lover and my life. Renita as my confidant and friend.

A challenge had been issued regarding the depth of our relationship. According to Destini, I failed. I suppose Destini was right from a personal standpoint. From a professional view, I believed Destini would have done the same had she been in my shoes.

The doorbell rang. I was expecting Renita to take me to the airport. Renita would be spending her Thanksgiving with Ernest.

Ernest had it bad for Renita and it looked as though Renita was warming up to Ernest. I suggested to Renita that she might want to pack her forty-five on that date. Renita thought I meant because of Ernest. I was referring to what Elma Louise might do when she found out. Renita didn't think much of my humor. I was only half-joking.

Renita had agreed to look after things while I was gone. I took one last look around to make certain everything was in order. I said goodbye to the twins asking them to behave which I expected they would not. I was stunned when I opened the door and there stood Destini.

"You didn't really think I would let you leave without me," she said. I had held onto the extra airline ticket in desperate hope Destini might change her mind. It was as if the world opened anew when Destini smiled at me. I felt like a child on Christmas who had his deepest wish fulfilled.

"Forgive me," I said.

"Time C. J.," Destini said. "I'll need time to heal." Her face was sober her eyes lucid and still.

"It'll never happen again," I said.

"We both know that's not true," Destini said. "If the same circumstances surfaced tomorrow you'd do it again in a heartbeat. I hate to admit it but that sense of commitment is one of the things I love about you."

My smile was slight. It symbolized a heavy burden being lifted from my heart.

"What I did learn," Destini said, "was I can trust you even when you won't trust me."

"Trust had nothing to do with it detective," I said. "Respecting the confidentiality of a client was at stake. If an investigator doesn't have his reputation he's not worth spit."

"I didn't come here for a lecture, especially about something I know as much about as you."

"Sorry," I said.

"Let's not talk about it anymore."

"Agreed."

Destini initialized a kiss, sweet and gentle. It was not a spark of passion but a seal of our mutual love.

"I'm glad you could make it. It means a lot to have the woman I love with me on the holidays."

"You said it!" Destini said.

"What?"

"The 'L' word without any prodding from me."

"It may be tough for me to say but it's always in here." I pointed to my heart. My last words made Destini smile for an instant. "We'd better get moving or we're going to miss our flight," I said suddenly feeling embarrassed.

"What are you waiting for," Destini said. "I wouldn't dream of disappointing your parents because of one stupid mistake their son made." Destini stepped inside and grabbed my suitcase. A taxi awaited us at the curb.

I locked up my home. Destini took my arm as we walked to the taxi. Out of what had become a habit, I looked around. No one was watching us. It was over. Getting into the taxi Destini said, "We have a lot to talk about Mr. Cavanaugh."

"Yes detective," I said.

"C. J."

"Detective?"

"Call me dear. At least until we return to Portland then you can call me detective again."

Destini took my hand in hers on our way to the airport. It was warm, soft and silky. The essence of home.

"Now C. J. tell me everything there is to know about your family."

"What can I tell you, you don't already know?"

"I want to hear it fresh, and don't leave anything out."

I told Destini everything about the Cavanaugh clan that came to mind.

www.ingramcontent.com/pod-product-compliance
Lightning Source LLC
Chambersburg PA
CBHW020344120726
47904CB00002B/441